INK AND BONE

ALSO BY RACHEL CAINE

Prince of Shadows

THE MORGANVILLE VAMPIRES NOVELS

Glass Houses
The Dead Girls' Dance
Midnight Alley
Feast of Fools
Lord of Misrule
Carpe Corpus
Fade Out
Kiss of Death
Ghost Town
Bite Club
Last Breath
Black Dawn
Bitter Blood
Fall of Night
Daylighters

Rachel Caine

Ink and Bone

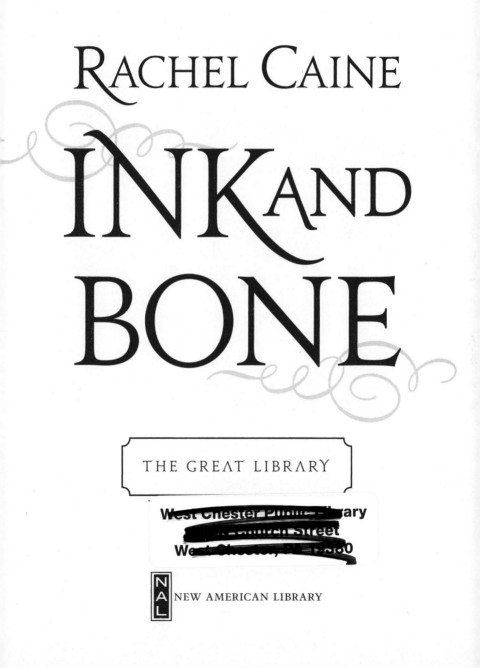

THE GREAT LIBRARY

NAL

NEW AMERICAN LIBRARY

New American Library
Published by the Penguin Group
Penguin Group (USA) LLC, 375 Hudson Street,
New York, New York 10014

USA | Canada | UK | Ireland | Australia | New Zealand | India | South Africa | China
penguin.com
A Penguin Random House Company

First published by New American Library,
a division of Penguin Group (USA) LLC

First Printing, July 2015

 REGISTERED TRADEMARK—MARCA REGISTRADA

LIBRARY OF CONGRESS CATALOGING-IN-PUBLICATION DATA:
Caine, Rachel.
Ink and bone: the Great Library/Rachel Caine.
p. cm.
ISBN 978-0-451-47239-7
1. Libraries—Fiction. 2. Alexandrian Library—Fiction. I. Title.
PS3603.O557I55 2015
813'.6—dc23   2015001509

Printed in the United States of America
1   3   5   7   9   10   8   6   4   2

Set in Bembo
Designed by Elke Sigal

To Carrie Ryan and Kami Garcia.
This one's for you, my friends.

ACKNOWLEDGMENTS

Thank you to my early readers, especially Carrie and Sarah, who made me dig so deep into Jess's world.

Thanks to the audiences who sat through early readings when I was trying to capture ideas too big to put into words.

Most of all, thanks to those who work daily to put words in the hands of those who crave them: librarians, teachers, booksellers, and writers.

You don't just make the world better.

You make the world.

INK AND BONE

EPHEMERA

Text of a historical letter, the original of which is kept under glass in the Great Library of Alexandria and listed under the Core Collection.

From the scribe of Pharaoh Ptolemy II, to his most excellent servant Callimachus, Archivist of the Great Library, in the third year of his glorious reign:

Great King Ptolemy, Light of Egypt, has considered your counsel to make copies of the most important works of the Library to be housed in daughter libraries, hereinafter to be called Serapeum, for the access and enrichment of all men. Pharaoh, who is as wide as the Nile in his divine wisdom, agrees to this proposal.

You shall therefore survey the contents of the Great Library and create for him a listing of all works housed therein, which shall serve ever after as the accounting of this great storehouse of the knowledge of the world.

You shall then consult with the Library's Editor to make exact copies of items suitable for the use of the Serapeum, being mindful of the need to provide works that elevate and educate.

By these means shall we further preserve the knowledge we have gathered and hold in trust from ancient times, to be preserved for the future of all who come after.

Pharaoh has also heard your words regarding the unaccompanied admission of females to this sacred space of the Serapeum, and in his divine wisdom refuses this argument, for women must be instructed by the more developed minds of men to ensure they do not wrongly interpret the riches that the Library offers. For a perversion of knowledge is surely worse than a lack of it.

Pharaoh and the gods will grant eternal favor and protection to this great work.

A handwritten annotation to the letter, in the hand of Callimachus.

His divine wisdom can kiss my common arse. We blind and hobble half of the world through such ignorance, and I will not have it. Women shall study at the Serapeum as they might be inclined. Let him execute me if he wishes, but I have seen enough of minds wasted in this world. I have a daughter.

My daughter will learn.

PROLOGUE

Six years ago

"Hold still and stop fighting me," his father said, and slapped him hard enough to leave a mark. Jess went quiet. He hadn't meant to fidget, but the pouch strapped to his bare chest felt hot and dangerous, like some animal that might turn on him and bite.

He looked up at his father as the man snugged the harness bindings closer. When it was suffocatingly tight, he tossed Jess a filthy old shirt.

He'd done this often enough that, while it was still frightening, it was no longer strange . . . But there was a sense that this time, this run, was different. Why, Jess didn't know, except that his father seemed more tense than usual.

So he asked, hesitantly, "Da—anything I should know?"

"Doesn't matter a damn what you know. Lose that book to the Garda and you'll hang, if you're lucky. If I don't get you first. You know the route. Run it flat and fair, and you'd best damn well die before you give it to any but the one that's paid for it."

Callum Brightwell cast a critical eye over his son's thin form, then yanked a vest from a chest and shoved it over Jess's shirt. There was only one button on it. Jess fastened it. It hung two sizes loose, which was the point: better concealment for the harness.

Brightwell nodded and stepped back. He was a smallish man, runted by poor nutrition in his youth, but now he was dressed well in a bright yellow silk waistcoat and trousers of fine cotton. "You look the part," he told Jess. "Remember to stay with the cutters. Don't split off on your own unless the Garda spring a trap. Even then, keep to the route."

Jess ducked his head in acknowledgment. He knew the route. He knew *all* the routes, all the runs that his family held against competitors throughout the vast city of London. He'd trained since he was old enough to walk, clasping the hand of his father and then later toddling behind his older brother, Liam.

Liam was dead now. He'd been seventeen when he was taken in by the London Garda for running books. His family hadn't stepped up to identify him. He'd kept the family's code. He'd kept his silence to the end.

And as a reward for that loyalty, the city of London had tossed him in an unmarked pit, along with other unclaimed criminals. Liam had been seventeen, and Jess was now ten, and he had no idea how he was supposed to live up to that legend.

"Da—" He was risking another slap, or worse, but he took a deep breath and said, "Today's a bad day to be running—you said that yourself. The Garda are out in force. Why can't this wait?"

Callum Brightwell looked above his son's head, at the sturdy wall of the warehouse. This was one of many bolt-holes he kept for rarities and, of course, the rarest treasures of all, *books*. Real, original books, shelves and crates full. He was a wealthy, clever man, but in that moment, with the light coming harsh on him through a high, mullioned window, he looked twice his age.

"Just get on with it. I'll expect you back in two hours. Don't be late or I'll get the cane." His father suddenly scowled. "If you see your feckless brother, tell him I'm waiting, and there'll be hell to pay. He's on the cutters today."

Even though Jess and Brendan had been born as identical twins, they couldn't have been more different inside. Jess was bold; Brendan tended to be shy. Jess was self-contained; Brendan was prone to explosions of violence.

Jess was a runner. Brendan . . . was a schemer.

Jess knew exactly where Brendan was; he could see him, hiding up on the thin second-floor catwalk, clinging to an old ladder that ran toward the roof. Brendan had been watching, as was his habit. He liked to be up high, away from where Da could lay hands on him, and he liked to avoid risking his hide as a runner when he could.

"If I see him, I'll tell him," he said, and stared hard right at his brother. *Get down here, you little shite.* Brendan responded by silently swarming up the ladder into the darkness. He'd already worked out that Jess was the one running the prize today. Knowing Brendan, he'd decided that his skin was worth more than just acting as his brother's decoy.

"Well?" his father said sharply. "What are you waiting for, a kiss from your mam? Get on with you!"

He pushed Jess toward the massive reinforced warehouse door, which was opened by three silent men; Jess didn't know them, tried not to learn their names because they died quick in that line of work. He paused and took deep, quick breaths. Getting ready. He spotted the mob of cutters ranged about in the alley and on the street beyond; kids, his age or younger, all ready to run their routes.

They were waiting only for him.

He let out a wild war cry and set off at a sprint. The other cutters took it up as a cheer, thin arms and legs pumping, darting between the startled pedestrians in their workaday clothes. Several lunged out into the street, which was a hazardous adventure; they darted between steam carriages and ignored the angry shouts of the drivers. The cutters re-formed into a mob of twelve or so kids at the next corner, and Jess stuck with them for the first part of the route. It was safer in numbers, as the streets got cleaner and the passersby better dressed. Four long blocks of homes and businesses, then a right turn at a tavern already doing good business even so early in the morning; smooth running, until a hard-looking man darted out from a greengrocer and yanked a girl out of his crew by her long hair. She'd made herself too easy to grab; most of the girls knotted up their hair on top of their heads or shaved it short.

Jess had to fight his urge to slow down and help her.

The girl screamed and fought, but the big man wrestled her to the curb and backhanded her into a heap. "Damn cutters!" he yelled. "Garda! Garda! Runners on the loose!"

That tore it. *Always some busybody do-gooder trying to save the day,* was what Jess's father always said; that's why he sent the cutters in packs, most with worthless decoy trash in their harnesses. The Garda rarely scored, but when they did, they paid any informants off rich who put them on the trail of the smugglers.

Citizens turned, eyes avid with the idea of free cash, and Jess tucked his chin down and ran.

The cutters wheeled and broke up and re-formed like a flock of birds. Some carried knives and used them when grabbed; it was chancy to do that, very chancy, because if a kid was caught with a bloody knife it'd be the rope for sure, whether it was a flesh wound on the man he'd cut or a mortal blow. The boy to Jess's left—too big to be running, though he was probably younger than Jess's age—veered straight into a wall of oncoming drunks. He had a knife and slashed with it; Jess saw a bright ribbon of blood arcing in the air and then didn't look back.

He couldn't. He had to concentrate on escape.

His route split at the next corner; they'd all break up now, running separately to draw the Garda's numbers thin . . . or at least, that was the plan.

What happened was that when Jess reached the corner, there were Garda bunched up *on his route.* They spotted him and let out a fierce, angry yell.

He made an instant decision he knew his da would beat him black for making: he left the route.

He almost banged into two other cutters as he veered right; they gave him identically startled looks, and one yelled at him to get off their patch. He ignored her, and despite the ache growing in his chest, the smothering drag of the book, he put on a new burst of speed and outpaced them both.

He heard a cry behind him and glanced back to see that the Garda were pouring out from alleyways. Bloody lobsters in their grimy red coats. They swiftly caught the others.

Not Jess, though. Not yet.

He dodged down a dark, twisting passage too narrow to even be named an alley; even as small as he was, his shoulders brushed brick on both sides. A rusted nail caught at his shirt and ripped the sleeve, and for a heart-stopping second he thought the leather of his harness might catch, but he kept moving. Couldn't go fast now, because of the inky darkness in the shadows, but his nose told him it was a popular dumping ground for rotting fish. The bricks felt slimy and cold under his fingers.

He could still hear the Garda hue and cry behind him, but they couldn't fit their thick bodies through this warren, and for a moment, as he spotted a thin slice of light at the end, he wasn't so sure he could fit either. It narrowed and narrowed, until he had to turn sideways and edge along with the rough brick tearing at his clothes. The book wedged him in as tight as a cork in a bottle, and he fought the urge to panic.

Think. You can get out of this.

He let out his breath and flattened his chest as much as he could, and it gained him the extra half inch he needed to edge free of the crush.

He stumbled out between two fancy buildings onto a wide, clean street he knew he should recognize, and yet it seemed odd, out of place . . . until it snapped into focus.

He'd come out only three blocks from his family's town house, where his mother and father took such pains looking gentrified. If he was seized here, there'd be some who'd know him on sight, and that would mean much, much worse for not just him; his whole family would be brought down. He had to get out of here. *Now.*

He rushed out into the street, directly under the wheels of a steam carriage, and into the darkness of another alley. It led in the right direction but twisted wrong soon enough. He'd not explored all the alleys near his home; he had enough to do with the routes the runners used. That was why his father had always ordered him to keep to the route—because it was so easy to be lost in complicated London, and getting lost while carrying contraband could be deadly.

At the next street he spotted a landmark a few blocks away: the glittering dome of St. Paul's Serapeum, the physical presence of the Great Library in London, and one of the largest daughter libraries in Europe. It was beautiful and deadly, and he averted his eyes and made a vow to never, *never* go that way.

But he didn't have a choice.

A Garda emerged from a doorway, clapped eyes on him, and shouted. Behind his pointing finger, the Garda was young, maybe the age Liam had been when he'd taken the rope. This young man was blond and had a weak chin, and his secondhand uniform fit about as well as Jess's disguise.

But he was fast. Too fast. As Jess took off running he heard the slap of the Garda's feet behind him, and the shrill, urgent toot of his whistle. They'd be coming from all around him. If they boxed him in here . . .

He took the only clear path out of danger. It was another dark, cramped alley, but the Garda was no side of beef and slipped through almost as easily as Jess did. Jess had to keep running, though his weary lungs were pumping fire, and the long legs of the Garda gained on him when they reached open street again. The watery London sunshine seemed to beat down on Jess's head, and he was dripping with sweat. He was terrified that he might damage the book with it.

Not as terrified as he was of being caught, though.

More whistles. The Garda closed in.

Jess had no choice at all. They were driving him in one direction—

toward the Serapeum. If he could get past the Garda barricades there, it was Library territory and under entirely different laws. The London Garda couldn't trespass without clearances.

Up ahead, he saw the orange-and-black wood of the Garda barricade across the street, and the line of supplicants waiting to have their credentials checked. Jess pulled for his last reserves of speed, because that damned rabbit-heeled Garda was close enough to brush fingers on his shirt. He lurched forward, aimed for a hole in the crowd, and threw himself bodily forward toward the barricade. As the Garda behind him yelled for help, Jess grabbed the painted tiger-striped wood and vaulted over it in one smooth motion, hit the ground running on the other side, and heard the shouts of surprise and dismay echoing behind him. Someone laughed and yelled at him to keep going, and he grinned fiercely and risked a look back.

The Garda had stopped at the barricade—or, at least, one of his fellows had stopped him by getting in his way and holding him back. The two were scuffling, the younger man shouting angrily. His blood was still up from the chase, or he'd have had more sense. Jess knew he didn't have long; they'd be sending a message to the High Garda, the elite guards of the Library, to intercept him. He needed to get through, and fast.

The street ahead had but fifty people on foot, including at least ten Scholars stalking in their billowing black robes. No steam carriages; they weren't permitted here anymore, not since the Library had closed this road to through traffic. The golden dome rose serene and gleaming overhead, and below it, a waterfall of steps flowed down from it.

There were still scars on the steps, despite all efforts to clean it, from the last Burner explosion. Stains from the Greek fire and the burned bodies of those who'd been killed. A mound of dying flowers marked the spot, though a groundsman was in the process of shoving them into a bag for disposal. The mourning period was over. Time to move on.

Jess slowed to a jog as he caught sight of the lions. Stone, they resembled, but they had the feral look of life—something caught in a moment of violence, of fury and blood and death, about to spring. He'd heard of the automata, machines that moved on their own, but they were far, far more terrifying in person, now that he was close enough to really see them.

Jess risked another look behind. The London Garda would be organizing men to meet him beyond the barriers on the other side, if the Library's High Garda didn't bestir themselves to get him first. He needed to run, as quick as lightning, but despite that knowledge his feet slowed down to a walk.

He was smothered by dread. Fear. A horrible sense of being *hunted*.

And then one of the automaton lions turned its head toward him. The eyes shone red. Red like blood. Red like fire.

They could smell it on him, the illegal book. Or maybe just his fear.

Jess felt a wash of cold terror so strong it almost loosed his bladder, but he somehow managed to hold the lion's fiery gaze as he kept walking on. He left the sidewalk and took to the middle of the street, where the authorized pedestrians seemed more comfortably gathered, and hoped to hide himself from those feral eyes.

The lion rose from its haunches, shook itself, and padded down the steps, soundless and beautiful and deadly. The other beasts woke, too, their eyes flickering red, bodies stretching.

A woman on the street—someone who'd been passed through the checkpoint—shrieked in alarm, clutched her bag, and ran for it. The others caught the fever and ran, too, and Jess ran with them, hoping they'd cover him like cutters even though they didn't know they were part of his gang.

When he glanced back, two lions were loping behind them. They weren't hurrying. They didn't have to work very hard to overtake mere humans.

The first lion reached the laggardmost of the fleeing people—a female

Scholar, dressed in clumsy robes and burdened with a heavy bag that she'd foolishly not abandoned—and leaped. Jess paused, because it was the most graceful and horrible thing he'd ever seen, and he saw the woman look back and see it coming and the horror on her face, her shriek cut short as the lion's bulk crushed her down . . .

. . . but the lion never took its eyes off Jess. It killed her and left her and came on, straight for him. He could hear the whir and click of the gears inside.

He didn't have time to feel the horror.

He'd thought he'd run himself flat out before, but now, *now*, seeing the death that was at his heels, Jess flew. He felt nothing but the pressure of the wind; he knew there was a crowd around him screaming for help and mercy, but he heard none of it. At the far end of the street stood the other Garda barrier, another crowd of people waiting for their turn, but that crowd was starting to scatter. The lions weren't *supposed* to chase anyone past the boundaries of St. Paul's, but nobody was going to take that risk. Not even the Garda, who abandoned their stations with the rest.

Jess was the first to the barricade, and he vaulted over it as the lions caught and crushed two more behind him. He tripped and fell and knew—*knew*—he would feel death on him in the next heartbeat. He flipped over on his back so he could see it coming, gagged for breath, and held up his hands in an entirely useless defense.

There was no need. The lions pulled up at the barricade. They paced back and forth and watched him with cold, red fury, but they didn't, or couldn't, leap the thin wooden line to come after him.

One roared. It was a sound like stones grinding and the screams of those it had killed, and he saw the sharp fangs in its mouth . . . and then both the lions turned and padded back up the street to the steps and back to the landing, where they settled into a waiting crouch.

He could see the bloody paw prints and human wreckage they left in their wake, and he couldn't forget—knew he never would—the look of despair and horror on the face of the woman who'd been the first to be crushed.

My fault.

He couldn't think about that. Not now.

Jess rolled over, scrambled to his feet, and melted into the panicked crowd. He cut back onto his route after another few long, tense blocks. The Garda seemed to have lost the will to chase him. The deaths at the Serapeum would be explained away in the official news; nobody wanted to hear that the Library's pet automata had slipped their leashes and killed innocents. Whispers said it had happened before, but this was the first time Jess had believed it.

He stopped at a public fountain to gulp some water and try to stop his shaking, and then a public convenience to check that the book was still snug and safe in its harness. It was. He took a slower pace the rest of the way and arrived at the end of the route just a few minutes late—exhausted but weak with relief. He just wanted to be finished, be *home*, for all the cold comfort it would offer him.

Buck up, boy. He could almost hear his father's rough voice. *No one lives forever. Count the day a victory.*

It might be a victory, Jess reckoned, but it was a hollow one.

His instructions were to look for the man with a red waistcoat, and there the man was, sitting at his ease at an outdoor table. He sipped tea from a china cup. Jess didn't know him, but he knew the type: filthy rich, idle, determined to make themselves important by collecting important things. Everything the man wore seemed tailored and perfect.

Jess knew how to make the approach. He ran up to the man and put on his best urchin face and said, "Please, sir, can you spare a bit for my sick mum?"

"Sick, is she?" The man raised his well-groomed eyebrows and set down his cup. "What ails the woman?"

This was the key question, and Jess held the man's eyes as he said, "Her stomach, sir. Right here." He placed a careful finger on the center of his chest, where his harness formed the bulge beneath.

The man nodded and smiled. "Well, that would seem to be a worthwhile cause. Come with me and I'll see you right. Come on, now, don't be afraid."

Jess followed. Around the corner waited a beautiful steam carriage, all ornate curls of gold and silver and black enamel, with some coat of arms on the door that he got only a quick glance at before the man boosted him up inside. Jess expected the buyer to follow him in, but he didn't.

The inside of the carriage had a glow tube running around the top that cast a dim golden light, and by it Jess realized that the one he'd taken for the flash client was really only a servant.

The old man sitting across from him was ever so much grander. His black suit seemed sharp enough to cut, the shirt the finest-quality silk, and he looked effortlessly pampered. Jess caught the rich gleam of gold at his cuffs and the shine of a huge diamond on the stickpin piercing his silk tie.

The only detail that didn't fit with the image of a toff was the ice-cold eyes in that soft, wrinkled face. They looked like a killer's.

What if this isn't about the book? Jess thought. He knew kids could be taken for vile purposes, but his father always took precautions and punished those who took advantage of cutters . . . which was passing rare, these days, as even the toffs knew they weren't safe from the long, strong arm of the Brightwells.

But looking at this man, nothing seemed so safe as all that. He glanced at the wide windows, but they were blacked out. No one could see inside.

"You are late." The toff's voice was soft and even. "I'm not accustomed to waiting."

Jess swallowed hard. "Sorry, sir. Only by a minute," he said. He unbuttoned his vest and pulled off his shirt, and worked the buckles behind his back to release the harness. It was, as he feared, dark with sweat, but the book compartment had been well lined, and the book itself wrapped in layers of protective oiled paper. "The book's safe."

The man grabbed for it like an addict for a pipe and ripped away the coverings. He let out a slow breath when his trembling fingers touched the ornate leather casing.

With a jolt of shock, Jess realized that he knew that book. He'd grown up seeing it in a glass case in his father's deepest, darkest secret treasure trove. He didn't yet read Greek, but he knew what the letters incised on the leather cover meant, because his father had taught him that much. It was the only existing hand copy of *On Sphere-Making* by Archimedes, and one of the first ever bound books. The original scroll had been destroyed by a Burner at the Alexandrian Library ages ago, but there had been one copy made. This one. Owning it carried a death penalty. *When you steal a book, you steal from the world,* the Library propaganda said, and Jess supposed it might be true.

Especially for this book.

He'd been running the rarest and most valuable thing in the entire *world*. No wonder his father hadn't dared tell him what he carried.

The man looked up at him with an insanely bright gleam in his eyes. "You don't know how long I've waited for this," he said. "There's nothing like possessing the best, boy. Nothing."

As Jess watched in numb horror, the man *tore a page from the book and stuffed it into his mouth.*

"Stop!" Jess shrieked, and snatched for the book. "What are you *doing*?"

The old man shoved back and pinned Jess against the carriage wall with a silver-tipped walking stick. He grinned at him and ripped another page loose to chew and swallow.

"No," Jess whispered. He felt horror-struck, and he didn't even know why. This was like watching murder. Defilement. And it was somehow worse than either of those things. Even among his family, black trade as they were, books were holy things. Only the Burners thought different. Burners, and whatever this perverse creature might be.

The old man leisurely ripped loose another page. He seemed relaxed now. Sated. "Do you understand what I'm doing, boy?"

Jess shook his head. He was trembling all over.

"I have fellows who spend fortunes to slay the last living example of a rare animal and serve it for a dinner party. There's no act of possession more complete than consuming the unique. It's *mine* now. It will never be anyone else's."

"You're mad," Jess spat. He felt as though he might spew all over the fine leather and brightwork, and he couldn't seem to get a clean breath.

The rich man chewed another page and swallowed, and his expression turned bitter. "Hold your tongue. You're an unlettered guttersnipe, a *nobody*. I could kill you and leave you here, and no one would notice or care. But you're not *special enough* to kill, boy. Ten a penny, the likes of you." He ripped out another page. When Jess tried to grab for the book again, the old man pulled it out of his reach and smacked him soundly on the side of the head with the cane.

Jess reeled back with tears in his eyes and his head ringing like the bells of St. Paul's. The man rapped on the carriage door. The flash servant in his red vest opened the door and grabbed Jess's arm to haul him out to sprawl on the cobbles.

The toff leaned out and grinned at him with ink-stained teeth. He tossed something out—Jess's ragpicker shirt and vest. And a single gold coin.

"For your troubles, gutter rat," the old man said, and shoved another page of something that had once been perfect into his maw to chew it to bits.

Jess found he was weeping, and he didn't know why, except he knew he could never go back to what he'd been before he'd climbed in that carriage. Never not *remember*.

The man in the vest climbed up to the driver's seat of the carriage. He looked down on Jess with an unsmiling, unfeeling stare, then engaged the engine.

Jess saw the old toff inside the carriage tip his hat before he slammed the door, and then the conveyance lurched to a roll, heading away.

Jess came to his feet and ran a few steps after the departing carriage. "Wait!" he yelled, but it was useless, worthless, and it drew attention to the fact that he was half-naked and there was a very visible smuggling harness clutched to his chest. Jess wanted to retch. The death of people crushed under the paws of the Library's lions had shocked him, but seeing that deliberate, horrifying destruction of a book—especially *that* book—it was far worse. St. Paul had said, *Lives are short, but knowledge is eternal.* Jess had never imagined that someone would be so empty that they'd need to destroy something that precious to feel full.

The carriage disappeared around a corner, and Jess had to think about himself, even shaky as he was. He tightened the buckles on the harness again, slipped the shirt over his head and added the vest, and then he walked—he did not run—back to the warehouse where his father waited. The city swirled around him in vague colors and faces.

He couldn't even feel his legs, and he shivered almost constantly. Because the route had been burned into him, he walked by rote, taking the twists and turns without noting them, until he realized he was standing in the street of his father's warehouse.

One of the guards at the door spotted him, darted out, and hustled him inside. "Jess? What happened, boy?"

Jess blinked. The man had a kind sort of look at the moment, not the killer Jess knew he could be. Jess shook his head and swiped at his face. His hand came away wet.

The man looked grave when Jess refused to speak, and motioned over one of his fellows, who ran off quick in search of Jess's father. Jess sank down in a corner, still shaking, and when he looked up, his mirror image was standing in front of him—not quite his mirror, really, since Brendan's hair had grown longer and he had a tiny scar on his chin.

Brendan crouched down to stare directly into his brother's eyes. "You all right?" he asked. Jess shook his head. "You're not bleeding, are you?" When Jess didn't respond, Brendan leaned closer and dropped his voice low. "Did you run into a fiddler?"

Fiddler was the slang they used for the perverts, men and women alike, who liked to get their pleasure from children. For the first time, Jess found his voice. "No," he said. "Not like that. Worse."

Brendan blinked. "What's worse than a fiddler?"

Jess didn't want to tell him, and at that moment, he didn't have to. The office door upstairs slammed, and Brendan jumped to his feet and disappeared again as he climbed up a ladder to the darkened storage where the book crates were hidden.

His father hurried over to where his eldest son sat leaning against the warehouse wall, and quickly ran hands over him to check for wounds. When he found none, he took off Jess's vest and shirt. Callum breathed a sigh of relief when he saw the harness sat empty. "You delivered," he said, and ruffled Jess's hair. "Good lad."

Approval from his father brought instant tears to Jess's eyes, and he had to choke them down. *I'm all untied,* he thought, and he was ashamed of himself. He hadn't been hurt. He hadn't been fiddled. Why did he feel so sullied?

He took a deep breath and told his father the truth, from the lions and the dead people, to the toff in the carriage, to the death of *On Sphere-Making.* Because that was what he'd seen: a murder; the murder of something unique and irreplaceable. That, he began to realize, was what he felt that had left him so unsettled: grief. Grief and horror.

Jess expected his father—a man who still, at heart, loved the books he bought and sold so illegally—to be outraged, or at least share his son's horror. Instead, Callum Brightwell just seemed resigned.

"You're lucky to get away with your life, Jess," he said. "He must have been drunk on his own power to let you see that, and walk. I'm sorry. It's true, there are a few like him out there; we call 'em ink-lickers. Perverts, the lot of them."

"But . . . that was *the* book. *Archimedes's* book." Jess understood, at a very fundamental level, that when he'd seen that book being destroyed, he'd seen a light pass out of the world. "Why did you do it, Da? Why did you sell it to him?"

Callum averted his eyes. He clapped Jess hard on the shoulder and squeezed with enough force to bend bone. "Because that's our business. We sell books to those who pay for the privilege, and you'd best learn that what is done with them after is not our affair. But still, well done. Well done this day. We'll make a Brightwell of you yet."

His father had always been strict about his children writing nightly in their journals, and Jess took up his pen before bed. After much thought, he described the ink-licker, and what it was like seeing him chew up such a rare, beautiful thing. His da had always said it was for the future, a way for family to remember him once he was gone . . . and to never talk about business, because business lived beyond them. So he left that part out, running the book. He only talked about the pervert and how it had made him feel, seeing that. His da might not approve, but no one read personal journals. Even Brendan wouldn't dare.

Jess dreamed uneasily that night of blood and lions and ink-stained teeth, and he knew nothing he'd done had been well done at all.

But it was the world in which he lived, in London, in the year 2025.

⁓〽℗

EPHEMERA

Work submitted by the Scholar Johannes Gutenberg, in the year 1455. Restricted to the Black Archives under the order of the Archivist Magister, for use of Curators only.

One thing is certain: the foundation of the Great Library itself, from the Doctrine of Mirroring forward, rests the safety and security of human knowledge upon the work of Obscurists, and this system cannot be long sustained.

I propose a purely mechanical solution. The attached designs show a device that can efficiently, accurately reproduce text without the involvement of an Obscurist, through the simple use of hand-cut letters, a frame in which they would be placed, ink, and plain paper. Through this method, we may eliminate the Doctrine of Mirroring and instead create fast, easily made reproductions of our volumes.

I have created a working model, and reproduced the page you hold now. It is the first of its kind, and I believe it is the future of the world.

Tota est scientia.

Annotation in the hand of the Archivist Magister.

It is unfortunate that Scholar Gutenberg has fallen prey to this unthinkable heresy. He fails to realize the danger of what he proposes. Without the Library's steady guidance, this device would allow the uncontrollable spread of not only knowledge, but folly. Imagine a world in which anyone, anywhere, could create and distribute their own words, however ignorant or flawed! And we have often seen dangerous progress that was only just checked in time to prevent more chaos.

The machine is to be destroyed, of course, and all such research inter-dicted. Sadly, it becomes obvious that Scholar Gutenberg cannot be trusted. We must silence him and put this lethal heresy out of our minds.

I realize that Gutenberg is a great loss, but we cannot be weak if the Library is to resist this invasive, persistent disease of progress.

CHAPTER ONE

Present day

The first clue Jess had that his hiding place had been discovered came in the form of a hard, open-handed slap to the back of his head. He was engrossed in reading, and he'd failed to hear any telltale creak of boards behind him.

His first instinct was, of course, to save the book, and he protectively curled over the delicate pages even as he slid out of his chair and freed his right hand to draw a knife . . . but it wasn't necessary.

"Brother," he said. He didn't take his hand off the weapon.

Brendan was laughing, but it was a bitter sound. "I knew I'd find you here," he said. "You need some new hiding holes, Jess. No telling when Da will sniff you out of this one. What are you buried in this time?" They no longer looked quite so identical, now that they were older. Brendan wore his hair in a shaggy mess, which half concealed another scar he'd gotten during a run, but they'd grown at the same pace, so their eyes were on a level. Jess glared right back.

"*Inventio Fortunata*. The account of a monk from Oxford who sailed to the Arctic and back hundreds of years ago. And Da won't find this place unless *you* tell him about it."

"Sounds boring." Brendan raised one eyebrow. It was a trick all his own, one Jess hadn't been able to master, so Brendan used it all the time, just to be irritating. "So make it worth my while not to sell you out." Brendan was already as ruthless a deal maker as their father, and that was no compliment. Jess dug in his pockets and came up with a sovereign, which Brendan took with evident satisfaction. "Agreed." He walked the coin back and forth in an expert ripple over his knuckles.

"Damn you, Scraps. I was *reading*." Jess called his brother *Scraps* only when he was really annoyed, because it was a bit of a cruel name: Brendan was the younger by a few seconds and had been born dangerously small. A leftover, an afterthought.

Scraps.

If Brendan minded the use of that once-loathed nickname, he hid it well. He just shrugged. "Like Da always says, we deal the stuff; we shouldn't use it. Waste of time, what you get up to."

"As opposed to what you do? Drinking and gambling?"

Brendan tossed a wet copy of the London *Times* on the floor between them. Jess carefully put down *Inventio Fortunata* to take up the flimsy newssheet. He wiped the beads of water from the page. The top story had an artist's illustration of a face he recognized—older, but he'd never forget the bastard's leering grin. Or the blackened teeth, chewing up priceless words written by a genius thousands of years before.

Brendan said, "Remember him? Six years late, but someone finally got your old ink-licker. Mysterious circumstances, according to the official story."

"What's the real story?"

"Someone slipped a knife between his ribs as he was coming out of his club, so not as mysterious as all that. They're hushing it up. They'll blame it on the Burners, eventually, if they admit it at all. Don't need a reason to blame Burners."

Jess looked up at his brother and almost asked, *Did you do it?*, but in truth, he really didn't want to know the answer. "You came all this way to show me?"

Brendan shrugged. "Thought it might cheer your day. I know it always bothered you, him not getting his due."

The paper was the morning edition, and it must have just turned evening, because as Jess handed it back, the newspaper erased itself, and filled line by line with new words. The ink-licker stayed front-page news, which probably would have pleased the vile old creature.

Brendan rolled the sheet up and slipped it in his pocket. He was making quite a puddle on the floor, and Jess tossed him a dirty towel he kept for wiping his own boots. Brendan sneered and tossed it back. "Well?" he asked. "You coming home?"

"In a while."

"Da wants a word."

Of course he did. Their father didn't like Jess's disappearances, especially since he'd hoped to train him up to inherit the family business. Problem was, Jess had no real love for it. He knew the smuggling trade, but Brendan was more eager and a better choice to take on Callum Brightwell's mantle. Hiding himself away gave Jess freedom, and it also gave Scraps a chance that younger sons didn't usually get.

Not that he'd ever admit, to Brendan or to anyone, that he was doing it as much for his brother as for himself.

"Stuff him. I'll be home when I want to be home." Jess sank down in the chair again. It was a dusty old thing, discarded from some rich banker's house, and he'd dragged it half a mile to this half-collapsed manor off Warren Street. Too much of a wreck for buyers and too flash an area for squatters. It was a good place to hide out, with no one to bother him.

Especially sour, then, that Brendan had found him, because despite the sovereign, Jess would need to find himself a new reading room. He didn't trust his brother not to drop hints . . . for his own good, of course. That meant dragging the chair with him. Again.

Brendan hadn't moved. He was still dripping freely on the old boards.

His eyes were steady and fixed now, and there was no humor in him. "Da said now, Jess. Shift it."

There was no arguing when Brendan took that particular tone; it would come to a fight, no holds barred, and Jess didn't particularly want to lose. He always *did* lose, because deep in his guts, he didn't want to hurt his brother.

Brendan never seemed to have the same limits.

Jess carefully wrapped the fragile book in waterproof layers, then put it into a smuggling harness. He stripped off his loose shirt and fastened the buckles himself with the ease of long acquaintance, only half thinking about it, then put on the shirt and a vest carefully fitted to conceal the secrets beneath. No longer the ragamuffin cutter he'd once been; his shirt was linen now, and the vest well sewn with silk embroideries. He added a thick leather coat, something to keep the rain off, and tossed a second coat at his brother, who fielded it without a word of thanks.

Then the two of them, sixteen years old and mirror images, yet worlds apart, set off together across the city.

Brendan peeled off as soon as they arrived at the family town house; he ran upstairs, past a startled housemaid, who shouted at him about muddying the carpets. Jess tidied himself in the foyer, handed his wet coat to the parlormaid, and made sure his boots were clean before he stepped off onto the polished wood floor.

His mother was coming out of the formal parlor, though the visiting hours were long past. She gave him a quick head-to-toe assessment. He must have been dressed to her satisfaction, because she glided over and delivered a dry kiss on his cheek. She was a neat, pretty woman approaching middle age, with streaks of silver at her temples barely visible in her ash-blond hair. She smelled like light lavender and woodsmoke. The dark blue dress she wore today suited her.

"I wish you wouldn't vex your father so much," she told him, and put her hand lightly on his arm. "He's in one of his moods again. Do try to be civil, for my sake."

"I will," he said, which was an empty promise, but then so was her show of concern. He and his mother weren't close and never had been, really. In this, as in so much else in his life, Jess was alone.

He left her standing there, already engrossed in adjusting a fresh arrangement of daisies and roses, and walked down the hall to his father's study. He knocked politely on the closed door and heard a grunt that meant permission to enter.

Inside, the study was all dark wood, warmed by the fire blazing in the hearth. Prefilled books with the seal of the Library on the spine lined the shelves, color-coded by subject; his father favored biographies and histories, and the maroon and blue leather bindings dominated. He'd purchased a dispensation to have a permanent collection in his home, so most of the books would never expire, never fade or go blank again.

There was not a single original hand-copied work in sight. Callum Brightwell gave no hint here that he was anything but a successful importer of goods. He modeled the Far East today, in the form of the red-orange Chinese silk waistcoat he was wearing beneath his jacket.

"Father," Jess said, and waited for his da to look up and notice him.

It took a few long seconds of Callum's pen moving across the surface of his personal journal before he said, "Sit, Jess. I'd have a word with you."

"So Brendan told me."

Callum laid down his pen and tented his fingers. His desk was a richly carved mahogany thing, with fantastical faces and giant clawed feet that reminded Jess, always, of the Library lions.

Jess took a chair well back from it. His father frowned. He probably thought it was disrespect. Jess would never want to tell him it was bad memories.

"You need to stop this running about," he said. "The weather's not fit for loitering about, and besides, I had work for you."

"Sorry," Jess said.

"Any idea where my copy of *Inventio Fortunata* has got off to? I had a client ask for it."

"No," Jess lied, though the slight weight of the book beneath his shirt and vest seemed to grow heavier as he did. His father didn't usually care about an individual book, and Jess was always careful to take the ones that weren't on consignment. "Do you want me to have a look around for it? Probably misfiled."

"Never mind. I'll sell him something else." His father pushed his chair back and stood up to pace around the desk. Jess resisted the urge to stand, too. It would seem too wary. He didn't sense danger, but his da was a master at sudden violence. Staying alert was better than signaling weakness. "It's time for you to start paying your own way, my boy. You're of an age."

As if he hadn't built up enough credit risking his life his entire childhood. Jess noticed that each step brought his father closer to him, in a roundabout but purposeful way.

"Not going to ask what I'm about, are you? Well played. You're like your brother in that way: both thinkers. Means you're sharp, and that's good. Need a sharp mind out in the cold, cruel world."

Jess was ready, but even so, his father was faster; he lunged forward, hands gripping the arms of Jess's chair, and loomed over him. For all his sixteen years, all his height and strength, Jess suddenly felt like a gawky ten-year-old again, bracing for a blow.

He willed himself to take it without flinching, but the blow never came. His father just stared at him, close and too personal, and Jess had to steel himself to hold the gaze.

"You don't want the business. That's clear enough," his father said. "But then, you're not suited to running it, either. You're more like some *Scholar.* You have ink in your blood, boy, and no help for it. Books will never be just a business to you."

"I've never failed to do what you asked," Jess said.

"And I never asked anything of you that I didn't think you could do. If I told you to throw that book you're smuggling under your shirt on the fire, you'd fail me in *that*, sure enough."

Jess's hands clenched hard, and he had to work not to shout his answer. "I'm not a bloody *Burner*." He somehow kept it to a calm statement.

"That's my point. Sometimes, in our business, destroying a book to keep from being found out is expedience, not some daft political statement. But you couldn't do it. Not even to save your own skin." His father shook his head and pushed away. The sudden freedom made Jess feel oddly weak as his da sank back into his desk chair. "I need to make some use of you. Can't have you sponging off of us like some useless royal for the rest of your life. I spent my coin buying you the best tutors while your brother was earning an honest wage, and I admit, you've done us proud at your studies. But it's time to look to your security."

It was strange, how the idea of his father's approval made him go hot and cold at the same time. Jess didn't know how to take it, and he didn't know what he was supposed to say. So he said nothing.

"Did you hear me?" Callum Brightwell's voice was unexpectedly soft now, and Jess saw something new in the man's face. He didn't know what it was, but it made him sit back in his chair. "I'm talking about your future, Jess."

Jess swallowed a sudden surge of unease. "What sort of future, if not in the business with you?"

"I've bought you a placement in the Library, provided you make the training."

"Do me a favor!" His scoffing didn't change his father's expression, not even with a flicker of annoyance. "You can't be serious. A *Brightwell*. In the Library."

"I'm serious, boy. Having a son in Library service could do the clan immense benefit. You go on a few smuggling raids, set a few of those priceless volumes aside, and you'll make us fortunes. You can send us advance word of raids, High Garda strategies, that sort of thing. And you'd have all the books you could ever lay your eyes on, besides."

"You can't be serious," Jess said. "You want me to be your spy?"

"I want you to be our asset—and advocate, maybe, in the dire event the Brightwells should need one. Library rules the world, son. Best to have a seat at that table. Look, you've more spine and cunning than is comfortable for a father. You could do well at many things, but you could do better for your brother inside the Library. Maybe save his life one day."

Of course his father would try to play on his heartstrings. "I'd never pass the entry test."

"Why do you think I've been paying for those tutors, boy? You'd have to take care to answer only with what any young man your age could learn from the Codex, though. You've got all manner of unlicensed knowledge stuffed in your head. Flaunt it, and they'll do worse to you than send you home disgraced."

His father really *was* serious, and Jess's anger faded with that knowledge; he'd never even considered working in Library service. The idea terrified him on one level; he'd never forgotten the trauma of those Library automata, crushing innocents under their paws. But the Library still held everything he'd ever wanted, too. All the knowledge in the world, right at his fingertips.

When he didn't answer, though, his father sighed, and his voice took on an edge of impatience. "Call it a business deal, boy; it gets you what you crave, and it lends us advantage. Give it an honest go. Fair warning: should you go and give it up, or fail, you'll get nothing else from this family from this day on. Not a penny."

"And what if I stay here?"

"Then I still can't be feeding and clothing a useless lout who's got no loyalty and no usefulness, now, can I? You'll work for us or be on the streets that much sooner."

His father looked hard and unforgiving, and there wasn't any doubt

that he meant what he said. Library test, training, and maybe service, or
out on his own at the age of sixteen, scraping a living any way he could
on the streets. Jess had seen how that served other young men. He didn't
want it.

"You're a low kind of man," Jess said. "But I've always known that. *Da.*"

Callum smiled. His eyes were like cold, dry pebbles. "Is that agreement I hear?"

"Did you really give me a choice?"

His father came forward and dug his fingers hard enough into Jess's
shoulder to leave bruises. "No, son," he said. "That's why I'm good at my
business. See you become just as good at yours."

B uying a placement to Library training was expensive. Most families
couldn't afford to dream of something like that; it was a privilege for
the filthy rich and the noble. The Brightwells were rich enough, but even
so, it was a staggering sum to come up with.

Jess couldn't help the thought that his future had been purchased by
Archimedes's ancient text, chewed up in that dark carriage when he was
ten. Another thing he didn't dare put in his personal journal, though he
did fill pages with careful, tightly inked script about what it felt like, being put under such pressure to succeed. About how much he both loved
and resented the opportunity.

His father paid the fee, and then it was up to Jess. The first step, and in
many ways the hardest, was to report to the London Serapeum for the entry test. He'd avoided the place since the day with the lions, and he didn't
look forward to going there again. To Jess's relief, he was driven by steam
carriage to the public entrance on the west side. There were still a few of
the statues, but they were positioned up on pedestals, so he wouldn't have
to come eye to eye with them.

He felt safer until he noticed the automaton of Queen Anne, staring
down with blank eyes on those trudging up the steps. She held the royal

orb in her left hand, and in her right, a golden scepter pointed down at the heads of those who passed below her pedestal.

She looked eerily human. He had the disquieting feeling that, like the lions, she stood in silent, merciless judgment, and for a giddy moment he imagined her eyes flaring bloodred and that scepter slamming down onto his head. *Unfit for service.*

But she didn't move as he hurried past with the rest of the Library's aspiring postulants.

The test was given in the Public Reading Room's choir stall, and a Scholar robed in black with a silver band on her wrist handed out thin sheets to each of them as they sat down. There were, Jess estimated, about fifty sitting for the test. Most looked terrified, though whether they feared failure or success was open to debate. Failure, most like. They were all richly dressed, and no doubt their futures were riding on their performance. *Today's wealthy second son is tomorrow's penniless lout,* his father had always said.

The test page on Jess's desk began to fill with text. It was in old Library script, designed to be attractive and ornate, and reading it was half the battle . . . but he'd seen and deciphered text far more difficult for fun. The opening questions, while designed to test the limits of a postulant's knowledge, were laughably easy.

He took too much comfort in that, because when the next section came it was *much* harder, and before long, he began to worry and sweat in earnest. The Alchemical and Mechanical sections tested him to the limit, and he wasn't so certain he did as well on the Medica portion as he'd intended. So much for thinking he would glide through without challenge.

Jess hesitated for a long time before signing his name to the end, which inked his final answers. The sheet went blank, and the elegant writing that next appeared told him that results would follow soon and he was free to depart the Serapeum.

When he left, Queen Anne was still judging those who passed, and he tried not to look directly at her as he took the steps two at a time. The day was warm and sunny, pigeons fluttering up in the front of the courtyard, and he looked for the Brightwell carriage, which should have been parked nearby. It had moved down the block, and he jogged toward it. He was nervous, he realized. Actually *nervous* about how he'd done on the test. He cared. It was a new sensation, and one he didn't much care for.

"Sir?" Jess's driver looked anxiously from his perch, clearly wanting to be gone; he was one of his father's musclemen and had spent most of his criminal career staying well clear of the Library. Jess didn't blame him. He got into the back, and as he sat down, his Codex—the leather-bound book that mirrored a list of the Core Collection straight from the Great Library in Alexandria—hummed. Someone had sent him a note. He cracked the cover to see it spell itself out in ornate Library script, one rounded letter at a time. He could even feel the faint vibration of pen scratch from the Library clerk who was transcribing the message.

> *We are pleased to inform you that JESS BRIGHTWELL is hereby accepted for the high honor of service to the Great Library. You are directed to report tomorrow to St. Pancras station in London at ten o'clock in the morning for transportation to Alexandria. Please refer to the list of approved items you may bring with you into service.*

It was signed with the Library seal, which swelled up in raised red beneath the inked letters. Jess ran his fingers over it. It felt slick like wax, but as warm as blood, and he felt a tingle to it, like something alive.

His name stood out, too, in bold black. *JESS BRIGHTWELL.*

He swallowed hard, closed the book, and tried to control his suddenly racing pulse as the carriage clattered for home.

His mother, much affected (or feeling that she ought to be), presented him with a magnificent set of engraved styluses, and his father gifted him with a brand-new leather-bound Codex, a Scholar's edition with plenty of extra pages for notes. Handsomely embossed with the Library symbol in gold.

His brother gave him nothing, but then, Jess hadn't expected anything.

Dinner that night was unusually calm and festive. After the half measure of brandy his mother allowed, Jess found himself sitting alone on the back garden steps. It was a clear, cool night, unusual for London, and he stared up at the swelling white moon. The stars would be different, where he was going. But the moon would be the same.

He'd never expected that the prospect of leaving home would make him feel *sad*.

He didn't hear Brendan come out, but it didn't surprise him to hear the scrape of his brother's boots on the stone behind him. "You're never coming back."

It wasn't what Jess had expected, and he turned to look at Brendan, who slouched with his arms crossed in the shadows. Couldn't read his expression.

"You're clever, Jess, but Da's wrong about one thing: you don't just have ink in your blood. It's in your bones. Your skeleton's black with it. You go there, to *them*, and we'll lose you forever." Brendan shifted a little but didn't look at him. "So don't go."

"I thought you wanted me gone."

Brendan's shoulders rose and fell. He pushed off and drifted away into the darkness. Off doing God knew what. *I'm sorry, Scraps,* he thought. But he wasn't, not really. Staying here wasn't his future, any more than the Library would be Brendan's.

This would be his last night at home.

Jess went inside, wrote in his journal, and spent the rest of the evening reading *Inventio Fortunata*.

Which rather proved his brother's point, he supposed.

The next day, his father accompanied Jess to St. Pancras and waved off servants to personally carry his case to the train . . . all without a single word or change of expression. As Jess accepted the bag from him, his father finally said, "Make us proud, son, or by God I'll wallop you until you do." But there was a faint wet shine in his eyes, and that made Jess feel uncomfortable. His father wasn't weak and was never vulnerable.

So what he saw couldn't be tears.

His father gave him a hard, quick nod and strode away through the swirl of passengers and pigeons. The humid belch of steam engines blew toward the vaulted ceiling of the station and intertwined in ornate ironworks. Familiar and strange at once. For a moment, Jess just stood on his own, testing himself. Trying to see how he felt caught between the old world and the new one that would come.

Still twenty minutes to the Alexandrian train, and he wondered whether or not to get a warm drink from one of the vendors in the stalls around the tracks, but as he was considering tea, he heard a commotion begin somewhere behind him.

It was a man raising his voice to a strident yell, and there was something in it that made him turn and listen.

". . . say to you that you are deceived! That words are nothing more than false idols at which you worship! The Great Library may have once been a boon, but what is it today? What does it give us? It *suppresses*! It *stifles*! You, sir, do you own a book? No, sir, not a blank, filled only with what *they* want you to read . . . a real book, an original work, in the hand of the writer? Do you dare, madam? The Library *owns our memories*, yet you cannot own your own books! Why? Why do they fear it? Why do they fear to allow *you* the choice?"

Jess spotted the speaker, who'd climbed on a stone bench and was now lecturing those passing by as he held up a journal. It wasn't a blank from the Serapeum, stamped with the Library's emblem. What the man brandished was far finer, with a hand-tooled leather cover and his name on it in gilt. His personal journal, in which he would write daily. Jess had one quite like it. After all, the Library provided them free on the birth of a child, and encouraged every citizen of the world to write their thoughts and memories from the earliest age possible. Everyone kept a record of the days and hours of their lives to be archived in the Library upon their deaths. The Library was a kind of memorial, in that way. It was one reason the people loved it so, for the fact that it lent them a kind of immortality.

This man waved his personal journal like a torch, and there was a fever light in his face that made Jess feel uneasy. He knew the rhetoric. The Garda would be on the way soon.

People gave the lecturer a wide berth, scared off by his passion and his wild eyes. Jess looked around. Sure enough, a knot of red-coated London Garda was heading toward the spot. The Burner saw them coming, too, and Jess saw his face go pale and set under that untidy mop of hair. He raised his voice even more. "A man cannot be reduced to paper, to lines and letters! He cannot be consigned to a shelf! A life is worth more than a book! *Vita hominis plus libro valet!*"

That last rose to a ringing shout of victory. The man reached under his coat and took out a bottle of poison green liquid, thumbed off the cap, and poured a single drop on the cover of the personal journal he held. Then he threw the book down to the stone floor, and in a second it ignited with a shocking burst of flame that burned emerald at the edges and bloomed in a towering column straight up into the air. Those closest stumbled back with alarmed gasps and cries of surprise.

"Greek fire!" someone screamed, and then there was a scramble, a full-on rush of people for the exits. It impeded the progress of the London Garda, who were heading against the tide.

"The Library wants you to live blind!" the Burner shouted. "I die to show you the light! Don't trust them! They lie!"

Jess should have run, he supposed; he was buffeted on all sides by those with more sense, but with frozen dread and—yes—fascination, he lingered to watch the man. The book, burning on the stones, held a ghastly echo for him of helpless fury and horror, as if the pages themselves were screaming for rescue. It was an original work, an *only copy*, written in ink on paper. It was the man's thoughts and dreams, and it was . . . dying. It wasn't *On Sphere-Making*, but Jess had to fight the impulse to rush to save it, regardless.

"Out of the way!" a Garda cried, and pushed him almost off his feet, toward the exit. "Get clear! Don't you know Greek fire when you see it, you fool?"

He did, and he also realized—all too late—that the Burner didn't have just the drop that he'd used on the book for his demonstration. The man had a full flask-sized bottle of the stuff, and he was holding it high. It glittered like a murky emerald in the dim light from the windows.

Jess took a step back and stumbled on his train case. He fell over it, still watching the Burner. *I should get out of here,* he thought, but it felt as if his brain had gone to sleep, lulled by the mesmerizing rush of the fire. He *wanted* to leave, but his body wouldn't respond.

"Cork that bottle, son," one of the Garda said as he approached the Burner. He was older, and he sounded authoritative and oddly kind. "There's no need for this. You've made your point, and if you want to destroy your own words, well, that's your burden and no one else's, sure enough. Cork that and put it down. No harm done. You'll only have a fine, I promise you."

"Liar," the man said, and for the first time, Jess realized that he was, in fact, only a little older than Jess himself. Twenty years old, at most. He looked serious and desperate and afraid, but there was something in his eyes, something wild. "You're a tool of the Library, and I will not be silenced by you! *Vita hominis plus libro valet!*"

It was the Burners' motto: *A life is worth more than a book.*

They were also his last words.

The young man upended the bottle of Greek fire over the front of his clothes and then poured the rest on his head, and the men who'd been advancing on him backed up, then turned and ran.

Jess saw the chemicals glow, spark, ignite, and consume the Burner in green fire that blew up toward the vaulted ceiling in an awful explosion of light. The sound was like nothing Jess had ever heard before—an indrawn breath of sucking air, and the crackle and fizz, and then the screams.

Oh God, the terrible screams.

One of the Garda grabbed Jess and bowled him over the edge of the platform to crash hard down onto the gravel bed of the tracks, only a few feet from the iron skirt of a locomotive. The man's weight crushed him down on a rail, and he struggled to breathe. From the corner of his eye he saw the firestorm billowing over their heads, a torrent of green and yellow and red.

The screaming stopped, and the horrible banner of flame drew back in, though the fire still raged.

The Garda who'd pulled him over the edge kept him down when he tried to stand up. "No," he said, panting. His face was pale under his black helmet. "Just stay down; the air's toxic up there until it burns completely out."

"But he's—"

"Dead," the man said, and held Jess's shoulder tightly. "And nothing we can do for him. The stupid boy, he didn't need to—" His voice was unsteady, and then it failed him altogether, and for all that Jess had grown up as enemies with the Garda, in that moment they were united in horror. "Damned Burners. No reasoning with 'em. Getting worse every year." The man blinked back tears and looked away.

Jess sat back against the rough stone wall and stared at the flickering glow of the fire above them until, at last, it died.

The Garda questioned him—not that they suspected him of anything, but he'd stayed while others fled, and he was of an age when young men might turn to such causes. He answered truthfully and showed them his Codex, which contained his travel papers to Alexandria and his official acceptance letter. He worried about missing the train, but nothing was running, not until the Garda were satisfied the danger was gone.

It took several hours, and he supposed they'd sent word to his family, but no one came. He remembered his da being told that his older brother, Liam, had been taken while running books, and the grief and resignation on his father's face. His father hadn't stood up to claim Liam. He'd not be visiting the Garda to retrieve Jess, either, should the worst come to pass.

Jess's nerves were as tight as wires, but the Garda finally let him return to the tracks, where scrubbing had removed all trace of the Burner's death, except for discolorations. *The book,* Jess thought, as he stood and looked down at the smaller stain on the floor. *This is where the book died.* It was the same ugly black scar as the one where the Burner had ignited himself on the bench.

Books and men left the same traces where they burned.

The idea that the young man had taken his personal journal with him into the flames left a sour taste in the back of Jess's throat: it wasn't just that he'd given up his life; it was that he'd given up any hope of people understanding his purpose. Maybe nobody would have ever read it; maybe his reasons would have been found utterly mundane and useless. But by burning it, he'd erased himself as completely as anyone could. To a modern man, growing up with the comfort of knowing the Library would keep his memories intact, it seemed . . . inconceivable.

Jess realized that he was getting strange looks as he stood there, and picked up his train case to move to his platform.

They'd delayed the schedules, and the station was once again full to bursting. Funny how normal it all was again. Trains chuffed their pale mist into the air, and men, women, and children strolled or bustled, absorbed in their own business. The pigeons had returned, too, to peck at crumbs falling from hastily eaten pies and sandwiches. The only difference, as far as Jess could tell, was that there were more Garda scattered around the station, looking out for more Burners come to imitate their newest martyr.

Brutal as it was, it seemed to Jess that the man's death had been nothing but a rock dropped in a fast-moving stream: a brief splash, then no trace left. He didn't know whether that was appalling or comforting.

He moved on to the platform and joined the long queue for boarding the long, sleekly silver train. At the gate, the elderly uniformed conductor said, "Best make yourself comfortable, my lad. Long journey ahead. Under to France, through to Spain, across to Morocco, then on to the city. Be sure to keep your papers handy to show at the last Alexandrian border. Sure you have everything?"

Jess thanked him and looked for his spot. He wasn't surprised his father had bought him a cheap fare; the fancier travelers had plush seats and tea trolleys, but the car he settled in was well used and smelled of mold and stale food and feet. Crowded, too; more and more bodies jammed on, taking space to pile their bags and cases. Jess rested his feet on his own luggage. He hadn't grown up trusting the good intentions of strangers.

He wrote in his journal about the Burner, about the trip and his fellow passengers, then put away his pen and slept and ate as the miles clacked by and stops ticked off. Travelers disembarked, and fewer got on than off, which was a relief. The makeup of those around him changed slowly as they left England through the underground tunnel to the Library territory of France; there was nervous talk of danger all the way to the coast, and many breathed a sigh of relief when they made it to the safety of the tunnel without incident; the Welsh army had been pushing in, closer and closer. No one took safe passage for granted, though so far the trains had been spared any threat.

By the time they pulled close to the Spanish border a full day later, most of those on board seemed to fall into two types: new postulants like him, young and mostly nervous, huddled in small groups, or self-assured Library employees, easily picked out even in civilian dress by the bands they wore on their wrists in copper, silver, and—a rare sighting—one in gold. Jess wondered what it would feel like, knowing you had a position that would last a lifetime. Would it free you or make you feel trapped? *Not that I'll ever know,* he thought. The Library offered gold to only a select few in a generation.

The rest of the trip was long but uneventful; some storms along the way, but a smooth enough ride all the way to the tip of Spain, where the entire remaining company disembarked, blinking in the fierce sun before boarding a large ferry for the trip across the water.

When they boarded the Alexandrian train in Morocco, a few new passengers entered. One of them was hard to miss. A blond, blue-eyed boy of about Jess's own age who looked big enough to bend iron . . . which made it odd how he moved so carefully past others and apologized for every bump. Too considerate by half.

Jess met his gaze for a second and nodded, and that was a mistake. The giant headed straight for him and said, "May I sit here?" His English was good but accented with German.

"Plenty of seats, mate. Sit where you like."

He thought that might be a sign to the boy to move on, but instead, Jess was presented with a meaty hand to be shaken, and the other boy said, "Thomas Schreiber."

"Jess Brightwell." They shook, and the boy wedged his big frame into the seat beside Jess and let out a lingering sigh of relief.

"Finally, room to breathe."

Jess didn't much agree with that, as Thomas had just taken up most of his. "Come a long way?"

"Berlin. You know Berlin?"

"Not personally," Jess said. "Nice place?"

"Very nice. And you? From?"

"London."

"In England? But that is a long way also!"

"It is, yeah. Guess you're off to Library training, too?"

"I am. I hope for a placement in engineering. My grandfather was a silver band for many years."

"Engineering . . . that falls under Artifex. Heard that was a hard one. Does having a silver-band relative make you some kind of legacy, then?" When he received a blank look from Thomas, Jess tried again. "Legacy means you didn't have to sit for the entry tests. Kids of gold bands get to go straight into training. Wasn't sure about silver."

"Would be nice, yes? No, no, nothing like that. I had to take the examination."

"Yeah? How'd you do?"

Thomas shrugged. "All right."

"I got seven hundred fifty. Highest score in London." He realized, as he said it, that it sounded like boasting. Well, all right. He was proud of it.

Thomas raised his pale eyebrows and nodded. "Very good." There was something in the carefully polite way he said it that made Jess glower at him.

"What was yours?"

Thomas looked reluctant to say it, but Jess's stare finally dragged it out of him. "Nine hundred twenty-five."

"What?"

"Students from Berlin have always done well on the examination." Thomas made it sound both proud and apologetic at the same time.

"Done *well*? Mate, I'm sure none of the Scholars in London could have scored that. Must be the highest score of the year!"

"No," Thomas said. "That would be hers." He looked around the train and nodded toward a young woman sitting near the back. Jess belatedly recognized her. She'd boarded earlier, with a flurry of relatives who'd clustered around her and departed only when the conductor had given them a warning.

She was as small as Thomas was large, and from the little Jess could see of her, she seemed darker skinned, with a closely pinned black cloth covering her hair. Hard to see anything, really, because she was engrossed in a book.

"That one," Thomas said. "She was the first in the history of the examination to have a perfect score, they say. Not the first girl. The first *anyone*." He sounded impressed and respectful. As Jess stared behind him, the girl lowered her book and returned their gazes with forthright brown-eyed intensity. Thomas, embarrassed at being caught out, quickly turned face forward again.

Jess, on the other hand, kept looking. She was pretty, not beautiful, but there was something about her that he found interesting. She cocked one eyebrow higher than the other, just like his brother's favorite trick, and he tried to mirror it back. Still couldn't.

So he settled for standing up and climbing past the mountain range of Thomas's knees.

"Where are you going?" Thomas whispered.

"To say hello," Jess said. "Smartest girl in the world? Worth knowing."

"I wouldn't . . ."

Jess was already walking back toward the girl, who was still watching him with that challenging dark stare, when a man moved over to take a seat next to her. He was a rounded fellow, older, expensively dressed in traditional Arab robes.

Jess stopped and bowed politely to the girl. She nodded back. "Wanted to introduce myself," he said. "Jess Brightwell. That's my mate Thomas Schreiber, the big shy one back there."

"Khalila Seif," she said. "May I present my uncle Nasir? He is accompanying me to the Alexandrian border."

The uncle gave Jess a warm smile, rose, and gave him a bow in return. It was all very civil, but he wasn't leaving the girl's side—that much was obvious.

Jess turned back to Khalila. "Highest score on the test," he said. "You'd be guaranteed a place, I suppose."

"Nothing in life is guaranteed. I may not be able to handle the work, after all. Some people prove fragile."

"Fragile," Jess repeated. "Yeah, you don't strike me that way."

"You are also a student, sir?" her uncle asked.

"Nowhere near as bright as your niece, sir, but yes."

"And from where?"

"England, sir."

"Ah. Are you not at war . . . ?"

"Not the part of the country I'm from," Jess said. The man was too well-mannered to say it, but he clearly thought England was a hotbed of trouble. "Well, I'll let you read, then, Miss Seif. Pleasant trip."

"Thank you for your courtesy, Mr. Brightwell," she said. "I wish you a smooth journey as well." Very formal, but the smile less so. Not warm, exactly. But not afraid.

And definitely not fragile.

Jess climbed back over Thomas to his seat and said, "Well, that's one placement spoken for; she'll end up a Curator one day, if not the damned Archivist. My future's looking dimmer all the time." He didn't mean it. He liked challenges, and this . . . this was turning out to be one of the best challenges he'd faced in his life. It was boring, always being smarter. Already, he felt he'd have to work for it here.

You're never coming back. Brendan's words suddenly returned to him. They were prophetic; already his family seemed like a fading dream. He felt good here.

He felt right.

As the conductors outside the train windows cried last boarding, a rawboned young woman ran hell-bent for their car. Not a graceful sort of movement, but those long legs ate up the platform's length, and she leaped for the still-open door in the last second before the conductor slammed it shut and the train's whistle blew. She leaned against the paneling, flushed and sweating, and overbalanced and fell onto Jess's and Thomas's laps as the train lurched into motion.

No lightweight, this girl. And sharp elbows. Jess winced and rubbed his chest as she fought her way back to her feet and glared at him and Thomas as though they were guilty of an assault on her person.

"Welcome," Thomas said. "Thomas Schreiber. Berlin." He offered her a hand. She clawed disordered, curling brown hair back from her face, and her glare turned to an outright frown, but she shook. Grudgingly. "And you are . . . ?"

"Glain Wathen. Merthyr Tydfil." She shut up fast as her eyes fell on Jess.

"Jess Brightwell. London."

She gave him a sour look, then pushed off and found a seat near the back.

"She doesn't like you," Thomas said. "Does she know you?"

"No need," Jess replied. He could feel Glain's stare boring into the back of his head. "By the sound of her, she's Welsh. She's probably making a plan to stick a knife in my kidney before we get to the border." When Thomas just continued to look confused, he said, "I'm English. Blood feuds. Makes people irrational."

"Ah," Thomas said, but he didn't seem particularly illuminated. Not up on his current wars, Jess thought. Or didn't seem to understand that the Southern Conflict had been going on for more than fifty years, with bloody losses on both the Welsh and English sides. Of late, the Welsh had been handily winning the day.

Glain looked like one of those unpleasant firebrands who couldn't just leave it at the border. Jess didn't mind, really. At least that was one fellow student he wouldn't mind cutting out in competition for a spot.

The miles clacked on, toward their uncertain future.

The Alexandrian border crossing meant that anyone without commissions into Library territory had to disembark, which meant the departure of Khalila's uncle. He clearly didn't like leaving his girl to the unwashed masses—and to be fair, they were all fairly unwashed, at the moment, on this train—but he went with good grace.

Jess nodded a polite good-bye, then turned and winked at Khalila. She ignored him. She'd fallen into a hushed, intense conversation with the Welsh girl, Glain, though whatever they had in common he couldn't imagine. Glain was as plain as Khalila was pretty, and her manners seemed rude where the Arab girl had grace and charm to spare. No accounting for taste, he supposed. He and Thomas played cards, drawing in a few more players as the hours clicked by; even one of the Library's silver bands sat in, and though his English was dodgy and spiced with a Chinese accent, he was a right madman for a bet, and Jess lost half his cash before he bowed out and slept.

When he woke up, Thomas had won back most of the money and had a contented, cherubic look on his face, and they were pulling into Alexandria, in Egypt.

Jess wasn't the only one gawking out the windows; most of those in the car were doing it, even adults with their bands of service on their wrists. Because this city . . . it was worth seeing.

They were arriving at Misr Station, all gleaming white marble and buff-colored stones; it was blinding in the noonday glare. The station itself rose three graceful stories of fluted columns, with ancient Egyptian statues of the old gods reaching to the same height. When the carriage stopped, they were facing hawk-faced Horus's massive feet, and Jess craned his head to look up. The beaked head blocked out the sun, and the gold leaf and blue enamel gleamed brighter than anything Jess had ever seen.

"Amazing," Thomas breathed. "Do you think it's an automaton? At that size?"

Jess shuddered. "Perish the thought."

Thomas scrambled up, grabbed his bag (twice the size of Jess's, but then, he was twice Jess's size), and rushed for the train car door. He was onto the platform before Jess could pull his own case from beneath his seat, but he caught up with the German quickly, and against his will, his steps slowed and stopped. The two of them stood together, just drinking it in. The sun felt different here: relentlessly hot but strangely welcoming just the same. Humid ocean air blew in and ruffled Jess's hair, drying the sweat that was already beading on his face. And the silent, majestic rows of gods stretched on in a cleanly ordered march that seemed to go for miles, each one of them different. *They've all got stories,* Jess thought. *I need to know them.* Best of all, he *could* know them. He could learn anything here.

It felt like limitless possibilities.

Khalila had joined them, he realized, and was gaping just as openly. Even Glain seemed stunned as she climbed down off the train steps and landed in this new, alien, intimidating land.

It seemed so *clean.*

Soon enough, they'd drawn a real cluster around them, as new postulants disembarked. Maybe it was just because Thomas was so tall and made a good center pole, but when Jess looked around there must have been thirty of them together, and they were all milling about, uncertain of their next steps . . . until a man strode out from the shadow of Horus's feet toward them.

He drew everyone's attention: black Scholar's robes that billowed around a plain black day suit. A gleaming gold band on his wrist, chased with elegant hieroglyphs and the Library seal. Dark shoulder-length hair swept back in a mane from a fiercely intelligent face. Narrow dark eyes and nut-brown skin. The students fell silent as he approached, and pulled closer together. *Gazelles facing a lion,* Jess thought.

The Scholar looked them over with unforgiving assessment. The silence stretched until Jess thought it might shatter poor old Horus's legs, and then the man said, "My name is Scholar Christopher Wolfe, and I take it you are incoming postulants. Let me be clear; most of you might as well turn around and board the train now for home. I have six slots to fill, *if* I decide to fill them at all, which at first glance is unlikely. Does anyone want to book a return now and save themselves the time and pain?"

No one stirred, though several made twitchy moves, as though they were considering it. Not Jess. Nor Thomas, nor Khalila, nor Glain. Rock solid. *For now,* Jess thought.

This had just gotten very interesting.

EPHEMERA

Text of a letter by Thomas Paine of the Territory of America, written in 1795. Consigned to the Black Archives; not available to the Codex. Access strictly controlled. Marked as SEDITIOUS CONTENT.

There are three parts to learning: information, knowledge, and wisdom. A mere accumulation of information is not knowledge, and a treasure of knowledge is not, in itself, wisdom.

The Library holds itself to be the keeper of both knowledge and wisdom, but it is not true. So much should never be held in the hands of so few, for it is a natural, venal habit of men to hold to power. And knowledge is the purest form of power.

The Curators mete out knowledge and progress in drips and drops, and see their duty to the people as that of a parent to an infant. As a parent will keep danger from his child, so then does the Library seek to protect us from what it deems dangerous knowledge.

But there is no wisdom without knowledge, no progress without danger, and I am not the Library's child! I must acquire my own information, build my own knowledge, and, through experience, transform it to the treasured gold of wisdom.

To this end, I say that the greatest good that can be done for mankind is to shatter the doors of the Great Library and make off with its storehouse of knowledge, spread it far and wide, for though the Library's history is vast and deep, even the greatest invention can turn upon its creators. And so the very institution we thought would bring the most light to the world has instead drowned it in shadows, and claimed that shadow as full sun. And we, poor blind creatures, have believed the lie.

It is a fine thing to preserve knowledge, but to set the Great Library above men, above nations, above life? This is not wisdom.

I will not believe that life is worth less than ink on a page. Let that be our rallying cry. Let us shout it where we can. Let us raise our hands against the false idols of the Serapeums wherever they rise.

Let us burn our life's work before they seize upon it and lock it in the darkness.

Let us burn it down and bring new light into the world.

A handwritten annotation to the tract, in the hand of Archivist Magister Alessandro Volta, 1795.

The American Territory has become a fetid jungle in which grows a dangerous heresy. See that it is rooted out by whatever means are necessary.

The Burner philosophy must, for our continued survival, be destroyed.

CHAPTER TWO

L ondon had been, to Jess, a sprawling modern metropolis. It had been impossible to imagine anything more majestic than the buildings that had challenged that low, gray sky. On some very basic level, he had always believed that England, and London, was quite simply *better* than the rest of the world.

His first indication that he was wrong had been when his new friend Thomas shared the news that students in Berlin regularly scored far better than he did on the tests, but that might have been simply a fluke . . . until he began to talk to his fellow postulants and began to realize that every one of them—*every one*—was as good as he was, or better.

And then there was Alexandria. Oh, Alexandria.

London had been a warren of narrow, winding streets, tiny alleys, blind corners. Crowds. Dirt that never quite seemed to be scrubbed away, even in the cleanest of places. It was a wonder, but a wonder that had the sweat and dirt of humanity ground deep for more than two thousand years.

Alexandria, for all its long, turbulent history, gleamed like heaven. Everywhere it was sparkling and spotless, with broad avenues for steam carriages and wide, flat pedestrian walkways that led past preserved ancient monuments. Priceless gold-decked statues commemorated a rich and ancient legacy, and it stunned Jess, once he thought about it, that no one sneaked about at night to pry the precious stuff away. Even the poor seemed to have respect for history here. Every building was carefully maintained and fresh painted each year in what he was told was a riotous public festival, and the streets were lined with beautiful gardens, flowers, trees, fountains, all carefully groomed. The city even *smelled* good.

For the most part, the people matched the place: exotic, clean, attractive, polite. Cosmopolitan.

He felt like a rude country lout, compared to most of those he saw on the trip to their lodgings. Scholar Wolfe had commissioned a large carriage to carry them all, and as it chugged smoothly along past overwhelming wonders, Wolfe stood in the aisle and talked.

"You will be quartered at Ptolemy House," he said. "You are treated as adults; there are no childish rules, no one to coddle you. You will share rooms. The accommodations are not luxurious. There will be a staff on duty, but they are not your servants and they will not clean up your messes. Tomorrow you will begin your studies. Am I clear?"

They all murmured agreement, then shouted it when he demanded more volume. And when the carriage parked, he was the first off, gone before Jess could think of a single question to ask. Not, he sensed, that Scholar Wolfe would have been inclined to answer one.

Ptolemy House proved to be an unremarkable squared-off building near Alexandria University. It was not luxurious, as Wolfe had said, but Jess had dossed in far worse places in his life. It was clean and cool, and that was what counted.

Room assignments were posted in the hallway. He found his number, opened the matching door, and half carried, half dragged his train case inside before he collapsed boneless on the first bed he came to.

It never occurred to him that it might not be his *own* bed until the bathroom door opened and an impossibly good-looking young man in a crimson robe said, "*¿Quién diablos es usted?* Who the devil are you?" The maroon of the robe went well with his bronzed skin, and his eyes were almost as dark as his hair.

Jess had already met his fill of new people, but he dragged himself upright to a sitting position, rubbed sweat from his palm, and offered it to the new boy. "Jess Brightwell," he said. "I suppose we're to share the space."

"No," the other boy said. "I have a private room. Get out."

That was it. Nothing but the cold words. Jess slowly lowered his hand back to his side and wondered for a moment what exactly the right move would be, and then he just let himself fall back to the pillow. It felt good. "I'm too tired for it, mate," he said. "I claim this bed for England."

That lasted about five seconds, before the Spaniard grabbed him by the collar of his shirt and heaved him bodily upright again, and threw him on the floor. "Out!" he said, and showed very white teeth. "Final warning. This is my room. I don't share."

Jess had his measure now, and the shove hadn't actually had much force behind it; the boy clearly never expected to *really* fight. He'd been born rich and was used to those around him deferring to whatever he wished.

Jess rolled into a crouch, exploded upward, and slammed the boy hard against the wall with a forearm like a bar against his throat. "Let's start again," he said, and bared *his* teeth this time. "*I live here* because my name's posted on the bloody list outside. If that's your bed, I apologize, and I'll take the other. Fair enough?" He emphasized it by leaning forward. The Spaniard struggled a little, but their gazes locked, and he must have seen that Jess was serious.

"Keep the bed," the other boy said. His voice sounded rough and strangled under the pressure of Jess's arm. "You've gotten your sweat all over it. I wouldn't touch it now."

"Fine." Jess let go and stepped back. He offered his hand, again. "Let's start over. Jess Brightwell."

The Spaniard continued to stare at him with a slight frown grooved above those sharp eyes, and he finally took Jess's hand and gave it a too-firm squeeze. "Dario Santiago," he said. "We won't be friends."

"Probably not," Jess said. "But we *will* be sharing this room."

Dario's lips suddenly curved into a truly amused smile. "You may not prefer that, in the end."

For some reason, Jess had assumed that Library classes would be held, well, in the *Library*, though that institution was more of a sprawling, vast complex than any single building. He'd expected a steady diet of classrooms and essays and tests, the same as he'd had back in London at the Library-administered public schools.

But Scholar Wolfe wasn't so predictable.

At dawn the next morning, shrill bells rang throughout the dormitory, throwing Jess groaning from his bed, still sore and stupid with exhaustion. He hadn't unpacked, and he struggled with the suitcase locks for far too long before he remembered how to work them properly. Inside, his clothes smelled of damp, of London, and he felt a strange pang of homesickness for a moment, though not for his family so much as for familiarity.

He grabbed a clean pair of trousers, a shirt, underwear, and a vest, and hurried for the bathroom.

Too late. Dario was already inside, with the door firmly locked. Jess cooled his heels and seethed as Dario took his sweet, leisurely time. He was still waiting when Thomas banged on the outer door, cracked it, and said, "Coming, English? You're late!"

"I'm still waiting for the shower! He's slower than my mother."

"You'd better come anyway. Scholar Wolfe is not a man to keep waiting."

That was certainly true, just from the first acquaintance at the train station. Jess cursed softly and stripped down as Thomas politely turned his broad back. He was pulling on his boots when Dario finally unlocked the bathroom door and stepped out, wreathed in an herb-scented cloud of steam. He looked fresh, perfect, and every inch a gentleman.

Jess felt like an unwashed, grainy-eyed lout, but he yanked his boots in place and followed. Thomas stood aside to let Dario pass and raised his pale eyebrows at Jess. "Is there a problem?"

"Don't ask," Jess said.

"The key must be to get up before him," Thomas said.

"Thank you for spotting the obvious."

Thomas just grinned and held the door open. He was big enough that Jess hardly had to stoop to walk under his outstretched arm.

The common room on the ground floor was already filled, and Jess felt even worse, seeing that everyone else had managed freshly washed faces and neatly arranged hair. He tried to finger comb his into some semblance of order, but from Thomas's mournful headshake, it wasn't a success.

Scholar Wolfe didn't come for them. Instead, he sent a tall man dressed in the intimidating black of the Library's High Garda elite, with a gold band on his wrist. The weapons he kept on his belt looked well cared for and, perhaps more significantly, well used.

Thomas nudged Jess with an unsubtle elbow and leaned close to whisper, "He is a Library soldier!"

"I know that," Jess whispered back. "What's he doing here?"

Thomas shrugged. "Perhaps frightening us?"

Accurate observation, because the man swept them with an indifferent, middle-distance stare that was more intimidating than a glare. He took a swift count and said just two words: "With me." Then walked down the hall, leaving them all to scramble along in his wake.

Outside, there were no waiting carriages, and the High Garda soldier led them down the boulevard at a quick-march pace. The sun was just rising, but it was already unreasonably hot and damp, and clothing that had seemed comfortable in London quickly felt smothering in Alexandria. Jess thought that it was an advantage to have skipped the shower, in all, because while he was sweating through his clothes, so were the others, even Dario, and by the time they finally came to a halt in front of a nondescript low building, Jess seemed no worse off than his fellows.

They'd walked all the way to the harbor, Jess realized; he could see the steamships bobbing beyond the low roofs, and the large passenger ships moving in to the docks, ready to disembark their travelers. He longed to see all that; he'd always loved being on the docks in London, with all the noise and activity. The half-reeking, half-fresh smell of the sea seemed like home.

But instead, their guide led them to a silent, darkened building with a single entrance. No windows. Going inside it felt like walking into a tomb . . . and the floor slanted down.

"Where are we?" he asked Thomas, but the bigger young man just shook his head. The ceiling was low enough that Thomas had to stoop. The walls were plain, but they seemed to have dirty smudges on them, and the whole place reeked of an acrid, chemical smell. Not that he had time to ponder it, because their High Garda guide was still walking at a brisk martial pace.

Then, suddenly, they emerged into a much wider, taller room. Jess took three steps inside and stopped, craning his head upward to admire the vaulting height of it. Someone shoved him from behind, and he moved out of the way to a spot on the side of the room. It was rounded and, like the hallway, bare of decoration. Their small group of thirty didn't take up much room in the relatively vast space.

The room seemed very sparse. Impressive, but empty; the walls had the same dark smudges, and the air still carried that sharp, chemical tang. It reminded Jess of something, but he couldn't think what.

In silence, they waited. Their High Garda guide had disappeared, leaving the rest of them staring at one another. Jess had met most of the postulants, though the names escaped his tired brain at present; he most vividly knew Dario, of course, and Thomas. He spotted Khalila standing off on her own, looking fresh and calm in her headdress and loose robes, while the Welsh girl, Glain, towered over the other females by several inches.

None of them spoke. A few shifted from one foot to the other in discomfort from the long walk, but by common consent, they understood this was not a place for conversation.

And then Wolfe emerged from the single entrance and walked into the center of the room. He looked just as he had at the train station: dark, dangerous, and impatient. He took a moment to look around the room at each of them, and then said, "Here begins your first lesson. You stand in the first daughter library of Alexandria, the first Serapeum. In this room, copies of works from the stores of the Great Library were first made available to anyone who cared to come and read them . . . even women, though that was not common practice at the time. Alexandria was the first place in the world to encourage common people to read and learn. The first to educate without regard to status, creed, sex, or religion. You stand in the birthplace of our history."

He let that sit for a moment, and in truth, Jess could feel the weight of it bearing down on him. The walls had been renovated, obviously, but the floor had not. It was ancient stone, worn smooth by millions of steps taken across it. *Archimedes might have walked here,* he thought. *Might have scratched out that first copy of* On Sphere-Making, *sitting at a table right over there.*

It gave him a chill, as if he was surrounded by ghosts.

"The reason I am here as your proctor is to teach you who we are. What we do. And we begin here in this place where the Great Library took the first steps toward what it has become." He paused, studying them. "Do you understand what the job of a librarian is?"

It seemed like a stupid question, and hands shot up. Wolfe sighed. "You are not children," he said, "and I will not favor the shy. Speak out if you have an answer."

A riot of voices. Wolfe scanned the crowd and pointed a finger. "You," he said. "Step forward, give your name, speak your mind."

A pretty young girl with glossy red hair and a confident smile moved forward with perfect grace. "Anna Brygstrom, sir, from Denmark. Librarians run the daughter libraries, the Serapeum."

"Postulant Brygstrom, I did not ask for your nationality. You have no homeland here, because once you enter Library service, it is your nation. We are your countrymen." He paused, and there was a cruel glitter in his eyes. "If you've come all the way here to learn the mundane details of how to create a work schedule and properly fill a patron's request, then you are in the wrong place. A properly trained marmoset could run a daughter library, since it is merely a mirror of what is concentrated here, in Alexandria. Step back."

She no longer had a smile, confident or otherwise, as she disappeared back into the circle.

Someone else stepped forward to take her place, and Jess recognized in the next second that it was the Arab girl. Khalila.

"Postulant Khalila Seif, sir. We are not here to learn how to run a daughter library. We are here to learn how the Great Library itself runs."

Wolfe stared at her for a long few seconds, then nodded sharply. "Correct. Step back, Postulant Seif. On the highest possible level, the Library exists because each nation of the world benefits from it, and because the Library favors none, relies on none. It took time to free ourselves from the tyranny of politics, kings, and priests; it took time to assemble the wealth and the force to defend what we have. But most of all, it took a miracle. And what was that miracle?"

Jess took a chance and stepped forward. "Jess—Postulant Jess Brightwell, sir. The discovery of mirroring." He kept it short and to the point; it was Scholar Wolfe's job to lecture, and if he tried, he could tell it would only lead to a bloody scar on him. At Wolfe's precise nod, he moved back again.

"In 1029, the Serapeum of Rayy in Persia was utterly destroyed, with the devastating loss of more than fifty thousand original works. It was an orgy of looting and fire that destroyed thousands of years of knowledge. We credit the four hundred and second leader of the Great Library, Archivist Magister Akkadevi, with the discovery of mirroring, by which the contents of any book, any scroll, any document, may be written into a similarly treated Library blank. The benefit of mirroring? You." Wolfe didn't wait for volunteers. He picked someone out of the circle.

"Postulant Glain Wathen, sir. It freed the Library from risking original books and scrolls. It doesn't matter if a blank is damaged or lost; it can always be requested again."

"Correct. The destruction of Rayy taught us that calculated politics and unthinking rage—make no mistake, the two are sometimes hand in hand—are the greatest threats knowledge can face. The Doctrine of Mirroring was the first great advance of the Library, the foundation on which all others were built. It ensures protection of knowledge while also giving free access to all, and this was an unquestioned good. But what followed?"

No one stepped forward this time for a moment, and Wolfe didn't point. He waited. Finally, Thomas stepped forward from his spot beside Jess and cleared his throat. "Postulant Thomas Schreiber, sir. The next doctrine issued was the Doctrine of Ownership."

"The Doctrine of Ownership states that the Great Library must, for the protection and preservation of knowledge in trust for the world, own all such knowledge. Which means what, Postulant Schreiber?"

"It's illegal to own an original," he said. "Sir."

"Illegal," Wolfe repeated. "And do you agree with this doctrine, Postulant Brightwell?"

Jess flinched; he hadn't expected that, not at all. He stepped forward. Thomas didn't seem to know whether or not he should move back, so it left both of them together, side by side. That made it a little easier.

"Sir?"

"I asked your opinion of the doctrine. Do you agree it should be wrong to own original works?"

Of course, Jess knew he ought to say; it was the standard answer. The Library was never wrong. But something made him say, "I'm not sure."

That woke a glint in Wolfe's eyes. "Why not?"

"I'd like to hold one," Jess said, quite honestly. "To feel the weight and history of it in my hands. A blank can't be the same, sir."

"No," Wolfe agreed. "A blank is a poor, pale imitation, though the words are arranged in precisely the same order; it is the difference between an idea and a physical thing. And some crave the physical thing, legal or not. Which is why there are such things as shadow markets, and the black trade, and ink-lickers."

Jess went cold inside because he felt—perhaps wrongly—that it was a very personal message to him, from Wolfe, that there was no hiding who he was or where he'd come from.

Wolfe motioned for the two of them to step back, which was a deep relief. He paced around the circle, meeting the eyes of every student.

"While the Doctrine of Ownership is logical, it led to our current age of unrest. At first, it was merely sentimentality that led people to conceal books in their homes; perhaps it had been an ancestor's gift or a favorite and well-loved volume. But then profit entered into it; in the early days, whole caravans of books were stolen. Even today, when new discoveries of original documents come to light, it becomes a race between criminals and the Library to own them. Once something enters the black trade, it may disappear forever—damaged, lost, greedily hoarded. And that robs all humankind of something precious."

"What about the Burners?" said a soft voice.

"Step forward, Postulant."

A slender young woman with sleek black hair and the delicate features of Japan moved out from the group and bowed her head slightly to Scholar

Wolfe. "Izumi Himura. Do not the Burners present a greater threat than the smugglers, sir?"

"Explain your reasoning."

"Smugglers would wish to preserve originals; it is their trade. To Burners, it is a political statement, because they wish to break the Library's hold on originals."

"Inadequate analysis, Himura. You must go deeper to understand the real source of the Burner movement. But I will not ask any of you to probe that wound today. Congratulations, Postulants. Not a terrible showing for your first lesson."

Jess heard a collective sigh of relief. He felt one rush out of him as well; being fixed by Wolfe's dagger eyes felt like being pinned up for dissection.

The class began to shuffle toward the single exit, but that exodus quickly halted because the High Garda soldier was blocking the way, arms folded.

Wolfe's voice had a dark amusement in it when he said, "Did I tell you to leave? Never assume you are dismissed until I tell you that you are. You'll remain here until you work out the problem I have left for you. I warn you, there is a time limit. You'd do well to spot the danger quickly. Try to work together."

Wolfe cut through them like a knife, and he and the High Garda soldier walked down the hall and out.

"What are we supposed to do?" The redhead, Anna, sounded annoyed. "He didn't tell us what to do!"

Jess looked around and found it was still the same featureless, unremarkable room as before. No other exits, besides the one. No windows.

"What does he mean, danger?" Dario asked. "There's nothing here. It's an empty room."

Jess hated to admit it, but it seemed that Dario was right. The class spread out, pushing on walls; Glain touched the stained surface and frowned as she rubbed her fingertips together. She sniffed them. "There's something odd here," she said. "Oily. Chemical."

"The whole place reeks of it," Dario agreed. He came to look at the spot she was examining. "You would think if this was *sacred space*, they would keep it in better order. But what kind of danger does that put us in? Ruining our shirts?"

It was a clue, Jess realized. This was the first place he'd been in Alexandria that hadn't been kept utterly spotless. Why leave it in disrepair? It was, as Wolfe said, *sacred space*.

The smell was familiar.

"These stains could be torch smoke. Maybe they have ancient ceremonies here," said another student. It was a decent guess, but Jess thought it was very, very wrong. A growing tension was gathering in his chest, and his heart was pounding faster. His body understood something that his mind was still trying to work out.

What had been the point of Wolfe's lecture today? Original books. Original books being destroyed in the looting of the Serapeum of Rayy. The development of the Codex and blanks. Original books.

The dangers of owning books. Smuggling.

Burners.

Jess looked up, because everyone else seemed to be looking down . . . and saw that a panel had silently opened at the top of the dome, and now a bulbous glass bottle dangled there, spinning slowly in place. It was hard to see it, but Jess spotted a telltale green liquid inside.

He went cold.

"Out," he said, and shoved at Thomas, standing baffled beside him. "Get out *now*! Go!"

Thomas stared at him. "But the Scholar said—"

"Just get out! Go!"

He made Thomas move by force of shoving as hard as he could, and he grabbed others along the way and pushed them to the exit, all protesting. Dario shook free of him and bared his perfect white teeth. "I'm not going anywhere, fool. You may voluntarily fail yourself if you like, but I'm staying. There's a puzzle, and I'm solving it."

Jess met his eyes and said, flatly, "I already did." He pointed up and lowered his voice. "*That* is a bottle of Greek fire, used by Burners. It could drop anytime, and by the smell and state of this place, they've dropped it here before to prove a point. Now, *help me get them out!*"

Dario moved faster than Jess would have given him credit for, helping chivvy the class on, down the narrow little hall, amid a constant drone of complaints. Jess hurried after him. He could vividly imagine that bottle dropping, tumbling, shattering on the smooth worn floor, and bursting into toxic flame.

But there was no fire.

Instead, when he emerged from the long hallway into the glaring Alexandrian morning, he found the class clustered in the shade of a taller building, while Wolfe and the High Garda soldier consulted a timepiece.

"All out," the soldier said. "Not bad."

"Not good, either," Wolfe said. "But I suppose we will call it acceptable."

Jess stared at Wolfe so hard he thought his eyeballs would burst. "You could have killed all of us!"

"Only the ones too slow to move," Wolfe said. "I do give you marks for first noticing the bottle, Postulant Brightwell."

"How do you know? You weren't there to see it!" That, of course, was Dario.

Wolfe gave him a long, silencing look and said, "Because I have a report from Santi's man, who was watching from the top of the dome, and don't try to convince me that *you* should earn that honor, Santiago. Brightwell. One question: why not shout a general warning to the class to clear them out?"

"If I had yelled about Greek fire, with that small exit, it would have been a crush. None of us might have made it out."

"True," Wolfe said. "But then, life is risk."

Khalila's face was set and pale, and she stepped forward to ask, "Would you have dropped the bottle? If we'd missed it completely?"

"Not on the first day," Wolfe said, in a deceptively pleasant tone. "Here ends the lesson: smugglers bite away at the Library a little at a time, like termites on wood, but you must be constantly vigilant for Burners. Some of you come from countries rotten with the heresy; some come from lands untouched by it. It doesn't matter. The first purpose of a librarian is to preserve and defend our books. Sometimes, that means dying for them—or making someone else die for them. *Tota est scientia*."

Knowledge is all. It was the Library's motto, and they all murmured it in response, as they had from the earliest school days.

"Now. Everyone but Seif, Santiago, Wathen, and Brightwell, draw a tile from the pot. There are numbers in it ranging from one to six."

The High Garda soldier was holding out a small clay pot filled with numbered tiles. He passed through the ranks of the students. Thomas stared at the tile he drew out in puzzlement and silently asked Jess for hints; Jess didn't have any to give.

Then the High Garda man took out a set of ivory dice and tossed them to Wolfe. Wolfe rattled them and cast them on the flagstones. "Anyone with two or five, step forward."

Only two students did, holding up their tiles. One of them was red-headed Anna. The soldier collected the tiles and put them back in the pot.

"You can pack your things," Wolfe said. "Go home. You're done."

"But—" Anna had gone bleach pale. "But we just got here! It's the first day! It isn't fair!"

"Eminently fair, and random. Only Seif and Wathen had fully formed and correct answers to my questions; only Brightwell noticed the Greek fire, a threat that all librarians must always guard against at all times. I generously gave Santiago credit for helping clear the room. The rest of you were bystanders, and the fact that I did not dismiss you all is a mark of my generosity of spirit."

"I'll—I'll appeal! You can't do this!"

"Certainly you can appeal. The Archivist Magister is always available to listen to whining, spoiled children who think they've been unfairly judged. However, if he finds I acted within my authority, you'll be fined for wasting his time, your placement fee will be forfeited, and you'll be paying your own way home. How confident do you feel?"

Jess felt a twinge of sympathy, and a larger bolt of fear, as he looked at the ashen faces of the two who would be leaving on the first day. *There but for the grace of God,* he thought. *And my early acquaintance with the Burners.*

Their walk back to the dormitory was all too silent, and Jess couldn't wait to get back to his room, take out his pen, and fill his journal with how much he genuinely was beginning to loathe Scholar Wolfe.

The first day set the tone. Wolfe was a merciless taskmaster, ruthless in dismissing those he thought were not worth his time. The first week was a brutal parade of failure. Of the thirty-two who'd moved their bags into Ptolemy House, twelve were gone within the first seven days. One left of his own accord, without a word to anyone. Jess understood that. He felt the pressure like a weapon to his head, and he knew it would be easy to let it crush his spirit.

But he wasn't in the habit of failure.

Wolfe did not take them back to the ancient chamber again . . . not that first week. Instead, he carried out his classes at Alexandria University in a conventional classroom, where he endlessly grilled them, one by one, on obscure points of Library history. After being caught out on the second day, and surviving the resulting dismissal lottery by sheer luck, Jess put himself to work.

So did all the rest of them. Even Dario.

"This is foolish," Santiago complained the next night. It was direly late, and Jess's whole body ached from it. Apparently, the bells were set to clang every morning at dawn, and classes began before any of them were properly awake, but the amount of study that needed to be done left them with little chance of sleep. "I thought he said we'd be learning real skills. He's doing nothing but stuffing nonsense in our heads. Who cares about the name of the forty-second Artifex Magnus?"

Khalila lifted her finger without looking up from the blank she studied. She had claimed a chair in the corner, while Jess had contented himself with sitting against the smooth white wall near the hearth, legs crossed. "Sarenpet."

"How do you do that?" Thomas asked. Even Thomas, usually sunny, seemed clouded over and tired. "Can you name all the Archivists as well?"

"There was an emphasis on study in my household," Khalila said. "And I had little interest in more traditional things, like cooking. So yes, I can name them all. You should probably try."

"Better history than distasteful conversations on smuggling," Dario said. "*That* is unnecessary information."

"Scholars frequently investigate the black trades and markets, looking for rare books," Izumi said. "At least where I come from. Don't they have such in your country? Or are you so virtuous no one sells originals?"

"Well, it's like kissing one's sister," Dario said. "If you have the bad taste to do it, you don't talk about it."

Khalila laughed and reached for the tea sitting on the table beside her. "I'm not afraid to talk about it. There's a flourishing black trade near the docks, I hear. I've heard a few names."

Jess deeply hoped that she was exaggerating. Khalila was mostly honest, but sometimes her stories stretched too far. "You'd better stay well away from those people." *For my sake,* he added silently. Those were *his* contacts, after all. He'd been given a list of names and addresses before his father had sent him off on the train, and he still recited them nightly before he went to sleep.

"I am a woman of many parts," she said. "And one of them is the ability to look to the future. Should I become a Scholar like Wolfe, I will need such resources, won't I?"

"Rough company," Dario said. "Unsuitable for an innocent flower like you."

"You sound like my uncle. One can be innocent and not be ignorant, after all." It was, Jess thought, nearly impossible to hate her, even when she sounded so smug. "I'm warning you: at least *try* to memorize the Archivists. It's just the kind of thing Wolfe will keep asking."

"We *are* trying," Jess said. His eyes burned, and he couldn't stop a yawn. It spread to the rest of them crowded in the common room, and he got muttered curses for it. "We're just not as good at it as you, Khalila. You should probably get used to hearing that."

"Did I give you permission to use my first name?" she asked, but it was a mild sort of tease, not offense.

"Forgive me, Postulant Seif," Jess said, and bowed as low as he could without really putting an effort in. "Your unworthy servant."

"Finally," Dario muttered. He'd claimed the most comfortable chair and had a strong little group of followers fanned out around him. "The scrubber knows his place at last."

Jess looked up and met his roommate's eyes. Dario's were challenging and bitter, and his smile matched. No jokes there. And no quarter.

"Oh, I do know my place, Dario," he said. "It's ahead of yours. What was your test score again?"

That woke hushed laughter from some of the others and a smile from Khalila. Dario seemed to let it drop.

But of course, he didn't.

Jess slept like the dead, when he had the chance, and that proved to be a mistake. When he woke the next morning, after a bare three hours of rest, the bells were clanging in the dark and Dario's bed was already empty. He'd missed his chance at the shower, again.

When he opened his chest to grab fresh clothes, it was empty.

The shock echoed up from his toes, hit the top of his skull, and shot back down again. He was no longer sleepy. *You bastard.* He thought about kicking in the bathroom door and dragging Dario wet and naked out to kick his arrogant arse, but that seemed too easy.

Dario had a lock on his chest, and clearly he'd foreseen the need to fasten it, but Jess had come from a family of smugglers, with a dash of thieving thrown in. He knew how to pick locks, and this one wasn't even much of a challenge.

Dario's silken shirt felt good against his skin. Definitely a step up from his own wardrobe. He took the other boy's trousers, which were a bit long, and tucked them into his own boots. Dario hadn't bothered to steal those, at least.

Then he took his Codex and strolled down to grab a breakfast of fruit and thick, hot Egyptian coffee in the common room. He was early, but the room had filled with students by the time Dario burst in the door, hair still damp, face flushed. His bitter black eyes fixed on Jess, and he advanced on him. Fast.

Jess sat at his ease, peeling an orange. "Good morning," he said. He didn't try to defend himself and didn't stand. Dario reached down and grabbed hold of the shirt, then froze and let go, probably because he remembered that he would be manhandling his own expensive garments.

"I should have known someone with your gutter manners would be a filthy little thief."

Jess dropped a piece of peel into his bowl. "When my clothes are in my chest, I'll give these back," he said. "Until then, I'll assume you mean to share."

Dario cursed at him in fluent, liquid Spanish and reached for a sharp knife on the breakfast table. Jess got there first and slapped it down with a clatter.

"Think," he said, and leaned forward. "Which one of us knows how to use this better, little prince, you or the one with gutter manners? And which one of us is more likely to be sent home packing after the crying's done?"

Khalila eased up and put a gentle hand on Dario's arm. "Dario," she said. "Please. We have to struggle enough to survive already. Fighting among ourselves is foolish."

Dario turned his head and glared at her. "Are you calling me a fool?"

"Yes," she said, very calmly. "Now, *stop*."

He blinked, and there was a twitch of a frown on his high forehead, and then the smooth, noble façade came down. He gave her an elaborate bow. "For you, desert flower, anything."

Khalila gave him an unreadable look, picked up a bread roll, and carried it to the farthest corner of the room, where she pointedly opened her blank to read.

Jess took his hand off the knife and went back to freeing his orange from its thick prison. He wanted to goad Dario, but he knew it wouldn't be wise; he could see Thomas silently beseeching him not to push his luck, and of course, Thomas was right.

The day's session with Wolfe was in the classroom—a normal enough place, with narrow windows, desks, chairs, and a large flat blank sheet mounted on the wall for Wolfe's use, should he need it. He didn't. It was five hours of relentless questioning, which ranged from history to geography (Jess had failed to memorize the locations of *all* of the daughter libraries, but the weight of that question had crushed three other students) and on to the proper usage of a Codex to conduct advanced research.

They were all exhausted and fearing the reappearance of the lottery tiles when Khalila suddenly said, "Are you going to teach us about the Iron Tower, Scholar Wolfe?"

It put a stop to everything for a few seconds, and then Wolfe slowly turned toward her. His expression put chills through Jess; he couldn't imagine how it felt to be on the direct receiving end of it. "Excuse me?"

"The Iron Tower?" She said it with slightly less confidence this time.

There was a darkness in the way Wolfe was looking at her, and a calculation, as if he was trying to decide what she meant by the question.

"If you wish to learn about the Iron Tower, so be it. Tell me what you
know about it, Postulant Schreiber."

It was an unexpected lash of a question, but it didn't seem to bother
Thomas at all. In fact, he seemed delighted to answer. "It was built by engineers from Artifex in the year 1789, to the specifications of the Obscurist Magnus at that time. It was made from a rare type of iron, which,
quite remarkably, does not rust—the Iron Pillar in Delhi is made from the
same, and the process has been under study for—"

"Fascinating, I am certain," Wolfe cut him off in an utterly bored
voice. "I was referring to those who reside inside the tower, however extraordinary the exterior might be."

Thomas was on firm ground when speaking of the accomplishments
of engineers, but less so now, and Jess saw him hesitate before he said,
"You mean the Obscurists?"

"The Obscurists would be a correct answer, if woefully inadequate,"
Wolfe agreed. "Expound."

"They . . . maintain the Library's Codex system."

"How?"

"Sir?"

"Postulant Seif wishes to discuss the Obscurists, and so we shall discuss them. Can you explain to me exactly how they accomplish the mirroring of the Library's information across so much distance? The exact
mechanism they use to perform this miraculous feat?"

"I—" Thomas swallowed. "No, Scholar."

"Then what else do they provide to the Library?"

"They . . . provide the spark to power the automata that guard the Serapeum?"

Wolfe let him dangle in silence for a moment, then crossed to stare out
the window at the Iron Tower with his hands clasped behind his back.

"The burning of the Serapeum at Rayy, as we discussed on the first day, changed everything," he said. "Prior to that loss, alchemists worked in secret; after, they began to work together. Their discoveries led to the Doctrine of Mirroring, but they also found something curious: alchemical successes were not a simple matter of chemicals and potions and the time at which they were combined, as everyone had thought. The formulae worked for some earnest masters and not others, because there was a spark in only some, a talent that could imbue formulae with real power."

"And those people became the Obscurists," Khalila said.

"The most valuable resource in the world." Wolfe suddenly rounded on Khalila and stalked directly to her, and Jess saw the fine tremble that went through her that marked a desperate desire to retreat. It was a significant achievement that she held her ground; Jess wasn't sure he could have done the same. "Do not *ever* bring up the Obscurists again, Postulant Seif. Your idle curiosity will not be so well rewarded."

She was silent for a second, and then—remarkably, to Jess's eyes—she drew herself up and held Wolfe's gaze quite steadily. Then she said, with only a tiny hint of a tremor in her voice, "With the greatest respect, Scholar Wolfe, I do not ask from idle curiosity, but from a desire to more fully understand the duties of a librarian. Librarians instruct, assist, research, develop, create . . . and protect, do they not?"

"Yes. Your point?"

"You said they are our greatest resource. Does that also not make the Obscurists our greatest weakness?"

That sparked a sudden, common intake of breath, because it seemed more than daring, that question.

It seemed seditious.

Wolfe stepped back without blinking. Smiled. It was a strange expression on him, unnatural, almost brittle. "Explain," he said.

"All of the other specialties of the Library—Medica, Artifex, Historia, Lingua—are positions to which we can aspire. But alchemy cannot be taught in the same way. None of us can become Obscurists, because they are born with a special gift. That makes them rare," Khalila continued. The tremor in her voice was more obvious now, and she stopped to swallow. "We must know if we are to help protect them."

"And when you rise to the rank of a Senior Scholar, you might be granted that knowledge," he told her. "Until then, the question is a waste of your time. Obscurists do their work in seclusion and protection within the Iron Tower. That is all you need know."

"But without them, documents can't be added to the Archive—isn't that true? Without them, the automata that guard our daughter libraries cannot have the spark of life. Without them—"

She seemed to run out of courage, suddenly, and her voice fell silent.

Jess finished the thought. "Without them, the Codex doesn't work," he said. "And if the Codex doesn't work, the Library falls."

That got Wolfe's attention. Jess instantly regretted opening his mouth. The room was hot and still, and when he gritted his teeth in order not to flinch under that stare, his jaw ached tightly in the corners.

But he didn't look away.

"Remember," Wolfe said. The word was silky soft, almost gentle. "Even here, you can ask the wrong questions and speak the wrong truths, Postulants. Here ends today's lesson. *Tota est scientia.*"

Their murmured response followed him as he turned and walked from the room, blending with the whisper of his black robes on stone. Finally, after the doors closed, Jess let out his breath in a rush.

"*Scheisse*, Jess," Thomas said. "Did he just threaten you?"

Khalila was looking at him in concern, and her face was several shades too pale. "I'm sorry," she said. "I didn't mean—"

"Never mind," Jess replied, and picked up his Codex from the desk. "It was a good question."

Outside, Wolfe's High Garda friend was waiting with the pot of tiles. Jess automatically reached for one.

The man pulled it back and gave him an unexpectedly friendly grin. "Not you," he said. "Pass."

Somehow, Jess thought, that only made it seem more ominous.

The day's lottery yielded no losers, by some miracle. By the time they made it back to Ptolemy House, the sun was down, they were all soaked with exhausted sweat, and Jess stood in the shower for well on an hour, wondering whether he could survive this grueling process and, more, whether he *should*.

When he came out of the shower, his missing clothes were back in his trunk. Stained, muddy, and filthy, but returned, and fair point, he hadn't told Dario they had to be in the same condition as they'd left. Jess silently brushed the worst of the mud from of a shirt and trousers, donned them, and then pondered taking revenge to the next level. His brother would have, until it came to knives and someone dead on the floor.

He wasn't his brother. For that reason, he decided to just let it go. Dario had kept his end of the bargain . . . exacted some petty revenge, but a little mud didn't bother Jess much. Benefits of an urchin childhood. Jess even wrote something that was almost civil about his roommate in his personal journal that night, simply because he believed they might have reached an understanding.

It was premature, as he found out the next morning when Dario roughly shook him awake.

"Where is it?" Dario growled. Jess blinked spots from his eyes and tried to sit up. Dario pushed him back down. "*Now*, scrubber!"

"Where's *what*?"

Dario lunged for him, and Jess, on his side, delivered a quick elbow to Dario's face and was on his feet and balanced for a fight in seconds as the other boy staggered away. Dario, however, went down hard on his arse and stayed there, breathing hard and holding his nose. It wasn't broken. It wasn't even bleeding.

"I'll kill you," Dario growled. It came up from the depths of him, and Jess believed he meant it.

"For *what*?" Jess asked. "Other than just on general principles? What do you think I did?"

"My Codex," Dario said. "You took it, out of revenge. Give it back."

That was serious. To steal someone's Codex was to cut off access to the Library, and even under normal circumstances that would be a vile thing to do; now, with Wolfe's class reaping a daily crop of failures, it was catastrophic.

"I didn't take it," Jess said, and held out his hand. Dario stared at him for a second, then took the offer and let Jess haul him back to his feet. "I'd do a lot of things. Thought of sending your entire wardrobe to Barcelona, in fact, and making you beg for it back. But I didn't do that, and I didn't take your Codex."

"Unfortunately, I believe you," Dario said. "But admit it, you were the most likely suspect."

"I'm flattered. Where did you leave it?"

"Are you going to be my mother now, and tell me to look in the last place I saw it? *¡Vete al diablo!* It was *here*. On my desk. And now it is not."

Jess went to the door. It swung easily open. "I locked the door. Someone opened it."

"I—might have done that when I came in."

"Left it unlocked?"

Dario shrugged. "Maybe . . . also not closed. There was wine involved. But I didn't lose my Codex. I've never been *that* drunk."

"Just buy a new one. You're not poor."

"My father gave it to me," Dario said. He looked away. "When I was ten. It was the last gift I had from him. I want it back."

Jess pulled in a breath and let it out.

"All right. Let's look," he said. "In case you really were that drunk."

He was checking the tangled bedding when Dario, over by the desk, said, "I think I know what happened." His voice sounded odd. As Jess came toward him, Dario handed him a piece of paper with a handwritten note.

> *You shove your money and nobility and privilege down our throats, and expect us to smile and thank you. We've had enough of you. Take the next train home, and we'll return your Codex. Stay, and you'll never see it again.*

No signature.

"It's not from you," Dario said. "You'd tell me to my face." He sank into the desk chair, staring out at the thick orange dawn smudging the eastern horizon.

"Who else have you tried to bully out of here?"

Dario's shrug said it all. "Everyone, at one time or another. I earned this, didn't I?"

"You did." No reason to lie about it. "What are you going to do, then? Give in and leave?"

Dario sat silently for a moment, then took in an audible breath and said, "It's just a Codex. I'll get another, as you said." But there was something broken in his gaze. "Leave me alone, scrubber." He pulled out his personal journal and pen. Jess understood the impulse, all too well, to spill out the bile and hurt into ink, where no one could see it.

He didn't waste the opportunity to be the first into the bathroom.

EPHEMERA

Text of a note sent via Codex to Jess Brightwell from his mother, Charity Brightwell.

My dearest boy:

I pray this message finds you well and happy in your exciting new life. Your father and I miss you awfully each day, as does your brother, who likewise sends his best wishes. Business is going well, he says, and he hopes that one day you will be able to participate in it in a more meaningful way.

Your father received an appointment to a select committee on the beautification of our borough. As a consequence, Lord Peter Foxworth had us to dinner the other night to discuss hedges. It was a lovely event, and I know you would have greatly enjoyed meeting his daughter Juliet, who is quite lovely. Your uncle Thaddeus has retired and moved to his country home in the north, and has made it known that we are always welcome there. He fears that London may fall victim to the Welsh advance, but we don't believe that could ever happen, of course. Surely the army will stop them.

I am eager to hear all of the news of your brilliant success, Jess. Please do write, and know that I send my love.

Fondly,

Your mother

A separate note from Callum Brightwell, attached to the same message. Suspected of hidden coded messaging and reviewed by Obscurists. Found to be inconclusive.

Greetings from your old da, boy. Always remember the words of Descartes:

The reading of all good books is like conversation with the finest men of the past centuries. Take full advantage of your opportunities at the Great Library, and do your family proud. All your siblings, living and dead, count upon you to prove your worth to the world. And don't forget your cousins. They're eager to see you again.

CHAPTER THREE

When Jess got the letter from home, he knew his father was finally calling in the debt. Mother's letter was mere camouflage, but his father's scribble . . . that was different.

Father had mentioned Descartes in his note. It was an urgent code, quoting Descartes, who was his father's least favorite philosopher. Jess, as he read the message, felt his pulse quicken. *All your siblings* . . . Brendan and Liam, but Jess knew there had been a third child born after Liam and before him and his brother. Stillborn. So that made three siblings. Descartes's third work was on the subject of optics and refraction, which meant his father was telling him to *look* . . . but look for what?

Worth to the world. An odd turn of phrase for his father, and Jess read it several times before the meaning sank in. It was a quotation, hiding in plain sight. He couldn't quite place the work in question by memory, and he didn't dare an obvious request to the Library to track it down.

His father wanted him to obtain the book where that quotation was to be found and deliver it to his *cousins* . . . names his father had made him memorize before he'd boarded the train for Alexandria. Distant relations, some of them, but just as often trusted colleagues in the trade.

In that one message, his father had ordered him to search for a particular book and to deliver it to contacts in the Alexandrian smuggling trade . . . and by using a quotation by Descartes, he'd indicated how urgent the acquisition was.

Very.

His first real job, on behalf of the Brightwells.

Jess had expected to feel exhilarated in that moment, useful at last, but instead, he felt . . . used. *Nothing different about that,* he told himself. He'd been used by his family since the day he'd been old enough to run. *You don't have to do it,* some little part of him whispered. *He can't punish you now. He's got too much invested.* What if he was caught? Not only would he be dismissed, but this time, he wasn't just an anonymous cutter in the streets of London. He'd be known. Identified.

Turning down his father had just as many risks.

"Everything all right?"

Jess flinched and almost fumbled his Codex, because Thomas was right at his shoulder, and Jess hadn't sensed his approach. Too stealthy by far, for such a solid young man. Jess shut the book. "Family business," he said. "Nothing."

Thomas sat down across from him on an old divan that wasn't meant to hold someone of his size; it creaked alarmingly and the ornamental legs bowed, but he didn't seem to notice. Glain, who was sitting on the other end, got up to ease the load on the furniture, with a typically grim scowl at the both of them. She went to the water jug in the corner of the common room and then found another seat farther away. Apart from Glain and a rowdy group playing dice in the corner, they were almost alone. It was far later than any of them should have been awake.

"My family messages don't make me so grim in the face," Thomas said. "Is it bad news?"

Jess shrugged and forced a smile. "It's always bad in my family. Can you think of a book that has the phrase in it *worth to the world*?"

"No, why?"

In truth, Jess couldn't; he didn't dare. He shrugged. "Not important. I just heard it somewhere, and it sounded familiar."

"It's from one of the Lost Books," Glain said, which was unexpected; he didn't think she was even listening. "A play by Aristophanes burned in the sack of Rayy. I thought you were supposed to be the expert, Brightwell."

"Not tonight, apparently," he said. "Thanks." He was genuinely grateful. His father wanted him to find a Lost Book by Aristophanes, urgently, and deliver it to the shadow market contacts. A book that was somewhere in Alexandria.

Somewhere in Alexandria wasn't a reasonable area to search.

Jess yawned, stretched, and closed his Codex. Thomas, who'd put his head back against the divan's cushions, cracked a blurry eye and said, "Off to bed?"

"Yeah, dawn's coming fast, and Wolfe has no mercy," Jess said. *"Gute Nacht."*

"Your accent is still terrible, you know."

"You taught me."

Jess didn't go to bed. He slipped up the stairs to the second floor, which was now mostly deserted, thanks to the early departure of some of their classmates. He took the route he'd scouted earlier through the back corner window of a little-used storage room. From there, it was a short drop to a ledge, then down to the alley behind Ptolemy House. Even this late, the streets were still busy, and he'd been out enough to know his way.

It took most of the night to find a shadow market "cousin" who knew the book in question, and who in town possessed a copy: he found it was in the collection of a man named Abdul Nejem. Nejem, he was told, wouldn't sell it; it was the prize jewel of his treasure chest of books.

It didn't matter, because Jess didn't have the funds to buy it in any case. His father had only instructed him to *get* it.

So he stole it.

It was an easy enough job, though it was near dawn when Jess delivered the Aristophanes scroll back to his market contact . . . but the cousin in crime who'd been waiting to receive the book was gone, and someone new waited in the darkness.

That was almost never a good sign, new faces. Jess stopped and took a step back, getting ready to run.

The figure stepped into the light with a tight, guarded smile on his face. "Hello, brother," Brendan said. "See you haven't lost your touch. That's good. Thought this place might make you turn honest."

He stepped forward and pulled Jess into a hard embrace. Hard to admit how good that felt, to see family. "I'm as honest as I'll ever get," Jess said. "Which will do fine, thanks. What are you *doing* here?"

"Came for that," Brendan said, and gestured to the ornate scroll case in Jess's hand. "Aristophanes, right? Never cared for him, but I don't care about personal taste when hard currency's involved. Any problems getting hold of it?"

"Brendan . . ." Jess took a deep breath and shook his head. "What are you doing *here*? In Alexandria?"

"Told you already. Were you followed?"

"No, I'm not an amateur, and answer the bloody question!"

"Da wanted it in the safest possible hands," his brother said, "which happen to be mine, of course. It's a trip to the buyer; he didn't want it entrusted to anyone else along the way. Including our cousins."

The idea of Brendan strolling as bold as brass into Alexandria and smuggling out a book made Jess feel sick to his stomach. Physically ill. "It's not simple death by hanging here, brother. They've got a long, inventive tradition of finding ways to make people die in pain. Let the others take the risk—that's what Da pays them for!"

"Da's *orders* were for me to do it personally," Brendan said. "I know what I'm getting into, ta for caring."

"I—" *I do care,* Jess wanted to say, and it was true, but he knew neither one of them felt comfortable with having that said aloud. "If you're caught, I'm in it, too. You know that. Same face."

Brendan's smile had teeth now. "Well, can't have my brutal torture and death get you failed out of your class, can we? Stop worrying, brother. I'll be fine. Best get back to your school before you're missed."

"Brendan—"

"At least you've learned not to call me Scraps. Thought I'd have to beat that out of you, one day." The smile faded, and his brother looked like half a stranger now. Someone he loved, but someone he wasn't sure he could ever really trust. "I'll give Father your love."

There was just enough sarcasm in it to sting, and then Brendan was gone through a hidden door at the back of the empty shop, and Jess was left alone to hope that the next time he saw his twin, Brendan wasn't dying. Or dead.

He made it to Ptolemy House just as the bells clanged, summoning them to another day with Scholar Wolfe.

"You look terrible," Thomas said, as Jess went straight for the common room, and coffee. "Bad night?"

That was, Jess thought, putting it mildly.

The Aristophanes book was valuable, but sending Brendan was stupid. Reckless. He wondered what his father was thinking . . . and then he wondered if it had really been his father's idea at all.

"This is impossible!" Izumi burst out the next morning, when their Codexes all flashed and chimed in unison; Jess opened his to find instructions from Wolfe. "We get so little sleep, he asks so much, and for what? Now this?"

"What?" Jess asked her. "Mine says report to the classroom. What's yours?"

Her mouth was set in a grim straight line. "He wants me to report to the Medica headquarters. I'm to receive special half-day training *on top* of classroom study."

Jess looked around at those in the common room. "Anyone else?" About half the class raised hands, including Thomas. "Where are you off to, then?"

"Artifex," he said. He was trying not to seem happy, but as usual with Thomas, he couldn't conceal it. "I am to study the making of blueprints."

The rest were similar; it was apparent that Wolfe had identified specific traits in them he felt needed cultivation. Khalila had special study with another Scholar versed in sophisticated mathematics and the study of the heavens. Dario seemed fairly content to be studying intensively in history. Glain, not surprisingly, ended up training with the High Garda.

Jess had nothing additional. It seemed ominous, as if Wolfe had simply given up on him. *Jack of all trades, master of none*, was another favorite saying of the Brightwell household. He'd always thought knowing many things gave him strength.

Now it made him feel vulnerable.

The day's classroom training, though, was also curiously individual. They were kept waiting in the room and told to read on the internal structure of the Library hierarchy, which Jess could already recite in his sleep, and then were taken one by one to a smaller side room where Wolfe waited. When it was Jess's turn, he felt that it was a critical moment: either he would impress Wolfe today or he would be struck off.

He was in sixth place in the class rank, and sixth place would be impossible to hang on to without standing out in some way.

"Sit," Wolfe said, and nodded to a simple wooden desk and chair in the middle of the room, with a box on top of the desk. "Do you understand the theory of translation?"

"Yes, sir. It is an offshoot of mirroring, but instead of just creating a copy of a thing, you actually move the thing from one place to another."

"Simplistic, but accurate. Part of the job of a librarian is that as you locate an original work, whether that is just a personal journal surrendered on the death of the owner, or recovered materials, it must be added to the Library's collection. I assume you understand how this happens."

This, then, was the test. "In theory. I've never done it."

"You will do it now," Wolfe said. "Open the box."

Jess stood up and folded back the leaves. Inside, there was a stack of volumes—twenty or more. Originals. The smell of them was hauntingly familiar. He took the first one from the stack, then looked at Wolfe, who was leaning against the wall with his arms folded.

Wolfe raised his dark eyebrows. "Don't wait for me, Postulant. You said you knew the process. Try the desk drawer."

Jess opened the drawer and inside found a jumble of clips. Simple things, spring hinged, with the Library symbol embossed on a seal at the top. They looked no different from anything a clerk might use to fasten some papers. Mundane.

He took a clip and put it beside the book, but his mind went blank. *I put the clip on next? Or . . .*

"I'm waiting, Brightwell."

He was missing something, and it flashed into his mind in the same second. He removed his Codex from his pocket and put it on the desk, opened it, and . . . again, hesitated. Was it the clip first? Or Codex? Or . . . *Stop thinking so much,* Jess told himself. *You know the steps; Wolfe's quizzed you on it enough. Just do it.*

He picked up the clip and slid it carefully down onto the front cover of the book, then opened the book to the interior to find the title. Once he had that, he checked the Codex. The title was already listed. He picked the book up and tapped the seal on the clip to his postulant's bracelet, and a dim light woke inside the seal. It started to glow.

"You may want to sit back," Wolfe said. Jess did. He was still holding the book, watching the glow brighten. There was a feeling inside his head, a kind of strange light static. "You may also want to place the book on the table, unless you want to lose a hand."

Jess quickly put it down. The glow brightened, and brightened . . . and then flashed red. He felt a suction of air, a strange *pop* that sounded more in his head than in the room, and the desk was bare.

The book was gone.

"Congratulations," Wolfe said. "You have successfully sent a book to Archive. Now do it again. Faster."

He did. This time, he didn't hesitate. It was a smooth process: clip, Codex, desk, *pop*, gone.

Wolfe said nothing. Jess reached back in the box and did three more in quick succession, one after another. The last title wasn't in the Codex, so he took the time to take out his stylus and carefully enter the title and author on an empty page before sending it on.

"Stop," Wolfe said, when Jess reached for yet another book in the box. He was frowning. "I think that's enough."

"Thank you, sir," he said, and stood up. Felt strangely dizzy for a moment, but braced himself and got his balance. His stomach growled.

"What you feel now is the energy the Obscurist's alchemical transfer takes from you. The tags work on the same principle as the Codex; they exist both here and in the Archive, and through manipulation of the essence of the object, an Obscurist's process can physically move it from one place to another. You're simply providing fuel." Wolfe continued to study him with an intensity Jess found unnerving.

"Am I dismissed, sir?"

"Yes," Wolfe said. "Send in Danton next. No discussion of this with anyone."

"Yes, Scholar."

That, Jess thought, was one of the simplest things he'd been asked to do so far, and it cheered him that he'd found something that made Wolfe look at him with real interest. He wrote it down in his journal that evening: *I think I might have finally found my place now.*

And he was, of course, wrong.

The next morning, when the Codex instructions came, Jess *still* had no individual study. It felt deeply unfair, especially since he was one of only four who didn't.

"It doesn't really help," Thomas told him later, when they were all back in the common room at the end of the day. "Individual study only makes me know how little I understand. And it seems no matter how much we know, Wolfe will always know more." He was trying to cheer Jess up, which was kind of him, but it wasn't going to work. Jess was in a completely dark mood. "It only allows us more opportunities for failure, *ja*? So perhaps you are better off. We will be lucky if any of us survive to get a placement."

"Speak for yourself," Dario said from where he sat near the fire. "I intend to wear the gold and become Historia Magnus one day. If you feel that way, Schreiber, you should save yourself humiliation and slink home to the land of . . . cabbages, isn't it?"

Thomas, busy with a clock that he'd disassembled and laid out for inspection, ignored him. His big hands worked with delicate precision as he sorted and cleaned the tiny cogs. Dario was playing dice with one of his cronies, Hallem, while the other, Portero, looked on.

Jess, despite his foul mood, had agreed to a strategy game of red and white stones with Khalila. He'd learned not to challenge her at chess, at which she excelled, but she'd not mastered the game of Go quite so readily. He was able to hold his own, which helped his mood a little. The rest of their classmates were clumped in groups around the room. Some studied, looking pinched and worried; some buried their fears in games or dozed in the somewhat worn armchairs. He wondered what Dario was up to. He didn't like the calculating look in his roommate's eyes.

"You're not paying attention," Khalila chided him, and he focused back on the game board. Indeed, he hadn't been, and she'd almost succeeded in trapping him. He made his countermoves and almost laughed when her expression turned thunderously dark. Had she been Glain's size and temperament, he'd have been right cautious, but on Khalila, thwarted ambition looked about as intimidating as a puppy's snarl. "I shouldn't have played fair and warned you, I suppose."

"Not if you plan to win," he said.

"I do like winning." She smiled, the fit of pique gone in an instant, and Jess realized why Dario was staring his way. Dario did *not* like it when Khalila smiled at someone else. *Jealous,* Jess thought. *That could be useful.* Dario had few weak points, other than his tendency to believe everyone was inferior to him. Khalila could be a sore spot.

Jess was ashamed of that in the next heartbeat, and concentrated hard on the board in front of him. In six moves, he'd driven her into a corner, and Khalila declared defeat with good grace. "Next time, we play chess," she said.

"Don't play to your strengths," Jess told her. "Strengthen your weaknesses."

When he pointed to the board, silently asking for another turn, Khalila shook her head. "No, I've got more work from Scholar Zhao to do." As soon as she said it, he saw the flash of contrition in her eyes; she had additional study, and she hadn't meant to rub that in his face. "Sorry."

"Maybe Brightwell's not just stupid. Maybe he paid Wolfe off, and that's why he's got no tutoring," Portero said as he rattled his dice. He'd taken Hallem's place across from Dario. "Though I doubt a scrubber like him has two Romans to rub together." The official coinage was a *geneih*, but everyone called it a Roman, for the portrait of Julius Caesar on the face.

"Maybe he's giving a different service," Dario said. "Have you finished licking our esteemed Scholar's arse yet, or are you merely pausing for breath?" There was an edge to Dario's voice, and Jess understood why.

He'd seen Dario vulnerable, when his Codex was stolen. They'd hardly exchanged a word since, unless it had that sort of confrontational teeth embedded.

Khalila looked up sharply at him, frowning, and Thomas dropped a wrench loudly on the table.

Jess poured himself a glass of wine from the decanter on the sideboard. "Sorry, was I taking your turn polishing his apples?"

Dario's smile was a flash of teeth from a dangerous animal. "Honestly, Brightwell, I don't know why you keep trying."

"Dario," Khalila said, "please shut up."

Dario shrugged and leaned back, spreading his arms extravagantly wide. One of the other students was passing and jostled him. Predictably, that focused Dario's attention. The boy who'd trespassed was a quiet one, pale, with flaxen hair and eyes more silver than blue. From America, Jess remembered, but with a very French name.

"Pardon," the boy said, and moved on.

"Danton, isn't it? You're related to the famous French Burner."

"I'm American."

"No, you're a pitiful French expatriate. Do you go to Paris for the re-enactments? The mass beheading of the Burners?"

Danton had no readable expression on his face, but his body language was guarded. "I've never been."

"Very educational. Living history. No stomach for watching your an-cestor's head coming off?"

"Dario," Glain said, and shut the book she was reading. "Leave him alone. Someday, someone is going to teach you a real living history lesson. It'll hurt."

"It's all right," Danton said. His voice was as level as ever, and as un-settlingly calm as his expression. "It's common knowledge. He didn't have to dig far to get to a sore spot. But then, Master Santiago never works very hard at anything he does."

"I was just pointing it out. Burner sympathies run in your family," Dario said. "I'm sure they're keeping a close eye on you, *Guillaume*. Feeling nervous yet?"

"Maybe *you're* nervous," Jess said. "Where are you in the class ranking now, Dario? Number ten?"

"And where are you? In my shadow. As usual."

"Rankings change. I'm in for the long run, not the sprint."

"Yes, of course, you would be a *runner*," Dario said, and Jess fell cold inside. Dario had resources, and he valued whatever dirt he could dig on all of them . . . but he relaxed as Dario went on. "You *would* be a runner because you don't have the stomach for a gentleman's fight."

"Your version of a gentleman's fight means a knife in the back, so no, I don't fight like a gentleman," Jess said. "I fight to win. Want to play?" He gestured at the Go board, eyebrows raised. Dario pushed back from the dice table, gave him a long and measured look, and then shrugged.

"Why not. Portero's almost bankrupt anyway."

Portero's faint "No, I'm not!" was generally ignored. Danton, released, pushed away and toward the back of the room, where he sat beside Glain. Dario stood up, stretched, and settled into the chair across from Jess . . . all without breaking the steady, measuring stare.

"I'll take red," Dario said. That wasn't a surprise.

What did surprise Jess was how acutely *smart* Dario Santiago was at the game. Jess was good—he knew he was—but it felt almost as if Dario could see directly into his mind. Every clever move he made, it seemed Dario had seen it two moves before. Jess thought he could almost *feel* the young man's intelligence at work. Dario had left his ego to one side, which made it an interesting match indeed.

They worked in silence. No barbs. Jess became aware that others had moved to observe. Even Thomas gradually stopped fiddling with his bits of metal and stood motionless as he watched.

Gradually, Jess became aware of vulnerability in Dario's approach. It was subtle, and Dario played fast and fierce to draw Jess's attention away from it, but at last, Jess had him. He heard an indrawn breath from the crowd around them as he sprang the trap; one single stone placed in exactly the right place, and Dario's strategy collapsed. Now Jess was the aggressor, Dario the defender, and as Jess played through the moves in his head, there was no possibility that Dario would win.

Dario came to the same conclusion. Jess saw the flash of recognition go over his face, followed by a swift wave of anger . . . and then it was gone, and Dario played it out to the bitter end, until he'd no more moves to make.

Then he rose to his feet, bowed slightly to Jess, and said, "Well played."

Jess stood as well and bowed in turn. "Well matched."

They stared at each other for a moment, and Jess had the feeling that for the first time, Dario was actually *seeing* him . . . not as an obstacle or a victim, but as someone worthy of notice. He wasn't entirely sure he liked it.

Dario must not have, either, because he smiled an entirely too brilliant smile. "Doesn't make us friends." He turned on his heel and walked from the room. His usual acolytes fell in behind him, but some cast glances back, as if recognizing that the balance of power seemed to have undergone a subtle shifting.

Thomas clapped a large hand on Jess's shoulder. Not gently. "That was impressive," he said, and sank down in the chair that Dario had vacated. "How did you learn to play this game?"

"My brother taught me," Jess said. "So he could beat me at it."

"I'm surprised he could."

"I didn't say it turned out the way he planned." Jess swept the board. "Let's play."

They were twenty postulants when he went to bed, yet somehow, when Jess woke the next morning, there were twenty-one in Ptolemy House. He'd adjusted to sharing schedules with Dario, and the advantage of taking his bath in the evening before bed meant that he could go straight to breakfast and be there first.

But not today.

Today, there was a girl there that he'd never seen, writing in her personal journal. When she saw him, she put her pen and book away.

She was pale skinned, with lustrous brown hair pinned up tight in a style he hadn't seen since leaving England, and she was wearing an English dress too heavy for Alexandrian weather. He was struck by the shape of her, trim and smoothly curved, and by her eyes, which were a striking light brown. She looked intelligent and guarded . . . and deathly tired.

Jess stopped. He knew he was staring, but he couldn't think what question to ask first. She spared him by offering her hand. "Morgan Hault," she said. Her palm was warm and soft, but her fingers seemed cold. Nerves, he thought. "They said I could eat here."

"Are you visiting someone?"

"No, I just arrived. I'm a postulant."

Jess cocked his head and considered that as he reached for a fresh, hot roll—benefits of coming early: the food was much better at this hour. "How's that possible? Our class was formed weeks ago."

"And I was supposed to be in it," Morgan said. She chose a pear and took a small bite. "I was delayed. Fighting around Oxford."

He recognized the accent then. *Oxford.* She must have had a devil of a time getting out. She was thinner than she should have been; that, too, would have been a souvenir of the war with the Welsh. Food was getting scarce, last he'd heard. And hadn't there been a siege?

She finished off the pear quickly. He silently handed her a bread roll, which she bit into with sudden ferocity, and made a delighted sound in the back of her throat as she chewed.

"Bread must have been scarce," he said for her. "Fruit, too, I'd imagine."

She swallowed as she nodded. "Everything was scarce," she said. "Is there any meat?"

He silently indicated the section at the end that held fish and fowl. No pork, and he missed bacon, but it wasn't a common dish in this part of the world. She loaded a plate and found a table. He brought her a cup of Egyptian coffee, which she tried politely. She clearly didn't care much for it.

"I'm Jess Brightwell," he said. "From London."

"Any other of our countrymen here?"

"There was, but he's already packed off home. First rule of Ptolemy House: don't get attached. We've lost twelve students already." Her wide-eyed look spoke volumes, and he shrugged, feeling suddenly like an old, wise veteran. "Wolfe is a very tough proctor."

"I've heard stories. Is he as bad as they say?"

"You'll see. How are you on history?"

"Fairly good. I'm still working on memorizing the Core Collection on the Codex."

"Memorizing the *Codex*?" She'd caught him by surprise with that one, and he took a bite of his bread to cover it. Chewing and swallowing allowed him time to consider. "Why would you do that?"

She smiled. "I come from a war zone, Mr. Brightwell. The Codex doesn't always function as it should. I'd think you'd know, as an aspiring librarian, to plan for the times it fails."

He'd never considered it, not for a moment. The Codex was simply *there*, available, a living document mirrored from the original in the Library. Had been all his life. It was how he located books and loaded them into blanks; it was how everyone did it. Why would the Codex not *work*?

And yet, clearly, that was possible. Even Khalila had that blind spot; she'd never so much as mentioned it, and Jess knew she wasn't studying for it. Quizzing them on the contents of the Codex they all took for granted was exactly the kind of nonsense that Wolfe would pull.

"Interesting," Jess said, and tried not to show the new girl how much she'd just taught him about his own assumptions. "I suppose that might be useful. When did you leave Oxford?"

"Almost a month ago," she said. "It was a long, hard journey to get to safety." Morgan took another bite of bread, then followed it with some spiced chicken. "I need sleep. And a new wardrobe. Is it always this hot?"

"Afraid so," he said, and fetched her another plate.

Before she finished what was in front of her, others had started filing in, still yawning. Glain made it as far as the coffee urn before she turned and stared at the newcomer.

"Allow me," Jess said, when Morgan began to speak. He stood up. "Everybody, this is Morgan Hault. She's new, so be kind."

"New?" Portero came closer to inspect her. "New and gone tomorrow. Doesn't look like she can stay the course."

"Who says *you* can?" Glain shot back. "Stop breathing on the girl."

"She's too far behind," Guillaume Danton said quietly, as he put an inordinate amount of bread on his plate, along with smoked fish. "She can't make up time unless Wolfe gives her breaks, and you know he wouldn't."

Morgan said, "I can keep up. So if you think you'll get rid of me that easily, get ready for disappointment."

"Morgan, if you are coming with us, you should get changed," Khalila said. "We're scheduled for the field today."

"The field?"

"The High Garda compound." Khalila set her plate down on a corner of the same table Jess and Morgan occupied. Jess took the hint and got up, since he'd finished, and Khalila gracefully slid into his spot. "Wolfe is a great believer in the idea that we must be able to defend ourselves, and Library property, at all times; I think he takes the Burners too seriously, but we all must complete a basic High Garda training course. You will want looser, lighter clothing if you're coming." Khalila had dressed in her version of that: a summer-weight pair of ankle-length gathered trousers under a long tabard, split on the sides. She still wore the headscarf, but today's was light, opaque silk. "Stay with me; I'll see that you—"

There was a sudden, audible intake of breath from across the room, and a clatter of utensils on plates, and Jess looked up to see the dark, foreboding presence of Scholar Wolfe in the doorway of their common room. That was bad enough, but behind him loomed Captain Santi, Wolfe's High Garda shadow. Jess's fellow postulants had gone very still, and Jess knew why: inside Ptolemy House, they'd always felt free from any interference by authority . . . until now. Now it was abundantly clear that Wolfe, or any Library authority, could enter without warning or announcement.

Their home was not their sanctuary.

Wolfe's gaze raked the room and settled on Jess . . . no, not Jess. Wolfe moved on to Morgan.

"You. Come here," Wolfe said.

"Sir?" She had gone milk pale, and Jess saw, with a pulse of sympathy, that the heavy dark circles beneath her eyes stood out even more starkly. She looked exhausted and quite sensibly afraid.

Wolfe didn't feel like explaining himself, clearly. He exchanged a look with Santi, who came forward and put his hand on the girl's shoulder. When she didn't get up, he pulled just enough to guide her to her feet.

"Where are you taking her?" Jess couldn't quite believe he'd opened his mouth to ask; he usually had a better sense of self-preservation. But he had done it, and the question hung in the quiet air.

"Did I make it your business, Postulant?" Wolfe asked.

Jess mutely shook his head. Morgan sent him a quick glance and a half smile that struck him as surprisingly brave, under the circumstances. "It's all right," she said. "I should have reported to you first thing, Scholar Wolfe. Here are my documents."

She reached into a pocket of her dress and brought out her Codex, which she flipped open to show a familiar shape: the same acceptance letter that Jess carried upon one of the pages of his own book.

Wolfe took the book and studied the page, then snapped it shut and handed it back. "You're late."

"I know, sir. The war—"

"You're late, and I don't care about excuses. You may ask anyone here how forgiving I am, and how likely it is that you'll be staying, Postulant Hault. But as I am a kindly soul at heart, you may take the day to recover from your travel. I expect you to present yourself with the others tomorrow, and I expect you to be fully prepared in every way. You'll get no further consideration. Understood?"

Morgan didn't speak. She only gave him a single, sharp nod. If she was afraid, she concealed it better than Jess would have thought possible, and when the soldier let go of her arm, she calmly sat back down to finish her breakfast.

Wolfe watched her for another few seconds, then walked to the coffee urn and poured coffee for himself. *Oh God,* Jess thought, appalled. *Now he's going to hang about.* He must not have been the only one who feared it, because the students closest to the door began furtive moves toward it.

Wolfe said, with studied casualness, "Don't bother to flee, students. Today I've decided to cancel the scheduled weapons training. We will be assigning you into teams shortly."

"Teams? Doing what?" Khalila was the one who asked, probably because she was the only one safe enough to question him, and Dario—who surely would have—hadn't yet arrived.

"Confiscations," Wolfe said. "And since you asked, Postulant Seif, you will be with me, along with Brightwell, Portero, and Danton. The rest of you, Captain Santi has your assignments. You will be working with other Scholars."

Khalila looked at Jess with wide eyes and mouthed, *Confiscations?* As if she'd never heard the word before.

Jess understood it all too well. His father had never been raided, but he'd seen it happen to others in London.

He'd just never expected to have to be a Library minion carrying one out.

At least you'll get to handle some original books. Despite his best efforts, his pulse quickened at that thought. *Maybe Da was right. Maybe I do have ink in my blood.*

Across the room, Guillaume Danton was exchanging a look with Joachim Portero, and it was clear that neither one of them thought being added to Wolfe's personal team was in any way a compliment. It was an opportunity, but only one to fail even harder.

Morgan Hault was watching Jess, and when he met her eyes, she gave him a small nod. "Good luck," she said.

"You'll need it," Wolfe said. "You have five minutes. I will be outside. Anyone late draws a tile."

He left, trailing Captain Santi. There was an immediate, hot buzz of talk in his wake. Breakfast was mostly ignored. Disappointingly, Dario somehow made it downstairs and outside just in time.

Jess joined the group with Wolfe.

He'd have expected to spend the day talking with Khalila, but that wasn't to be; she fell into close conversation with Guillaume Danton instead as they boarded the steam carriage, and the two of them sat whispering as the vehicle lurched into motion. Jess had no choice but to sit next to Dario's friend Portero. The Portuguese boy was shorter than Dario, darker in skin tone, and he cultivated a thin little mustache that failed to be a convincing balance to his heavy chin.

They didn't talk. Partly, that might have been the ominous, unspeaking presence ahead of them of Scholar Wolfe and Captain Santi.

Mindful of what Morgan had said about the Codex, Jess reviewed the list of Core Collection titles. No one (not even Khalila) could hope to remember every book on the list, but he concentrated on the oldest and rarest. Smugglers and collectors delighted in those, and thanks to his background, he had more than a passing acquaintance with what sold best in the shadow markets.

Portero idly stared out the window as the wide, clean Alexandrian streets rolled by. They'd all gotten used to the sight of the teal blue harbor and white-sailed mountains of ships floating there, but Portero was staring out at the old Egyptian gods that lined the roadway, still mighty under the sun after so many thousands of years. He clicked beads between his fingers, and Jess finally realized they were part of a rosary.

"Does it bother you?" he asked Portero, and nodded out at the gods on the street. Portero shot him an unreadable look.

"Shouldn't it? They're false gods."

Jess shrugged. "Real enough to the Egyptians," he said. "And they're beautiful, in their way."

Portero was already sweating from the intense heat; even the carriage's cooler interior couldn't keep it all out, especially next to the windows. "They should have been pulled down ages ago," he said. "The Christians and Muslims agree on that much."

Jess flashed back to the death of *On Sphere-Making* and felt a slow roll of revulsion. "That sounds like a Burner talking," he said. "Destroying what offends them, and never mind legacy."

Portero turned on him angrily. "I said nothing of the kind! I would never harm a *book*! Never!"

"Not all knowledge is books. Those out there, they're history in stone. Men carved them. Men sweated in this sun to put them there, to make their city more beautiful. Who are you to say what's worthy for men to see today, or tomorrow?"

"You're an irreligious bastard," Portero said. "I knew you would be."

"I'm as good a Catholic as you," Jess said. "I just don't hold with making the world into copies of what I like."

Khalila and Guillaume had stopped talking, and both were staring at him. Guillaume raised his eyebrows and said, "You'd better stop or you'll be failed out for this kind of talk, Portero. Not that I wouldn't enjoy it."

Guillaume was right. Portero glared back, then went back to staring out the window, while Jess picked up his book again. Guillaume and Khalila went back to their whispered conversation, too indistinct to be clearly heard, and Portero clacked his beads.

It was too long a ride. By the time the carriage slowed and stopped, Jess was ready to strangle the lot of them.

Then the carriage halted, and Jess stepped out and wished immediately for the cooler comfort of the interior again. The heat rose in waves from the stone, and in the shimmering air, Jess spotted Wolfe's black robe billowing wide as he jumped down from the conveyance's front cabin. Captain Santi joined him, and Jess noticed that this time, he was dressed in full High Garda uniform, with the Library's symbol embossed in gold. Armed to the teeth.

Wolfe took a look around them, and Jess followed his example. It was a gracious street, shaded here and there with spreading trees; the flat-roofed, square houses were neatly plastered and well kept, and the one that Wolfe seemed most interested in was painted a clean, pale yellow. It was larger than its neighbors, and discreetly set back behind a wall of a slightly lighter color. The walkway was inset with hieroglyphs of protection and benediction.

"Always survey the area first," Wolfe said. "Identify anyone in the area who might interfere or be on the lookout. Look, listen, feel. It might save your life." The same things, Jess thought, that a smuggler would do. Maybe it was that thought that woke a strange sense of familiarity. Déjà vu.

Khalila, Guillaume, and Joachim were all silent, so Jess stepped forward and stopped a respectful distance from the High Garda soldier. "Pardon, Captain Santi, but . . . could you explain how this is supposed to go?"

Santi turned toward Jess, pivoting with smooth grace. He was not overly tall but had the build and poise of a fighter. Must have been a *good* fighter, since his sharp-chinned face was unmarked by any scars or disfigurements; he had a long straight nose, heavy dark brows, and close-cropped hair. His skin held the deep brown shade of an Italian who spent a lot of time in the sun, and the deep lines at his nose and mouth betrayed his age . . . older than his still-dark hair would suggest.

"Don't *sir* me. I'm not your father, and you're not under my command." He said it pleasantly enough, but there was a distance in his eyes.

"Sorry, Captain," Jess said. "What do you want us to do?"

"Assist," he said. "You search and carry away what illegal materials we find. You'll learn how to spot a contraband hiding place. And stay out of Wolfe's way."

It sounded simple enough, and Jess felt on firmer ground. Contraband was his specialty, after all.

Khalila seemed disturbed. "Will . . . will the family be there?"

"Of course," Santi said. "If they've nothing to hide, they'll be fine. If we turn things up, their sentences will depend on what we find. Could be confiscation; could be arrests. But that's not your concern. Just follow Wolfe's lead and let me take care of any trouble."

She nodded hesitantly and glanced over at Jess. He tried to give her a reassuring smile, but in his guts, he felt this wouldn't be pretty. She was about to have a harsh introduction to the darker underbelly of the Library . . . the one that Jess had grown up knowing. It wasn't all clean reading rooms and fancy Scholars debating the merits of Plato's views of comedy. The Library might have brought the wisdom of ages into the lives of the common folk; it might have kept humankind from falling into the darkness of ignorance and despair and superstition. But that didn't mean the hands of those in charge were clean.

Just the opposite, in Jess's experience.

Wolfe didn't speak to them. He abruptly strode forward down the peaceful little walkway toward a yellow house, and a hot breeze caught his robe and snapped it like a pirate flag behind him.

As Jess got closer, it hit him like a bolt why this street seemed so familiar. *I've been here.*

He'd been at this *house.*

As Alexandrian custom dictated, Wolfe touched his fingers first to the small inset statue of the household god Bes on one side of the doorway, and then to the goddess Beset on the other.

Then he knocked and was answered in only a moment by a young servant girl, neatly dressed. He showed her a page in his Codex, and her mouth fell open in shock. She had absolute terror in her eyes.

"Please get the master or mistress of the house," Wolfe said. She dashed away on bare, silent feet; it was the Egyptian custom to go without shoes on the polished tiled floors that helped keep the houses so cool within. Wolfe followed her in and drew the rest of them along.

Alexandrian homes were almost oriental in their simplicity, with a few luxuries showing like gems against the plain walls. A fluted lamp cast a yellow glow in a dimmer corner with a Roman-style reading couch, and there was a bookcase in plain view . . . filled with Library-stamped blanks, of course, as could be found in any home, no matter how rich or poor.

Disconcerting. Jess *did* know this house, but he'd seen it only in the dark. Deep night, when all the lamps were doused or lowered.

This was the house of Abdul Nejem, and he'd stolen the Aristophanes scroll from it for his father. That . . . couldn't be a coincidence.

The servant girl didn't reappear; instead, he heard the confident slapping footsteps approaching of a much larger person, and a man rounded the corner from what must have been the courtyard garden. He'd been in the pool, most likely; he'd wrapped himself in a Japanese-style robe of rich blue silk that had been cut twice as large as usual to fit around his bulk. He had shaved Alexandrian style, hairless head to toe, and if he hesitated a little when he saw Wolfe at his door, he covered that discomfort well.

"Scholar," he said, and gave the deepest bow his belly would allow. "I am honored, of course, to entertain such an esteemed visitor. Please, be welcome to our home. May I bring you food and drink?"

Wolfe brushed aside the courtesies. "Are you Abdul Nejem?"

"Yes, of course. How may I assist you?"

Wolfe extended his Codex and displayed the warrant. He handed the book to the man, who scanned it, read it again, and looked up to say, "But this is a terrible mistake! There is no contraband here!"

"Perhaps," Wolfe said. "But we have a job to do. You'll wait with Captain Santi while my team searches."

"But I must protest!" the big man said, and jabbed the book back toward Wolfe like a sword. Wolfe deftly intercepted it and put it away. "This is outrageous—I am no criminal! I would *never* . . ."

Santi stepped forward then, and the man's bluster drained out of him, and something like fear crept across his face. "Please take a seat on this very fine couch," Santi said, and led the man to it. "Who else is at home today?"

"My—my wife, Nabeeha," the man said. "But she is unwell. In bed."

"Postulant Seif," Wolfe said. "Please go find the lady Nabeeha and bring her here, if she can walk. If not, we will go to her in a moment."

Khalila wavered, then bowed her head and went quickly down the hall. The house was built in a square, with a central sunlit courtyard made serene with a bathing pool, fountains, flowers, and sheltering trees; the thick-walled house stayed cool and funneled breezes that carried the pleasing scents throughout the rooms.

Jess wondered if he should follow Khalila, to be sure she was all right, but before he could make that decision Guillaume Danton said, "Sir, should I explore the other rooms?"

"Go," Wolfe said. Danton disappeared after Khalila. When Jess made a move in that direction, Wolfe extended a sharp finger toward him. "Thorough search of *this* room, Brightwell," Wolfe said. "Portero. Check out there."

Jess didn't really need to search at all, because he knew exactly where the compartment was; he'd recently spent an hour finding it in the dark of night. He wished that Wolfe had sent him off to search somewhere else, because now he had to make an elaborate production of *not* finding the spot . . . at least, not quickly.

Jess started on the wrong wall, tapping and probing. It felt like elaborate theater. He'd gone more than halfway around the room when he finally arrived at the tiny piece of fabric stretched tight and plastered in place that hid the switch.

"Found something, Scholar," Jess said, and pressed hard. There was a muted *click*, and a section of the wall about four feet square sagged inward and rose. Inside, the alcove was covered by a layer of plastered fabric that was cleverly secured at the corners.

Jess peeled the fabric back, and behind it were the treasures. Seen in full daylight, they would have been breathtaking to most—stacks of original books and a honeycomb of scrolls. The smell of the old ink and vellum and parchment . . . it smelled like home to him, and for a dizzy moment, Jess just wanted to touch those smooth leather bindings, those crisp rolled edges.

He stepped away and met Wolfe's gaze. Wolfe nodded, looking far too thoughtful. "Good, Postulant Brightwell," he said. "You have a knack."

"That's—that's not mine!" the fat man in the corner blurted, and Niccolo Santi pushed him back down on the couch as he tried to rise. "I swear, I am innocent! This is a house that honors the Library in all things!"

Guillaume Danton had returned, Jess saw; he was supporting the bowed weight of a woman of about the same age as the house's owner. She seemed old before her time and moved as if each step pained her. Her eyes widened when she saw Jess standing at the wall, and the uncovered cache of books. Her knees loosed, and she would have fallen if Danton hadn't held fast to her.

Or at least, that was how it looked at first, until the seemingly frail woman snatched a hidden knife from her belt, straightened, and threw Danton off-balance. He had no real chance to react before the woman had whipped an arm around his throat to choke him and pull him up to his toes, while the knife hovered over his vulnerable, fast-pulsing jugular.

"Let my husband go or this boy dies," Nabeeha Nejem said. Santi exchanged a glance with Wolfe, who'd not moved so much as an eyebrow,

and stepped back to let the fat man stand up. The husband seemed unsteady and out of his depth. "Abdul, get the books. *Go.*"

"There's nowhere you can run," Wolfe said. "You must know that."

Jess moved aside as the fat man came toward him, and made sure that
as he did, he angled closer to the woman and Danton. The other boy's
face was even paler than usual, but he didn't struggle. She was pressing her
arm like a bar over his throat, and he was likely to lose consciousness if it
continued. The London Garda had favored that move, and it was usually
successful. Danton might be stronger than Nejem's wife, but she had better leverage.

And she had the knife.

She also wasn't stupid, and as Jess shifted his weight, her dark eyes cut
toward him. Suddenly, the knife pressed hard enough against Danton's
neck to slice a thin line of red. But she didn't speak to him—instead, she
spoke to her husband. "Abdul, *move!* We have little time!"

Abdul Nejem was already hurrying, but he was clumsy and nervous,
and there were far too many books for him to carry. There must have
been twenty volumes, not including the scrolls. Abdul had to pick and
choose, and it was clear he was too frightened to do it well.

As he reached for another volume, the five he already had stacked in
his left hand slipped, and two of them crashed to the tile floor. Abdul gave
a little cry of alarm and tried to pick them up, but that only created more
of a landslide . . . and in the distraction, Khalila Seif slipped up as silent as
a ghost behind Abdul's wife and grabbed the woman by her long braid of
hair. Nabeeha cried out, unprepared for the sudden attack, and then froze.
From Jess's angle, he could see that Khalila had pressed her own blade into
the woman's back.

"Let my friend loose, or this goes into your liver," Khalila said. "It
might not kill you, but it will certainly make you wish you were dead."
What seemed most effective about it—and, Jess had to admit, most
chilling—was the calm way Khalila said it. She didn't raise her voice.

There was no sense of tension or excitement. It was as casual as if she'd commented on the lovely garden just visible beyond the other doorway.

Nabeeha must have known she had no chance. She waited long enough that Jess began to calculate his chances of disarming her, but then she suddenly lowered the knife and let Danton fall. The boy, only half-conscious, dropped to his hands and knees, gasping for breath. Blood dripped slowly from his cut neck—a flesh wound, from the look of it. Lucky.

Khalila stayed where she was, one hand clutching the other woman's braid and the knife pressed against her back, until Niccolo Santi stepped forward to take charge of the captive. Then the girl let go, sucked in a deep breath as if coming out of a deep sleep, and shuddered all over. Jess watched her as she tried to resheathe her knife; her hand trembled too much to hit such a narrow target. She finally put the blade down on a small table near the wall and knelt down next to Guillaume Danton to see how he was. Jess understood. Always easier to see to another than face your own fears.

Abdul Nejem, meanwhile, stood indecisive in the center of the room with his arms filled with a tottering stack of illegal books. He stared at his now-captive wife with shock, as if he couldn't quite believe that she hadn't won the day, and when Wolfe stepped up and took the books from him, the man deflated like a punctured balloon. He sank down on the only other furniture in the small room—a chair that groaned beneath his weight—and buried his face in his hands. "You've killed us," he wept. "You've killed us all, you greedy woman!"

"Shut up, for the love of heaven," Nabeeha said. "We claim academic privilege!"

"Really," Wolfe said, in that ominously silky voice that Jess recognized from classes. He turned toward Nejem and tilted his head to one side. "Regale me with your credentials. I will be fascinated to hear of your work." The man only sputtered, clearly unable to manufacture anything useful. "Niccolo, I believe we're done. Secure them both."

"Wait! I—I can tell you where she got them! I swear, it was my wife who did this, not me! I am *innocent*!"

"Abdul!" Nabeeha's shout held all manner of vicious threat, and her husband shuddered.

"Take the lady outside," Wolfe said, and Niccolo muscled the struggling woman out her own front door. Now that the game was up, she seemed about as weak and infirm as a cobra. "Continue, Master Nejem. I really *am* fascinated."

"It was my wife's idea. I never read them, I tell you! I never *touched* them until today! She—her family—" Nejem gulped air again. "Her family is full of black market criminals. I can give you names, Scholar, I swear that I can, if you will show mercy . . ."

It was, Jess hoped, a bluff and a lie, because if it wasn't, there could be consequences. The community engaging in black trade here in the very shadow of the Great Library was small and close-knit. It wouldn't take much for it to come apart . . . and that would affect him, too.

It might even implicate him.

"How many in your household?" Wolfe asked. He was thumbing through the books that he'd taken from Nejem, and he sounded distracted. "Besides your wife."

"My two sons are grown men and live with their own families. It is only me and two servants."

"The servants may go. You *did* know of her activities. That makes you complicit in the . . ." Wolfe stopped talking and concentrated on the book he'd just opened. He read for a moment, then looked up and gestured to Jess. "Take these. All of them. Scrolls as well. Catalog them and tag them for removal."

Nejem paled still more. "Please, Scholar, I beg you—"

"It's not for me to decide your fate, Master Nejem. That will be up to the jurists. But if you want my advice, hire yourself an advocate, and don't attempt to leave the Library's precincts unless you want to try to outrun a sphinx."

Jess took possession of the books. The man was openly weeping now, and the servant girl they'd met before came in from the garden door to offer him a soft cloth to wipe his face. She glanced at Jess, then quickly down, and he realized that she was afraid of *him*.

He'd become the enemy, the terrifying specter of authority.

Don't think about it. Just do what you're told.

"Sir," Jess said, "I need tags."

Wolfe handed him a bag of them without comment. Jess paused to give him a look. "Are you still grading me?"

"Of course," Wolfe said. "You disappoint me by asking."

It was no different than it had been in training, except that he thought it would be better, given the urgency of the situation, to place all the tags on the books at once and activate them all at the same time. The Obscurists had created the things, after all; he was only triggering the potential held within the seal. Sending them all together was more efficient. Wolfe said nothing to indicate he was making a mistake as he placed the tags, activated them all quickly, and stepped back as the glow brightened around the clips.

Even at the safe distance, Jess felt the tingle of energy sweep through him as the tags—all of them—activated at once. It felt vastly more powerful than in training, a jolt like being struck by lightning, and he smelled a peculiar, sharp odor of burning that vanished almost as quickly as it came.

He turned to see that Khalila and Danton were standing behind him, watching. They seemed riveted.

"How many did you send at once?" Khalila asked him. "Are you all right?"

"Yes, I'm fine . . ." That was an automatic response, but then he realized that he wasn't, not at all. He felt disoriented, exhausted, and suddenly, violently sick. In fact, it was all he could do to control his nausea long enough to stumble out of the room to the peaceful garden, where he dropped to his knees to void his stomach. He remembered Wolfe's curious stare when he'd done so many, one after another, at the original training. That hadn't seemed to hurt him at all. He'd had no idea that it would drain him so much to activate twenty at the same moment.

Danton and Khalila had followed him, and as Jess knelt there shaking and chilled, Danton passed him a cup of clean water and an orange. "Here," he said. "It should help."

The food and water did do him good, and Jess regained his balance after a few moments. Khalila offered him a cloth with which to wipe the sweat from his face, and the two of them helped him to his feet. "That was impressive," Danton said. "I've heard librarians sometimes pass out from managing five tags one after another, never mind twenty at the same time. I got sick from just *one* in Wolfe's training."

Jess hadn't even considered it, really. Training hadn't made him feel much, just a brief dizziness that had passed in seconds. Since it had been an individual process, with only Wolfe in attendance to show him the steps, he hadn't even known the others felt sick.

"Next time, group them in fives and rest between," Khalila said. "It might avoid the discomfort."

"Good advice," Jess said. "Thanks."

He pulled free of them and stood on his own. Shaky, but manageable. As he stood there testing himself, their fellow student Portero sauntered through another door, looked around, and said, "Nothing in the rest of the rooms. Nice place, isn't it? What did I miss?"

Khalila patted him on the shoulder. "Nothing," she said. "Absolutely nothing."

EPHEMERA

Text of secured Library correspondence between the
Obscurist Magnus and Scholar Tyler, stationed at the
Oxford Serapeum.

Greetings to my fellow servant of the Library. I trust this message finds you well.

I regret troubling you at this time, given the unsettled state of affairs in England, but this is of the utmost importance.

Recently we detected unusual activity on the Codex, which indicates the possible existence of a budding Obscurist in Oxford. We are striving to trace this incident back to the young person—for, as I am sure you are aware, Obscurist talent begins to manifest before the age of twenty in every case—so that this individual may be properly secured and conveyed to us here at the Iron Tower. We believe this incident, which may well have been visible to another, occurred within the Oxford Serapeum in the past three days. I shall require from you a detailed listing of all persons under the age of twenty who visited the Serapeum during that time so that we may more closely investigate, and shall also require that you quickly and quietly inter-view all staff to find out if anyone was witness to an unusual incident.

I am sure you understand the urgency of this matter.

No reply to this message has been found.

Handwritten paper message from Scholar Tyler in Oxford to Morgan Hault.

As I feared, your efforts to remove the traces you left on the Codex were un-successful. You are no longer safe here. The Obscurists, when they send the

High Garda, will be looking for you in Oxford, and so you must leave immediately. I can buy you passage out, but you must leave tonight. Go to London. It is possible at the London Serapeum you may have both more time and concealment to alter the records and hide yourself, but stay on your guard at all times.

If London does not serve, I fear you may have to go into the heart of the Library itself, in Alexandria. I have been told that the closer you can come to the Iron Tower, the easier access is to the formulae of the Codex and the records. It may be the only place in the world where you can remove all traces of your talent from their sight, and secure your freedom.

I pray, for your sake, that you don't have to resort to this extreme. Try London first, and be safe.

CHAPTER FOUR

J ess expected the day to be over when they left Abdul Nejem's home; after all, as far as he could tell, they'd all passed the test. But instead, after a stop at Ptolemy House to allow the other three to exit, Wolfe ordered him back inside the carriage and climbed in after him.

What did I do? Jess wondered, and felt new, sticky sweat crawl down the back of his neck. *Did I give it away that I'd been there before? Does he know one scroll was missing?*

And perhaps the biggest question of all: how had they known about Abdul Nejem? Because he didn't think it could have been luck that his father had urgently wanted him to steal a book, just in advance of a Library raid. His father must have known something was on the way.

"You did well," Wolfe said. "But I warn you that what you did today was a mistake."

Jess froze. *This is it, the end of it.* He was being taken to a Library prison cell, and somehow, he'd betrayed not only himself, but his family, too. He imagined his father in chains, his mother, Brendan. *No. I'll take the blame. I won't implicate them.* If his older brother, Liam, had found the courage to go to the chop without selling out his family, then Jess could live up to that example.

If Wolfe was waiting for him to confess, he'd wait a long time.

Wolfe finally continued. "It was my own fault. I failed to instruct you on the danger. Most students have little tolerance for the drain, so they only attempt one, perhaps two at a time. You tagged and sent twenty. At once. That is impressive, and quite stupid. You might have sustained real damage from the drain . . . but you seem to have fully recovered."

Jess drew in a sudden breath because the weight that had been crushing him lifted. This wasn't about smuggling. It was about what he'd done with the tags.

He wasn't going to prison. Not yet, anyway. "I didn't realize it would be any different," Jess said. "It didn't bother me in training."

"No," Wolfe said. "And I was curious to see how you would approach the task today. I did not expect you to send them all at once, and I was frankly even more surprised that you handled it with so little trouble."

"I'm—not an Obscurist, am I?"

"Not at all. Merely capable of withstanding the drawing of energy by the Obscurists' processes better than most."

"Oh." That seemed oddly disappointing. Then again, a lifetime locked up in the Iron Tower didn't seem attractive, either.

"It's a curious talent you have, Postulant. It could well be valuable." Wolfe seemed to be weighing something as he looked into the middle distance, and then Jess sensed a decision being made. "Given what you did today, I expect you will also find it easier than usual to use other Library tools. That is why I asked you to come with me. I want to test a theory."

"So . . . it's another test."

"In a way." Wolfe's lips curved in something that wasn't quite a smile. "And I warn you, it will most certainly hurt."

When the carriage hissed to a stop, they were somewhere familiar . . . a low, small building that Jess vividly remembered near the harbor. Santi joined them as Jess stepped down from the carriage.

"What are we doing here?" Jess asked.

Wolfe walked ahead of him, down the stained narrow hallway. Lights flickered on dimly, triggered by his motion. Jess swallowed and wondered if it would be possible to run . . . but he knew, as Abdul Nejem had known, that there was nowhere safe he could go. Wolfe held Jess's fragile future in the palm of his hand, and it would take little effort to crush it.

The last time he'd been in this place, Wolfe had threatened to drop Greek fire on their heads.

Santi gave him a little tap from behind. "Go on, boy," he said. "He doesn't bite. I do, though. It's a benefit of the job."

The inside of the domed room looked exactly the same, and it still stank of that peculiar chemical reek. Jess couldn't tell if the dark swirls on the walls were from new burns or old, but when he looked up, he was relieved to see that nothing dangled from the top.

Santi was blocking the only exit, behind him. Wolfe stood in the center of the room, holding a golden double loop of thin rope with a flat Library seal in the middle. "Do you know what these are?"

Oh, Jess knew. He felt a sick twist in his stomach at the sight of them, and swallowed before he said, "Restraints for criminals. You didn't use them on the couple back at the house, though."

"I didn't see the need," Wolfe said. "They weren't capable of outrunning us. We use these for more dangerous sorts. However, they do take skill. Santi?"

Jess's breath turned solid in his lungs as Santi walked forward, took the restraints, and turned to him. *This is it,* he thought. *I'm done.*

Santi slipped the loose binders over his own wrists and held them out to Jess, who was too puzzled to move. He looked over at Wolfe.

"Use your Library identification band," Wolfe said. "Touch it to the restraints."

"And do what?"

"Let's see what happens."

What happened was that as soon as Jess touched his wristband to the restraints, they snapped together, binding Santi's hands so tightly the soldier winced. The seal on them shimmered in a strange, hot orange. "Sorry," Jess said. "Did that hurt?"

"Did it hurt you?" Wolfe asked.

"No."

"Did you feel it at all?"

"A little." It had been just a tingle of numbness, as if his hands had fallen asleep. Gone in seconds.

"Interesting," Wolfe said, and tapped a finger on the cover of his Codex.

"Not the word I'd use for it," Santi said. "This isn't how I'd planned to spend my day, Christopher."

Christopher? Wolfe had a first name, Jess remembered, but he couldn't imagine anyone using it. Especially not so . . . casually.

"I appreciate your help, Captain," Wolfe said. "Time for a run."

"One day, we'll have to trade spots. You could do with a run."

"Not today." Wolfe made a gentle shooing motion, and Santi turned and jogged down the hallway, out of sight.

"Where is he going?" Jess asked.

"No idea. Now you're going to find him," Wolfe said. "But I'm going to give him a head start. Seems only fair." He consulted his book. "Take out your Codex."

Jess pulled it from his pocket and held it closed in his hand until an annoyed look from the Scholar prompted him to open it to a blank page.

"Touch your band to the page," Wolfe said. "Normally, you would do this immediately after securing the bindings."

Jess pressed his wrist to the paper, and it quickly drew him a map . . . a street map, highly detailed, with one thick splash of ink in red on it. He didn't know how it worked, but he assumed it was something like the Codex—mirrored in real time, only instead of showing a simple list of books available for duplication, it showed an item. And how to find it. "The restraints are showing where he is," Jess said. "Isn't that right?" Activating the map, and the restraints, had made him feel weak and unsteady. Jess stared at the map, trying to focus on the crawling dot that must surely be Santi, on the run, and felt a sudden stab of pain behind his eyes. He shut his eyes a moment, and it went away. He opened them again and focused on the map, where the ink splash steadily crawled on. The headache returned.

"Exactly." Wolfe was studying him closely now. "How bad is it? The pain?"

"Not so bad," Jess lied. He looked away from the map, and the headache faded almost instantly. "It's only when I look at it. Is that all?"

"No. I want you to find him," Wolfe said. "And you'd better be quick about it. Santi's very fast."

Jess took in a deep breath of the tainted air and walked down the hallway, out into the bright Alexandrian sun. He risked a quick glance at the map. The dot was three streets away and still moving toward the edge of the page. He didn't know what would happen when it got there—would it just vanish? Or would the map adjust to follow? He decided it wouldn't be wise to find out, and set off at a run. The headache didn't go away quite so quickly this time when he looked up from the map; it throbbed in time with his pulse and sat like a thick, hot stone behind his eyes. It came with a twist of nausea deep inside, but for the first time in a long time, Jess felt on strangely familiar ground.

After all, he knew how to run. He was good at it, and as he ran through the streets of a hot foreign city, dodging between carriages and past startled, swearing pedestrians, he felt at home. His body was in its element, and the pump of blood and wind whipping his hair made him remember what it had been like back home, running alone and testing his wits against the London Garda and all comers.

Even the headache couldn't spoil the thrill of it, though it sank claws deeper with each necessary glance at the map on his Codex. It was changing, he saw, moving with him. The dot of ink that was his fleeing prisoner didn't have as much of a head start anymore, and as Jess rounded one of

Alexandria's sharp, clean corners, he saw the enormous, ominous stretch of the Iron Tower looming ahead on his left, surrounded by tall fences, gates, and guards. His fugitive wasn't making for that. He'd swerved right, toward the university grounds. The Alexandrian Serapeum's gigantic pyramid rose in clean angles beyond that, blurred by distance, and Jess slowed his run just a step or two to check the map.

Santi's course seemed to be taking him toward the Serapeum.

Jess knew the university grounds by now; he'd walked them daily, to and from Wolfe's classroom, and he knew the broken path that Santi would have to run between the buildings. *I can cut the corner,* Jess thought. *If I'm right. If he's making for the pyramid.*

He checked the map and watched the progress, just to be certain. The headache suddenly pounded harder, and the flare of it blinded him with black flashes. He tore his gaze away from the map, but the pain didn't subside this time. Not at all.

Jess slammed his Codex shut and shoved it in his pocket. Headache or not, all he had to do was run—run flat out, the old London way, for the pyramid. He'd be either spectacularly wrong or absolutely right. It felt good, letting go, letting his legs warm and his stride lengthen, flashing past shops and blurred faces, down a market lane full of exotic silks and spices, through a cloud of steam exhaling from a building's pipes . . . and ahead, he saw a flash of black that was moving faster than everything around it.

He'd spotted Santi, and he knew Santi hadn't spotted him. Right-handed people didn't generally look to the left when they were trying to avoid pursuit; they looked forward and back and toward their dominant side, unless something drew their eye.

He was going to catch him.

He did catch him, coming at a wide angle from just behind Santi's left shoulder, and knocking the still-bound man off-balance to roll several feet off the path of buildings and onto a shaded patch of rocky dirt. Santi let out a frustrated yell, which Jess only half heard, because there was something wrong with his ears. And his eyes, because the black flashes that had been constantly crowding his vision were worse now, and the nausea had taken full hold. He couldn't feel his feet, and the overwhelming, thudding agony of his headache took away the last of his strength.

Jess didn't feel himself collapse, but when his vision cleared from black to a thin, gray, ghostly mist, he saw the world had tilted on its side, and his prisoner was free, looking down on him and scratching a message into a Codex with a stylus. Jess shut his eyes. He heard a buzz of sound and felt something that might have been a hand on his shoulder, but all he really felt was the pain.

Words filtered through. Lights. Someone was telling him to keep his eyes closed, and yes, they were right, the pain was just a shade less in the darkness. It was spreading out of his head, into his neck, shoulders, chest, arms, legs. He was made of pain.

And then, finally, he felt a cool, sharp bite on his wrist, and the darkness took on weight, and crushed him down.

He woke up in his bed at Ptolemy House, and the whole thing might have been a bad dream except for the weak trembles of his muscles and the throbbing remains of the headache. He swallowed and tasted blood.

Someone was sitting in the dark with him, and he instinctively knew it wasn't Dario Santiago. When he tried to sit up, a hand gently pressed him back down again, and a girl's voice said, "Stay still."

"Khalila?" It didn't sound like Khalila, but he couldn't imagine Glain being so kind to him, either.

"Morgan," the voice said. "Close your eyes; I'll turn the light up just a little. Tell me if it's too much."

It was, at first, but he held back his wince. After the first few heartbeats, it wasn't so bad, and he could make out the features of the new girl.

It seemed like years since he'd met her, but he supposed it had only been since breakfast.

"What happened to me?"

"You were brought in by Scholar Wolfe. He said you were not to get up. I was drafted, since I don't officially have class until tomorrow. The rest are all downstairs." She must have read his feeling of abandonment, because she smiled a little. "Don't blame your friends; they wanted to be here. Wolfe summoned them all to give them some kind of news. Do all his lessons end with someone unconscious?"

"Wait until you hear about the Greek fire," he said. It seemed like a long speech. "Is there water?"

She silently fetched a pitcher and glass from the small table, and poured. He drank in convulsive gulps and held it out for more. She re-filled, but only halfway. "Drink slower," she said. "You'll make yourself sick."

"Yes, Mother."

She laughed, and it sounded low and tired. He remembered how she'd looked at breakfast. A day hadn't been enough time to recover, and now she was spending it tending to him. "Definitely not your mother, though I've been called worse— Wait, what are you doing?"

"Sitting up."

"Wolfe said—"

"I thought you weren't my mother." She didn't try to stop him as he struggled up into a half-reclining position. "You should go and rest. I'm fine."

"I've been sleeping, on and off."

"In Dario's bed? That's punishment enough. I don't think he's changed the sheets since he got here. He's used to having servants for that."

"Believe me, dirty sheets are luxury compared to where I've been sleeping."

She'd come out of a war zone, he remembered. His eyes had adjusted to the light, and as he sipped the rest of the water, he studied her more closely. Still tired, with bruised circles beneath her eyes. "I'm *fine*," he told her. "Go. I promise not to get out of bed until morning."

Morgan frowned at him a moment, but her weariness was more of an argument than anything he could say, and she finally nodded. "You promise?"

"My word on it."

She got up, stretched, and left, shutting the door behind her, and before the latch clicked, he was already swinging his feet down to the floor. They were bare, and he hunted for his boots with one hand as he turned up the intensity of the lights. Bringing them up slowly allowed him to cope with the still-ringing gong of his headache. That, and more water. He drained half the jug before he tried to stand.

It was, he decided, a limited success, and after holding himself up for a while, he walked slowly. The hallway beyond was empty. He got to the stairs and rested, then descended.

There were voices coming from the common room, a confusing tangle of them . . . but they all died away when he appeared in the doorway. Jess tried to look casual about it as he leaned there, and hoped he didn't appear to be on the edge of collapse.

"You're supposed to be flat on your back." Santiago, surprisingly, was the first one to say something. As if he realized that might smack of concern, he said, in a studiously disinterested tone, "Trust you to get special treatment, though."

"Sit down," Thomas said, and dragged a chair over for Jess to sink into. "You should be in bed. Wolfe said—"

"I'm fine," Jess lied. "What did I miss?"

"There's a lottery tomorrow," Khalila said. "We all have to draw tiles."

For a moment, he thought the headache had permanently damaged his brain, because that made no sense. He repeated it. "All of us? We *all failed*?"

"Every damned one of us, apparently," Dario affirmed. "Including Khalila. I can only think that the rest of you were so miserably bad that our sweet desert flower suffered by association."

"He didn't explain *why* we failed?"

"Not a word," Khalila said. The mood in the room was dark and heavy, and someone had broken out a bottle of Scottish whiskey that Jess suddenly wanted very badly. "I was there, Jess. We found the books— well, you found them. And we arrested the guilty. How did we *fail*? What is he trying to teach us?"

"Wait," Jess said. "When is the lottery?"

"Tomorrow morning," Thomas said. He was sitting, and his whole body spoke of how dejected he was, from the curve of his back to his low-hanging head. "It's entirely unfair."

"No one said life was fair," Danton said; coming from France, Jess supposed he had a unique perspective on that. "He needs to reduce the class; he told us from the start that he'd only accept six in the end. I suppose this is how he goes about it. Unfairly."

"He doesn't have the right!" Glain was, predictably, incensed.

"He has every right," said Dario. "He's our proctor. They turned away tens of thousands when they accepted thirty of us. The Library has a surplus of people with *promise*. We're ten a *geneih*."

"So why do *you* think he failed us all? He must have some reason!"

Dario shrugged. "I think he did it because he can. And resents us. A Research Scholar like him, slumming with us? Why? I can only guess it was a punishment for him to be put in charge of rank amateurs like us."

That was an interesting thought, and it made a certain amount of sense. Research Scholars, like Wolfe, were constantly on the move out in the world, conducting research, experiments, doing the work of the Library. Having him as nursemaid to students seemed . . . wasteful, and the Library wasn't known for that.

"I know why we failed," said a quiet voice. The conversation slowed, then ceased, and they all looked around for who'd said it. Near the fire, Izumi raised her head. She almost always spoke softly, even diffidently, but she was rarely wrong. "We failed because we didn't ask."

"Ask what?" Jess said.

"What would happen to the books we confiscated."

"We know what happened to them. We sent them back to the Archives. We used the tags, just the way he taught us," Dario said. "It would be a stupid question."

Izumi finally raised her head and looked at him directly. There was something unexpectedly fiery in her steady gaze. "Were the books you found unique?"

Dario shrugged. "Rare enough."

"But already in the Codex." Izumi looked at the rest of them, a quick sweep of her gaze. "Did *anyone* find a unique book?"

No one spoke. Jess ran it over in his mind; he'd found rare volumes, but nothing that wasn't listed.

"What does the Library do with rare volumes that *aren't* unique?" Izumi asked. "We sent them to the Archive, using the tags, but what does the Archive do with them once they arrive?"

"Preserve them," Portero answered. "That's their job."

"Is it? Why should they? They have the originals. They mirror them to blanks. What use do they have for another copy?" She paused for a moment and then plunged on. "I have heard they destroy them. In a furnace."

"That's a lie!"

"Is it? Why not just destroy it? One less copy for the smugglers to trade!"

"It's not possible," Thomas said. "The Library, destroying books? It goes against everything they teach us!"

"Yes," she said. "It does. But so does a lot of what they do here." Izumi tapped the blank she'd been reading to clear it, and walked over to put it back on the shelf. Then she left.

"She can't be serious," Glain said. "The Library can't be destroying books in secret."

"But we didn't ask. She's right about that," Jess said. "We don't know anything that happens once the books go to the Archive."

The students erupted in a frenzy of debate, which turned to resentful speculation about just which of them would be leaving in the morning. Some were outspoken about not playing Wolfe's game this time. There were two sides forming: some who thought this was a ploy by Wolfe to see who would stand up for themselves, and some who didn't want to risk his wrath.

Jess was just too disheartened to care. He didn't even record it in his journal.

There didn't seem to be a point.

The next morning, Wolfe wasn't there. Neither was breakfast, which usually was laid out on the common room sideboard before the bells clanged dawn. When Jess came down to claim his portion, it was a portion of nothing.

Instead, there was a blank sitting on the empty sideboard, open to the first page, and Jess walked over to read what it said.

It simply said, *Draw a tile.*

The lottery jar was sitting next to the blank. Jess stared at it for a moment without moving until he heard footsteps behind him. Heavy ones. He knew whom they belonged to even before Thomas said, softly, "*Mein Gott*, he meant it, didn't he?"

"He meant it," Jess said. He was seething inside for the unfairness of it . . . He'd gone along with Wolfe, done everything he asked, even chased Santi down with that damned map. He'd driven himself half-dead for the man. And this is what he got in return . . . a good chance at being dismissed for *nothing*.

Thomas joined him in staring at the words on the blank, and then at the jug, which had a scene on it of Horus and Ma'at. For the first time, seeing it this close, Jess realized that both the jug and the tiles were old . . . very old. The smooth ivory pieces were worn and yellowed by the touch of thousands of sweaty, nervous hands.

Then Thomas sighed and reached out to take a tile.

Jess grabbed his arm to stop him. "Don't."

"If I don't take one, I will be finished anyway," Thomas said. "We should do as Wolfe says."

Thomas fished around in the jug and drew out a single tile, which he clenched in his fist. He didn't look at it. When Jess mutely gestured to it, Thomas shook his head. "There is no point in looking," he said. "Either I will stay or I will go, and it is beyond my control now. Come, Jess, choose and let's sit down by the fire. It's damp this morning."

Because Thomas was with him, a calm and silent witness, Jess didn't think there was any way out of it, and he didn't want to seem afraid, though he was, down to his bones. His future rode on this single, stupid, meaningless chance.

He didn't look. He just plunged his hand into the jar, fumbled blindly, and yanked free a tile. He shoved it into his pocket, next to his Codex, because if he'd held on to it he wouldn't have been able to resist the temptation to stare at the number on it, as if it was some mysterious fortune-teller in the market.

Morgan was the next one into the room, with Izumi; the two girls seemed to have struck up a friendship, though a quiet one. Morgan looked better rested, Jess thought, and she'd changed from her stifling English clothing into a loose linen dress in a pale Mediterranean blue. It suited her, he thought. There was color in her cheeks now, and he watched her stop in the doorway with Izumi, taking in the room. Morgan's eyes met his, and she nodded a little, without smiling. He nodded back.

"Is it normal to have tiles for breakfast?" she asked.

"Every Thursday," Thomas said, all too cheerfully. "Crunchy. Good for the digestion."

Izumi rolled her eyes, walked over, and chose a tile. "I wish they'd at least brought the coffee," she said. "I don't think I can face this without coffee."

Morgan was staring at the jug doubtfully, and Jess could tell that she was wondering whether or not she should pull a number. It was, after all, her first official day as a student; if she was unlucky, she wouldn't even have a full day of it before dismissal.

"You shouldn't have to," Jess said, and Morgan turned to look at him. She gave him a strange, fleeting smile and then reached into the jug and pulled a tile.

"I'm in the class," she said. "Scholar Wolfe said everyone draws a number. Therefore, I draw a number. I'm one of you."

Jess was almost sure he wouldn't have made that choice; he'd have argued for the fact that he shouldn't be blamed when he hadn't even been present for the failures. He wasn't certain whether he was impressed by her courage, or confused.

He certainly wasn't bored.

The rest drifted in, one by one, and each had a different reaction. For most it was anger, as if they'd expected Wolfe to have been joking, which was, to Jess's mind, as unlikely as a snowstorm. Glain complained bitterly before she picked her tile, and Dario seethed and promised to use his family's influence to ruin Wolfe if he ended up dismissed. Some cried. Some tried to seem as if they didn't care, but Jess knew they did. They'd all fought to be here. They'd all fought to stay.

It felt deeply unfair to every one of them.

About half of them refused to draw tiles at all. Hallem first. Some who'd drawn put them back in the jar.

"You'd better take them," Khalila said, as she drew her own. She was the last in the door; Jess had counted heads, and they were all present now. "Once he gets here . . ."

And all too suddenly, he arrived. Wolfe appeared in the doorway, all black robes and judgment. The very sight of his impassive face made Jess feel angry.

"No doubt you're all cursing me for the unfairness of this," Wolfe said. "Or at least the lack of breakfast. Food will be delivered once we finish the unpleasantness at hand."

"We're not going to draw lots when we did nothing to deserve it." Hallem stepped forward out of the half of the room that hadn't taken tiles. Hallem was a tall, rawboned boy, with a mean streak that they'd all learned to avoid, but this seemed out of character for him, publicly confronting Wolfe. At least, until Jess spotted the sweat on his face and dampening his shirt collar, and the wide, eerie pupils of his eyes.

He'd taken something this morning to give himself false courage, and it had swallowed his good sense.

"Step back, Postulant," Wolfe said.

Hallem didn't. "Tell us what we did wrong. You owe us that."

"I owe you nothing. Step *back*," Wolfe said. It was calm enough, but freighted with real, quiet menace. Hallem took another step forward. Jess exchanged a quick look with Dario, who seemed as surprised as anyone else—and, curiously, Dario wasn't standing with the rebels. Neither was his other henchman, Portero.

"The Library doesn't need sheep. It needs people who think for themselves. People who can stand up to a challenge." Hallem bunched a shaking fist, and for a moment, Jess thought he'd lose control and hit the Scholar, who stared at him so calmly. "You think you're some pagan god! You think you can lord it over our lives and ruin us for nothing but your whims! No more!"

"Hallem," Jess said. "Easy."

"Easy?" Hallem turned on him, and his whole body was a bundle of clenched muscles, racked with rage. "*Easy?* Do you know what I've got to go home to, scrubber? Do you know what my father will do to me?"

"If he locks you in a room to sweat off whatever you've taken, it would probably be a good start," Thomas said. He stepped forward and stared down at Hallem. Placid and kind as he was, Thomas could still be intimidating when he wished. "Fair or not, Scholar Wolfe is our proctor. What do you think you'll accomplish by this?"

"He can't fail us all!"

"I think he can," Thomas said. "Worse, I think the Archivist would agree. Stop and think what you're risking. All of you. *Think*."

Wolfe shifted his attention to the middle distance, as if Hallem no longer mattered at all. "Tiles," Wolfe said. "Everyone should have drawn one. Take them out."

Hallem crossed his arms. "I didn't draw one. None of us on this side of the room did. We're standing up to you."

"Then I'll draw for you." Wolfe reached into the jar and held up a tile. "Three, Postulant Hallem," he said. "I hope for your sake it's a lucky number. Last chance. Take your tiles."

Behind Hallem, his group of rebels—the majority of the remaining class, Jess realized—stood unified behind him. He knew and liked most of them. *I'm on the wrong side of this,* he thought. Jess had the smooth ivory tile in his hand and kept turning it over and over, feeling the lines incised on the surface. It would feel good to take a stand. Do something powerful for a change.

He wanted to throw it back in the pot.

Captain Santi had joined Wolfe, leaning casually against the doorframe as he peeled an apple with a sharp knife. As Jess considered his choices, he realized that Santi was looking directly at him, and though he said nothing, made no significant motions, something in him stopped Jess cold.

"Does anyone else wish to join Postulant Hallem's protest? He does have a point. I might be looking for those willing to think for themselves," Wolfe said. "Or, of course, I might have another thought altogether."

No one moved. He withdrew two dice from his pocket and tossed them on the table. Jess watched as they rolled, tumbled, clinked off the pottery of the jug, and finally came to a stop—too far away for him to see the numbers. Santi took a bite of his apple and moved to take a look.

"Two and four," he said as he chewed. "Check your tiles."

Next to Jess, Thomas let out a long, slow sigh and opened his hand.

On it lay a tile with the number four.

"No," Jess said. "No!" *Thomas?* Thomas couldn't go home. It wasn't even remotely fair.

Khalila let out a choked cry, and Jess spun to look at her. Her trembling palm held the number two. Wolfe couldn't dismiss Khalila; she was unbelievably good at this. She was *meant* to be here.

Jess closed his eyes and reached for his own tile. He ran his fingers over the engraved surface, as if he could read it blind, and then pulled it free and looked.

Four.

He was finished. A slow, oily sickness rolled through him, and he felt suddenly very tired. The anger was gone now. All that was left was an overwhelming feeling of loss. *I wanted this,* he realized. *I liked this. I liked these people.*

And now it was all over. He'd go home in disgrace, if his father let him come home at all, and he would never see this place again, walk these streets again, feel this friendship again.

Morgan was holding her own tile in her palm, staring at it. The color had faded again from her cheeks. Like Khalila, like Thomas and himself, she held one of the fatal numbers. *At least she didn't have time to get used to all this,* Jess thought, though the unfairness of it ached. *At least she hasn't worked so hard and lost so much.*

Some people were sobbing. Some were gasping in relief. The rebels were muttering, clearly unsure what their next move should be.

All except Hallem, who looked triumphant. "You're finished, Wolfe.

If you dismiss those of us who didn't draw and those who hold the wrong numbers, you'll be down to only *three students*. So this lottery can't possibly count." He looked elated now, and he was right. The math of it was on his side.

Hallem had *won*. Wolfe couldn't possibly drop the class all the way down to three. The Archivist wouldn't allow it.

Wolfe said, "Solidly reasoned, Mr. Hallem. But I still expect all who refused to draw a tile to be at Misr Station within the hour. Leave your trunks. We will have them shipped home to you. I want you gone."

"You can't!" Hallem said. "You just said—"

"Your mistake, former postulant," Wolfe said, "is assuming that I was ever going to dismiss *anyone*. I said you would all draw tiles this morning; I never said it meant anyone would be dismissed. It wouldn't have mattered what number you drew, as long as you drew a tile. I knew some of you would let your outrage override your good sense, because yesterday, for the first time, every one of you was a *complete success*." He shook his head. "A pity you didn't trust me. But then, I haven't given you any reason, have I?"

Silence fell heavy in the room. Everyone seemed stunned—those who'd held on to their tiles and thought they'd survived, those who thought they'd drawn losing numbers. Those who'd refused to play at all.

None of them had seen it coming.

There were nine of them left, Jess realized. Nine who hadn't joined the rebellion.

However improbably, he'd survived another round.

EPHEMERA

An excerpt from a work entitled On Press-Printing: A New
Beginning by Research Scholar Christopher Wolfe,
submitted to the Artifex Magnus for peer review and
brought by him to the Curators of the Library. Marked as
SEDITIOUS CONTENT and sent to the Black Archives by
order of the Archivist Magister, for his eyes only.

. . . *foundation built in those early days, when the Library was at its most*
vulnerable, was flawed by one thing: the relative scarcity of the Obscurists
themselves. It is a skill which can be taught only to a point, and then there
must be a real spark of talent with which to bring the alchemical theories
into active life.

Fewer of these rare, bright talents are born now than ever before, and
even within the Iron Tower itself, there is a growing knowledge that so
few Obscurists cannot long sustain the massive burden of the Library,
which calls on them for mirroring, for translation of books, objects, and
even people, and for many more similar demands.

Without the Obscurists, the Library falls . . . unless another method of
purely mechanical duplication of knowledge is put in place.

I propose the immediate and widespread use of a device I call a press-
printer, which uses a system of movable letters that may be arranged into
any grouping to form words, lines, and pages of text. Once inked, these let-
ters are then pressed by means of a mechanical arm upon an individual
sheet, which may then be bound up into books.

By this means, we can distribute the knowledge of the Library in repro-
duced form, endlessly, in a way that removes the burden from the fragile
shoulders of the Obscurists.

I have included full schematics of this press-printer and a sample page produced from the prototype device. I look forward to demonstrating this device to you at your convenience.

An annotation from the Artifex Magnus to the document.

The pernicious heresy that began with Gutenberg once again appears among us, as if some great and sinister force insists on destroying the greatest institution of learning humankind has ever known. That it should spring from the mind of one of our most valuable and well-regarded Scholars, one so closely connected to the Iron Tower itself, makes it even more disturbing.

As with Gutenberg and all others who have followed, we must destroy this heresy immediately and completely. We have no choice.

A following annotation from the Obscurist Magnus to the document.

The work that Scholar Wolfe has done must be destroyed, there is no question of it, but I cannot and will not agree to the destruction of the man himself. All his research, even that unrelated to this heresy, can be interdicted from the Codex and sent to the Black Archives. He can be effectively erased without the need of his death.

He should be taken to a place of questioning and there made to see the error of his beliefs. Once he has been so instructed, he may then be useful to the Library again, but only under the close and constant watch of the Artifex Magnus.

He must, of course, be made to understand that this extraordinary mercy will not come again, and he lives on the sufferance of the Archivist and Curators.

I leave this in your hands, Artifex.

CHAPTER FIVE

P tolemy House went from claustrophobic to uncomfortably empty, with only the nine of them left to rattle around inside. That included a few Jess wished had dropped by the wayside, like Santiago and Portero and Glain . . . but the addition of Morgan to their ranks made up for it. Jess enjoyed her company. More than he should, he knew. With nine of them left, three would have to leave by the end, and they would all be fighting for the six spots left.

On the morning of the third day after the false lottery, Jess was up before the bells, but he found Khalila in the common room ahead of him, already sipping coffee and reading a blank. She was always reading now. It was probably why she would survive them all in the cutthroat world of the Library.

"What is it?" Jess asked, as he poured his cup. She shrugged. "Khalila, you're never early. You sleep until the last moment and arrive exactly on time. You're precise about it."

She shut the book. "I wanted to talk to you in private, and *you* get up early."

"Talk about what?"

She gave him a significant look.

"If you're waiting for me to guess, I haven't got a clue," Jess said, hand-ing her a piece of pastry he knew she particularly liked. It had raisins. He loathed them, but she bit into it with enthusiasm.

"You should be more careful," she said.

He froze cold inside. *She knows. She knows about my family.*

But that was proven wrong when she continued. "I assume you already know better, but anyone can see that you're paying far too much attention to the girl."

"Glain? Well, she's very tall. She's hard to ignore." Khalila only sighed in response to that, so Jess conceded the point. "You mean the new girl? Morgan? All right, I like Morgan. At least she isn't Glain."

"Glain is all right. She's just very direct."

"And what do *you* think of Morgan, then?"

Khalila considered him over the lip of her coffee cup. "She is a mystery, and mysteries are dangerous, especially here. You should remember that. This is not a time to be distracted."

"I like mysteries."

"You like *challenge*, Jess. And I assure you that she is well aware of it. She's very clever. Too clever by half. Maybe you cannot see that, but I do."

"So you don't like her?"

"Oh, I do, very much. I just don't trust her, and neither should you. The rest of us, we've spent time together. Sweated together. Failed together. She . . ." Khalila tapped a fingernail on the heavy pottery of her cup. "She is a blank, and until we see what's on her pages, I would keep my distance."

"There are only nine of us left. Three of us are leaving anyway. Maybe I should be worrying more about the devils I know."

Khalila conceded that with another shrug and a rueful half smile. She was different now, Jess thought. More mature. More comfortable in her skin, and with her own brilliance. Here, among people who respected her, she shone like a diamond.

He might have also been drawn to *her*, except that she had made it all too plain to everyone that she was not available. Only Dario pursued her, and she found it, Jess thought, flattering and exasperating, in turns. But he didn't think she would ever return Dario's affections. She was too aware of the same advice she was giving him. *Three of us will leave.*

She didn't want to be one of them . . . or have to give up someone she loved. And she didn't want distractions.

They ate without talking more about it. He enjoyed Khalila's ability to say what she meant and move on. Efficient.

Portero was the next one in, yawning and surly; he grunted a greeting to them and loaded his plate up before taking a seat far away. Dario settled for coffee and a spot with Portero. Glain avoided them all, still, and sat solitary, at least until Morgan arrived with Izumi, and both infringed on her space. Glain suffered it, though not happily.

Thomas was almost late, and as he reached out for a pastry, Izumi—back at the food, which was remarkable for such a slender girl—slapped his hand away. "Wash your hands before you touch anything, Thomas," she said. "You're filthy."

He was. His fingers were dark with grease, and he blushed a hot red and left the room. When he came back, his skin was scrupulously clean, and he retrieved a light breakfast before crowding into a seat beside Jess and Khalila. *"Guten Morgen,"* he said. "Will we survive the day?"

"Depends," Jess said. "We don't know what Wolfe's got for us. What were you working on down there?" Thomas had established his own space downstairs, in a corner of an old storage room, where he rebuilt things that he rescued from dumps and market stalls. How he found the time was a mystery, given the work Wolfe piled on them, but Thomas insisted it was soothing.

"Something amazing," Thomas said, and the delight in his face had a sly cast to it. "I think you will especially like it, Jess. You see, I've been thinking about how the Codex functions."

"The Codex functions through the Obscurists, and Wolfe made it very clear that the details of just exactly *how* it functions remain the secrets of Obscurists," Khalila said. "Thomas, I thought you would know all this by now."

"I do! But only imagine if we could make all that unnecessary!"

"Make *what* unnecessary?"

"The Codex. Obscurists. All of it."

"Unnecessary? Thomas! It's the basis of the Library!" Khalila had lowered her voice, and Jess saw the flash of worry on her face. When he tried to speak again, she gestured for him to speak more quietly.

Thomas's version of quiet was a hoarse whisper, and Jess didn't know that it helped much. "It's inefficient, yes? Obscurists are rare. It is an unstable resource—you said that yourself in class. Safer to find another method. What if we could eliminate the need for the Codex?"

"You're barking mad," Jess said. "The Codex is necessary. Always will be."

"What if I could show you something else? Something better?"

"You'd be the bloody Archivist Magister in a day. *If* it worked."

"It will," Thomas said, with complete confidence.

"Then show us."

"Not yet. It isn't finished. But when it is, I will be able to make the Codex obsolete."

Khalila was still frowning. "Thomas, I don't know about this. It sounds like heresy to me. Be careful, will you? Please?"

"I am *not* a Burner!"

"I said it *sounded* like—"

Jess's Codex flashed and hummed. He pulled it free, and all the others' buzzed as well.

From Wolfe.

It had an address listed, and nothing more. No instructions other than that, but it was clear what Wolfe wanted from them. Jess drained his coffee, and around him, everyone else was doing the same.

"Come on," Glain said. She was the first to the door. "It's a long walk. We'd better hurry."

The heat beat down from a shimmering molten sun, with no hint of clouds; the ocean breeze didn't help much, since it came weighted with moisture. Jess was getting used to the climate, but in the half hour it took to follow Glain's long, fast strides to the address Wolfe had messaged them, he began to really miss the bone-chilling days of a London winter. The light cotton shirt he wore stuck to his skin in uncomfortable patches, and the crown of his head felt as if someone held a hot metal plate to it. When Thomas took a swig of water, his face brick red from the exertion and heat, Jess remembered to do the same.

"Up there," Glain said, and indicated a nondescript shop on the street. She paused, and when Dario would have pushed past her, she grabbed his shoulder to pull him to a stop. Unlike the rest of them, she didn't seem tired, or even overly warm. Jess wasn't even sure she was sweating. "Wait. This seems wrong."

"What do you mean, *wrong*? Wolfe sent for us. He gave us this address. What are you afraid of?" Dario pushed her hand away and kept walking.

They all followed him. Jess watched Glain, because she positioned herself near the back of the group, and he thought, *She's using us for cover.*

She really did sense something. He had no idea what, but it woke a stinging prickle of alarm on the back of his neck.

Dario had almost reached the front of the shop when Guillaume Danton said, "Wait!" Dario came to a halt and looked back, frowning.

Guillaume drew in a sudden, sharp breath and said, "Step back, Dario. Carefully. Now."

"Don't be stupid. There's nothing . . ." Dario looked down, and his voice faded away to nothing.

His leg was just touching a thin, almost invisible, silver wire that stretched across the doorway. Guillaume moved forward and crouched down, face close to the wire. He straightened up. "I can't see where it attaches. It may be an alarm, or something worse. Burners sometimes rig up Greek fire to fall using this method." When they all looked at him, he shrugged. "I never said my family didn't know things."

Dario took a very careful step back from the wire.

"We should go back," Khalila said.

"Wolfe gave us the address," Thomas said. "I think he means for us to go inside."

Izumi sighed. "Why does he insist we do these things? Why can we not just learn—learn how to run a Serapeum for a change? I came to be a Scholar!"

"Haven't you paid attention?" Glain snapped back. "That isn't why we were chosen. If they'd wanted us to be librarians, we wouldn't be here; we'd be taking training in our home cities and signing one-year contracts for a copper band. If you want to be a Scholar, you have to be *better*. You have to be able to handle yourself, out in the world."

Glain was right. Absolutely right. Jess knew Thomas was right, too; retreat from this would mean a black mark. Wolfe wanted them inside.

"We have to go," Jess said. "You know we do."

"By all means, go," Danton said, and backed away. "I'll be waiting out here. Better failure than funeral."

"Coward," Portero said. Danton raised his eyebrows and folded his arms with no evidence of caring. "Fine, stay here. I'll take the lead."

"Wait," Jess said. "Not through the front. There's another way."

That got all their attention, and Dario said, "How do you know?"

"Because there's always another way." He hadn't lived his entire childhood running from one thing or another without learning *something*. "Stay here. Let me scout it."

Jess spotted the alleyway only when he was almost past it; it was hardly wider than his shoulders, and the walls converged into an optical illusion that was hard to distinguish unless you were looking for it. He kept his eyes open as he moved that way, but there were no tripwires below, no traps dangling above. The alley led around to the back of the shop, and he backed up and gestured for the others. They followed him to the small courtyard in the back.

The shop's door was shut. "Now what?" Khalila asked. She was, for once, out of her depth. This wasn't a problem that would be solved by anything in her experience.

Glain turned to Jess. "Locked. Can you open it?"

"Yes. Probably."

She searched around and helped him locate pieces of wire, which he stripped and bent to the necessary angles. It was a simple lock. His da would have been disappointed in how long it took him to crack it, but the others seemed suitably impressed. When he started to open it, Glain caught hold of the latch and shook her head. "Step back," she said. "Everybody. Back and to the sides."

She was right. Glain kicked the door open with a sudden, violent movement and darted off to the right, and a glass bottle that had been balanced inside crashed down on the stone floor inside. The chemical reek of it hit Jess an instant before he saw a single, vividly green flame flare up. Greek fire, but the bottle had been almost empty. It wouldn't have killed anyone, but it would have left a scar.

Glain swept the glass fragments aside with her boot and stepped inside . . . and froze.

"What is it?" Jess asked.

She let out a fast, huffing breath and stalked into the room to glare at Scholar Wolfe, who was sitting in a chair, calmly enjoying a hot cup of tea. "Slow, but acceptable," he said. "Glain, well done."

"*Greek fire?*" Glain stood right in front of the Scholar and glared. She had a fairly magnificent glare. Jess had to give her that. "What kind of test was *that?*"

"An hour ago, it wasn't a test at all," Wolfe said. "Santi and his men arrested a nest of Burners in this shop this morning and defused a series of traps, many of which they have left in place for you to discover, though they rendered them relatively safe. You did well in avoiding the tripwire in front and the Greek fire at the rear door. Now join Postulant Danton and search the rest of the shop."

"Danton?" Jess turned and saw that Guillaume was behind them, already going through boxes. "I thought you were staying outside."

"I waited to see if you died back there," Guillaume said. "You didn't. So I thought it was safe enough to come in." He lifted a box from the pile next to him and carried it over to put it in the center of the room. "I found this: copper igniters. Burners use them for large Greek fire containers. They might have been planning something big."

"They were," Wolfe said. "I leave it to the rest of you to work it out for yourselves."

They gathered up anything they found that seemed out of place; the shop was supposed to be a pottery-making enterprise, but it had been closed up for months, and any trace of clay or wheels was long gone. Jess found a box of what looked like loose papers, but he realized, with a sickening jolt, that they were the interiors of books . . . ripped out of their bindings and tossed in sheaves into a pile. Not rare works; he knew most of the titles and checked the rest on his Codex. Common black market copies, every one.

Why destroy them? Burners burned books in protest, as statements. It seemed strange to destroy them in private.

It was Thomas who put the puzzle together, from scraps of metal and paper, leather and glue. He looked at everything they assembled in the center of the shop and said, "They built Greek fire containers into the covers of hollowed-out books. Why would they do that?"

Wolfe rose from his chair and looked at the tangle of clues, and nodded. "You bait a trap with what the creature you're hunting likes best.

Scholars love original books. The firebombs would have been layered un-der real ones, inside of containers. All they have to do is arrange for the lot to be confiscated and tagged back to storage."

Khalila put a hand to her mouth. "If Scholars had sent them to the Archive . . ."

"The Archive might have been damaged," Wolfe finished for her. "It's always a goal of the Burners, though it's very rare to find such a plot within Alexandria itself. They usually target outside the city, but this knot of snakes seems unusually venomous. I wanted you to see this. Rea-son it for yourself."

Jess remembered with sudden, vivid clarity the dark, smoky scars and gouges left on the steps of the London Serapeum, the day he'd run from the lions. The Burners had been going after St. Paul's for years, long be-fore his birth; they'd killed hundreds in that particular attack when he was nine. He'd been a long way off and had still seen the smoke rising, heard the distant screaming. It had been the worst attack anywhere, ex-cept for the assaults that went on constantly in America, where the Burners had succeeded in shutting down four of the largest of that coun-try's daughter libraries. Technically, those Serapeum remained open, but no one dared to visit.

"They're getting bolder," Glain said. "Every year, more attacks. Why can't the Library stop them?"

"We try," Wolfe said. "They've learned to avoid the Codex; when they make plans, it's through paper message or messengers. Never any-thing an Obscurist can track or see."

"Sir?" Thomas looked up from his contemplation of the pile in front of him. His face was set and very serious. "How close did they come?"

"Not close this time." Wolfe looked around at them, and for the first time, Jess felt he was treating them as genuinely worth his effort. "And yet, they are here, and that is troubling. Some of you may have grown up in places where the Burners are tolerated, even encouraged, but believe this: if you wear the band of the Library, you are their enemy. That is why we are putting so much time into training you to be vigilant."

"Scholar?" Izumi raised her hand, a little hesitantly. She waited for his nod to continue. "Isn't it the job of the High Garda to pursue them? Not Scholars?"

"It was," Wolfe said. "Now it's ours as well. I don't like it, either, but that is the world in which we live. That is the world I am training you to enter." He walked toward the door, only looking back to say, "Mind the tripwire. It still has a bite."

They had a silent, grim walk back to Ptolemy House. Jess could still smell traces of alchemical compounds from the Greek fire, a ghost of the man burning in St. Pancras station. *That is the world I am training you to enter.* Jess had grown up a smuggler, understanding that books were a precious commodity, understanding that his family catered to a basic human hunger.

He didn't understand the Burners. He didn't *want* to understand them. He wanted to go back to a safe place where he didn't have to think about these things anymore . . . but he was honest enough to know that there were no safe places. Maybe never had been.

And maybe that was why his father had sent him, to learn that lesson, as much as anything else.

Jess dreamed of automaton lions running at his heels, but when he turned in the dream, slow and weightless, it wasn't lions after all. It was a young man carrying a bottle of Greek fire, who upended it over his head, screaming.

It was his own face.

Dario stumbled in drunk in the middle of the night and set to snoring. He sounded like a broken chain being beaten on metal, and it didn't stop. Jess thought wearily about smothering him, but that seemed imprudent, so he dressed in the dark and slipped downstairs.

The common room sofa would do just as well for tonight. Tomorrow, he'd move his small chest of belongings to one of the empty rooms. Should have already done it, he thought. Dario would be pleased to have his private room again.

When he got to the common room, the door was closed. He tried the handle. Locked.

He put his ear to the door, but it was as silent as the grave on the other side. Someone might have locked it by mistake; it had happened more than once, but if Portero had brought one of his girlfriends back, they were going to get a nasty surprise. Jess didn't intend to let anything stand between him and the few meager hours of rest he had left.

He stretched up for the key on the ledge above the door. After the first few times of being locked out, Thomas had provided a key, which had come in handy more than once.

The door opened without so much as a creak. He expected to find the room empty.

Instead, he found Morgan Hault.

She was dressed in a thick Egyptian dressing gown, and her brown hair was plaited into a rope that hung over her left shoulder. He hesitated in the doorway. Her back was turned to him, and as he started to say her name, something made him stop.

There was a strange buzzing feeling in his head. He recognized it. It was the same feeling he had when one of the Archive tags was activated and drew energy away from him in the process. The same as the drain he'd felt when using the map to track Santi, only that had been so much worse.

"Morgan?"

She turned, fast, and he saw something he couldn't comprehend. It didn't make sense. She was holding a blank, but the letters were not on the page of the book. Not ink on paper, the way that the Codex mirrored them from the original book in the archive. The ink was there, but ghostly. Shimmering.

The letters were floating in gold and orange, sparking and turning, twisting in slow, fluid patterns. Rows and columns, cubes of them, all shifting and whispering and moving as much as a foot above the blank, and the storm in his head reached a sudden horrible intensity just as Morgan dropped the book.

As the blank slid free of her fingers, something followed it—a kind of *string* was how he thought of it, except that it was a string of strange, pulsing light. Almost like a static shock, but too delicate, too lingering.

A string of orange light that broke just as the blank thumped to the carpeted floor.

She didn't say a word. Her eyes had gone wide, but then they narrowed in calculation and she backed slowly away.

He staggered and braced himself against the doorway. Just breathed for a moment, and then reached over and closed the common room door. Then he locked it and pocketed the key.

"What was that?" he asked, and when she didn't answer, he pushed free and stepped forward. She backed up. "You're not leaving until you tell me."

"I don't know what happened," she said. He could see her trembling. "The blank must be—"

"Don't try it. The blank isn't defective, and I'm not a fool."

"Jess—"

"I can only think of one explanation for what I just saw, and that is that you're an Obscurist," he said.

"I'm not!"

"Don't lie to me again."

He saw her whole body go tense and still. She was considering whether or not to come at him for the key, and whether or not she'd win if she picked that battle. It lasted a long few seconds before she took in a breath and said, simply, "Yes."

Now that she'd admitted it, the shock rolled over him. *Obscurist.* But they weren't supposed to ever leave the confines of the Iron Tower. What was someone like that doing *here*, disguised as a student?

Maybe that's the point. Maybe it's another test, and we're supposed to find her out. "Does Wolfe know what you are?"

She snapped the answer back too quickly. "He doesn't know anything."

"Bit of advice: if you're going to lie, learn to do it better." Jess's pulse was racing, but it was as much with adrenaline as with fear. *I've seen an Obscurist at work.* That seemed as impossible as petting a unicorn. "Relax. I won't hurt you."

That made her frown, and her voice turned firmer. "Do you realize how arrogant that makes you sound? If I'm an Obscurist, do you really think you have the *ability* to hurt me?"

"Probably," he said. "They don't keep you in the Iron Tower because you can easily defend yourselves, now, do they? You're not some sorcerer out of a story. What you do is alchemy, not magic. You're not going to throw a spell at me. Alchemy requires preparation."

"I wasn't talking about magic," Morgan said. "I can look after myself. And, if you push me, I will." She had a knife now, and he hadn't even seen her draw it. From the way she held it, he could see she was comfortable with the weapon . . . and she would be, if she'd actually survived a war to get here.

But there really would be no advantage in fighting, for either of them. He held up his hands. "Good point. Maybe I should just call the High Garda and have you escorted to the Iron Tower."

He'd hit a nerve. A big one. She took a tighter grip on the knife, and he saw the flash of panic in her eyes. She didn't want to go there. Not at all.

"All right," she said, and tried to make it sound casual. "Wolfe knows all about me. Happy now?" He might not have believed her if he hadn't just seen her lie, but that, surprisingly, was the truth. Though *why* Wolfe would help was another thing entirely.

"What are you going to do?" she demanded.

"I don't know." He nudged the blank on the floor with his foot, but it was back to just a plain volume, no different from any other he'd ever held. "Is this thing dangerous?"

"It's a *blank*. Why would it be dangerous?"

"Because I just saw it do something I've never seen a blank do before."

"That's not the book," Morgan said. "It's just simple manipulation of the formulae behind the mirroring. I can do that with any blank. They're all connected to the Codex, by their nature; it's the principle of similarity. As above, so below. It's what the Doctrine of Mirroring is based on. I was finding a way in."

She said it as if that was self-explanatory, which maybe it was, to her; it was the same offhand way Thomas talked about engineering, or Khalila about dizzying levels of mathematics, as if anyone ought to be able to see how it worked.

It made him feel stupid, and annoyed by it. "So you're an Obscurist who came here to pretend to be one of us," he said. "Why? Is this another one of Wolfe's bloody stupid tests? Are we supposed to discover your secret? Then I think I win. Though it was stupid of you to be down here doing this."

"It's not a *test*! I wish it was. That would be so . . . simple." The flush was fading from her cheeks now, and she walked over to the fire to warm her hands. "And I didn't do it here by choice. The blanks work best when they are near each other. Principles of similarity, the sympathetic energy grows stronger. I locked the door. What are *you* doing here?"

"Looking for sleep," he said. "Which I'm not going to get. If you're not here to test us, why *are* you here? Shouldn't you be in the tower?"

"I'm not going to the Iron Tower," she said, very quietly. "That's the whole point of this. They were looking all over England for me by the time I made it past the border. I won't be here long. Once I have what I came for, I'll be on my way again."

"Khalila was right. She told me not to trust you," Jess said. He sat down on the divan because he didn't think he had the strength to keep standing; too many surprises today, and not enough rest. "What are you after?"

"What do you think? I want my *life*! I want to erase any trace of . . . what I am." She wrapped her arms around her body, as if she was chilled to the bone, despite the fire. "I was coming here, you know; that wasn't a lie. I'd already been accepted for training when I first accidentally opened up formulae; Scholar Tyler in Oxford saw me do it when I was reading a blank at the Serapeum. He told me opening the formulae leaves a kind of—record that the Obscurists could trace back to me, eventually. I had to destroy my record in the Codex itself if I didn't want to end up in the Iron Tower."

She paused, but Jess didn't say anything. Her voice had the ring of truth. More, it had the ring of desperation.

"I could open formulae, but actually altering them was impossible to do from Oxford, and even from the London Serapeum; I tried. Scholar Tyler told me that the closer I could get to the Iron Tower, the better chance I had of changing them. I already had an opening here in the training class. It was my only choice; they were looking for a stray Obscurist in London by the time I left." That struck some kind of thought in her, and she looked at him with sudden, real distrust. "Did someone send you here to find me? Did you suspect me?"

"Not me. I was just looking for a quiet place to kip. You should have put a sign up. *No entrance—alchemical sabotage in progress.*"

"Was that a *joke*?"

"Not a very funny one." Jess still couldn't quite take it in. An *Ob-*

scurist. He'd come to think they weren't real, or if they were, that they were incredibly old, with beards that stretched to the floor. He'd never imagined one his own age. Or a girl, for that matter. "You said Wolfe knows. How did he find out?"

"He caught me," she said. "I tried my best, but if I'm not concentrating, sometimes I reveal the formulae without meaning to do it, and . . . he saw. I thought he'd send me straight to the tower. Instead, he told me to do what I needed and get out as soon as possible. He warned me my time was running out, and he couldn't protect me."

The idea of Wolfe protecting *any* of them made Jess feel oddly off-balance. Wolfe was their enemy—or, at least, their judge, jury, and executioner. What would move him to keep Morgan's secret?

He didn't think she knew or, if she did, that she'd tell him. "If you came just to remove this—record from the Codex, it means you won't be staying once you do it. Right?"

She was watching him with just as much wariness as he felt himself. "All I need is a few more days. Are you going to turn me in?"

He should, he knew; if anything would get him a posting at the Library, completely eliminate any chance that he'd be sent off . . . there she was, his golden goose. A stray Obscurist, the rarest of all birds, by her own admission.

He knew that was how he should see her, but all he could see was a girl. He'd spent his entire childhood as a fugitive from one thing or another. From his father. From the Garda. From his future.

So he said, "No. I won't turn you in."

"As simple as that?"

"As simple as that. I understand what it's like to run. Besides, you said Wolfe already knows. Who would I tell?"

Morgan closed her eyes tight in sudden relief. Now that she wasn't looking at him, he could stare freely. It was the same face, but there was something different about her, too. Something subtle and strong she'd taken great pains to hide and wasn't hiding anymore. Not from him.

"Morgan. How old are you? Really?"

"I didn't lie. I'm sixteen," she said, and opened her eyes again. He looked away. "I've been running for months. Training in secret."

"Training with who?"

"I won't tell you that, Jess. I know you have secrets of your own, so let me keep mine."

"All right. Are you really from Oxford?"

He met her eyes again, briefly, but it didn't help. If she was lying, she was better prepared to do it well now. "I was born there," she said. "My father's still there. And I'm going back as soon as I'm done. Another day or two, I promise. You won't have to keep my secret for long."

"How do you plan to get out of Alexandria?"

Her lips curled a little on the edges, making shadows. "I'll fail one of the tests and lose a lottery drawing, and I'll be off. No one will suspect a thing, and by that time the records will only show that I'm Morgan Hault, failed student. No one will know I was ever anything else."

"Well, while you're altering records, put me at the top of the class. It'd be a nice change."

She crossed to sit down on the divan, and pulled her feet up beneath her. Graceful and easy, and deceptively familiar; he'd seen her in this pose many times. *It's a role. She's just playing at being one of us.* But it didn't seem that way. It seemed to him that she'd genuinely relaxed in his presence, as if she felt safe.

"Do you know what you're giving up?" he asked. "I know you didn't ask for it, but being an Obscurist must be important work. You'd be part of the Library for life, automatically a gold band . . . They'd pamper you like a queen."

"You really don't know anything about it, do you?" She rested her chin on a fist and braced her elbow on the worn velvet arm of the divan.

Across the room, the fire cracked and sparked; the room felt warm and peaceful. Strange, given what they were discussing. "I told you, Obscurists are *taken*. Dragged from their families as soon as they're identified. Forced into the Iron Tower. Those gold bands you speak of? For an Obscurist, it's a collar locked around your throat that never comes off. No freedom. No way to leave." She studied him for a few silent seconds. "I'd rather die. You would, too. I know that much about you, Jess."

"I expect you do," he said. "If you're using the blanks to get into the Codex and alter your records, that means you can *read* those records," he said. "Which means you also know everything *they* know about all of us. You're too sharp not to have done your research."

That got him a sudden, sharp look, as if he'd unnerved her. "And?"

"I need to know what it says about me."

"Not much. Your father should be more careful when he writes to you. I could tell that it was some type of code. I don't know what it meant, but if I thought he was sending you instructions, someone else might have guessed it, too. They could be watching you." She picked at a loose thread on the arm of the divan. "I haven't been able to get deeper than that. It takes time, I told you, and I've been more concerned about finding my own records than yours."

"Aren't you going to ask me what that suspicious message was about?"

She shook her head. "It's not my business."

"How do you know I'm not some kind of Burner, here to blow up the place?"

"Are you?"

"I think the better question is, are *you*?"

They were suddenly locked in a wide-eyed stare, and it occurred to Jess that it was just . . . insanely ridiculous. A spy for smugglers and a hidden Obscurist, and all they could do was ask each other if they were *Burners*.

It was so sad it was actually funny.

Jess got up and searched behind the blanks on the far wall, where he knew Portero had hidden a half-empty bottle of wine. He poured two glasses and handed one to Morgan. "Cheers to well-kept secrets."

She tipped her glass vaguely in his direction. "So you're not here for the obvious reasons, either."

"Doubt it's even just the two of us. Danton seems to know quite a lot about Burner tactics. Even Khalila worries me from time to time." He took a deep gulp. Cheap stuff, but it didn't matter.

"Did you *want* to come here? To the Library?"

"I was sent. Mostly my father's idea. He's . . ." Jess shook his head. "It's not something I can talk about."

She shrugged. "I'll be gone soon. It won't matter. And I know how hard it is keeping secrets. Sometimes, you just *need* to tell them." She let out a strange little laugh, fragile and oddly charming. "I should be terrified because you know about me. I haven't trusted anyone in so long. But instead I feel . . . I feel better that you know." She took another drink and didn't quite look at him. "I feel safer."

He hadn't known, until that moment, how desperately he craved that feeling . . . the feeling of letting down his guard, of having someone *see* him for who he really was. Not the Jess Brightwell he'd constructed over the years, his silent lie to everyone outside his family. *Go on,* some mad little voice inside him said. *Who can she tell? You can send her to the tower with a wrong word.* He could tell a little. Just the worst of it.

"Do you know what an ink-licker is?" he asked her, startling her. She turned toward him, eyes going wide.

"Not really. Only that it's—"

"Perverted? Yeah. It is." He pulled in a deep breath and let it slowly trickle out. "I saw one eat a book. The rarest book in the world, Archimedes's *On Sphere-Making.* And I gave it to him. Wasn't supposed to go that way; I thought he was just—just a collector. But he chewed it up, like it was a treat. Sickest thing I ever saw."

She covered her mouth with her hand, stricken, and he liked her the better for that. For the horror in her eyes. "That's appalling," she said. "I'm so sorry. How—when—"

"I was ten," he said. "Ten years old. He's dead now, the ink-licker."

"How did you get your hands on an original book like—" She stopped herself and studied him for a long moment, then shook her head. "I think I can guess. Don't tell me."

He waited for the inevitable look of shock or revulsion. When it didn't come, Jess said, "Now you can turn me in, too. I suppose that makes us even."

Morgan didn't say anything. Her expression said volumes, though. She understood being out of place. Being alone, always. Burdened with secrets and afraid of every wrong word.

They had a great deal in common. How strange.

He finished his wine in the warm, comfortable silence. For the first time in a long time, he felt relaxed. *I probably just made a terrible mistake,* he thought. *But it might have been worth it to feel this way. To feel . . . free.*

He finally said, "Aren't you afraid? Being in the enemy camp?"

Morgan gazed at him for so long he thought she wouldn't answer, and then she slowly smiled and sipped her wine. "Yes," she said. "From the moment I left Oxford until now, I've been absolutely terrified."

She didn't elaborate. He didn't, either.

Until now.

He wouldn't dare break that trust.

They didn't speak again. They finished their glasses, and Jess closed his eyes, half reclining on the couch. *I'm daft,* he thought. *Daft to trust someone who's done nothing but lie to me from the start. She could go straight to the High Garda. Turn me in.* She was probably thinking the very same thing of him.

He didn't mean to, but he drifted off to sleep. He just barely sensed something like the soft brush of fingers across his face, and then he was off in dreams.

Quiet, pleasant dreams.

He was lying on the couch alone when the bells rang.

Not the usual morning bells. These had a different tone altogether. Jess bolted upright, because these bells sounded like emergency tones to him, and they didn't shut off. *Fire?* No smoke, but he supposed it was possible.

By the time he made it to the common room door, others were coming out of their rooms, breathless and just as alarmed. Only some were already dressed for the day. One of them was Morgan, neat and tidy in her pale blue linen dress, with her hair up.

He looked at her for too long, and she returned it. *We should watch that. Someone will notice.* But what would that matter? What was wrong with noticing a girl?

Thomas came from downstairs in the basement, rubbing grease from his hands onto his trousers. He looked as if he'd slept in his clothes, if he'd slept at all.

"Is it a fire?" Khalila shouted over the alarms, as she ran toward them. She'd thrown on her clothes, but her headscarf wasn't pinned as neatly as usual. Bits of smooth dark hair poked out. Glain, behind her, wasn't just dressed; she looked as if she'd been up for hours. "Please tell me it's not a fire!"

The bells cut off and left a deafening silence.

"It's not." The answer came from the front door of Ptolemy House, where Captain Santi was just entering. "It's a summons. You're to report to the Scholar's Reading Room in the Serapeum. Don't waste time. This isn't a test."

Jess believed him. There was something deadly serious about the way he looked at their little group. Serious—and regretful.

"The pyramid?" Dario said. "We're going to the *pyramid*?"

"Right to the top," Santi said. "Hurry up. The carriage is waiting."

Those who weren't already dressed scattered to remedy that; Thomas muttered something under his breath in German and went to clean up. Jess, Glain, and Morgan remained in the hall with Santi.

"Sir," Glain asked, "what is this about?"

"I'm not here to answer your questions. I'm here to get you where you're going."

"Is it—is this where we get our final ranking? Where we get our appointments?"

Santi stared at her in a way that clearly said question time was over, and Glain gave it up. Jess's pulse quickened, though. She could be right.

This could be Wolfe's final decision.

He saw Morgan's face then, and realized that there was another option, a far worse one.

Maybe this hadn't come from Wolfe at all. Maybe one of them was about to be found out.

The hissing progress of the carriage carried them past the familiar borders of Alexandria University, and close to the Iron Tower, which dominated almost everything in view, except the pyramid. *It doesn't rust,* Jess remembered Thomas saying, and this close, he could see that his friend was right. The iron was black, pitted, and almost unmarked by streaks of dark red, for all its age. Massive. Forbidding. *Why iron?* Jess wondered. *Does it help them in their work?* He'd avoided alchemy as best he could; he didn't care for being shut away in labs, smelling foul chemicals all day, but he remembered that iron was an important alchemical symbol, all bound up with blood and the earth. Morgan would know.

Morgan was sitting beside him, and the backs of their hands brushed. Just lightly, just the backs, but the warm softness of her skin was distracting.

So were her secrets.

The Iron Tower fell behind, and the massive bulk of the pyramid grew and grew. "I knew it was big," Danton said, staring out the window next to him. "I never knew it was *this* big." He sounded awestruck, and Jess thought that maybe he'd been wrong about the boy being a Burner. He seemed impressed, not outraged.

The carriage arrived at the Serapeum. Santi got them all out, and Glain looked around with the same care she'd taken on the street the day before, when they'd been scouting the Burner house. "Which way?" she asked Santi.

He nodded at the steps.

The breath went out of Jess just looking at them. They were *endless*, straight up, though there were a few landings along the way with benches for those who needed respite. At the top, the rising sun sparked gold from the pyramid's capstone. It seemed ridiculously far up.

"Fantastic," Dario said grimly, and led the way on the long climb.

Dario's lead lasted to the first landing, and then Glain's long, seemingly tireless legs pulled her into the front. Jess was content to let her have it anyway; the steps were shallow, but mindlessly eternal. He looked up and paused for breath . . . and for the first time realized that there were automata reclining on the marble on either side of the landing.

Sphinxes.

The statue to his right turned its head and stared at him with flickering red eyes. Jess had to fight the instinctive urge to back away, because these creatures were even more disturbing than the lions of London; the sphinxes had eerily human faces, set off by the ancient Egyptian headdresses of pharaohs. A human face on an automaton was infinitely more disquieting, because it was all the more inhuman.

The flickering red in the eyes continued and grew brighter.

"Hold up your wrist," Dario said from behind him. He sounded as out of breath as Jess felt. "Your sleeve covers it, and they need to see the band. Do it."

Jess did, slowly, showing the statue his Library postulant wristband. The sphinx's eyes flashed white, and it settled back into its crouch. Morgan was hastily rolling back the sleeves of her gown on the other side of the landing, too, since that automaton was restless as well.

"Maybe Wolfe's hoping the creatures will remove a few more of us for him," Thomas said. He meant it for a joke, but it was a dour one. Despite all the differences—the gleaming pyramid, the rising Alexandrian sun, the clean, orderly city laid out beneath with its flat roofs and statues of lost gods—Jess felt like he was back in gray London, stalked by lions.

Danton had stopped next to them now. He was shorter than most of them, and the steps must have been even more of a challenge, since he was the last one up. "What are you afraid of? They're just automata. They're on every street in America." It reminded Jess of an ancient Greek text he'd read once: *The animated figures stand, adorning every public street, and seem to breathe in stone, or move their marble feet.*

He'd always found it chilling, not thrilling.

"If you didn't have so many Burners in your land, perhaps there wouldn't be so many statues," Thomas said. "We have very few in Germany, you know."

"Maybe we have so many Burners *because* the Library keeps adding more automata."

"Chicken, egg, omelet," Jess said. "Stop arguing, the both of you."

"And stop talking about breakfast," Dario groaned. "I'm starving."

"Climb," Thomas said. "You'll forget."

He was right. By the time Jess achieved the second of the three landings, food was the last thing on his mind. His legs burned, and so did his lungs, and he still had hundreds of steps to go. Glain was halfway up the last set, and not slowing. Good for her.

Morgan joined them on the steps, and as Thomas and Dario took the last set upward, she held Jess back to fiercely whisper, "Do you think this is a trap?"

"For you?" he asked. "Or for me? I don't know. Maybe."

"What can we do?"

He nodded to the sphinxes, gazing off into the distance. "Nothing," he said. "We can't run, can we?"

Morgan followed his motion and stared thoughtfully at the automaton. It turned its head and met her gaze.

"Morgan. Come on."

She didn't seem to want to move, but he grabbed her elbow and forced her up for a few steps.

When he looked back, the automaton had turned its head almost completely around at an utterly disturbing, inhuman angle.

Watching them.

Jess climbed faster.

They joined the others at the top in the shadow of the ancient stone portico, Portero, Himura, and Danton behind them, the last still laboring up the stairs. Next to him, Morgan leaned forward, bracing her arms on her thighs; her chest heaved for breath. Jess was just as exhausted, but he held himself upright and tried to slow his breathing as he gazed out over the city. It *was* a magnificent view . . . all of the glittering, elegant glory of Alexandria laid out around the pyramid like spokes in a wheel. The harbor was a silken teal blue in the growing morning light, as perfect as a jewel, and the ships drifting there as small as toys. The breeze up here was fast and cool on his sweating face.

Staring down from the pyramid's golden capstone was the Library symbol, and the motto: *Tota est scientia.* Knowledge is all. A multitude of sins could hide in that all-encompassing shadow.

When the last three joined them, the nine of them looked at one another. "Well?" Glain demanded. "Anyone?" When no one moved, she shook her head and stalked to the closed marble door under the capstone. It glided open under her touch.

"You first," Dario muttered, but he immediately followed second.

The hall they passed through was lined with the portraits of ancient librarians. Not a single one looked as if they'd ever learned to smile. It took almost a full minute of gloomy progress before Glain arrived at a massive set of square wooden doors set with iron bands and intricately carved with the seal of the Library.

The portal opened at her push, and buttery light from the room spilled out over them. Ranks of amber lights cast pools of brilliance down from a high, pointed ceiling onto gleaming wooden tables and books.

The Scholar's Reading Room.

The shelves surrounded the room, floor to high angled ceiling— blanks already filled with Codex information in a permanent collection, like the ones Jess's father had in his office. And there, on the far western wall, stood an entire case of originals. Not, Jess thought, anything rare, but enough to allow Scholars to touch real paper, smell real ink, weigh real history. Handling originals was an important part of a Scholar's life— finding them, saving them, preserving them for the future.

Defending them.

The room was empty. No sign of Wolfe. No sign of anyone, in fact. Tables stretched out across the room, some stacked with untidy piles of blanks as if those who'd been here had left in a hurry.

It seemed unnaturally quiet.

"Should we sit?" Thomas asked. When no one answered, he shrugged and took a chair at one of the tables. They all followed suit. Jess wanted one with easy exits, but Dario beat him there, and Danton claimed the other logical choice. He chose a seat next to Morgan instead.

Then they waited. Time ticked by, and with every silent moment, Jess felt the tension crank tighter. *This is wrong,* he thought. *Why now? Is it because I found out about Morgan? Is it even Wolfe we're waiting for?*

It was.

Wolfe arrived, dressed, as always, in Scholar's robes, so that was comforting in its own cold, familiar way. What wasn't so comforting was the fact that he didn't come alone. Santi was with him and took up a post near the door, but Santi was only one of an entire contingent of High Garda men and women, all dressed in full uniform, who filed in and took up positions.

In the middle of that parade of force came a new form in billowing robes, but his weren't black.

They were a brilliant purple.

Jess had never seen one of them, but he knew that only the seven Curators of the Great Library wore that color, by law.

Beside him, Morgan took in a breath and whispered, "That's the Artifex Magnus."

Artifex. Mathematics, engineering, the practical arts. Jess studied the man as he moved forward, and if he'd had to boil his thoughts down to a single word, it would have been *intimidating*. The man's white hair was shorn close to the scalp, and his face was square and lean and strong beneath a shocking white brush of beard.

He looked grim. Impossible to tell if that was his usual manner or a sign of what was coming.

"I am honored to introduce the Artifex Magnus," Wolfe said. "Attend to his words."

That made Jess's stomach go tight and his mind go still. There was something ominous in Wolfe's stiff posture, the distant glitter of his eyes. The presence of the Artifex alone made it an earthshaking event that no one could possibly have predicted. Someone in the position of a Curator, charged with the preservation of the Great Library itself, could not be here just to impress students.

"We have a pressing issue," the Artifex said; he had a deep, resonant voice, one that must have delivered thousands of speeches. "Oxford has been under siege for some time. All negotiations have failed. The English king has ordered that no surrender be given, and both sides have informed us, as is required by the accords, that the Serapeum at Oxford may be damaged in the conflict. They've agreed to the standard evacuation cease-fire so that we may withdraw Library personnel."

Morgan's body trembled, just a little, but her expression didn't flicker. She was from Oxford. She had family there. This was personal to her.

"The Library staff have been guaranteed safe passage from the city, and most have exited, but therein lies our problem," the Artifex continued. "The staff left before the discovery of a cache of rare books beneath the Serapeum. Since most of our librarians are already gone, those who remain cannot possibly handle the removal of so much. To make it more critical, if the English forces discover we are in possession of such a treasure, they might use it as a bargaining chip."

"Bargaining chip?" Thomas seemed stunned by the idea. "But surely they would want to save the books, not put them at more risk! That is in the accords!"

"In theory," the Artifex agreed. "In the fog of war, such things become fluid. So we must send in additional staff to assist in tagging and archiving the books."

"And you're sending us," Jess guessed. "Why?"

The Artifex's frosted blue eyes fixed on him. They were the color of unforgiving winter, and Jess felt a chill go through him to match. "In part because of you, Brightwell," he said. "There are only a few among us capable of handling the transfer of so many books, so quickly; your skill then becomes essential. Likewise, Postulant Hault's familiarity with the city benefits us. Even Postulant Wathen's Welsh connections may come in handy for the fulfillment of the mission."

"For the record," Wolfe said, in a deceptively casual voice, "I don't agree. Postulants are not librarians. They cannot be asked—"

"They are not being asked," the Artifex snapped. "They are being ordered. You've narrowed the class to nine; there are six placements available. At the end of every postulant class is a field examination. This will serve."

"Artifex—"

"Enough, Wolfe. I've heard your arguments. There is no place in the world for librarians who lack the will to defend books against wars, rebels, and Burners. Books cannot fight for themselves. Postulants or not, it's still their duty to defend them."

Wolfe took a step forward. "I strongly object to this—"

The Artifex snapped his fingers, and his High Garda escort pushed off the wall, ready to move. Santi moved, too, walking around the tables to stand alone with Wolfe. Two sides, and the students caught in the middle, Jess realized.

And it was very clear who was on the winning side.

The Artifex pointed a sharp finger at Wolfe. "Leave. Another word, and you bring down a great deal of pain. Not just on yourself."

Wolfe's dark eyes glittered and his hands clenched, but he nodded sharply, turned, and walked out of the room. Santi followed, but not without a look back.

That, Jess thought, was a killer's stare, and it was fixed on the Artifex with real intensity.

Then they were gone, and the door shut behind them.

Portero cleared his throat. "Artifex? With the greatest respect, sir . . . what happens to us if we . . . don't agree to go?"

"You fail," the man said. "And you go anyway. Never fear. I won't send you alone. You'll have a troop of High Garda with you. And Scholar Wolfe, of course. I wouldn't dream of keeping him from the action."

Smug bastard, Jess thought. As much as he'd always disliked Wolfe, what he felt for the Artifex was an entirely new level of loathing.

"When do we leave?" he asked. *"Sir."*

"Immediately. Wait here for instructions. And no messages out. I will keep your families apprised of any necessary details. You are dismissed. *Tota est scientia*."

They said it back, mostly by rote, and watched him depart, drawing his High Garda escort along with him.

Wolfe didn't come back.

"What should we do?" Izumi asked.

"That's not the right question. The right question is, what *can* we do? And the answer to that is, nothing." Dario got to his feet, but even he didn't seem to know where to go from there. "We refuse, are failed, and go anyway, or we go and hope we don't fail."

"My father won't stand for this," Khalila said. She seemed stunned, out of her depth for the first time since Jess had met her. "The Library can't just *send us*. Not to a war zone! We aren't High Garda!"

"They can do whatever they want," Jess told her. "They always have. You're just seeing it that way for the first time." He offered her a hand, and she took it to stand. Her fingers were cold, but she offered him a small, unsteady smile. "It'll be all right. We'll look out for each other."

"Yes," Glain said. "We will. It's time to stop biting at each other, and that means you, Dario, and you, Jess. We have to depend on each other from this moment on. No secrets. Agreed?"

Jess's gaze brushed over Morgan's. *No secrets.*

"Agreed," Jess said.

One by one, they all echoed it.

The door to the room opened again, and Captain Santi looked in on them. "Down the hall. Wolfe's waiting for you," he said. They all filed by him, but when Jess passed, Santi took hold of his arm. "Brightwell. A word."

Thomas gave him a worried look, but at Jess's nod, he left with the rest. The door swung shut behind him with a solid *boom*.

Santi let him go. "Do you recognize this?" He pulled a folded piece of paper from his pocket. Written on it, in ink, was a message that had no name or signature, but Jess recognized the hand. Brendan never had been very skilled with a pen.

Pay respects to your cousin Charlie. You'll find him beneath the sod. Lay some flowers for us.

It was a family message, and it was in family code. *Cousin Charlie* meant his cousin Frederick, in Oxford; *beneath the sod* meant a particular spot in that town to find the man. *Lay some flowers* meant that Jess could ask for help there . . . at a price.

Jess looked up at Santi's impassive face and felt a real stab of fear. Brendan had written this, so had his brother been taken? How else could that note be in the possession of a High Garda soldier? He deliberately fought down those fears and handed the paper back. "Nothing to me, mate. No idea what it means."

"Ah," Santi said. His tone was light and pleasant. "Good thing. One of my eager young soldiers found it in the possession of a black trader. Barzem. Know him?"

"Never heard of him," Jess said. Barzem had been the contact who'd sent him to steal the Aristophanes play from Abdul Nejem. He was a good liar; he'd trained at it his entire life.

But he didn't think Santi believed a word of it.

"Just as well," Santi said. "He's dead. Knifed in the back on his way out of a coffee shop. What's the world coming to? Well, might as well dispose of this." He ripped the message up into tiny pieces and put it back in his pocket. "I'll burn it at home. Wouldn't want anyone to find it here."

That was confounding. And disturbing. "Are we done?"

"I doubt it," Santi said, but he opened the door for him to escape.

Jess found the others, who were waiting in the hallway. Thomas sent him a questioning look, but Jess just shook his head. He edged closer to Morgan, who ducked her head and said, "What was that?"

"Nothing you need to worry about," he said.

"But something you should?"

He wasn't sure yet. He knew that he *ought* to be worried; Santi obviously knew the message had been meant for him, and yet he'd shown it to him. He'd destroyed it.

Brendan knew he was heading for Oxford. He'd known even before Jess did somehow, and that was worrying indeed. His father had extensive networks of contacts around the world—every book smuggler did. But he'd never had contacts inside the Library itself, not before Jess. So how had Brendan known? Who'd told him?

There was something familiar about what Santi had just said about the dead man, Barzem. *Knifed in the back on his way out of a coffee shop.* It was a strong echo of something his brother had once told him, long ago it seemed, back in rainy London. *Slipped a knife between his ribs as he was coming out of his club,* his brother had said.

The ink-licker's murder. Something Brendan would know Jess couldn't forget.

Brendan hadn't gotten a message *through* to Barzem. He'd left it on his body.

His brother had never left Alexandria.

EPHEMERA

Text of a message in the hand of Scholar Wolfe, directly to the Artifex Magnus.

I've done all that you have asked of me since my release. I've stood silent when you threatened my friends, my lover, destroyed my life's work. I've borne every punishment.

I will go to Oxford and preserve the books. If it becomes necessary, I will lay down my life for the Library and all it represents, as I'm sure is your plan.

But I warn you, you have crossed a line I cannot forgive. These students were given to me to train. They are my responsibility. You may have made me proctor as a bitter joke, since I have always been a miserable teacher at best, but even so you have no right to risk the lives of an entire generation of Scholars to punish me.

I will take this to the Archivist himself.

Response to Scholar Wolfe from the Artifex Magnus.

By all means, appeal. I have already spoken with the Archivist, and he understands the urgency of this mission. And the risks.

Your life belongs to us, Wolfe. Don't test my patience again. As to your postulants, we both know that there will always be another crush to fill those empty spaces.

CHAPTER SIX

J ess expected that they'd leave the Serapeum and board carriages for the train station. It was a long journey back to London, and then to Oxford.

But Wolfe didn't lead them outside. He put his wristband against the painting of Callimachus, the first Archivist under Ptolemy II, and the painting melted into flowing orange symbols. Symbols Jess recognized, after having seen them moving under Morgan's fingers. *Formulae*, Morgan had called them. What were they doing here, hidden inside a painting?

Then the wall next to it slid open, and Wolfe stepped into another, hidden corridor. The eye of Horus was inscribed on the tiles that lined the hall.

"I had heard this place had secret tunnels," Thomas said. He kept his voice low, but it echoed all the same. "I thought they were all ancient. Abandoned."

Not this one. It was modern, and lined with inset statues that melded Greek, Roman, and Egyptian influences in the odd style that Alexandria had developed; the first, a Scholar in a Greek tunic, held a scroll. The next, in a Roman toga, held an open book. The third was one of the Egyptian deities . . . Thoth, who had invented writing, and served as the god of scribes. He held the feather of Ma'at.

All, Jess realized, were automata. If a threat was found in the hall, it would never make it out alive.

Jess got all of this in hurried glances, because Wolfe was moving at a quick pace to the end of the hallway, which ended in another empty wall. He used his Library band on it, waking more symbols, and another entrance opened.

The Obscurists built these passages. He looked at Morgan, who'd put her hands in her dress pockets as she walked, as if she was cold. He remembered how the string of orange light from the blank had clung to her fingers. She was afraid to touch anything, for fear she might call something up that others could see.

Jess followed her into a small, plain anteroom lit by amber glows. No books here. No blanks. No reading tables or couches. In one corner was a stack of black canvas bags.

"Pick up your packs," Wolfe said. "Your names are on tags."

Thomas got there first. Even for his bulk, the pack he selected seemed large. When Jess grabbed the one with BRIGHTWELL on the tag, he was staggered by the weight. He slipped the straps on his shoulders. It fit well enough, and having the load distributed made it feel more manageable.

He wondered how Khalila would fare with it, but he needn't have worried; she shouldered it just as easily as the much more muscular Glain. Only Izumi, the smallest of them, seemed overwhelmed, but she didn't complain.

"Watch out for each other," Wolfe said, when they were all ready. "This will not get any easier, I can promise you. I didn't want you involved in this, but since you are, I need all of you focused. Follow orders without delay, and stay alert."

It was Wolfe's concern, Jess thought, that was the most unsettling part of this.

"I thought we were going to Oxford," Thomas said. "What are we doing here?"

Wolfe said, "You are in the Translation Chamber. That is how we will travel."

Jess had heard of it, but only in whispers . . . the same principles that allowed for the mirroring of documents and the movement of books back to the Archive could allow different kinds of things to be physically moved from one spot to another . . . with the direct participation of an Obscurist. It wasn't something he'd ever expected to see.

There was a brief hesitation before Dario said, "I thought the Translation Chamber was only used to send supplies."

"It is," Wolfe said. It sounded casual, but Jess wasn't deceived. "But it can also be used to send people, in emergencies. I will warn you, it can take years of practice to grow accustomed to translation; some never do."

"We—haven't had years of practice," Thomas said. "Or any practice."

"I'm aware," Wolfe said. "But needs must. It's a simple enough process, one that requires little from you but to clear your mind. If all goes well, you'll appear in the Translation Chamber in Aylesbury, which is the closest safe point to Oxford."

"And if all doesn't go well?" Khalila asked.

Wolfe ignored the question. He reached out and pressed his gold band to the matching Library symbol embossed on the far wall, and a hidden door swung open.

On the other side was a dizzying array of wires, tubes . . . a tangle of metal and harsh lights. So different from everything else Jess had seen here. Massive and intimidating, this . . . machine, he supposed he should call it. In the center of it was a clear space, and an old man in a white robe stood with a bronze metal helmet in his hands. The helmet was connected to wires that led into the tubes.

There was a sudden, loud hiss, and white steam billowed up over their heads. Jess ducked. So did everyone else, except Wolfe.

Niccolo Santi stepped into the room and edged past them to Wolfe.

He had on a pack, too, but his looked well-worn. "Let me go first," he said. "Show them how it's done."

Wolfe nodded and put his hand on Santi's shoulder. *"In bocca al lupo."*

"In bocca al lupo," Santi said, and walked to the center of the room, where the old man was waiting. "I'm ready."

The old man sighed and fitted the helmet down over Santi's head. It looked tight and left only a small part of his face showing.

Santi's easy smile faded, and he closed his eyes. Stood very still.

"Ready?" the old man asked. Santi nodded. "The connection isn't good. It will hurt."

"Always does. Get on with it."

The old man put his palsied, unsteady hands on the metal helmet Santi wore.

A column of orange symbols rose into the air around the two of them and began to revolve. Slowly at first, and then faster and faster, until it was just a blurring tornado of light. The old man suddenly jerked his hands away, and the light contracted into a tight, whirling circle around Santi's body.

The circle drew in on itself into a single, brilliant orange point of light, and Santi . . . *folded*. There was a flash of something horrible, something so fast Jess hardly saw it: sprays of blood and torn flesh and the fragments of bones. A powerful wave pushed through Jess's flesh, and he felt the hair rise on his head and arms in response to something alien, terrifying, and wrong.

The metal helmet fell with a heavy *thud* to the floor. Empty. Then it was silent. Dead silent.

The Obscurist—he had to be one; there was a golden collar around his throat—staggered backward, breathing heavily.

Khalila let out a choked cry and pressed both hands to her mouth as if she felt sick. Jess knew exactly how she felt. How were they supposed to endure that?

In the silence, the Codex in Wolfe's pocket buzzed. He checked it. "He's through," he said. "Next."

It was abruptly very real, Jess thought; the pack dragging on his back, the Translation Chamber, the future opening wide and unknown at his feet like an abyss. His feet felt frozen to the spot.

It was somewhat surprising that it was the quiet Guillaume Danton who stepped forward and said, "I'll go." He didn't sound frightened, but Jess caught the telltale tremor of his hands.

Wolfe put a hand on Danton's shoulder and guided him forward. He picked up the helmet and placed it on the boy's head. "Think about the sky," he told him. "Close your eyes. Think about the blue sky and clouds moving over it. White clouds. Moving over a blue sky." Wolfe's voice seemed different now, slow and soothing, and Jess saw Danton's body actually *relax*. Wolfe nodded to the Obscurist, who placed his hands on the helmet. "Blue sky."

"I see it," Guillaume said, and smiled.

The orange light formed around him. Symbols swirled. Wolfe took a step back. "White clouds," he said. "Watch them move."

"White clouds—"

The light snapped in on itself, and Danton screamed. It was a horrible cry, ripped right out of the core of him, and Jess started forward, but Wolfe was in his way, holding him back.

"You can't help him," he said.

Jess stared as Danton's body was ripped apart, folded, *gone*. The horrified shrieking cut off clean, and that wave of power flashed over his skin like a burn.

The empty helmet clattered to the floor.

Wolfe checked his Codex. Something changed in his expression, just a brief flash: anger, anguish, fury—hard to know. He said, "Next."

Going next was the very last thing that Jess wanted to do. It was all he could do not to bolt for the exit.

Khalila said, with forced cheer, "Better to get it over with." She walked toward the Obscurist, who was picking up the helmet.

Morgan had a horrified look on her face. She rushed to Wolfe. Before she could speak, he turned on her and snapped, "Wait your turn, Postulant."

"But I saw—"

"*Postulant.* Control yourself, or go." Wolfe's stare burned, hot enough to melt the Iron Tower itself, and she finally nodded and bowed her head. Stepped back. "Postulant Seif, you may proceed."

Khalila squared her shoulders as the Obscurist settled the helmet over her hijab. When Wolfe moved forward, she shook her head. "Blue skies and clouds. Yes. I know. Just let me do this."

Dario made a twitch of a move toward her, as if he wanted to drag her back, but he held himself still. "*In bocca al lupo*, desert flower."

"I'm from Riyadh," she told him. "It's not the desert; it's a modern city, with roads and carriages. And desert flowers have spikes." She somehow managed to smile beneath the weight of that helmet. "What does it mean?"

"In the mouth of the wolf," Dario said. "Forget the clouds, and keep your eyes on me. I'm much prettier."

"And much more empty in the head," she said. "*In bocca al lupo*, Dario."

The old Obscurist put his shaking hands on her head. Dario continued, somehow, to hold her stare and smile, though Jess couldn't imagine what that cost him. She didn't look away, either, even as the light began to swirl.

Even as it snapped in and broke her apart.

She didn't scream. Jess felt the power blow over him, disorienting and visceral, and he wondered how the old man could bear that lash, time after time.

Dario must have felt honor bound to go next, because he strode up and donned the helmet without a word. At the last second, he threw a dazzling grin at Jess. "Don't ask me to look at you, scrubber," he said. "I'd rather think of the damned clouds."

A soul-deep shriek of mortal pain and terror, blood, shock, and then he, too, was gone.

When Izumi's turn came, it did not go the same. The Obscurist laid on his hands, and there was the same scream, the same whirl of blood and bone and flesh, but instead of collapsing inward, the whirling orange light exploded *out*. It washed over them in a wave of heat, and this time Jess ducked as if it was an actual, physical threat. He wasn't the only one. Even Wolfe flinched.

When he looked back, Izumi was still there. Facedown, sprawled on the marble, buried beneath the weight of her pack. Jess got to her at the same time as Wolfe, and helped loosen the pack straps to get the weight off of the slender young woman while Wolfe stripped off the helmet.

Wolfe turned her over.

Izumi's eyes were open and staring, but . . . empty, of everything but a mute horror. Over their heads, a red light began to flash, bathing the whole room in flares of crimson. A torrent of steam hissed out of valves and pipes in a deafening roar.

The old Obscurist was on his knees as well, but not to help. He was gasping for air and shaking like an autumn leaf in a storm. His face was the color of gray mud. He looked like he might drop dead. When Jess reached out to help him, the old man flinched back, as if he expected to be hurt. "No," he said. "Leave me alone. Not my fault. Not my *fault*."

Wolfe pressed fingertips to Izumi's neck, then his ear to her chest. "Help is coming," he told her. "You're not alone. Can you hear me, Izumi? Show me you can hear me." She seemed frozen and unable to move, but her eyes cut toward him, and she blinked. His austere face softened into a relieved, fully warm smile. "Good girl. You'll be fine."

She swallowed and managed to whisper something Jess couldn't catch, but Wolfe clearly did. He shook his head. "Don't," he said. "Some can't tolerate it. There's no shame in that."

The door they'd entered slid open, and a two-man Medica team carried in a stretcher. They loaded Izumi on and whisked her away before any of them could comprehend what had really happened.

It was left to Jess to say, "She failed, didn't she?"

Wolfe's smile was gone now, and his face closed and stony. "There's nothing I can do. The Artifex made it clear that anyone who fails on this journey loses their place," he said. "Not her fault."

"Has anyone ever died?" Portero asked. His voice sounded higher than it normally did, his face two shades off his normal dull bronze.

"Yes," Wolfe said. Just the bare word. He turned his eyes to Jess. "Are you ready?"

Jess realized that he was already standing in the center, beside the fallen helmet. He felt the urge to bolt away. Instead, he raised his gaze to meet Wolfe's and said, "I'm ready."

The helmet felt suffocating and as heavy as granite as it pressed down on him. It smelled of sweat and burning metal. *Think of clouds.* He couldn't. He couldn't think of anything but the torment his friends had endured before him.

"Jess."

He opened his eyes. Morgan had stepped forward, and she was holding out her hand to him.

He took it, and she squeezed his fingers. *"In bocca al lupo."*

He said it back, and then she was gone.

The Obscurist shuffled forward and pressed those shaking hands down on the helmet. The old man's robes smelled of stale curry, and his breath was rank with it, too. *He's too old,* Jess thought. *Maybe it's his fault, what happened to Izumi. Maybe he'll kill me.*

He felt something rising around him like a storm of needles, and caught and held his breath. He squeezed his eyes shut, like a child hiding from a monster in the dark.

Somehow, he managed to hold on to the tattered remains of his courage as the needles turned in and began to rip him apart. It was an awful, horror-filled second of utter destruction, and he heard a scream wrenched out of his mouth that he couldn't control. His vision went bloodred, and he felt himself convulse, and then . . .

Then he was falling to hands and knees on a stone floor, still crying out. Nothing worked. He flailed and rolled onto his back, managed to silence himself, and tried to breathe. Someone grabbed hold of his shoulders and was dragging him away . . . Dario? Yes. It was Dario Santiago, gripping him hard enough to leave bruises.

Dario propped Jess's back against a wall and left him there. For the first time, Jess was grateful for the pack weighing him down; it felt as soft as a feather bed now, a familiar anchor in a world that seemed to still tremble and dance in front of his eyes.

"Easy," Khalila was saying to him, and her hands were holding a cup of water in front of his face. "Drink. You'll feel better in a moment."

He took the cup mindlessly; his hands shook so badly that he spilled half of the water on his face and down his shirt, but he got enough of it into his mouth to choke down, and as she'd said, it helped. The world steadied slowly into an off-kilter wobble, then finally righted itself.

Thomas arrived while he was still struggling to adapt, and Dario's job evidently was to grab and drag the newcomers, which wasn't an easy job, given the German's bulk. Jess handed the cup back to Khalila, and she filled it from a jug and moved to administer the same kindness to Thomas. *She* didn't seem to have any problems; she moved with calm grace, and her hand extending the cup was rock steady.

Jess still felt a horrible conviction in the back of his mind that some part of him was missing, lost in that bleeding whirl, though as he ran his hands over himself he couldn't feel any wounds.

He was better off by far than some of the others. Dario and Khalila seemed to have done best; Guillaume Danton, first to arrive, was lying still off to the side. A woman dressed in the sand-colored overcoat of a librarian was tending to him—a Medica specialist, by the red blood-drop symbol on the lapel of her uniform. Guillaume looked icy pale, his face slack.

Jess tried to stand up, failed, tried again, and slid down the wall to where Dario had dragged Thomas. He dropped in place next to his friend. Thomas lost his grip on the cup, which slipped free and dumped water all over Khalila's dress. She calmly refilled it and tried again. This time, Thomas managed a sip, then another. The look in his eyes was appalling, and Jess had to find something else to study for a while. There were things too private to watch.

One by one, the rest came through. Portero vomited and wept, but more of the Medica attendants were arriving and took firm charge. Portero and Guillaume seemed the worst affected; Glain seemed to hardly even need the water once she'd arrived, and she recovered fast.

Jess hated her for it. He wasn't entirely sure he'd *ever* recover, in some very deep and visceral way. She seemed to have simply taken it in stride and moved on.

Like Khalila, who hardly seemed to have missed a breath.

"That," Thomas whispered, "that was the worst thing I have ever felt." He seemed truly shaken. Jess slapped him on the shoulder and nodded. "I am not cut out for this. Not if *that* is required."

"It's only for emergencies. And Wolfe says it gets better, with practice."

"It will never get better, and I will never practice." Thomas looked around and spotted the motionless form of Guillaume. A frown line creased his brow and pulled his eyebrows flat. "Is he all right?"

"Doesn't look like it," Jess said. "Here. Drink more."

Khalila hadn't spoken, but she was quietly waiting for Thomas to finish the cup; he did, handed it back, and she moved on to the next who needed it. Suddenly Jess wondered if her glacial poise really *was* a sign that she was all right; maybe it was a form of shock as profound as his own, only expressed very differently.

"*Mein Gott,*" Thomas said. His voice sounded different, flatter, and Jess looked away from Khalila to his friend. He was staring across the room.

The two Medica staff with Danton were standing back, and Captain Santi was making the sign of the cross over the body. As Jess stared, Santi slowly pulled the cover over the boy's face.

"Christ above," Jess blurted, and crossed himself; it was a long-forgotten habit, but shock drew it out of him. Couldn't be true, could it? That Guillaume was *dead*?

Dario swore viciously, quietly, in Spanish. Morgan, who'd arrived when Jess's attention was elsewhere, was up and moving, and she tried to go to Danton's body, but one of the Medica staff caught her and led her away. She was weeping. Jess wanted to get up and go to her, but he wasn't sure his legs were ready.

In a violent clap of air and movement, Christopher Wolfe arrived. He didn't collapse. He didn't even *pause*. He strode on, as if he'd simply stepped from one place to another, and walked past Jess and Thomas toward the place where Niccolo Santi still knelt next to Guillaume's covered body.

Niccolo Santi looked up just in time. He lunged up to halt the Scholar's relentless advance. When Wolfe tried to push past, Santi grabbed hold and held him. "No," he said. "*Christopher.* No. He's gone."

Wolfe took in a deep breath, turned away, and used his Codex to send a message. His stylus moved in fast, vicious jerks as he wrote it down. It hummed in answer a moment later, and he put it away and stalked to a darker corner of the room.

That, Jess thought, was the most emotion he'd ever seen from Wolfe.

Or Santi, for that matter. It felt like an earthquake on previously steady ground.

Santi stepped forward in Wolfe's absence. "Up," he said. "We've got to move."

"What about Guillaume?" Khalila asked.

"He'll be returned as quickly as possible to his family," Santi said. "Does anyone want to say a word now for him?"

For a frozen moment, no one moved or spoke, and then Dario Santiago said, "I didn't like him, but he went through first when I wouldn't. Brave. I think that says enough."

Santi nodded. He glanced toward Wolfe, who still hadn't moved. "Outside," he said. "Go on."

Most of them had already gone when Wolfe finally turned and stalked for the door, but Morgan had lingered. She caught Wolfe's sleeve as he passed, and although her whisper was very soft, Jess was close enough to hear it. "Scholar, I saw it. I tried to tell you. I saw—"

Wolfe turned and gave her a fierce, almost wild stare. "You couldn't have saved him," he said. "Even if you were an Obscurist, *which I remind you, you are not.* This wasn't your doing." He yanked his robe free of her hand and pushed on and out the door.

Morgan nodded. She seemed flushed now, and tears sparked in her eyes.

Wolfe was telling her to keep her secret.

But Jess wondered if he was telling her everything.

EPHEMERA

Text of a letter under the name of Scholar Christopher
Wolfe to Aristede Danton, father of Guillaume Danton.
Not written by him.

*It is my sad duty to inform you that your son Guillaume has succumbed
to injuries that he suffered during his translation from Alexandria to the
front lines of the Oxford expeditionary journey. Such events are rare, and
unforeseen, and while Medica experts were immediately at his side, there
were no measures to be taken that could prolong his life.*

*A stone shall be consecrated in his name in the Library's Great Hall of
Knowledge, and his name and legacy will live on.*

*We have included his personal journal, which was up-to-date to the
morning of his passing, in the record of the Library, and the days he lived
on this earth will enrich the days of those who come after.*

*Please accept the Library's condolences upon this sad occasion. A funer-
ary representative from the London Serapeum will accompany your son's
remains home.*

Message sent the same day in the hand of Scholar Wolfe,
addressed to the Artifex Magnus.

*This blood is on your hands. Whether it was deliberate or accidental, you
caused this to happen. I will not forget it.*

A reply from the Artifex to Scholar Wolfe, received the
same day.

Don't be a fool. We both know it wasn't an accident. We both know why it was a necessary step.

I hope you will not forget, because accidents can happen. Even to someone you care more about than a Burner spy.

CHAPTER SEVEN

G uillaume's death left Jess feeling oddly empty inside. He watched as the Medica staff wrapped his friend's body in clean white sheets and tied them with careful, traditional knots. From there, they'd convey his body to a sarcophagus, which would be taken to the place of embalming, if Guillaume's religion allowed it. Likely did, Jess thought, since the boy had probably been a Catholic.

He thought of the practical order of these things to avoid thinking about more painful things—things that Thomas couldn't stop asking, like, "Do you think he suffered?" or "Do you think he knew he was dying?" Jess didn't see how he could possibly know those answers, and didn't see how the truth, even if they learned it, could be any comfort at all.

It didn't help matters that Khalila suddenly broke down in tears. Even Glain seemed emotional. Jess was a little surprised by that. *But the real question,* Jess thought, *is why I feel so little and they feel so much.* Maybe it was his upbringing. Maybe it was all the death he'd seen in the smuggling trade.

Or maybe he was just trying to keep it all locked in a small, dark box until he could face what he felt. It was the same bargain he'd made when he'd been nine and his brother Liam had gone to the gallows. He'd focus on the things that needed doing, for as long as he could.

Dario didn't weep, either. He and Jess had that in common. As Guillaume's body was carried out of the Translation Chamber, Dario leaned his shoulders against the wall next to Jess and said, "If any of us had to die, it might be best it was him. Burner ancestors from a rebel country. They'd never have let him stay."

It was a concise, cold, brutally truthful statement, and he said it low enough that only Jess heard. Jess nodded. "Given all that, it must have been incredibly hard for him to win a place here in the first place. Have some respect."

"I do," Dario said. "I also have clear eyes. He had secrets. So do you."

They were, Jess thought, more alike than either of them wanted to admit. He'd never realized that about himself before; he'd always thought of himself as a good person, at his core. But sitting next to Dario, hearing familiar tones and words out of a different mouth, he was forced to reconsider.

"I do have secrets. I secretly think you're a bastard," he said to Dario, though without much heat. "Shove off. I'm thinking."

"Well, that would take all your concentration," Dario agreed, and moved off to put his arm around Khalila. Jess watched as her body relaxed into his, and he realized he wasn't surprised that the two of them were drawing together. Not after what he'd seen in the Translation Chamber. She'd trusted the boy. Why she would was a mystery to him, but there was no doubt that some barrier had fallen between them.

Jess's gaze went to Morgan. They'd all recovered more or less quickly, though Jess was cursed with a hitching pain in his ribs and what felt like a wrenched knee—not bad enough to hobble him, just enough to make him hurt a bit. He'd walk it off, though. He'd had worse.

But it kept him from catching up to Morgan.

As he grabbed his pack and swung the weight onto his shoulders, Thomas joined him. The German already had his pack strapped securely, but he still had a hurt, lost look in his face. "We're just going to leave Guillaume?" he asked. "Just like that? No . . . service?"

"We're heading into a war zone, Thomas. Can't stop for services."

"Still, it seems . . ."

"Come on."

Jess knew he sounded impatient, but he couldn't control that; Thomas's grief rubbed like sandpaper and made him want to lash out.

Thomas gave him a sad-eyed look, but followed as Jess made his way toward the door. Morgan was following close behind Wolfe. Khalila was still escorted by Dario, though as they emerged from the Translation Chamber into a wide brick hallway, she broke away from him and took a quicker pace, chin raised. Independent once more.

Wolfe led their party—only seven now—into the Aylesbury Reading Room. Like the Alexandrian version, it was filled with shelves and tables, though Aylesbury needed a large, roaring furnace, where Alexandria rarely felt the cold so deeply. Jess hadn't thought about it until now, but the familiar English damp and chill were starting to close around him. He'd worn light clothing for the merciless heat he'd grown accustomed to, and now he was starting to feel the lack of wool.

This room had a different smell, too. Paper and ink, yes, and dust, but a faint trace of mildew, too. And the sharp oak scent of the fireplace, whose warmth didn't penetrate far into the space. Old ashes. Old sweat.

This place hadn't been built as a Library building; it must have been converted from a church, at some point, and still had the feeling of one. The shelves in the room looked oddly spaced, bolted in to replace sacred statues or shrines. The Library hadn't built new here, just repurposed.

"Everyone fit to travel?" Wolfe asked them, when they were assembled around him. One by one, they nodded. "Open your packs. In them, you'll find two things I want you to wear. One is a bronze temporary bracelet; it conveys on you the rights of a full librarian for the duration of this trip. The second item is a Library coat. You will all put them on and wear them unless I tell you to remove them. I want no claims from the English or Welsh that they mistook us for combatants."

Jess muscled his pack off again and dug inside, and yes, near the top was a metal clasp bracelet—bronze—embossed with the Library symbol. Unlike regular Library bracelets, it could be removed; the symbols that librarians wore had to be cut away at the termination of their contracts.

The bronze was the lowest of the levels. At the end of a bronze contract, a library employee would either move up, stay on, or move out. *It isn't a real one,* he told himself. *Just temporary.*

He removed his postulant version and fastened the new one, and felt a chill when he looked down at his wrist. *I'm one of them now.* He'd wanted it, and still did, but that didn't change the unease of a lifetime of running from that symbol, and fearing it. From knowing that the Library would relentlessly continue to pursue smugglers, and would cheerfully hang him, his father, his brother, even his mother.

When he donned the dull gold of the overcoat, he felt even more distanced from his past. The material weighed very little, though he was grateful for another layer to hold in the heat.

He looked like one of them now. Completely.

When they'd all properly fitted themselves out, Wolfe looked them over, made some adjustments here and there, and nodded. "You're ready," he said. "Do what I tell you. Obey the soldiers when they give you an order, and you'll come through."

That sounded suspiciously like concern, and that, more than anything else, made Jess start to worry about what was coming next.

Outside in the large, walled forecourt of the Serapeum stood a full squad of Library High Garda . . . about eighty of them. Men and women alike, laughing, talking, sitting, standing, playing cards and dice and other games he didn't immediately recognize. A relaxed atmosphere, except that they all wore the formal black of the High Garda and had heavy arms ready at hand. Santi was with them, talking to one of the others and reviewing a map laid out between them.

Santi rose from his crouch and folded up his map. As the captain rose, an instant change came over the company around him. Bodies straightened and stepped into neat ranks. It happened fast, and economically, from chaos to order in less time than it took Jess to recognize what was happening. Santi didn't so much as glance at his troops, but he bowed slightly to Wolfe and said, "In your service, Scholar Wolfe."

"Grateful for it, Captain Santi," Wolfe said. "What conditions?"

"Bad ones. Rain and flooding, but we've got the carriages to take us as far as the Welsh lines. From there, we'll have to play by the rules we're given."

"Which are?"

"They'll let us take one vehicle into Oxford. Even with all of my soldiers on foot, it'll be a tight squeeze to get all your students inside with even a small number of books, but I don't see an alternative. They didn't even have to allow us the one vehicle, technically. Asking for another is useless."

"Not ideal."

"Not even close. But it never is, is it?" Santi's white, even teeth showed in a sudden grin, and Wolfe's lips actually turned up at the corners. "I hope your children know which end of a gun to hold."

"They've been taught the basics."

"We're going beyond the basics. Costigan! Issue our new friends their arms, please."

One of Santi's men broke from the neat lines and grabbed a box, which he carried forward and opened. He gestured at Jess, who was closest, and as Jess stepped toward him, Costigan thrust a cloth belt, holster, and weapon at him. "Fully loaded," he said. "You're good for ten nonlethal shots, then switch the canister. Extras on the belt are charged. Try not to shoot your friends."

That was it. When Jess tried to buckle the belt on where he was, Costigan impatiently shoved him away to make room for the next person stepping forward. Jess retreated into the shadow of a portico to finish strapping on the weapon; his fingers were cold and didn't seem to work as swiftly as he wanted. He hoped to look smooth and confident, but he thought he probably looked scared.

Thomas fell in beside him and buckled on his own belt. He pulled out the weapon and looked it over with the avid interest of someone who truly itched to deconstruct it. "I've never seen one this small before," he said. The weapon didn't much look like the sleek, deadly projectile weapons that the regular High Garda carried; these were far bulkier and squared, and had visible tubing around the top. "It fires charged darts. I've seen them used; they can drop a man for almost an hour." Thomas turned it over. "How do you think they solve the overheating problem? Someone must have, if they could fit the coil here, you see?"

"It's colder here," Jess said. "Maybe it's a cold-weather weapon."

Thomas gave him a long-suffering look. "That's nonsense."

"I know."

"It's a perfectly good question!"

"It's an engineering question." Jess put a hand on his own sidearm but didn't draw it. It felt warm. That was probably just an illusion. "As long as they work, I don't care. Though I'd rather have the ones that do real damage."

"That's because you're insane," Thomas said. "I'm happy I *don't* have one."

"Well, you're a terrible shot." Jess realized the two of them were chattering at each other to pretend they weren't resisting the urge to run. All this had seemed better in concept.

Costigan had finished dispensing the weapons, and disappeared back into the straight, perfect lines of the soldiers. Santi nodded to Wolfe, who turned toward the students.

"Follow me," he said, and took them past the motionless, expression-less soldiers to a waiting steam carriage, one clearly painted with the Library's symbol. It hissed a steady white stream into the air from the exhaust pipe, and unlike most public or private carriages Jess had ever seen, it had no brightwork at all on it . . . just plain, dull paint, the bright metallic symbol standing bolder than ever.

When the door swung open for them, there was nothing inside it except a bare metal floor, and two seats up front for the driver and his escort gunner.

"Where do we sit?" Portero, the first one in, asked Wolfe.

"On the floor," Wolfe said, as patiently as if it wasn't painfully obvious. "It's a tight fit. Get comfortable. You won't have this much luxury on the way out."

Tight fit was right. Jess, who was last in, had hardly enough space to sit without making a home on the ill-placed feet of those around him. Poor Thomas was squashed in the corner, which couldn't have been half so comfortable. At least Jess had the door at his back to lean against. Could have been worse. Was, for those in the middle.

Morgan and Khalila had managed to find places at the back, against a wall. Jess nodded to Morgan, but she didn't seem to notice.

Khalila did, and gave him a brave smile. Which made Dario, intercepting it, scowl.

"Welcome to the war," their driver said, with frightening good cheer. "Water's in the canteens on the side. Drink up. We'll be on the road a while. If you get sick, try to spew on each other, not on me."

"How long is the ride?" Glain asked from the back.

"Four hours, more or less. Patience. We'll get you where you're going."

"Might even get you there in one piece if you're lucky," his gunner said, and did something to the large gun he held that made it give a sharp, metallic click.

The driver nodded to someone outside the carriage. "We're rolling."

"Rolling," the gunner confirmed, and the carriage moved forward with a sudden jerk. It picked up speed, rattling over old cobbles, and Jess gritted his teeth against the juddering motion.

As Wolfe had already promised, it was to be a hard trip.

By the time they reached the forward positions of the Welsh army, the pace of the Library carriages had slowed to a crawl, lurching over rough and broken roads, through mud, over debris that Jess was glad he didn't have to look at through the front windows. Someone in the back had asked what the smell was, and the gunner had answered, woodenly and accurately, "War." It was a foul mix of things that worked on the brain in terrible ways, and Jess was fairly certain that what they were smelling had to be the bodies of unburied dead.

When they finally ground to a halt, Jess felt as sore as if he'd been run through the same number of hours of Wolfe's brutal training, and he knew everyone felt the same.

"Everybody out," the gunner said, and slid open the door at Jess's back. Jess had to catch himself from tumbling to the mud. His legs had gone to sleep, and he endured the sharp-prick pain of blood reviving dulled, sleeping nerves. While he leaned against the muddy surface of the carriage and helped the others out, he realized that they were all being watched.

The Welsh were camped here in wide tents—hard, dangerous-looking men and women sitting on camp stools, cleaning weapons. Some were talking together, but they all had their wary, assessing eyes on the newcomers.

The Welsh wore dark green, dappled with brown, but the colors were camouflaged further by the ever-present mud. The only colorful spot on them were the red Welsh dragons embroidered on their shoulders. Jess returned their stares for a second before helping the others down from the carriage. When they were all assembled in a tight, anxious cluster, Wolfe arrived with Captain Santi. Santi, like his men, was dressed in black, with the Library's symbol prominently displayed in gold on the front and back. He was also armed to the teeth, and moved more confidently than Jess had ever seen him. This was Captain Santi's natural home, the battlefield, and his dark eyes missed nothing—not the tension of the Welsh troops, the muttering, the hands gripping weapons a shade too tightly.

"With me," Wolfe said to his flock, and they all scrambled after him and Santi as they strode through the muddy field toward the center of the encampment. When Jess looked back, he saw that the other Library troops had fallen into a guard formation around the vehicles. They'd also picked up a squad of High Garda men and women behind them.

"Do we need so much protection? We're armed, after all," Thomas said. He sounded a touch anxious, though he was fighting to press it down. Jess sent him a glance. The young German's face was tense, but still.

"So are the Welsh," Jess said. "And they've fired at real targets."

Thomas wasn't the only one feeling unsettled; every one of them seemed to be, even Dario, though the Spaniard covered it by returning challenging looks from Welsh troops with glares of his own. Khalila kept her head down, but that might have been only because of the treacherous footing.

Morgan pulled closer to Jess, close enough that their arms brushed as they walked. He sent her a sidelong glance. "Are you all right?"

"No," she said. "Why would I be?"

He hadn't thought about what it would feel like, coming home to this . . . to the war, the destruction, the ruin of everything she knew. The fact that she was bearing it with dry eyes and steady hands seemed remarkable to him.

Glain, on the other hand, looked pallid in the cold, damp air, with hectic spots of red high in her cheeks. It occurred to Jess for the first time that she was walking through her own country's men and women, and yet seen as an intruder. Could have even been her kin standing there, watching her, he supposed. It must have been as much of a shock to her as what Morgan was feeling.

No one menaced them on the march to the tent. A light rain started to fall, which was miserable in the cold; the Library's coat was water-proofed, at least, and Jess pulled up the hood to shield his face as the rain pattered harder, and then, without warning, cut loose in a silver flood from above. It made the muddy footing worse, but Wolfe and Santi kept a quick pace, and the rest of them stumbled along as best they could in their wake.

An immaculately turned-out Welsh soldier met them at the entrance and directed them to wipe their boots on the stiff mat before coming in; they all dutifully followed that instruction, not that Jess imagined it would help very much. The mud seemed determined to get everywhere.

Inside, the floor was a thick, stiff material, and within the canvas walls it was mysteriously warm. Jess hadn't realized how chilled he'd become until the heat began to chip it away. Wolfe motioned his students back against the walls, out of the way. Jess pulled his hood back and stood silently as Wolfe and Santi greeted the Welsh commander, who waited on a square of carpeting in the center of the room next to a large camp table. Plans and maps were still on it, but rolled away from prying eyes.

The Welshman was shorter than Jess would have expected, and not prepossessing; he wouldn't have glanced twice at him on any street in the world. The man's hair had receded to a thin fringe at the back of his skull, and though the life of a soldier wasn't one of ease, he still had a comfortable paunch on him. He greeted Wolfe and Santi with courtesy and hand-shakes, and offered them hot coffee, which Jess deeply envied.

"Scholar Wolfe, your reputation precedes you. By my information, this is your . . . tenth war zone?" the commander said, which was a sur-prise to Jess, and likely to the rest of them. "Given all that experience, do you really think it's wise to bring your little chickens into the fox's den?"

He meant the students, Jess thought. The commander sounded amused, and just a little grim.

"Our little chickens have sharp beaks," Wolfe said. "I'm informed that you have put more conditions on our safe passage. I hope you understand what trouble you're borrowing, General Warlow. It has a very high interest rate."

"Are we dealing exclusively in metaphors, or may I speak plainly?"

"Please."

"My troops will not help you," Warlow said. It was clear to Jess now why he was in charge, because there was a sharpness to the man that felt dangerous even at this distance. "They will not hinder you, but they will not help. I am *not* rescinding safe passage; I am simply telling you that once you leave this tent, you are on your own, and I can't answer for your safety."

That, Jess knew, wasn't the accepted code of conduct in war zones; the armies of both sides had always accepted Library neutrality and given protection to their parties. Or, at least, that was what they'd all been taught to believe. Yet neither Santi nor Wolfe seemed at all surprised at this turn of events.

"You know that should anything happen, Wales and England will share the blame," Wolfe said. "Are you prepared to face those consequences?"

"I'm up to my neck in a bloody war. I'm prepared to accept every consequence." Warlow sent a hard, telling look toward the gathered students. "I'd think you're the one who has something more to lose, Scholar. For shame, bringing children into this hellhole."

"It's a hellhole of your making," Santi said. It was the first thing he'd said, and Warlow's stare locked on him like a gun on a target. "You're the one declaring no quarter for the city. Are you also threatening a Scholar and his students now?"

"Am I?" Warlow and Santi were engaged in a full-on staring match.

Warlow's lips curved into a cold smile. "With one single command, I could make you, your Scholar, his students, and all of your troops and vehicles just . . . vanish. Just like that. No bodies. No wreckage. No trace. Strange things happen, in war. That's not a threat. It's a simple fact."

Wolfe and Santi had no reaction. None. Jess glanced at Thomas, then at Dario. Dario had moved his hand to his sidearm beneath the cover of the cloak, which seemed like a damn fine idea. Jess's palm was sweating, and now the warmth in this tent seemed overpowering. Smothering.

General Warlow let the silence stretch. And stretch. The sharp pound of rain on canvas grew louder and louder, and Jess found that he, too, had his right hand on the handle of his gun, and his left on the hilt of a knife. There were guards just outside the tent, but Warlow hadn't bothered to keep a single one in here, despite being outnumbered heavily.

It spoke volumes about his confidence.

Wolfe finally smiled. It seemed, to Jess, an easy, calm smile, and he sat back in his chair, entirely comfortable. "It's good we understand each other," he said. "Every single fallen Scholar in history has his or her name on a wall in the Great Library. Names that each of these students remember. You may ask them. They will flawlessly recite each name, each war, each instance." He raised his voice, just a bit. "Postulant Seif. Relevant example, please."

Khalila straightened her shoulders and stepped forward, and Jess felt an intense surge of pride in her, in that moment. Her chin was up, her gaze steady on Wolfe. "Yes, Scholar. Scholar Padma Dahwan was selected to close the Serapeum in the city of Milan during the war with Austria. She and her entire party were taken prisoner by the Austrian army and executed. The Serapeum was destroyed."

"And the Library's response?"

Khalila said, softly, "Austria no longer exists."

"And approximately how large was Austria then, in comparison with the area Wales now claims?"

"It was approximately thirty-three thousand square kilometers in size. Wales is now approximately eleven thousand square kilometers."

This time, as the silence stretched, it seemed heavier on Warlow's head.

"I wish you to understand that this is also not a threat," Wolfe said. "Only a history lesson. Thank you, Postulant Seif. You may step back."

Warlow cocked his head. Not intimidated, Jess thought; just made more cautious.

"I regret that your vehicles can't proceed any farther. My men will escort you to the gates on foot," Warlow said. "I can't answer for the actions of the English army, of course, once you get inside the city. They're violent and starving. And they are, by nature, a savage people."

Jess could feel Glain looking in his direction, and Morgan's—possibly in sympathy, possibly in agreement with her countryman's opinions. He also knew that Wolfe would be observing him, and he kept himself expressionless and still. If there was a little extra color in his face, well. He couldn't help that.

"I'm sure the English have interesting views on the Welsh as well," Wolfe said. He drained his cup of coffee in two gulps and set it aside, then rose. Santi had left his untouched, and that, Jess realized, was *also* a strategy; Wolfe had demonstrated he trusted Warlow, or at least that he had a reckless disregard for his own safety. Santi had simultaneously sent the message that he didn't trust the general a bit, and stood ready to avenge Wolfe's death should there be poison in the cup.

Jess was suddenly quite glad he hadn't been offered any refreshments. *Should have thought about poison, first thing.* Well, it wouldn't be far from his mind from now on.

So much going on in this tent. He probably hadn't even understood the half of it, and for the first time since being inducted into the Library's program, he began to realize how much he had to learn about how different the world was from the theory of it.

Wolfe and Santi led them out of the tent and into the rain. Neither man bothered with hoods, and after a hesitation, Jess left his down, too. The rain was already passing away again into a disinterested patter, though the clouds remained overhead, iron gray and oppressive.

"What now?" Jess asked Wolfe as they moved back toward the vehicles. Wolfe ignored him.

After a telling pause, Santi answered. "Now we walk."

"But I thought we were going to remain in the vehicles until we loaded the books . . ."

"It's war. Plans change," Santi said. "It'll be your job to get the books out now. Each of you can control tags to transfer volumes back to the Archive. Between you, what we have should be enough."

"Sir? Some of us can't manage more than a few at a time."

Santi's look turned sharp. "Then they'll get better with practice. Enough talking, Brightwell. Walk."

EPHEMERA

Private paper note from Obscurist Magnus Maryanna Sfetsos to Lingua Magnus Cao Xueqin, 1750.

My dearest friend,

By the time you read this, the doors of the Iron Tower will be shut on me, by the order of the Archivist. Do not try to reach me. The High Garda have orders to stop any who try to enter, even Curators, and I would not wish for you to risk injury on my behalf.

I fear for what is happening to us . . . and not only to the Obscurists, who have been steadily robbed of our power and freedom. The rot extends deeper, into every branch and root, for the Library now seeks not to enlighten, but to enslave. We are only the most visible casualties of a silent war, and as they lock collars on our necks and tell us it is for our protection, we know that worse will come.

Let this be our good-bye, for I will likely never see your face again, except in the company of the Archivist or his lackeys, but know this: I cherish you, my friend. Guard yourself at all costs, and when you can, fight for the soul of what we both love.

Do not let the Library become an evil shadow on this world.

Text of a message from Lingua Magnus Cao Xueqin, 1750, to the Archivist Magister.

Most esteemed Archivist, it is with a heavy heart that I take up my pen today, and I pray you will forgive this imposition upon your time. It is not the place of the head of Literature to question your wisdom, which comes from a place of divine Scholarship, and yet I feel I must tell you of my deep concerns.

I have been a lifelong friend of Obscurist Magnus Maryanna Sfetsos, as you know, and your most recent decree that no Obscurist may leave the Iron Tower without your express permission troubles me deeply. I hasten to absolve the Obscurist Magnus from any guilt; the disquiet I feel does not mean that she has in any way shown opposition to your decree. It is, perhaps, purely selfish that I grieve for the loss of the company of my friend, when we have all our lives been close companions.

I have been told that this is a temporary measure, for the protection of our Obscurists, and to allow their absolute concentration upon the work of the Library. If this is so, Archivist, may I respectfully ask when this seclusion will be complete? For it seems beyond comprehension that you mean for it to continue longer than the year.

With utmost respect and prayers for your good health,
Lingua Magnus Cao Xueqin

Text of a reply to the Lingua Magnus from the Archivist Magister, written the next day.

I regret to inform you that Obscurist Magnus Maryanna Sfetsos suffered a collapse within the Iron Tower last evening, and the best efforts of our Medica Obscurist were not enough to save her. We all mourn her passing. Her funeral rites will be held in three days.

The Obscurist Magnus, in her final communication with me, urged me to continue the seclusion of the Iron Tower, for the protection of those within, who are under special threat from Burners and other heretics. I shall honor her request, and I trust you will do the same.

CHAPTER EIGHT

The open ground between the Welsh front lines and the city walls of Oxford was nothing but mud . . . churned constantly by Welsh assaults, beaten and mixed by the rain that still fell, though it was more of an annoyance than anything else now. Jess labored under his pack, which felt like the weight of an extra person clinging to his spine. The constant, squelching, dragging mud made them all clumsy—even Wolfe and Santi, though they managed it better than any of the students. Pity about their new Library coats, Jess thought. They were already wet, lank, and miserably laden by muddy hems.

The sickly-rotten smell of the battlefield overwhelmed him to the point that he no longer noticed it; he had much more to concern himself with now. On top of the Oxford walls—new walls, strong walls, built of solid granite and reinforced with iron bands—stood English troops, and they pointed their weapons straight at the steadily advancing Library party.

Wolfe had taken a telescoping pole from his pack and attached the Library banner to it—black, with the symbol worked in reflective gold paint, it seemed to glow in the dim, oppressive light. The banner even had some kind of reinforcement to keep the flag straight and highly visible, despite the lack of wind.

The Library took no chances.

No one fired on them, but the massive metal gates didn't open, either. The road that had once brought the city's trade and travel had been destroyed, and fragments of it were buried in the mud, all too easy to stumble over; more than one of their number went down as they clambered through the rubble, but nobody seemed injured, and the students clustered at the gates behind Wolfe and Santi. Santi's High Garda soldiers surrounded them in a solid, black, heavily armed block.

Morgan looked small and cold to the bone as she stood there, staring up at the city that had been her home. Not a happy event for her, and she seemed very alone even in the middle of their group. Jess moved to stand next to her. He didn't touch her. He didn't think she would welcome it, or his pity.

Santi pulled a parade-ground voice from deep in his chest and shouted, "Open in the name of the Library!" It echoed and rang from the stone and metal, and with divine timing, thunder rumbled overhead.

Nothing happened. Jess felt as if he were sinking slowly into the mud, and tried to pull his feet out, but it only made him more uncomfortable. A minute crawled by. Black flies buzzed, and there was a worse stench to the mud here that pushed insistently at his empty stomach: death, blood, rotting flesh. Surely there were fallen men lost under that churn. Jess had a sickening feeling he might be standing on top of one. *We could join them,* he thought. *Under the mud. Forgotten. Just like Warlow said.*

He was understanding in an entirely new way what Wolfe had been trying to teach them . . . that the Library was not just the bloodless work of making vast stores of information available to the masses; it was defending that information against *this*. Death. War. Destruction. It had all seemed so much easier in the safety of a classroom, smugly discussing the days when the Library had been vulnerable to this kind of chaos, when knowledge had vanished in flames and the cries of fanatics.

It had been unthinkable that it could still happen in modern times.

Their party seemed so small, but that, too, was part of the message the Library was sending . . . that it didn't need to dispatch an army. Harm any of its people, and the army would surely follow, as Khalila's recitation of the story of Austria proved. The leaders behind this massive wall must have been weighing those lessons carefully.

Wolfe and Santi waited with patience, and Jess tried to imitate that calm certainty. It paid off at last as a voice called down, "Step back from the gates!"

Wolfe turned to them and nodded, and they all backed away to avoid the swing of the huge metal-clad doors as they moved open. They were on some kind of steam-driven mechanism, and behind the doors was a portcullis of steel mesh that slowly cranked upward as the Library party walked forward. As he came even with the gateposts, Jess realized there were soldiers standing on either side of them, arranged so as to avoid any potential cross fire. This was a killing zone.

The gates reversed course behind them and cranked shut with a heavy *boom* that Jess felt through his bones and boots . . . but all that faded away—the soldiers, the guns, the mud, the rain, the nerves—because crowded ahead, just beyond the next gate, were the people of Oxford.

There were so many, and they were so shockingly *thin*.

Khalila, who was pressed at his side, whispered, "How long has this siege been going on?" She sounded shaken, and so was he. The misery was written on their faces, on their shrunken bodies dressed in worn and dirty clothes. The children were the worst of it, and he had to look away, because children shouldn't be so thin and ill. Even in the worst of London, it hadn't been so bad as this.

"Too long," Thomas answered. He was on the other side of Khalila, and his expression reflected all the anguish he must have been feeling. "*Mein Gott*, look at them. They're dying."

"No quarter," Jess said. "They're all under a death sentence."

"Easy for their king to say, safe in London," Glain said. "He'd be begging for surrender if this was happening in Buckingham Palace."

"Stop your chatter," Santi snapped. "We have a job to do. Stay together and stay *quiet*." He sounded tense, and coming from the always-calm captain, it had the impact of a closed fist.

The gate cranked upward, and Santi led them into Oxford.

No one said a word. They moved in silence through the crowd. Hundreds of people pressed around them, staring with strangely empty expressions at these well-fed, armed strangers. It wasn't just hunger, Jess thought. It was the absence of hope.

Wolfe stopped them when an armed crew blocked their path. The English soldiers, presumably, though in contrast to the neatly uniformed Welsh, these men had only remnants of their former red and black about them—a grimy pair of pants here, a tattered scarlet coat there. They looked as dirty, tired, and near starved as the civilians. The man in front was of medium height, with close-cropped brown hair and cheekbones that would have been prominent even if he'd been well fed, but now jutted out painfully sharp, as if they might soon cut the skin. A thin-lipped mouth and gray eyes the color of the leaden skies. He looked every inch a warrior, and the very opposite of General Warlow . . . and yet this man was on the losing side of the war.

"Let us pass," Wolfe said.

"As soon as we're clear on the rules," the man said. "Scholar Wolfe. Yes, I know who you are. And you, Captain Santi. My name is William Smith, and I'm in charge of the Oxford defense."

"And what is your rank?" Santi asked.

That got him a humorless smile in return. "All the bastards with rank are buried. Call me the major general of walking corpses."

"You said there were rules," Wolfe said. "Let's get on with them."

"Simple enough. Straight to your Serapeum, get whatever you need, and get out. You have until nightfall. After that, your neutrality doesn't matter a damn."

"By the accords, Library neutrality doesn't have a time limit."

"It does today."

Wolfe merely nodded, as if he'd expected it. "I suppose there isn't much intimidation the Library can manage on the major general of walking corpses."

"Exactly," Smith said. "I'm giving you this day from the kindness of my cold, soon-to-be-dead heart. Use it well, Wolfe. Or I'll take you, your party, and your precious books, and use you for every advantage I can."

"You'd damn your entire country," Santi said. "But I suppose you know that."

"Do you think I care about that?"

It was simply said, but there was no question in Jess's mind that the man meant every word. Wolfe didn't try to negotiate. He just nodded, and when Smith gestured his men out of the way, Wolfe continued to lead the Library's party forward.

Smith called after. "Need a guide?"

"We know the way."

After that, no one blocked their path, though there were still those eerily silent Oxford citizens watching; some were standing in long, unmoving lines to get meager rations of food, medicines, clean water. Some were lying beneath lean-to structures to keep the rain off, alone and unfriended.

The city stank of waste and sickness and unburied death, which was an awful contrast to the beauty of it—clean, ancient buildings sturdy under the weight of history. The Serapeum was off of Catte Street, near the colleges, and as they neared it Jess was struck by its resemblance to a fortress. Heavy old iron gates blocked a large gray-stone courtyard, with the Library building itself towering over it and casting it into cold shadow. Battles had been fought here. Blood spilled.

It looked old, and it was. As they got closer, Jess was disquieted by the number of Oxford citizens who'd gathered at the gates: men, women, children of all ages. It was a press of them, blocking the way, and on the other side of the bars stood a contingent of the local Library Garda, armed and ready. There was muttering, and it grew louder as Wolfe's party approached.

"On your guard," Santi said to all of them. "This might be difficult."

He was right. The crowd didn't want to give way, and mutters quickly gave way to pleas. Jess swallowed hard when he saw a woman grab at one of the Library soldiers' sleeves; she was moved away, firmly but gently, by the soldier behind him. The voices rose around them as they pushed forward, and grew in desperation.

"Please, Scholar, let us have the food! We know they have stores inside!"

"We need shelter!"

"Please, only take the children inside!"

"Bastard! We know you're hoarding water!"

"Why do *you* get to leave? What about us?"

The guards formed a wedge that drove through the crowd to the gates, then pushed open a corridor to let Wolfe and the students advance toward the closed barrier. On the other side, a robed librarian turned the lock to open it.

As it swung aside, the voices rose to shouts, and Jess looked around to see that the soldiers who'd guarded his back were now defending themselves. They were shoulder to shoulder, two deep on each side, and formed a tight, strong arc to hold the crowd at bay.

"Inside!" Santi ordered, and shoved Thomas after Wolfe as the Scholar stepped inside the courtyard. "Go, go, go!"

Jess grabbed Morgan, and Glain grabbed him, and the rest of them hurried after. Dario brought up the rear, pistol out and ready, but he didn't need it. The lines held. Santi called retreat, and it was made quickly and efficiently, with the lines compressing into a thinner and thinner arc until the last of them was inside the courtyard, and the gate could be secured behind them.

Jess stumbled to a fast halt as he almost ran into a guardian statue. A lion, this one. Massive. It was on all four feet, head down, red eyes glowing like lava. A rumbling alert came from it, and Jess quickly held up his Library bracelet for scan. The lion brushed him aside and advanced to stalk into the courtyard.

The crowd stormed the gates. Bodies slammed against the unyielding iron bars, and it was a mass of screaming faces and flailing limbs. There was no speaking with this crowd, no reasoning with it. They could only hope that the gate would hold and that the guardian lion, which now paced the inside of the fence and roared warnings, would be able to help Santi's men hold the line.

"Come inside, quickly," the librarian who'd greeted them said. She was a tall, thin woman of African descent, with close-cropped graying hair and a bleak look in eyes that had seen too much. "My apologies, Scholar Wolfe. I am—"

"Senior Librarian Naomi Ebele," Wolfe said. "You've done very well under difficult conditions. You only need to hold on a little longer."

She caught her breath, and from the sudden shimmer in her eyes the relief was overwhelming, but when she spoke her voice remained steady. "Help is most welcome, sir. You'll see the extent of our problem inside."

"What about the gates? Will they hold?" Jess asked. The mob—and it was a mob now, mindless and violent—was trying to climb over. Santi's men were keeping them off.

"They have so far," Ebele said. "This isn't their first try getting in. They believe we're hoarding supplies."

"Are you?" Wolfe asked.

"No," she said. "We've barely enough to keep us alive another day or two. What we do have is books. You were told of the cache we found?"

"Yes. Black market?"

"If so, it's from ages ago. It seems more likely that some early librarian stored a valuable donated collection here intending to ship it on, but something happened and the storehouse was forgotten until we opened it looking for more supplies. It came as quite a shock, believe me. We'd already sent all but our core staff out of the city when the negotiations failed."

"How many do you still have here?"

"Three, including me. I sent our resident Scholar away to London a week ago, over her objections. But she was too old and frail to stay." Ebele walked them up a set of steps to the oak door, which looked stout enough to withstand a determined attack. She opened it with another key and led them into a hallway that seemed drenched in shadows, but then it opened into a vast echo chamber of dark wood, high arches, and shelves. Like all Serapeums around the world, this one was filled with blanks, ready to be served from the Codex, but in addition to those, the long polished tables down the center of the hall were piled with books. Originals.

So *many*. The room had a vividly familiar smell to Jess, a crisp, dusty aroma that woke memories of his fathers' warehouses. Of old books cradled in his hands or strapped against his chest.

The smell of history.

Even Wolfe took in a breath at the sight of what lay before them, because it was a *massive* number of written works, more than most of them would ever see in their lives. Jess, who'd touched more originals than they'd ever dream, was silenced by the sight, and felt a prickle not just of awe, but of actual alarm.

"As you see," Ebele said, "we have a problem."

"Agreed," Wolfe said. "Your message was cut before you could report the actual numbers of what you'd found, but we did gather that it was large. This is . . . not large. It is enormous."

"A rare prize," she agreed. "You see why I could not abandon my post, even under orders."

No librarian could, not when the Welsh army was poised to rain down fire and death on the city, and when everything in it had been named fair game. This wasn't a prize, these thousands of books burdening the tables of the Bodleian Serapeum of Oxford.

This was a holy treasure.

"We can't." Khalila's voice shook with emotion, and she took a breath to steady it. "We can't possibly manage to send so many, even if we have enough tags!"

"Then we sort and save what we can," Wolfe said. "Form into teams of two and sort into three stacks: unique, rare, common. Go. We have little time."

Khalila paired up with Dario, and they immediately went to work. Thomas had already chosen—unexpectedly—Portero. Jess looked for Morgan and didn't find her. He gestured Glain over and asked, but Glain just shrugged.

"Don't know. Come on, let's get started."

"I know most of the rare things," Jess said. "You organize and read me titles." *What did Wolfe have Morgan doing?* And where had Wolfe gone? He was nowhere in sight now, though the rest of them were clustered around the table, working as he'd instructed.

Glain sent him a silent look of gratitude and opened the first book. "*A Gentleman's Guide to the Cultivation of Wheat, Including the Diseases to Which It Is Prone.* Author Hywel Pryor."

"Common. And boring."

"Unless you like to eat," Glain said. *Touché.* "*On the Circumference of the Planets.* Author Ping Le. Translated from the Chinese."

"Rare. Careful with that one."

"*On Sphere-Making.*" He stopped dead, staring at her, and he could feel the blood draining from his head down toward his feet. Glain glanced up at him and gave him a hard smile. "We couldn't be that lucky. The title is *A Process of Iron,* by Gwen Neame. A novel."

"Rare, and don't do that again."

"Don't joke? What should I do, weep? Will it help?"

"It might," he said, thinking of those desperate walking dead outside the gates. "We're taking too long. Just read the titles."

Glain began a steady drone of them, and when Jess didn't know them, he used the Codex. He spotted Morgan, finally; she was off with Wolfe in a corner, arguing fiercely. He couldn't hear anything, but he knew that look.

She wanted to find her father, he guessed. And Wolfe wasn't risking her out on the streets. *Good,* Jess thought. From what he'd seen out there, the chances were high that if she found her father at all, he'd already be dead.

"Focus," Glain said, and snapped fingers in front of his face. "You're slowing down. Stare at your girlfriend later."

"She isn't my girlfriend," Jess said.

And got back to work.

I t took hours to work their way through the enormous stack; at the end, each team took their unique and rare book stacks and moved them to one of the end tables. It still formed a formidable mountain. As Wolfe examined each volume himself, and sorted them into two more stacks, he glanced up. His dark gaze landed on Jess. "Check outside," he said. "Santi hasn't been in to give a report. Not like him."

Jess nodded and hurried down the hallway. Glain preceded him, opened the locked door, and let him through. He glanced back as he stepped over the threshold, and said, "You're locking me out, aren't you?"

"Just for safety," she said, and smiled. "Good luck."

She shoved him on a step and slammed the wood at his back. He heard the locks grinding shut behind him, and took in a breath of icy, damp air as he saw the situation of the courtyard.

The weather had turned while he was in the timeless silence of the Bodleian building; overhead, the clouds were flat and low, and the rain had turned to spits of sleet. The ancient steps were coated and slick.

There was blood on the cobblestones *inside* the gates, in a wide, watery smear. New chains fastened the stout iron; the lock must have broken. Outside the gates lay bodies, at least ten of them—men, women, even the small, still form of a child. Jess stared at them, at the blood, and when he looked up, he saw Niccolo Santi.

The captain looked grim. There was a thin thread of blood on his cheek that wasn't his own, and cuts in the black cloth on the arm of his uniform. "What are you doing out here?" he demanded. Jess took in the rest of the scene in a hasty glance—one set of soldiers standing guard at the bars, another sitting against the courtyard walls, huddled in coverings. One was very still beneath his blanket—asleep, badly injured, or dead.

"Wolfe sent me to check."

"Tell him we were lucky. This old ironwork isn't likely to keep them back next time, and neither will our guns; if they come in numbers, they'll get into the courtyard this time."

"How many of your men—"

"Just tell him the sand's running fast," Santi said. "And leave someone stationed at the door to open it if we need to retreat."

"You think the mob will come back?"

"They're convinced the library is filled with sacks of food and fresh running water and fairy dust. They'll come." Santi looked in the direction of the gate, held shut with new chains. "Soon, I think."

Jess retreated back up the stairs. He banged on the door and listened to the scrape of the locks and bars being removed. He tried to imagine standing out here under vicious attack, killing the sick, the weak, *children*.

Knowledge is all. The Library's motto, and this was what it meant in the real world. It meant that nothing—nothing—was more valuable. Not even lives.

It seemed like mockery, looking at those desperate faces.

Jess shoved the door open the instant it was free, pushing Glain back. When she protested, he ignored it. "Keep it unlocked," he told her, "and stay here. Santi may need to retreat at any time."

"But—"

"Stay here!"

He stalked down the hall. The drag of his muddy Library cape on his shoulders made him feel older. Harder. More breakable than he had been just a few days before.

He reported to Wolfe. Wolfe had attention only for the books he was combing through, but he nodded. "Good," he said. "We're ready to start tagging. I need you."

"I put Glain on the door, sir."

"Good. She's well placed." Finally, Wolfe looked up at him. Jess's classmates were grouped together at the other end of the table with the Oxford Library staff, whispering; no one was obviously listening to him and Wolfe, yet he knew that all of them were paying attention. "How many tags can you handle?"

Jess's first impulse was to honestly say, *I don't know,* but instead, what came out was entirely different. "As many as you need."

"Do ten, rest, eat, do ten more. Keep going until you can't. Understand?"

"Yes, sir." Wolfe handed him a supply of tags. "We're supposed to enter them by hand in the Codex—"

"Skip the tick boxes. Seif! Santiago! Get over here. I'll want you to do three tags, break for food and five minutes' rest, then three more. When you start feeling sick, step out."

Jess started on the stack in front of him. *Ten, then rest.* Adrenaline carried him through tagging and sending the first set; he pushed it and kept going through another five. The books would be appearing in the Archive, into the hands of an Obscurist whose job it was to hand them off to Library staff for safekeeping. One by one by one, Jess kept sending.

He'd lost count when he felt weakness take hold, and staggered against the edge of the table. He grabbed it with both hands and held on until his head stopped spinning. Thomas handed him a pressed ration bar of nuts and honey and fruits, and Jess ate it without any appetite, then washed it down with a mouthful of water. "Easy," Thomas said. "You make us look bad. Sit."

Jess nodded; he suddenly realized his legs weren't holding him up anymore, and dropped into a chair. He watched as Khalila took her turn. She activated five in a row, staggered, and caught herself against the table. Dario steadied her with an outstretched hand on her back. She sent him a shaky, grateful smile. Dario sent his own books and managed not to seem affected, though Jess saw he'd gone bone pale. Jess stepped in and relieved him. "Here," he said, and passed Dario a cup of water. "Don't want you to get ahead of me."

"Quality, not quantity," Dario shot back, as he collapsed in the chair Jess had left behind.

They both knew that wasn't true. Not today.

It went on like that, though the players changed; Jess managed fifty tags more before he had to sit down for a long rest, head spinning, body too weak to stand. Keeping rations down was difficult. Librarian Ebele and Wolfe managed a hundred together, but she collapsed completely and had to be carried to a hard bed on a table nearby. Her skin had gone the ashy color of someone near death. Wolfe didn't pause, though he did step back to eat and drink and sit, and watch the next wave—Ebele's colleagues, with Morgan and Thomas—continue to steadily tag the pile of books back to the safety of the Alexandrian collection.

They'd managed almost all the stack when Jess heard the clamor echoing from the hallway. It rushed toward them, in the form of Santi, Glain, and the bloodied, hard-breathing bulk of the soldiers. Some of them were being carried, some dragged. Hardly any of them were unmarked.

"Lost the courtyard," Santi said to Wolfe. Over his words, Jess heard the angry roar of a crowd outside the heavy stone walls, and the thud of hands—or weapons—on the door through which Santi's men had come. "They've broken the lion. Leave the rest of this."

"No," Wolfe said. "We'll have to hand-carry them."

"You've got five tags left. Use them on the students, at least. Send them home."

"We both know the trip could kill them. Tags aren't designed for flesh and blood."

"We're past that. Send them." Santi turned toward the students, who'd clustered together again. Jess found himself standing with Dario and Glain, the others behind them. *Fighters in front,* he thought, and almost smiled. They'd done it unconsciously.

"I'll stay," Jess said, and heard both Dario and Glain saying it at the same moment, in chorus. They all looked at one another, and in the next instant, the rest were saying it behind them. Thomas. Morgan. Portero. Khalila. *All of them.*

"Let me phrase it differently. Who volunteers to take a tag and retreat back to Alexandria?"

"Is it worse than the Translation Chamber?"

"Infinitely worse," Santi said. "We use tags when there is absolutely no escape. I've survived it, though. You probably would."

Portero gave a regretful sigh. "The books come first, sir. Isn't that how it should be? Books before men?"

Wolfe almost smiled. "As you see. They're not children. They're librarians."

Santi didn't seem all that surprised, but he did seem even more grim, if that was possible. "Your *librarians* look like death chewed, swallowed, and vomited them up," he said. "We have bigger problems. Our major general of the walking dead changed his mind: he's not letting us walk out the front gates. He's offered extra rations to anyone who brings us in to him, alive. He intends to use us as hostages."

Wolfe nodded. He was silent a moment, and then suddenly looked at Jess. "We knew that might happen."

"And the Welsh aren't going to hold back," Santi said. "They'll kill us along with the English. We both know it. We need an exit, Christopher, and I don't have one now that you've used all the tags."

"I believe young Brightwell may be able to help with that."

Jess involuntarily took a step back, only to run into the solid bulk of Thomas standing behind him, and caught himself in the next instant. Of course Wolfe would know. Santi would have told him about the message, even if he didn't understand what it meant.

He'd worry about the level of danger later. Nothing mattered now but finding a way out of the rattrap they were in, so Jess said, "I may be able to get us out. It'll cost, though."

Wolfe didn't seem at all surprised. "Where do we go?"

Beneath the sod, Brendan had written in his message. "My cousin Frederick should be at the Turf Tavern, sir. Off of Hell's Passage. He'll have a way."

"Nic?"

"Map," Santi said, and one of his soldiers stepped up to open a round case that held the information. Santi spread the paper—not a blank, real paper, with the information meticulously drawn on it—on the table and anchored the corners with the tags that lay there. "We're here," he said, and pressed a fingertip to the small image of a building in a warren of others. "The Turf Tavern is here. Not far, but narrow, especially through Hell's Passage. Hell of a risk if this mob catches up."

"Not if we give them something else to focus on." Naomi Ebele rose slowly from the table on which she rested, and stood up. One of her fellow librarians took her arm, and she gave him a grateful smile in return.

"Scholar Wolfe, please send what you can, and take the rest. Help us move the rest back to the vault, and we'll let them have the Serapeum. They can search to their heart's content for our stores of food. It will keep them busy enough."

"They'll destroy the place," Khalila said. Her voice was hushed, and Jess felt the same dawning, dull horror . . . this ancient place, with its wood beams hundreds of years old, the gold-leaf ceiling lovingly made, the beautiful high windows. "They'll tear it to pieces when they don't find what they want."

"I know," Ebele said. There were tears in her eyes as she looked around, and she put a hand gently on a smooth, age-darkened shelf. "And we will build it again."

Santi said, to Jess, "Just who is this cousin of yours?"

"It doesn't matter," Wolfe said. "If he can get us out, anything else is moot. Postulants, help Librarian Ebele take books to the cellar. We don't have time to waste—no, not you, Brightwell. You're with me. We have five more tags left to use; then we take the rest and divide them up. Each one of you will take a few in your pack. Guard them with your lives."

The other students went with the Oxford Library staff, and Santi's troops dispersed to scout the exits and routes, and suddenly Jess was standing almost alone with Christopher Wolfe in the middle of the doomed Bodleian Serapeum. Wolfe calmly clipped the last of the tags to five more books and handed them to Jess to activate, one by one.

"How long have you known?" Jess asked. His voice came ragged and harsh, between deep breaths, as he struggled for the energy to send the last two volumes off to safety. "About my family?"

"Since the day you found that hidden compartment in Abdul Nejem's house," Wolfe said. "You did a good job of dissembling, but someone unfamiliar with the smuggling trade would never have found it. I admit, finding out about your family's business was much more difficult. I thought your father was merely a collector at first." For a moment, the

older man's expression was the usual harsh, empty mask, and then it softened as Jess wavered and almost dropped. Wolfe grabbed him and eased
him into a chair, then crouched next to him with his black robes pooling
like spilled ink on the floor. "Listen to me. I am prepared to overlook your
family and your past, and keep your secrets; I'm always ready to do that,
for talent that will serve the Library. But just now, it's your past, and your
family, that will save us. So use it. Use *them*."

"Just like you're using me?" Jess tipped his head back to stop it from
spinning. "Just like my father always did. Are you using Morgan, too?"

Wolfe was silent, but he put a warm hand on Jess's head a moment,
then rose and walked away.

Maybe he had nothing he could say in response to the truth.

EPHEMERA

**Directive from the Obscurist Magnus to the Aylesbury
High Garda commander. Confirmed in his reply, without
annotations.**

*We anticipate the successful completion of Scholar Wolfe's journey to Ox-
ford within twenty-four hours. When his party arrives in Aylesbury, you
are instructed to remove Postulant Morgan Hault from the party of
Scholar Wolfe, by force if necessary. Postulant Hault is not to be harmed
under any circumstances, but should Wolfe, Santi, or any of the others attempt to interfere with this order, you have the authority to do what is necessary.*

*You are ordered to deliver said postulant to the nearest Translation
Chamber, to be sent with armed escort directly to the Iron Tower.*

Confirm your receipt of this message.

CHAPTER NINE

Jess's backpack was heavier than it had been before, weighted down with as many books as he could safely carry; they were all burdened, according to their ability, though the outer rank of soldiers had the lightest burdens so as to fight effectively.

So far, though, luck was with them. They didn't need to fight.

Librarian Ebele had been right; once they'd abandoned the Serapeum, the mob had re-formed at the front, ripped through the old iron bars, and was busy tearing the ancient place to pieces as they hunted for the rumored caches of food and water. It was like listening to a murder, and they all moved as quickly and quietly as possible to get distance from it. The Oxford staff wept quietly. Wolfe kept Naomi Ebele close to him, and Jess could see why; she seemed distracted and almost feeble now. She'd pushed herself too hard.

They all had.

The sleet was falling more steadily now, a constant gray hiss, and Jess put up his hood to keep it out. The weatherproofed silk was already stiff with a thin, sheer coat of ice, and he was cold to the bones. They were in a narrow alleyway now, and able to pass through only two abreast. The cobbles were awash in slick mud, and it smelled like a sewer. He tried to breathe shallowly, but it did little good; that stench soaked through even the smallest gasp.

The small alleyway opened out onto another street, this one all but deserted. There were a few people at the far corner, but they seemed too disheartened to care about the passage of their party. The riot was still behind them. When Jess looked back, he saw what looked like black smoke rising to stain the gray clouds.

They made it to the tavern without incident, which seemed half a miracle. The Turf Tavern was a hallowed institution in Oxford, almost as old as the Bodleian Serapeum, and it usually served as a friendly gathering place for all levels of Oxford society.

Not now. Now it was surrounded by a group of hard-looking, scarred men armed with guns and knives. A few had even dragged out swords, maces, and axes for the occasion.

Jess pushed through to the front and took down his hood. "I'm Jess. Looking for Frederick."

The men—every one of them topping him by at least a foot, and broader by far—gave him identical looks of disdain, but at length one of them stepped back into the shadows of the open doorway beneath the low roof.

The man who emerged next had the Brightwell sharp features, though his eyes were lighter and his hair a different shade than Jess's family side sported. Frederick's gaze missed nothing—not the numbers of High Garda soldiers, the arms, the readiness—but he was all sunny smiles as he stepped forward and extended his hand to Jess. "Cousin," he said. "A warm welcome to Oxford. How has your trip been so far? Eventful, I'd guess, or you'd not be calling on me. Lucky thing, your timing, because we were about to take our leave of this death house of a town."

"So you do have a way out?"

"Naturally. For a price." Frederick grinned, and lines seamed his face. He was only three years older than Jess but seemed far more worn; maybe it was the smuggling life, or maybe it was the strain of watching his home city die by inches. "Family comes free, since I'm feeling generous, but as you're associating with the enemy these days, you have to pay for your . . . friends."

"And what's the price for them?"

"You're fresh from the Serapeum. You'll be carrying something worth my time. Make it good and we'll see how friendly I feel. After all, you've exposed me to not just the High Garda, but a damned Scholar. It had best be good enough to buy me a new life."

Jess was prepared for that. He'd already bargained with Wolfe for something that would be dear enough to pay for the lives of all of their party. So he shrugged off his pack and said, "We'd better do it inside. I'm not risking this to the weather."

"Good idea. I'd spot you a pint, except we drank all the ale ages back," Frederick said. He led the way into the dimness of the deserted tavern, which was a warren of small rooms, low ceilings, heavy dark beams. One of the walls was the only remaining trace of the original city fortifications, before it had grown so large, and it was worn from the passage of hands and shoulders.

It smelled of old spilled drinks and sweat, and a new, bitter scent of blood.

"Now, cousin, produce," Frederick said. He sat at a trestle table and leaned his elbows on it as Jess unfastened the pack.

Frederick talked like a back-alley tough, but he had fine hands, a musician's hands, and he cradled the book Jess gave him carefully in them. "Damn this light," he said. "Got a glow on you?"

Jess did. He tapped it and set the round ball on the table; it warmed up to a steady firelight shimmer and cast dark shadows around them. Frederick picked up the ball and held it close to the binding, then carefully opened the cover.

He took in a quick breath, let it out slowly, and looked at Jess with eyes that reflected the glow eerily. "You know what this is?"

"I know," Jess said. "It's enough to cover us."

"Your brother would *kill* you if he knew you let this go to me instead of him."

"I know that," Jess said, and smiled. "But it'll make its way to him, won't it? He told me where to find you. Means *he* knows how to find *you*, too. I wouldn't hold back if I were you."

Frederick raised his eyebrows and carefully closed the cover of the book. He tapped the aged leather with one soft fingertip. "I'm tempted to squirrel it away for leverage. I don't know what Brendan's game is. You watch out for your brother. He's a twisty one."

"He's family."

"I know. And if I were you, I wouldn't count on the embrace of your nearest and dearest."

"I'm counting on you," Jess said, reaching for the glow ball to tap it off, "but it's good that I'm supposed to make myself a home in the Library, then. Deal done?"

"Fair enough," Frederick said, and they shook on it. His cousin opened up a pack leaning on the wall and took out a familiar design of waterproof wrap—the specialty of the Brightwells, for their important volumes. He carefully packaged up the book and put it away, then shouldered the pack. "Let's get the parade marching."

"I hope we won't be quite that obvious."

"Trust me, old son, it's my trade to be inconspicuous—"

They were coming out the door of the tavern as Frederick said that, and his words were cut off by a raw, full-throated shout from one of his men. "On the passage!"

That brought a rush of realignment of Frederick's men, from guarding the tavern to guarding a particularly narrow alleyway off to the right.

"Wolfe," Frederick said, in a suddenly businesslike tone, "get your flock inside. Don't want to be seen in your company. Gives me a bad name."

Wolfe and Santi hustled all of them back into the tavern's dark, cramped interior, until everyone with a Library symbol was safely out of sight. Jess pulled his hood back and arranged himself at one of the windows; Wolfe and Santi had taken up similar posts.

"Will he sell us out?" Wolfe asked.

"No," Jess said, but he thought, *Maybe.* He didn't know Frederick well enough to say. He only knew that it was up to which side of the bread Frederick thought had the most butter, and that depended on things he couldn't know, like whether Frederick would keep a bargain.

He already had the book, after all.

"Back exit is clear," Santi said to Wolfe. "I had it scouted when we got here. Won't get us far, though. We'll never make it out the main gate, not with Smith setting the mob after us with the promise of food."

"Let's not give up on Cousin Frederick just yet."

Santi shrugged, as if he thought it was a foregone conclusion. Jess didn't blame him, given that he wasn't so certain about their prospects himself. If the mob came boiling out of that passage, he imagined Cousin Frederick might decline to put himself in deeper to save them.

It wasn't the mob, though.

It was one man. Old, graying, rail thin from the deprivations of the siege. He edged along, propped his left shoulder on the wall as a crutch, but he stopped when he saw Frederick's men arrayed before him.

He might have looked frail, but there was a dark intensity in his face.

"Welcome, friend," Frederick said from where he leaned against the Turf's wall, and gave the man a grin that didn't reach his eyes. "Sorry, pub's closed for business. Sad days, eh?"

"I want my daughter," the man said.

"No girls here, mate. Sorry."

"She's here. I followed." The man's voice was unsteady, and Jess realized, as he edged a little forward, that he was bloody, too, as if he'd been in a fight. "Bloody Library has her. Give her to me. I don't want to hurt anyone."

The threat woke a raw chuckle through the ranks of Frederick's very capable toughs. "Old man, just go back where you came from," Frederick said. "Your girl's not here, like I said. Ned, help him on his way."

The biggest man of Frederick's crew stepped up and put a hand on the older man's shoulder . . . and froze, then backed up one step. Two. He turned to look at Frederick and shook his head.

The older man raised his right hand over his head, and in it, he held a glass vial of liquid. The thin light caught it and turned the color to sour emerald.

"Don't touch me," he said. "Send my daughter out to me. If I toss this, a fair number of you are going to die."

"Easy," Frederick said, in a calm, low voice. "Easy there, nobody needs to end up crisped. Right? So put that down and I'll see about your girl. Come on, burning the Turf? Worse than setting the Great Library itself alight. Might be more of a loss to the world, even."

"Send her out," the man said. His voice went thready and faint. He pushed free of the wall, still holding up the bottle.

Frederick's men, who weren't scared of much, flinched and backed up to give him generous room.

"Got nothing to lose. Send my daughter out," the man repeated. "Morgan Hault. Or I drop it."

Jess saw the resemblance then . . . the same dark-honey eyes, though this man's had faded with time. The same pointed chin.

"Father?" Morgan's voice came from behind and to Jess's left, and he didn't have time to do more than turn in that direction before she was past him and out the door. "Father! Are you all right?" She ran to him and gave him a quick embrace, then pulled back when he winced. She hardly seemed to notice the Greek fire he was still holding over their heads, in the first rush of reunion . . . and Jess saw her body stiffen as she did. She took a step away. "What is this? What are you doing? You have to put that down—it's dangerous!"

"Damned right it's dangerous," he said. "I came to save you, Morgan."

She laughed a little. "I don't need rescuing, Father. I'm rescuing *you*. We're leaving. Now. Come with us."

"Us," he repeated. "You think of these people as *us*, as if you're one of them? You can't be. Not with the Library. The Library isn't taking you away." Her father, Jess thought, had a fanatic's burning eyes, and the look he sent toward Wolfe, toward them as they stepped out into the courtyard, was vicious with hatred. "Take their damned sign off. You're not their slave—" His voice died as he caught sight of the bronze Library bracelet gleaming dully on her wrist. "No. *No*. You're not one of them. You can't be one of them. I forbid it."

"Father—"

"Morgan, *take it off*!"

"I will. Just not yet. These are my friends. See? My friends. And we're all leaving here. You can come with us. Please, come with us."

Her father stared at her with an expression of contempt and revulsion, and said, "They've turned your mind. Made you believe they're on your side. Who did it, that one? That *Scholar*? What did you do to my daughter?"

"I've helped her," Wolfe said. "Which is more than you're doing right now. We have little time before the Welsh begin to destroy this city. If you don't want her to die, stop wasting it."

"She's coming with me," Hault said, and tightened his grip on the girl. "She'll never be yours. Tyler told me what happened, what *would* happen, if she went into the Library. Not my girl. Never."

"Father, stop! Where are you going?"

"Back," he said. "Back to burn that nest of serpents they call a Serapeum. Come on!"

Morgan broke free of his hold. "What happened to you? What are you talking about?"

"We have to burn it down," her father said. "It's the only way they listen." He was insane—Jess could see it. Feverish with it.

She backed away. "You weren't a Burner when I left you," she said. "What did they do to you?"

"They showed me the truth," he told her. "I can't let the Library have you. They'll use you. They'll make you just another one of *them*, and it's better—better if you're dead. Better that than life with them." He took in a deep breath. *"Vita hominis plus libro valet!"*

He threw the bottle.

"No!" Morgan screamed and lunged forward. Somehow, she got underneath the bottle, dived, and caught it in her outstretched hands just inches above the cold cobbles. The green liquid inside sloshed, but the thin glass didn't break.

It would have been the death of them all if it had.

Santi stepped quickly over to Morgan, helped her up, and took the bottle. He stored it in a padded pouch at his side and nodded to Wolfe. "Get behind me, Morgan."

She didn't argue. She was, Jess thought, too much in shock to even try. When she failed to move on her own, Jess took her by the shoulders and pulled her back; he held on, just in case she tried to run back to her father.

But she didn't.

"Go," Santi said. He pulled his pistol and leveled it at Morgan's father. "Go. Be grateful I'm not doing the Welsh's work for them."

"I'll get my daughter back," the man said. "I swear to God I will set her free."

He stared straight at Morgan with a bleak, awful expression, and then he turned and stumbled the other way.

Frederick shrugged and made a circle motion to his men. "Right," he said. "He was a treat. If he's got Burner friends and more Greek fire, I don't want to be here when he comes back. Sorry, lass. Can't pick your family. Believe me, I know."

Morgan suddenly turned and buried her face in Jess's chest. She didn't cry, but the hitching, awful pain of her breathing was worse. He could feel the loss in her, a terrible bleak emptiness that pulled like a magnet.

"He tried to kill me," she whispered. "He's my father and he tried to kill me."

Jess had nothing to say to that, because there were no words that were going to make it any easier to swallow. He remembered how it had felt in that awful moment of clarity in his childhood, knowing that his father would let him die.

At least with hers, it was a cause to blame. Not profits.

"You can weep about it later," Frederick said. "For now, get your wits back in your head."

"You English," Dario said. "So sensitive."

"We're a practical lot," Frederick said, "and you'll keep your tongue quiet if you want these practical men to get you out alive. Right?" He cast a sharp look at Wolfe, who nodded without any real expression.

"Yes," Wolfe said. "For better or worse, we're in their hands now." He suddenly gave Frederick one of those dark, cool smiles. "Don't ever speak to my postulants again."

It didn't take long before the scouts came back and reported the way clear, and Frederick said, "Then let's move on. All of you, lose those damned Library colors. Now."

"You heard the man," Wolfe said. "Students. Coats off." He was taking off his own Scholar's robe. That left him in plain black, like the soldiers, who were ripping away patches and symbols. "Nic. Give them guns."

"Real weapons? You sure?"

"We're past kinder methods."

Santi gestured to one of his men, who grabbed a pack and went to each of the students, taking their stunning weapons and replacing them with heavy, sleek, lead-firing guns. "Don't shoot unless you have to," he said. "It will get confusing out there. Too easy to shoot your friends."

Morgan's wet hair was out of its pins and falling in untidy strings across her face and neck. She looked lost.

"Can she walk, or do I have to risk a man carrying her?" Frederick asked Jess.

"I can walk," Morgan said, and turned toward Frederick. "And I can fight."

"Good," he said. "Do that. And if you want my advice, you'd best put a bullet in your dear old da's head before you let him near you again."

"Nobody asked you," Jess said. "Piss off. We're ready to go."

"You're really not, my dear coz," Frederick said. "Hold on to your knickers. This isn't the fun part."

Frederick's men and Santi's troops didn't mix well. After the second scuffle, Santi assigned his forces to rear guard, while Frederick's men led the way into an old, nondescript house with a ruined door. Inside, the place was wrecked—ransacked, Jess thought, for anything that would burn—but Frederick's men weren't interested in the contents of the place. They pried up a large, square stone in the center of the room, and beneath were steps heading down.

"Stay together," Frederick told them. "It's a rat's warren. You get lost, you'll stay lost, because we're not turning back for anyone. And for God's sake, put your guns away; bullets will bounce back on you. If you have to fight, use a knife. And keep it quiet. Sound carries."

It was claustrophobic on the stairs, and worse once they'd gained the tunnels. For some reason, Jess had assumed the tunnels would be newly dug . . . some sort of hidden smuggling system that Frederick had devised. Instead, they were *very* old. In some places there were markings chiseled into the stone, and Jess studied them for a few puzzled seconds before the light dawned . . . but he was well behind Khalila, who whispered, "These are Jewish signs. Escape tunnels, in the event of persecution. I've read of this."

"Smart girl," Frederick said. "Now, shut it. We're not the only ones that know about these tunnels."

"Do the Welsh?" Wolfe asked. He sounded calm and casual, but the question definitely had weight to it. Frederick gave him a wolf's grin.

"Not as of an hour ago," he said. "But things change."

They moved quickly and, as required, quietly . . . at least for a while. It got harder to move around bits of fallen masonry and seemed like an eternity of dark, narrow tunnels, alcoves, and the skitter of rats. Morgan stayed right behind Jess, and he glanced back frequently to see if she was all right. She seemed to be—as all right as any of them, at least.

The forward motion stopped, and Frederick sent two of his men up a set of narrow stairs off one of the alcoves. They'd made a dozen twists and turns so far, and Frederick hadn't been consulting any kind of map; he must have learned this warren, and learned it well, to be so fast and sure getting them where he wanted them to be.

But was it safe? It didn't feel safe.

The scouts came back down and whispered with Frederick, who nodded and turned to Wolfe. "Right," he said. "Up you go."

"No, you first," Santi said. "We insist."

"Age before beauty, and all that," Frederick replied. "Up. Now."

Frederick's men had drawn weapons. Jess's pulse began to beat faster, and he found the hilt of the knife in his belt. Close quarters in here. Bad conditions. It would be a slaughterhouse, and the only way out was up . . . and who knew what waited for them there?

Wolfe broke the tension by saying, "Nic. Take us up."

It was a calculated risk, but staying wasn't better. Santi gave the Scholar a dark, doubtful glance, but he turned and ordered his soldiers out.

They went without question.

Then it was the students' turn, with Wolfe, and Jess glanced back at his cousin, who was watching them mount the stairs.

"If you've sold us out—" he began, but Frederick shook his head.

"Family loyalty, Jess. I kept my word. There's a guide up top." He gave a sudden, luminous grin. "But it'll cost you later, I promise."

He gestured his men onward, farther down the tunnels. Where they were off to, Jess didn't know.

He followed Thomas up the steps, out into an echoing dark hallway. They extinguished their glows, because ahead was a barred gate, and cloudy, dying daylight.

The gate's lock had been snapped, and hinges oiled to keep it silent; they stepped through and out into . . .

. . . a graveyard.

"Well, this is comforting," Dario muttered. He put his knife away and pulled out his gun, which he held pointing down, the way they'd been taught. *Only raise it to fire when you're moving,* Santi had told them. *Better to shoot yourself in the foot than in the head if you trip.* Too much to remember, suddenly. Jess felt clumsy and very, very unprepared for this.

On one side, the graveyard was a sea of silvery grass and swaying trees, random movement muted by the hissing fall of ice. The bitter cold wind cut at Jess's skin. The gate through which they'd passed turned out to be a tomb, built like a miniature Greek temple, and as they left it they were surrounded on all sides by leaning granite and marble headstones, jutting like broken teeth from the jaw of the ground.

"We have a problem," Thomas said. He sounded grim, and scared. "Look."

They were close, but he was right; the new city's wall had been built on the borders of this cemetery, and stretched high up. No way over it. *You bastard, Frederick,* Jess thought. He must have known what he was doing, and he'd lied about it, right to Jess's face.

"We have a guide," Santi said, and nodded toward the left. Someone was standing at the far edge of the cemetery, waving in their direction—a scarecrow of a woman, as thin as a walking corpse. She was wrapped in faded layers of clothes but seemed half the size she should have been, even then. As the Library party approached her, she sniffled and wiped at her dripping nose with dirty hands.

God, she was *young*. Not much older than Jess himself. He could see that in the fine texture of her skin, the gold of her hair, but war had worn her thin and hollow. "Come with me," she said. "Hurry."

"Where are you taking us, girl?" Wolfe demanded, and she shook free of his grip on her arm and ducked her head, as if to avoid a blow he didn't give.

"To the gate," she said. "Frederick's taking it, but you've got to be quick."

"We should have gone with him," Dario said. "I knew it."

"Minute the mob sees you lot, they'll howl," the girl said, and wiped her nose again. "Redcoats said any who grab you get extra rations. Which is why Frederick went first. Nobody wants *him*, so he can get the gate open for you, like. He said move it quick."

"Show us," Wolfe told the girl, and she scampered off, faster than Jess would have believed possible for her thin, starved frame. The ice slimed the grass, and it crunched and slipped beneath his feet, but he kept up as Santi's men broke into a trot, then a run, in pursuit of the girl. They all kept up. He kept a hand on Morgan's arm to make sure they didn't lose her.

Portero lagged a bit behind, and he was the first to be caught. It wasn't his fault; Jess didn't see the men lurking behind the brick building on their left until they poured out, howling. Portero spun to face them, pulling his gun, but three of them were on him before he could fire more than once, and Jess saw two of them pulling him down.

Santi's men pivoted in a practiced, almost elegant formation and went at the attackers. There were only six or seven of them, but they were hard men, killers, and even as Jess grabbed Portero's wrists to drag him out of the fight, he knew it was too late.

Someone had stabbed him.

He watched Portero gasp for breath, his face turning a horrible shade of cream, and the blood that bubbled from his mouth seemed the brightest crimson Jess had ever seen.

Then he stopped breathing. His eyes fixed, his pupils relaxed, and the only thing that moved on him was the slow crawl of blood down his cheek and onto the icy grass.

Someone was pulling at Jess's shoulder. Thomas. It was Thomas who screamed in his ear words that Jess couldn't fully process. *Get up,* he thought stupidly at Portero. *Get up, you lazy bastard.* Portero had never been his friend, but he couldn't just leave him. Not like *this*.

Thomas rolled Portero over, grabbed his pack, and pulled it off. Portero's arms flopped limply as he fell back to the ground, and Jess tried to straighten him, but he was off-balance because someone was pulling him by the shoulder in a grip hard enough to make his bones creak, and the day seemed smeared and oddly silent . . .

. . . until it all snapped back, hard and loud and chaotic, and he was running, his arm gripped tightly in Dario Santiago's hand. Thomas loped next to him, and Khalila, and all the others. When Jess looked back over his shoulder he saw that Santi's men had broken free of the conflict and were coursing after them, with a growing mob on their trail like rabid wolves.

There was a low stone wall at the edge of the cemetery, and their guide was on the other side of it, screaming at them to hurry. Wolfe was the first to it, and vaulted up on it at the run; Glain's long legs scrambled her up to the top, where she crouched. Khalila stumbled, but Wolfe and Glain pulled her up and over. Each of them got the same help, boosted up, scrambling over. Jess went near the end, and only realized when Glain flinched that he'd smeared her with Portero's sticky blood, and then he was over, tumbling down a hill and up to his feet with the unwieldy weight of the pack on his back to overbalance him yet again when the cobbles of the street below proved slick.

The exterior gate the girl was talking about was one of those that had been closed, locked, and reinforced with steam-powered bulwarks; a gate that Oxford must have once hoped to use to launch their own attack when it had been built. One that had been heavily defended by a guard station of redcoats. Frederick's men had taken the guard station, shattered the layers of locks, and cranked the gate open. Not without resistance, though, and not without massive losses, judging from the men dead around them; Oxford redcoats were now desperately trying to retake the controls. The battle raged ahead, and it was no longer just Frederick's lot versus the soldiers; Oxford citizens had smelled a rare chance for escape, and they were fighting to get out before the gates cranked shut again. It was total madness, a boil of bodies and screams. Santi's soldiers pushed through to form a narrow corridor for Wolfe and his students, but it was a fragile protection and wouldn't last.

"Go!" Frederick shouted from atop a fallen block of stone, and fired into the face of a man lunging toward him. Santi's soldiers slammed back a rush of people trying to cut ahead of them. "We'll hold it!"

One of Frederick's men just ahead and to the left of Jess was felled with a club, and a wild-eyed woman stumbled over his body. She had a red-faced, screaming child in her arms, and she shoved the baby at Jess. "Take her!" the woman shrieked at him.

Jess didn't remember doing it, but suddenly the baby was squirming in his arms, and the mother was dragged aside to stumble and fall beneath another wave of desperate men and women surging forward. He pushed his way on. *I shouldn't have the baby. I can't put her down. I can't take her with me. I can't . . .*

Jess spun as someone clawed at his shoulder, and saw a boy about his own age with a knife; he slammed a fist into the boy's chin and sent him flying backward. The baby in his arms was wiggling so hard it was difficult to hang on, but he needed one hand free to deal with those coming at him. Frederick's lines were collapsing fast now, and the Oxford citizens were surging for the open gate . . . but the huge wings of the gate were cranking closed again. Oxford defenders had activated the steam engine.

They had to get through before it shut. He saw that the other students were ahead of him. Glain was scrambling over a mass of fallen bodies and dragging Morgan with her.

"Run, damn you!"

He turned at the shout in his ear and saw Wolfe next to him, armed with a gun; he took methodical, fast shots and was half-covered in blood. The crowd was screaming around them, pure chaos and fury, and somehow Jess stayed on his feet as he was pushed and buffeted. The gates squeezed forward. Screams of those on either side of them turned from fury to terror. Wolfe grabbed Jess's shoulder and shoved him into what seemed a solid wall of bodies. Some fell, and Jess realized now that there were bullets being fired from outside. The Welsh.

He almost turned back, but Wolfe's hand relentlessly drove him forward, over fallen bodies, and a woman dropped right in front of him, face forward in the mud. Jess leaped over her.

Behind him, the screaming grew worse as people were caught in the closing gate, unable to retreat, jammed too tightly together to rush forward.

Jess was out into the mud and icy wind, with Wolfe right next to him. They were out.

Santi's men—so few left now—formed around them and pushed them forward. There was an awful keening shriek of metal as the gate pushed closed, through the bodies of those caught, louder than the screaming.

Jess didn't look back. He couldn't.

Santi drove them together in a defensive band. He had the Library flag out and slammed it to its full height above their heads. His soldiers were slapping their Library symbols back on their chests and on each other. Out here in the mud, nothing moved but them.

The screams and shouts from within the Oxford walls were growing faint.

"What have you done?"

Wolfe was standing right in front of him. Jess stared, uncomprehending, until he realized that Wolfe was looking down at the child in his arms.

The baby.

She was still alive and squirming. Somehow, amazingly, she'd survived. He had no idea how. He didn't know how *he'd* made it through. How any of them had.

"We can't take her," Wolfe said. His voice was tight and strained, his expression very bleak. "Put her down."

"Down?" The mud he was standing in was almost knee-deep. She'd sink without a trace. "Where?"

There was a party of Welsh soldiers running toward them across the muddy open ground. They were all armed. "Halt!" one of them shouted, and the men and women all came to a quick stop in the mud with their weapons trained on the Library party. "Surrender *anyone* not in your party! You have thirty seconds to comply!"

"Put her down," Wolfe said.

"I can't!"

"You must, Jess." His voice had gone soft. Gentle. "They'll kill us all if you don't. You're violating the accords."

Jess looked around for somewhere to leave the baby. There was nothing. Nothing that wasn't churned bloody mud. "I can't," he whispered. He felt ice-cold now, inside and out, and he couldn't stop shaking. "I can't just—"

"Fifteen seconds!"

Wolfe took the baby from Jess's arms and turned toward the Welsh soldiers. "Let me talk to General Warlow."

"Five seconds, Scholar! Put that down! Four! Three!"

Wolfe held up one hand to stop the count, walked to the churned, bloody mud outside of the gate. He put the child down on top of the body of a dead woman lying there. The child screamed and reached for him with chubby arms, and Wolfe hesitated, crouched over her. Jess couldn't see his face.

"Scholar!" the Welsh commander shouted. "Step back to your group! I want to see bracelets, every one of you, right now, or we shoot!"

One by one, the students held up their wrists. Jess numbly followed suit, but he couldn't look away from Wolfe, who still hadn't moved from where he was crouched by the child.

"Scholar!" That wasn't the Welsh. It was from inside the gate.

Wolfe grabbed the child and ran that way. There was a gap in the gate, because the metal doors were still jammed on the bodies. Despite the continued shudder and whine of the engine, it was still open a little.

Just enough.

Jess's cousin Frederick—bloody, wounded, and somehow still alive— was on the other side, stretching out his arms.

Wolfe gave him the girl. She barely fit through the gap.

"Get out however you can," Wolfe said. "Hurry. I'll keep them talking as long as I can."

Frederick backed away, turned, and ran.

There was a damp crack as the flesh and bones of the dead finally failed, and the gate slammed shut.

Wolfe spun toward the Welsh troops and held up his arm. The gold bracelet flashed, and to Jess's eyes, it almost looked like a warning, not a surrender. "Safe passage," Wolfe said. "Now."

The Welshman didn't look happy but gestured for Wolfe to follow, and led his troops back at a jog toward the Welsh lines.

Wounded, bloody, exhausted, Jess and his fellows struggled after, stumbling and slipping in the mud, clinging to one another for help and comfort. So few of Santi's men and women had made it, Jess realized. He'd never even learned their names. Santi was wounded, but he was still supporting one of his soldiers as they limped their way toward safety.

Good luck, Frederick, Jess thought. He hadn't expected his cousin to be their unlikely savior, or to take that little girl. Selflessness wasn't a Bright-well family trait. He hoped it wouldn't end up costing Frederick his life.

A shout went up from the Welsh lines; it was an eerie, savage sound, and Thomas lurched forward toward Wolfe. "What is that?" he asked. Wolfe kept moving, head down.

"Signal to attack," Dario panted when Wolfe didn't answer. "The assault's started."

They *were* coming, those lines of troops. The first wave was racing toward them in armored carriers, and for a moment Jess thought, horribly, that they would simply be run down, lost in the mud, but the vehicle heading for them changed its angle and charged past, throwing up mud head high to flop over them in a stinking wave. Inside the carrier, the Welsh soldiers were cheering.

Jess looked up to see a container arcing over their heads. Something bright and burning and eerily green within.

It fell inside the walls of Oxford.

And Oxford began to burn.

Beside Jess, Khalila burst into tears and hid her face in her hands. Glain stood stock-still, staring at the destruction as more ballista-fired bottles of Greek fire landed and bloomed into hideous, toxic life.

"Happy you're winning?" Jess said. He felt sick inside, and angry, and he needed to hit the only target in reach.

Her gaze fell to lock on his. She didn't say anything. She turned and flailed on through the mud.

Jess, having hurt her, felt even sicker than before.

He grimly followed, hearing the distant high wailing from inside the walls of Oxford as the slaughter continued.

EPHEMERA

Codex message from Scholar Christopher Wolfe to the Artifex Magnus.

Two students and twelve High Garda dead.

We were lucky. Luckier than you'd prefer, as I am still alive.

The Welsh have refused to provide us escort back to Aylesbury, and the roads are too dangerous with our losses. We will make our way instead to London.

If you ever wanted to prove that the Library is full of coldhearted bastards who value books above lives, we have done that for you.

Response from the Artifex Magnus to Christopher Wolfe.

I know someone warned you not to go back to Aylesbury. You're only delaying the inevitable, and this is a battle you won't win. I advise you to pick another.

Let the girl go to her fate, which, I assure you, is sealed; there is ample evidence from Scholar Tyler and other discovered correspondence that the postulant Hault is, in fact, an Obscurist. A fact that you most likely already knew. If I prove it, you know it will be the last inch of your rope.

Family connections won't save you a second time.

CHAPTER TEN

T he Welsh encampment was mostly empty, but there were still enough troops around to take them into custody as one by one the Library party stumbled in. At least that meant being taken inside a tent and out of the sleet; it felt like luxury, and as Jess sank down on the tarp-covered ground he began to realize just how cold he *really* was. His fingers were almost blue, and his shivering was constant. His clothes were soaked through and crackling with ice.

Morgan was pushed into place beside him. One of the Welsh soldiers came around with cups steaming with hot coffee, and Jess gulped it down so fast he hardly even felt the burn on his tongue. It helped steady him, and by the second cup he began to be more aware of those around him . . . like Morgan, who was still shivering. "Can we get a blanket?" Jess asked the man who'd delivered the coffee. "She's half frozen."

"So are you, by the looks," the man said. "Blankets on the way." His brisk, impartial kindness suddenly struck Jess hard, and all out of proportion. He gulped down more coffee to hide his gratitude.

Morgan was trembling so much the coffee sputtered in the cup as she tried to raise it to her lips. Jess reached over to steady it. That was a mistake. She flinched from his touch and slopped the hot liquid over both of them.

"Sorry," Jess said. "I was only trying to help."

"I can manage," she said, and tried again. This time she gulp down a mouthful with only a little lost over the sides. "Thank you."

"For what?" He hadn't, he thought, been any kind of a hero, or even particularly brave. He'd just desperately wanted out.

She looked away and hunched her shoulders, and somehow, in that gesture, he remembered her falling against him in that courtyard, as she'd realized just how alone she was. "For not dying, I suppose."

He didn't know how to answer that, so he didn't.

The Welsh soldier was back with an armload of blankets, and as Jess reached out for his, he winced from a sudden, lancing pain. Strange. He hadn't felt anything until that moment. He could see wounds on the others: a slashing cut on Dario's arm, an injured left wrist for Glain, and Khalila had a bullet hole in her arm, but she'd been lucky; it had missed bone and done only minor muscle damage.

Jess felt a strange twinge in his side. He twisted to look down, and went suddenly, weirdly faint. There was a hole. He hadn't even felt it, but from the looks of the wound, someone had tried to skewer him with a knife. It hurt.

There was blood. It was spreading fast.

"Jess!" He hadn't realized that he'd fallen until Morgan's hands were slapping his cheeks. "Jess, wake up—someone! He's bleeding!"

"I'm fine," Jess mumbled. He was aware that he wasn't, really. His head felt oddly stuffed, and he just wanted to rest. Close his eyes. As he grew warmer, the blood flowed faster, taking the pain away with it.

He was flat on his back now, with no sense of transition, and there were faces leaning toward him. They looked strange. Thomas looked *very* strange, all out of proportion, and Jess wanted to laugh but he couldn't quite manage it. Wolfe was next to him, too, and barking orders that made no sense, something about a surgeon. Someone needed a surgeon.

He blinked, and it was night. The lights were low, the heater still casting warmth. He was tucked onto a camp bed, wrapped in a thick pile of blankets, and when he clumsily tried to move, pain paralyzed him. He managed to lift up the covers with his left hand. He was almost bare beneath them, and a glaring white bandage wrapped tightly from his waist and up onto his ribs. "Oh," he said. "Right. I remember."

His head fell back against the pillow, and he heard someone stir nearby. It was Thomas, who sat up and leaned forward. "Stay still," his friend said. "Someone stabbed you. The only thing that kept you alive was the cold, Wolfe said."

"I know," Jess said. He felt oddly disconnected, still. "Someone gave me medicine."

"Dario is jealous. He only got bandages. You have narcotics."

"It doesn't feel like winning," Jess said. "Is everyone else all right?"

"You're our worst." Thomas's face shut down. "The worst who lived. You saw Portero?"

"I remember." Jess thought he'd never forget it. Any of it. Not Portero's killing, not the run for the gate, not the child in his arms that he'd had to give up. "You heard anything about my cousin?"

"Nothing. They're still fighting inside the city. Not many have managed to make it. Dario thinks the Welsh will declare victory soon and spare the survivors; they have made their point to the English king. They could have killed everyone."

Glain wasn't far away, and now she sat up, too. "Not like English hands aren't bloody," she said. "This started with the slaughter of the Welsh during the Glyndwr uprising. Men, women, children . . . cut down by the tens of thousands."

"So killing each other is—"

"Stop," Jess said wearily. "It doesn't matter why, or who, or how long it's been going on. We're the Library. Left our countries behind, remember? Neutral. Where's Wolfe?"

"Off with the Welsh general."

"And Morgan?"

"I'm here." He turned his head and saw Morgan, on a bed a few down. "You frightened us. What were you thinking, not telling anyone you'd been stabbed?"

"I didn't know I had been," he said. "It didn't hurt at the time."

She shook her head and stared up at the dark, fluttering fabric of the tent above their heads. He couldn't see much of her expression. What he did see looked angry.

"I told her to rest," Thomas said. "She hit me when I told her to leave you alone."

"I just wanted to see how he was doing. You were in my way," she said. "And you're too big to go around."

"She has a point," Jess said. He wanted to laugh, but he knew it would be too painful. The impulse faded quickly. "So we survived."

Thomas patted Jess on the shoulder, too hard. "Go back to sleep, English. Wolfe said we can rest a while before we leave. He wants to be sure you can make the trip safely first."

Oh God, Jess hadn't thought so far ahead, but yes, there was a long, uncomfortable drive ahead across bad roads to Aylesbury, and then he'd have to face the trauma of translation again . . . and how they were expected to do *that* wounded, and remembering what had happened to Izumi and Guillaume, he didn't know.

"What about the books?" he asked. "Did we get them out?"

Now Khalila sat up, too. She winced a little as she did, but waved Dario's helping hand away. "Most survived. Dario might have bled on the ones in his pack."

"It wasn't *my* blood."

"I will grant you the possibility and state instead that Dario's books were bloodstained."

"That's better. I wouldn't want you to think I was so careless. Not like this one, getting his liver sliced for no good reason." Dario's voice wasn't nearly as harsh as his words, and Jess raised his head a little to look at him. In the low lights, it was hard to tell the other boy's expression, but Jess saw the slight inclination of Dario's head. From him, it was as good as a bow. "Remember, losing one pint of blood's an accident. Losing two is carelessness."

Jess extended his right hand. It hurt, but he managed to hold it up, and after a moment, Dario got to his feet and walked over to grasp it. "We're still not friends," Jess said. "Thank God."

"Imagine *my* relief." Dario went back to his bunk—limped to it, actually. He wasn't in the best shape of his life, either. None of them were.

Thomas must have been thinking on the same lines, as he watched Dario's painful steps. "What will they tell our families about this?"

"Doesn't matter," Khalila said, and pulled the blankets closer. "My father will *never* let me go on, after this."

"Wolfe won't tell him anything. It's not in the Library's interest to be honest," Jess said.

"Being stabbed has made you cynical," she said. "And you used to be such an optimist."

"Bite your tongue," Jess said. He was fighting to keep his eyes open, and he badly wanted to drift off again, away from the pain.

In a moment, despite the angry, burning ache in his side, the drugs dropped him as gently as a feather down into the dark.

It was two more boring days of lying still, with one of the Welsh surgeons poking and prodding him three or four times a day, though not very sympathetically. He requested an interim personal journal, which the Medica station had at hand; for the first time, he genuinely missed having his old journal, the familiar feel and smell of it, the thickness of its pages. This new one felt flimsy and unsatisfying, but he wrote it all down anyway, all the insanity and anguish of Oxford.

Words didn't cover it, he felt, but he did his best.

The others, one by one, were allowed to roam free; not Jess. The news came to him through bulletins delivered by various friends—Thomas, most often, but also Khalila, Dario, Morgan, even Glain. (And he wasn't sure when he'd begun to think of *Glain* as a friend, but perhaps it had been the moment that they'd lost Portero and he'd realized that all their petty grievances meant so little.)

Oxford had been devastated, according to Thomas; the death toll was staggering. The Welsh had declared a general truce and allowed the survivors to stream out of the ruins to flee as refugees for a full day after the escape of Wolfe's party and the initial attack, but after that, there'd been no mercy given.

No way to know if Morgan's father was among the survivors.

Thomas spared him the details of what the city looked like now, and Jess was glad not to know. He didn't want to think about it, any of it. When he shut his eyes, he saw the woman shoving her baby into his arms. None of it made sense to him, and trying to make it fit together inside made him feel worse.

He asked after Frederick, but there was no news of his cousin, either. The death inside the city meant that if he hadn't managed to escape, there was almost no chance his body would be identified; the Welsh were bound to shovel the corpses into mass graves and be done with it. No, he'd get news of Frederick only if that flash criminal had managed to escape.

Morgan stuck close to the tent, though she was free to roam freely; he wondered if Wolfe had given her orders to watch him. Except for trips out to collect food and to the privies, she sat on her camp bed and read—from an original book, one that she must have kept out of the cache they'd rescued. Jess was restless and frustrated, and she turned her pages at a pace that Jess could only envy while he scribbled down more detail in the journal. It still felt stiff and awkward in his hands, and he didn't like the pen they'd given him. It dragged too slowly on the paper.

It all combined to make him irritable. "You don't have to stay here," he said. "I promise not to run away if you take your eyes off me."

"Do you?" She turned a page. "I'm not sure I believe you. You're not someone who understands his limits. I personally saw you tag so many books you almost fell unconscious."

"I'm much better."

"That's exactly the issue. You *think* you are. It makes you foolish."

"So Wolfe assigned you?"

"I didn't say that." She calmly turned another page. "Would you like something?"

"I'd like to get up and at least go outside. See something different."

"My home, still burning? The corpses of my neighbors? Is that different enough for you?" She pulled her knees up closer to her chest. "Just shut up."

God, that was clever of me, Jess thought. He didn't know how to apologize for being so clumsy, so unthinking. "What are you reading?" he asked instead.

Morgan said nothing for a moment, then passed over the book. It was *Inventio Fortunata,* written long ago by an Oxford monk. He'd held another hand copy of this book once. He'd read it the last night he'd slept in his family's home.

"I'm not going back to Alexandria," she said. "Wolfe says the Obscurist Magnus knows, and she's issued orders for my immediate return. I have to run. Maybe to London; I can lose myself there."

"Ask for my father, Callum Brightwell," Jess said. "Tell him I said to help you."

"He won't—"

"Betray you? Not to the Library." Jess handed the book back, and their fingers brushed. It wasn't much of a touch, but it meant something that she didn't pull away quickly.

It meant something that she tried to smile through the brightness of her tears.

Wolfe stepped into the tent then, and whatever she might have said was lost. His dark eyes darted from Jess to Morgan and back to rest on Jess. "We'll be leaving in the morning," he said. "The Welsh have abided by the covenants, but they're not happy about it, and they want us gone. You're not well enough, but we need to move before their patience is completely gone. We will head for London." Wolfe's gaze passed from Jess over to Morgan. "They're sending the Express for us."

The Alexandrian Express was a special train, one that used technology only the Library possessed; it was as fast as lightning and ran on special rails that only the Express could use. It was reserved, Jess had thought, for only the most senior officials of the Library on diplomatic missions, or for the personal use of the Archivist; he'd never seen it himself, and he didn't know anyone who had.

It wouldn't stop from the time it left London until it arrived in Alexandria. Morgan would have no chance to escape from it.

"You could let me go on the way to London," Morgan said.

"No," Wolfe said. "I can't risk it. I'm sorry."

"Why were you even helping her in the first place?" Jess asked. "If you're just going to turn your back now?"

"I told you, Brightwell. I keep secrets. But not at the risk of my own life. Not anymore."

Jess sat up and swung his legs off the bed. He felt weak and hot, but much better now that the effects of the painkilling morphine had passed. The wound didn't ache too badly, but when he tensed his stomach muscles to stand, it escalated quickly. He managed, though his legs didn't seem any too steady.

"And where do you imagine you're going?" Wolfe asked him.

"I'm tired of using a pot. I'm going to the privy."

"The Welsh accommodations are about what you'd expect for a battlefield. I don't know that you'll find it an improvement." Wolfe watched him but didn't offer him any support. Jess leaned against a tent pole for a moment, then grabbed a clean, plain shirt that someone had left for him and pulled it on. That hurt, too, and required another pause for breath. A long one.

"You'll never make it on your own," Morgan said. She stood up. "I'll go."

"To the privies and back," Wolfe said. "Any deviations and the alarm sounds. And you know what happens then."

"You find me," she said. "I know."

Jess listened to that with total incomprehension and couldn't form the question before Wolfe stalked away, out of the tent. He turned his gaze on Morgan.

She shrugged. "I tried to run," she said. "While you were drugged. I got outside the camp before I was caught by the Welsh, and if Thomas hadn't come to help . . . it might not have gone well for me. It caused an incident."

"An incident?"

"The Welsh general demanded that Wolfe hand me over for punishment or give up Library neutrality. Wolfe compromised." She held up her wrist, and instead of the temporary Library bracelet, she was wearing something Jess recognized: two loops of gold wire, with the Library symbol on a seal in the middle. They were normally used as restraints across two wrists, but Wolfe had used it just on the one for her.

It looked like jewelry, but it wasn't. It was a tracking device. The same kind Jess had used to follow Santi in Alexandria.

"He knows where I go now," she said. "And if I try to leave. For my *safety*." Morgan came to Jess's side and took his left arm in a firm grip. "Lean on me," she said. "And watch your footing. It's still a mess out there."

It was. The rain had stopped, but the skies remained as heavy and gray as iron. The Welsh had put down boards in the thick mud, but even those slipped unsteadily around and were hardly broad enough for him and Morgan to walk together. Jess concentrated on the difficult job of placing his feet, one step at a time, and his whole body shook with effort by the time he'd reached the privy tent.

He pulled loose from her. Her bracelet was making a ringing sound now, low but continuous. A warning. She was approaching the edge of her allowed distance. "I can go alone," he said, and promptly stumbled when he tried.

She sighed and grabbed him as he lurched to one side, righted him, and shook her head. "Are all Londoners this stubborn?"

"I'm the soul of reason. Comparatively."

"I'd feel right at home there." She pulled back the flap and made a retching sound at the smell. "It's as lovely as last time."

"I really can do this myself," he told her. "Go on."

"And if you fall into the privy, it'll be my fault," she said. "At least let me help you onto the seat."

"No." He stared at her until she shrugged and dropped his arm. "Go on. Outside."

She left the tent, and he immediately wondered if he really *could* do this alone; he felt better, but the walk had taken it out of him. *Grit it up,* he told himself. He could hear his father's voice echoing in it. *Do for yourself; don't let anybody do it for you. Only way to stay strong.*

So he managed. Somehow. It wasn't the most pleasant experience, or the most painless, but just controlling his own body, after feeling mortally helpless, was good for his soul. He made it to the flap of the tent and expected to find Morgan waiting outside.

She wasn't there.

The camp was a busy place, with uniformed Welsh soldiers crisscrossing between tents and armored carriers grinding past through the mud, but she couldn't have blended in *that* well. Morgan was wearing a Library-gold shirt and pants and thick black boots. She'd stand out against the Welsh colors.

Not my responsibility to watch out for her, he told himself. *And besides, she has on a tracker. If she makes another run for it, they'll find her without my help.*

Convincing arguments, but he sighed and limped off in search of her anyway.

She hadn't gone far, and he spotted her as he came around the corner of the privy tent; she was standing still and looking off in the distance.

"This is as far as I can go," she told him.

"What are you doing?"

She didn't answer. He followed her gaze, and the first thing that struck him was the sullen, smoking glow of what had been the city of Oxford. The walls were broken, tumbled ruins; tongues of flames still licked the sky. No screaming now. Just the stillness of destruction.

The next thing that caught his attention were the Welsh troops massed outside the walls. They were loading something into carriers. He didn't say anything, and neither did Morgan. They watched as the carriage chuffed and clanked across the mud, and passed them.

It was filled with the dead. Not Welsh dead; none of the bodies wore those uniforms. These were dead civilians, headed for a shared grave.

"I don't know where my father is," Morgan said quietly. "If he's dead, I'll never be sure."

She turned and walked back toward the tent. Jess followed. She didn't slow for him, and he panted and sweated as he caught up. When he slipped and would have gone down in the mud, Morgan took his arm and steadied him. He didn't speak. Neither did she, all the way back to the tent.

"You didn't say you were sorry," she said.

Jess looked up and found her gaze full on him; the shock of those eyes, so intently focused, was like a lightning strike. She could outstare Wolfe, if she tried. "What?"

"Most people would have, you know. Said they were sorry about my home. My father. You didn't. Why not?"

He shrugged a little. It hurt. "What's the point? Does my being sorry for you make you feel better?"

"No," she said, and blinked away tears. "Nothing makes me feel better. But thank you for being honest about not caring."

"I never said I didn't care."

He left her to think about that, went inside, and collapsed back on his bed with sweaty relief.

Morgan said nothing else to him that day. She remained quiet while his classmates helped him to the Welsh mess tent, where he ate his first solid meal—tasteless, even if an improvement over the weak broth he'd been enduring. But it felt good to be sitting at a table with his fellows again. They were quiet, and he could tell that the time for idle jokes was past, at least for now. They were all healing, still.

Khalila and Dario held hands.

Wolfe sat with Santi at another table, and the two were in deep conversation. Serious conversation, it seemed.

Jess felt oddly divorced from it all, even as he was in the middle of it. Delayed shock, he supposed. Slow recovery. He found himself looking more at Morgan than anyone else—Morgan, who wasn't really one of them anymore. Morgan, who'd either slip away before London or be dragged to the Iron Tower once they got to Alexandria. Wolfe wasn't protecting her now.

I can get Brendan to hide her. Put her on a ship, away from here. Maybe to America. Jess wondered what price his brother would charge him for that and decided that it didn't matter.

Wolfe suddenly nodded at something Santi said, and stood up. He walked over to their table. The students' laughter and conversation died a quick, strangled death.

"I wanted to tell you that you've done well. All of you." Wolfe hesitated, then fixed his gaze on Jess as he continued. "I also want to make something clear. You all saw a harsh illustration of why it can be difficult to do this job. We can't take anyone from the city—child, family member, *no one*. The moment we stopped being neutral, we would have been dead. We had no choice but to leave the child Brightwell took."

"So you did it for the best reasons," Jess said. "Is that it?"

"I did it to save us," Wolfe replied. "And to preserve the tradition of neutrality of the Library."

"Neutrality? They tried to *kill* us in Oxford!"

"Desperate people do desperate things. You cannot be one of them. You must be better."

"You wanted me to leave her in the mud to drown," Jess said. "I don't call that *better*. The fact you changed your mind doesn't make me forget it."

Wolfe held his stare for a long moment, then turned and walked back to join Santi.

The others all looked at Jess, with varying degrees of alarm. Khalila leaned forward. "Jess . . ."

"There are six of us left now," he said. "Six. Wolfe's giving six placements. He's not going to fail me now. And if he does, I don't care."

EPHEMERA

Text of a private paper correspondence between Frederick Brightwell and his uncle Callum Brightwell, written in a family code for safety and decoded to read:

Safely out of Oxford with all the goods, though can't say much for the state of my men. Going to have to hire fresh once I get to the new setup in the north; I'm not staying anywhere near the damned Welsh, so don't try and bribe me into it. One close brush with them was enough, and I've got the still-healing scars to prove it.

On to family business: I saw Jess in Oxford. Boy's grown up well; I should say man, rather, because he's carrying himself more like one, and no coward, either, though coming from our family stock I'd not expect so. Seems comfortable with his new Library friends. Here's hoping he doesn't go native on you and turn his coat to Egyptian gold. Be quite the laugh on you if he did, wouldn't it?

Speaking of laughs, that fierce Scholar fellow who ran the show knew his goods, all right. He let Jess trade me a fine, rare copy of Aristotle's On Dreams. Would have been worth enough to ransom a half dozen kings under normal circumstances, but these weren't, and he didn't hesitate to give it up to buy my help for his escape.

More family news: I've become a father. Adopted a girl I took out of Oxford, just a tadpole of a thing. I know, you don't need to tell me about sentimentality. Maybe I'm just thinking of the future. Always good to have more kids to take on the trade, eh?

I'll write when I set up the new digs in Yorkshire. Until then, I remain faithfully yours,

Frederick

CHAPTER ELEVEN

The High Garda carriers clanked them away from the ruins of Oxford. It was a grim ride for Jess, even though he was given one of the padded front seats. It didn't help that he felt isolated from his friends, who were all in the back of the carrier.

What made it worse was that he found himself riding with Wolfe and Santi. He didn't want to talk to Wolfe. His somewhat irrational anger had gone from a boil to a simmer, but it was still on the stove.

"You're quiet," Captain Santi said after about an hour of bone-jarring progress. Jess didn't respond. He assumed Santi was talking to Wolfe. "I mean you, Brightwell. Wolfe's never a chatterbox when he's on duty."

"I took a pain pill," he said, quite truthfully. Half of one, not a whole one, but enough to file the edges off the knife he could still feel sawing at his liver.

"Is it working?"

"Not enough."

"That would explain the sullen silence," Wolfe said.

"Sullen?" Jess let the anger out in half a shout, and twisted in his seat to face him, never mind the burst of pain that hissed up and down his side. "Don't I have enough reasons yet? You used me, you bastard!"

Wolfe seemed completely unruffled. "Of course I did. I knew your

244 · RACHEL CAINE

family were criminals. I also knew that one of your fellow students was a Burner agent."

Jess opened his mouth and couldn't find anything to say. Wolfe waited. The question finally came down to, "Who?"

"It no longer matters, but you see why knowing so much is important. Your family business is of concern to me only as a very relative issue."

Burner. Jess tried to fit that on each one of his classmates, but he couldn't. "Portero?" he finally guessed.

"You only say so because you didn't care for him much. Not Portero, poor devil."

"Not Morgan."

"No. Morgan's father became a Burner after she left him."

"But—" Jess suddenly remember that long-back conversation in the study of the Ptolemy House, when Dario had tormented Guillaume with information about his long-dead Burner ancestor. "Guillaume." Had *Dario* known? Or had it just been a lucky thrust? He swallowed hard. "Was it deliberate, then? That translation accident?"

Wolfe didn't answer for a moment, and then he said, "It was either careless or immensely stupid. My plan was to allow young Danton to proceed and track his contacts. It would have given us a wealth of information. But I may have been overruled."

"That's all you have to say? Someone in the Library had him killed, and you *may have been overruled*?"

"If you're wise, that's all you'll say of it, too," Santi broke in. "Wolfe. Are you sure you should be telling him this?"

"Yes," Wolfe said. "Because I want him to understand the danger in which he stands. Because this time a Burner agent was eliminated. The son of a book smuggler might be an equally tempting target the next time someone wants to make a point."

"You want me to quit and go home."

"I want you to feel the knife at the back of your neck, because it will always be there. And I won't always be able to protect you."

Jess sank back against the seat. His body felt raw and full of aches, and though they were heading for London, he no longer felt that might be safety. "I suppose you want me to apologize for calling you a bastard."

"No need," Santi said. "You should hear what his *friends* call him."

"I have friends?" Wolfe said.

"They don't care to admit it in public."

"Did it ever occur to you that I might not care to admit to them, either?"

Santi cast him an odd look, which Wolfe avoided to stare out toward the road. They were almost to the train depot, where they'd catch the carriage on to London.

Jess said, "You put restraints on Morgan."

"Yes," Wolfe said.

"We're out of the Welsh camp. When are you going to take them off?"

Wolfe braced himself against a particularly hard jolt. "I'm not."

"Then I won't apologize for calling you a bastard. Since you well deserve it."

"Brightwell," Santi said, in a quietly warning voice, but Wolfe held up a hand to stop him.

"He's right. I am," he said. "In far more ways than I hope you'll ever know, Postulant. But believe me when I tell you that I am on the side of my students. Always."

Jess didn't.

There was no chance for Morgan to escape before they reached London.

But she tried anyway. And they caught her.

The train into London was almost a luxury, after the kidney-rattling progress of their Library transportation, and Jess found himself nap-ping, lulled by the clacking wheels. It felt like he imagined it would feel to fly. But they arrived quickly, and falling back into harsh, hurting reality was less pleasant, especially the long underground tunnel from King's Cross to St. Pancras, and then to the main boarding area. It was all, he began to realize, surprisingly empty. London Garda blocked each tunnel they passed, each entrance, and there was not a single fellow traveler in sight. Once they'd mounted the steps, he thought that he'd never seen the vast arc of St. Pancras so empty . . . No, no, he *had*. The day that he'd left for the Library.

The day the Burner had incinerated himself.

That made Jess extremely uneasy, and he looked toward the spot where the smear of the Burner's suicide had been. No sign of it now. The floor was clean, and—perhaps fittingly—a new massive bronze statue had been added of two librarians standing back-to-back, male and female, jointly holding a book above their heads like a torch. The base was inscribed all around with bas-reliefs of the locations of English daughter libraries, and with a pang, Jess recognized the Bodleian Library in Oxford. Most likely gone now.

Being here made him feel disoriented, and unexpectedly sad, as if he'd visited his childhood home and found it razed to the ground.

"Why is no one here?" Khalila asked Wolfe. "Isn't this one of the busiest stations in England?"

"It is," he said. "But they've been asked to keep it clear."

"For us," Santi said. "In case word's traveled. We're still carrying valuable books with us."

True, and Jess thought his father would have been very pleased to have seeded the King's Cross station with thieves and roughnecks if he could have gotten away with a volume or two from the Library's grasp. But of course, Wolfe would have thought of that. Hence their exclusive passage.

Morgan was next to Jess, and the back of her hand brushed his—by accident, he thought, but then he glanced at her and realized that she was still trying to think of a way out. Yes, of course she was. She'd counted on this as being her opportunity to slip away, but there was no crowd here. No way to lose herself.

She was just as trapped here, in the middle of a vast, sprawling city, as she had been inside an army's camp.

He took her hand and squeezed it, and she smiled a little. "Don't panic," he said, with his lips close to her hair. It brushed like silk against his cheek. "There'll be another chance. There always is."

Wolfe led them through a vacant, echoing tunnel that seemed to go on forever. The arched form began to seem to Jess like a throat, swallowing them whole, with the white tile gleaming like a lining of unnatural teeth. He felt smothered and—suddenly—as filthy as he actually was. He longed for a hot shower to wash the grime and stink of Oxford away, and looking at his companions (even Wolfe, who had managed to clean himself up) he could tell they all felt the same. They needed rest.

But the tunnel stretched on, and he had to put every ounce of concentration into the long, long walk.

It finally widened into a larger area that branched off into other tunnels, all empty; the Garda were present in force here as well, all the way up a short flight of steps and around a right turn through yet another set of archways.

And then they were in a different place altogether. The ornate brickwork on the left was for a booking office, with cathedral-window ticket booths. No one manned them.

"Sir," a man dressed in an extra-sharp London Garda uniform said, and pointed the way with an arm as straight as a ruler. "Up there and to the right. Your train's waiting."

Thank God, Jess thought, because he didn't think he could bear much more walking. His side felt as if it had been dipped in acid.

They rounded the corner, and there sat the Alexandrian Express.

It was gold. Not *real* gold, of course, though it had the sheen of it;

some kind of paint that streaked brilliant lines from the gold-washed engine down the sides of the sleek, rounded carriages. It looked fast. Very fast. Even the engine had the shape of something predatory and quick. It was hissing ever so slightly, but if it was steam-powered, it lacked the billowing white clouds Jess was used to seeing on the more square, serviceable trains that were common throughout the world.

There were only four carriages attached to this engine. Wolfe headed for the first, but he stopped by the side and waited for them all to gather. It didn't take long.

"The sensors will read your bracelets," he said. "I'll enter the code that will allow you aboard. There is a lounge, dining car, and bedroom carriages. Your names are on the doors. Each compartment has its own shower, toilet, and bed."

"Dinner?" Dario asked.

"Served in two hours. Our journey will carry us overnight. We'll arrive in Alexandria by noon tomorrow."

That seemed impossibly fast, and Jess struggled to calculate the speed at which they'd have to run, but his mind was as exhausted as his body, and anyway, he'd never been especially clever at math. He didn't even know the route, really.

But Thomas did, and he said, in a hushed voice, "We will move at *four hundred eighty kilometers per hour.*"

"You'll hardly notice, unless you look out the windows. If you do, I advise you to look to the horizon to avoid dizziness." Wolfe slapped a hand on a button that was hardly visible on the side of the carriage, and an equally disguised door slid open with hardly a sound. "As you enter, pause until you hear the chime. If you do *not* hear a chime, hold still."

"Or what happens?" Jess asked.

"It's the Archivist Magister's personal conveyance; given that, I assure you, you don't want to know."

Somehow, after that, no one wanted to go first, so with a sigh, Jess stepped forward and paused in the doorway. A pleasant chime sounded, and he limped forward, into a world where everything was right and orderly and beautiful, and in which he felt completely out of place. A graceful young lady in a perfectly tailored Library uniform was standing a few feet away, and she gave him a smile that made him almost believe he was welcome.

"This way, Mr. Brightwell," she said. "I expect you'll want to clean up first before you enjoy the other amenities."

He couldn't stop a bleak laugh. "I expect," he said, and limped after her down the clean little aisle, past tables and chairs, through an elegant dining car, and then into another hallway with gleaming wood all along one rounded side. She paused three doors down and opened one that had a blank inserted in it that had his name written in exquisite cursive.

"Thanks . . . What's your name?" he asked, as he edged inside. Her smile took on a slightly brittle quality.

"It's Gretel, sir. Should you need anything, please ring the bell. You'll find soap and toiletries in the shower for you."

Gretel was pretty, but he could read the revulsion in her hiding just beneath the surface. He didn't blame her. She must see powerful people here. Catering to some half-maimed, filthy students of no real repute must have been beneath her.

He shut the door and leaned against it for a moment, then opened his eyes and looked around. The bed was soft and tempting, but he needed cleaning far worse. The muck caked in his hair was driving him mad.

Though the Welsh doctor had assured him the waterproofing on his wounds would hold, and the healing had already advanced quite far, he was careful in the shower. The violent blue/black bruises circling his side and back, he realized, looked so frightful that if elegant Gretel had seen them, she'd have run screaming. The bruises seemed far worse than the relatively small stab wound.

The posh train had robes, thick, fluffy ones, and once he was clean he donned one and stretched out on top of the bed. The cool air drifted over him, and he felt, for the first time, as if he could really rest.

It didn't occur to him to lock the door.

He fell asleep, predictably enough, and woke up when his door clapped open with too much energy, and Morgan stepped inside to say, "I'm told to bring you to dinner— Oh. Sorry."

"No, it's all right," he said, and tried to sit up, but the brief nap had stiffened his sore muscles, and it was a clumsy process. He grabbed at the robe to keep it more or less closed. It was mostly a failed attempt, and it exposed the livid black-and-blue of his side. She took in a breath and came to help him rise. He yanked the robe back together and tied it shut.

"Don't apologize," she said. "I've seen worse."

"You mean the bruises, I hope."

"What else would I be talking about?" She sat next to him in quiet harmony for a moment. She'd washed herself, too; her brown hair flowed loose, and it crackled with energy when she pushed it back with one hand. "I won't go to the Iron Tower, Jess. I'm not asking you to help me, because . . . because I know they won't stop coming for me, and I can't put you in the middle. But I wanted you to know that I'll do whatever I have to do."

"The train's already moving," he said. "You'd kill yourself trying to escape."

"I know that."

"Once you get to Alexandria, you'll never get out of that tower."

"I know that, too."

"So?" She shrugged. Wasn't looking at him. He felt sick. "Tell me you're not thinking of killing yourself. Just tell me that much."

She turned and met his eyes. "I'm not thinking of killing myself."

He'd told her that she ought to become a better liar, and he was afraid that she'd taken his advice, because he couldn't tell what she was thinking at all.

"Hand me my clothes," he said. "I'm starving."

Dinner was a quiet affair, since he and Morgan were the only ones left who hadn't ordered; they sat together, and both had beefsteak. He needed it. He'd lost so much blood that he craved red meat like oxygen.

They ate without much conversation, though Morgan's golden brown gaze kept skimming up and over him. They didn't speak much, but then, there wasn't a lot of conversation among the other few left in the dining car, either. They were all too tired, he thought. Too relieved to still be alive.

When they were alone, and his plate neraly empty, he said, "Do you think Wolfe will help you?"

"No," Morgan said. "He left the tracker on." She held up her wrist. The restraints delicately crisscrossed there, with the seal in the middle, and it did look like an ornament.

"Maybe he forgot."

She didn't dignify that with an answer as she forked more steak into her mouth.

"All right, maybe he didn't forget. Check and mate."

"I'm glad you think my life is a game."

"It is, though. Winning, losing, doesn't matter. You can't give up, because whether you win or lose, you just set up the board and keep playing."

She let out an annoyed rush of breath. "Stop. You're very bad at this."

"At what?"

"Trying to comfort me."

"I wasn't," he said. "You deserve better than that."

"I'm just tired," she said. "You don't understand how *tired* I am." He saw something flicker in her eyes, spark, and flare . . . and go out. She started to get up.

"Wait. Morgan, *wait*. Don't. You can survive this."

"I know I can," she said. "That's not the problem."

"Then tell me what is."

She glared at him. "You! Your stupid *questions!*" She slid her chair back and walked away toward the bedroom carriages. He got up, quickly.

Glossy Gretel stepped in his way, with her manufactured smile. She offered him a menu. "Dessert, Mr. Brightwell? I recommend the sticky toffee pudding."

"Then you should have some," he said, and moved her out of his way.

Morgan was already out of sight.

She wasn't in her bedroom in the carriage. He knocked, and when she didn't answer, he tried the door. It was open. There was no sign of her, except for the disturbed sheets on the bed. He put his hand on them. They were cold.

She hadn't come back.

He tried all the other rooms. One by one, his friends answered. They hadn't seen her. *I have to tell Wolfe,* he thought. The idea that Morgan might do something drastic, that he might stand by and let it happen . . . He couldn't face that.

Wolfe didn't answer his knock, either, and when Jess tried the knob, it also swung open.

Empty.

He slammed the cabin door.

"Looking for something?" Santi was leaning out the doorway of the next cabin down, stripped to the waist.

"I need to find Scholar Wolfe—" Jess's words died in his mouth, because behind Santi, Scholar Wolfe stepped out of Santi's cabin door. Also half-dressed. Jess's brain went blank as all his assumptions tumbled and tried to fit together again.

Santi just looked amused. Wolfe . . . looked like Wolfe. Annoyed and impatient. He pulled a white shirt on over his head. "Well?" he said. "You've found me. Speak."

"I can't find Morgan," Jess said.

"You couldn't find *me*, and I was one door down. What business is it of yours where she is? She can't leave the train."

Jess sucked in a deep breath and said, "She's not going to let you just hand her over to the Obscurists, either. She told me that."

He wasn't saying what he was afraid of, but Wolfe didn't miss it, either. He froze for a second, then turned and grabbed his Codex. He flipped pages. "Her tracker is still active," he said. "Still on the train."

"Then where is she?"

"In the back." Wolfe tossed Santi a shirt. "Come on."

"She can't get out. It's suicide."

"She's an Obscurist; she can get out," Wolfe said. "And I hope to God it's not."

Jess followed them as the two men moved through the rest of the carriage. Santi turned on him at the door to the next section. "No," he said. "Go back. We'll find her."

"I want to—"

"Jess." Santi grabbed him by the shoulders and held his gaze. "Just go back. All right? I promise to tell you."

Before he could tell Santi to go to hell, the man stepped back and slammed the compartment door between them. Jess grabbed for the knob.

It felt like grabbing a sharp knife, and he was knocked back as if something invisible had punched him hard in the chest. He couldn't get his breath. When his eyes cleared again, he saw that the entire door pulsed red, like a beating heart.

He was locked out. The more he battered at the door, the more he shouted, the less it helped; Dario came stumbling out of his room, and Thomas, and Khalila. Glain. He didn't answer any of their questions.

Gretel finally came, still sleek and perfectly composed, and pushed her way through to where Jess stood. "Sir," she said, "that area is secured. You can't enter."

"Open it."

"Perhaps you should go back to your cabin—"

"Open it!" When she didn't, he grabbed for her wrist, pulled her forward, and put her hand on the compartment door.

The red warning light continued to flash. Gretel pulled free.

"I can't," she said. "Only the highest-ranking person on the train can open it now. Scholar Wolfe."

Jess wanted to hit her, but that wouldn't do any good, either, and so he hit the door again. Hard. The material looked like wood, but it felt like steel.

"Jess!" Thomas grabbed his arms and held him back. "Stop! What's wrong with you?"

"Morgan," Jess panted. "Morgan's in there. She's—"

The red light stopped pulsing, and the door's handle turned.

Wolfe and Santi stepped through. One look at their faces, and Jess knew.

Santi was holding a thin gold figure eight of wire, sealed in the middle. Jess stared at it until his eyes ached.

"She managed to open one of the doors," Wolfe said quietly. "She left this behind."

"She *jumped*?" Khalila's voice sounded puzzled, as if she couldn't work it out. "But how could she survive at this speed? We're going so . . . so fast . . ."

Jess heard the change in her voice, the sudden tremor, as it hit her. Hit them all.

"I'm sorry," Wolfe said again.

"You're *sorry*." Glain's voice sounded icy with contempt. "Again."

Jess didn't turn to look, but he heard her walk away and slam her cabin door. Khalila had turned away, and Jess thought that she'd found comfort, again, in Dario's arms.

Thomas tried to talk to him. Jess just pushed past him.

Reset the board and keep playing.

He wanted to laugh at himself for being so stupid. He wanted to scream until his throat bled.

As he opened the door of his cabin, he heard Wolfe tell Santi, "Make sure he's all right. He'll take it better from you."

Wolfe was wrong about that. Jess wouldn't take it from anyone. He'd had enough of these people. All of them.

Before Santi could get to him, he stepped inside and shut the door, then locked it.

It was dark inside, but he didn't want lights. He wanted the black. The silence. He remembered where the bed was, on his left, and walked over to sink down on it.

"Jess."

It was barely a whisper, and for a second he thought it was in his head. That he'd gone that mad, that he was imagining her voice now.

"Jess."

Something inside him went very, very still. He wasn't imagining it. He couldn't be. "Morgan?"

"I tried to make them think I jumped," she whispered. She was sitting on the bed, curled up in the corner. He could feel the warmth of her now. Smell the lavender of the soap she'd used in the shower. "Did it work?"

The relief came in a rush, and hard on the heels of it, the grim understanding. She'd used him. She'd led a trail for him, hinted at ending it all, pointed him at Wolfe to deliver the message. "Oh yes. Worked a treat. They think you're a smear of blood on the tracks. So did I."

"Jess—"

"How'd you get the restraints off?"

"It took some time, but I figured out how to get into the formula," she said. "The door wasn't hard, once I knew how to do that."

"And then you hid the one place you knew I wouldn't come looking for you. You needed me to be desperate so Wolfe would believe it. You wanted me to think you were dead."

"Jess!"

"It's all right," he said. He knew she'd believe *him*, because he was a very good liar. "You can stay here. Once we're all off the train, you can find some way off. Just keep running. You must be good at it by now." He swallowed hard and said exactly what had hurt him the most. "You used me."

"Jess!"

He stopped. He sat in silence, in the dark, and listened to her breath. It sounded fast, raw, and wounded. When her hand touched him, he flinched, as if she'd burned him. He shut his eyes, like a scared child in the dark, trying to shut her out, but he already knew he couldn't do it, no matter how much he wanted.

It had hurt so much when he'd thought she was gone, and so much more when he realized how she'd played him for a fool.

But he wanted her to touch him so badly his whole body ached for it. Stupid, *stupid*, because he shouldn't feel that way. She'd done the same thing to him every other person he'd begun to care about in his life had done: used him for their own purposes. His da, running him on the streets. His brother, using him as cover. He'd had to trade a book to his cousin for his life. Even Wolfe had only really wanted him for his family connections.

Somehow, he hadn't expected it from her. Should have, though. He should hate her. He should want to walk away. *Why can't I walk away from her?*

Her fingers touched his cheek and traced warmth on his skin. Behind his eyes, gold flashes sparked and flared and spun, and he felt his heart running fast, like an animal trying to escape.

"I'm sorry for doing that to you," she whispered, and she was so close now he felt her breath on his neck. "I'm so sorry."

When she kissed him, it felt like an endless, weightless fall. Her lips warmed and softened and parted, and he got lost in the taste of her mouth, darkly spicy and sweet. His blood was thundering through his veins, and all he wanted, all he *needed*, was to touch more of her.

It was so dark, and so bright, and he knew it was wrong.

Somehow, he pulled back from the drowning sensation of her mouth and sat back. He felt her start to reach out for him, but her fingers fell away as they brushed his shirt.

"I'm sorry," she said again, and he could tell that she was crying now, a broken sound. "I had to, Jess. Please don't blame me for it. I want to—I want to stay, but I can't go back. I can't be locked away. You can't want that for me."

He didn't. God help him.

"You can stay," he said. "I won't tell them."

He didn't speak again. He stripped off his boots and stretched out on his bed, fully clothed. He left room for her. After a long moment, she carefully laid herself down on her side behind him, feverishly warm but not touching him at all until she reached out and put a hand on his arm.

"Thank you," she whispered.

He said nothing. He didn't sleep for a long time, long after he heard her breathing change, slow, relax. Long after her body shifted and pressed against his.

Then, finally, he shut his eyes and let himself drift away.

It was still ink dark, and Morgan was curled against him, when he opened his eyes and tested himself. *This might be a dream. Just one of those dreams that make things so much worse when you wake up and find out she's dead and this was all just your mind playing tricks.*

But his side ached like he'd drenched it in Greek fire, and that, more than anything else, convinced him that he hadn't just dreamed it. He'd moved in his sleep and was now on his back. Morgan's hair had spilled heavy over his chest, and he breathed in the scent of it. His hand stroked slowly down her arm, and he felt her wake up. It felt comfortable . . . strange, but comfortable.

And a hateful little voice whispered deep inside that she'd set him to trick Wolfe and she was doing the same thing now. Making him believe something that couldn't be true. Making him believe she cared. *Doesn't matter,* he told that part of him. *If she doesn't end up with a collar on her neck, locked in a tower, it doesn't matter how much she lies to me. It's all that matters. She should be free, whatever it costs.*

He felt a sudden odd lurch run through the metal around them. Then another one.

Morgan raised her head. "Something's wrong," she said. "Did you feel—"

The train screamed, and everything began to slide.

A red light flashed on, off, on, and in the light Jess saw that things were moving inside the cabin, moving as if gravity had stopped. Every flash of the light, the things were in a different spot, but he couldn't really feel the motion anymore.

And then it was nothing *but* motion. He was weightless, tumbling off the bed and slamming into the wall, and he had to bite back a scream as pain sheeted through him. Morgan fell next to him and braced herself with outstretched arms above his head to keep from sliding into him as the train continued to shriek.

Not the train. The brakes, Jess realized. A scream of burning metals that were never meant to burn together like this, at this speed. The train lurched, let go, lurched again. He could hear shouts from other rooms now.

With one more massive jolt, the train squealed to a halt, and he coughed as he caught a breath of acrid smoke. Something was burning underneath.

He turned his head to look for Morgan, but it had gone dark again and he couldn't see her, but her warmth was still beside him. He could hear her gasp for breath, and cough on it. "Are you all right?"

"Yes," she said. "We stopped."

The Alexandrian Express never stopped.

One of the glows flickered on above the bed, and for the first time, Jess saw her. She looked frantic and grim.

"Why did we stop?" Morgan handed him the heavy, still-bloodstained boots he'd worn in Oxford.

"No idea." He jammed his feet into them. She retrieved her shoes from the corner, and was just snapping the catches shut when the train jerked hard, again, and it was good that he was sitting on the edge of the bed now and braced, because it might have thrown him even more violently than before. Morgan slid forward, and he grabbed her around the waist to brace her. She sent him a quick, all-too-fleeting smile. "Stay here. Stay out of sight. They still think you're dead, so whatever you do, don't let them see you."

She leaned her forehead against his for an instant. "Take care of yourself, Jess. Please. *Please.*"

He knew she was telling him good-bye. This was her chance. Her chance to disappear into the dark outside this train, to find a safe haven somewhere far away where the Library would never find her.

He wanted to go with her. It was a nice dream, and he let himself have it for the length of the kiss that followed, fierce and sweet and promising things that he knew would never be.

Kisses could lie as well as words.

He turned the light off again on his way out the door.

EPHEMERA

**Ciphered message sent via Codex. Sender and recipient
both erased in a manner that indicates tampering from
within the Library.**

*The Alexandrian Express departs soon from London. Wolfe is on board.
Take him alive and he will answer all your questions.*

**Handwritten message from the Artifex Magnus to the
Archivist, sealed and sent to the Black Archives. Marked
for immediate disposal.**

*All the pieces are in place. Wolfe is on the train; you were right that he
would try to protect the girl. It's a pity about her. We could have used another powerful Obscurist, but she was clearly going to be hard to make
useful. All that's left is to blame the Burners.*

*They've been told where to find the prize, and they will be in place. With
any luck, they will all be destroyed.*

*I hope you know what you're doing, crossing the Obscurist Magnus in
this; it's not just the girl she's losing, after all. She might never forgive you.
Or me.*

CHAPTER TWELVE

I f the Alexandrian Express hadn't been the best, most advanced piece of machinery in the world, built to carry no less than the Archivist Magister, they likely would have all been dead. Jess had said it himself: *nothing but a smear of blood on the tracks.* As it was, the train looked oddly twisted out of true, and he could feel the engines laboring unsteadily under the corridor floor. Jess looked out the windows as he stepped out of his room, but it was dead of night outside, nothing visible but hills and trees.

Dario emerged at almost the same moment. He had put on his boots and pants, but he'd never gotten to his shirt. It made him look even more piratical, as did the gun in his hand.

"Burners?" Dario asked. Jess shook his head because he didn't know, although it was a decent guess. "Where's your gun?"

"I turned over my pack. It should be in the rear of the train with the rest."

"Good thing for you *I* kept a gun, then," Dario said, and grinned. He seemed to *love* this, which made Jess want to hit him very hard. "Come on, let's make sure the others are all right."

A door opened on Jess's left. It was Khalila, who'd either taken the time to put on her headscarf or hadn't yet removed it. She seemed calm and unhurt, and like Dario, she held a gun. *Was I the only one not to stay armed?* Jess thought.

Thomas, who came pelting through the doors that separated the cars, looked rumpled and unkempt; he was also unarmed, which made Jess feel a little less foolish. "All okay?" he asked. They nodded. "Glain has hit her head. Wolfe is seeing to her, but he told me to take you all to the lounge. Gretel says it is the most secure place."

That seemed simple enough, until Dario turned to head in that direction, and the door in front of him opened to reveal a stranger—no Library uniform, and the man was armed with a gun of his own.

"Stop!" Dario shouted. The man—the Burner, Jess assumed—did, but only for an instant. He lunged forward, low and fast, and Dario's shot went wild.

Khalila's did not. She braced herself, aimed, and hit the Burner with one shot, right in the chest. The sound was shockingly loud in the enclosed space, loud enough to set up a ringing like bells in Jess's deadened ears.

Khalila calmly walked over to the man she'd shot and crouched down to press her fingers to his neck. "Dead," she said. She slid his gun over to Jess, and he picked it up. His ears were still ringing, but he could make out what she said. "He won't be the only one."

"Is he a Burner?" Dario asked.

"I don't know. But he meant to kill us."

Jess checked the doorway to the next carriage. Beyond the door, the dining room seemed empty, though darkened, and Jess took the lead forward. Chairs and tables were broken and scattered, white tablecloths slumped in tangles, crystal broken and crunching underfoot. Jess was glad he'd had the foresight to put on his boots. Something moved ahead, and Jess stopped, planted his feet, and aimed. It was just a shadow, and then he blinked and saw it was Gretel, the train attendant. Bloody, and injured.

He lowered the weapon and moved to her to help her up, and silently passed her back to Dario, who took charge of her.

There was no one else in the dining hall. He checked the exterior door; it was unlocked. "Gretel," Jess said, "how do I lock this?"

"You can't," she said. "Someone sabotaged the outer locks. That girl. The one who jumped."

Morgan. But she couldn't have known about this, could she? Not about an attack. She'd only wanted to make Wolfe think she'd died. She wouldn't risk their deaths like this.

He didn't believe it. Wouldn't.

"I'll keep watch," Khalila said. "Go."

"What about the train driver?" Dario asked. "Should we find him?"

"There is no driver," Gretel said, and swiped at the blood dripping from a cut on her forehead. "We don't need one."

"High Garda?"

"No, they were not assigned this time. Only when the Archivist is traveling."

"I am less impressed with this train now," Dario said, "given that we will probably all die on it."

"Dario," Khalila said, "shut up."

"Yes, desert flower." His voice became serious. "Will you be all right here?"

"I will be fine," she said. "You missed, remember. I didn't."

"You might want to give her that one," Jess said. "Come on, Dario."

The two of them went to the next door. The lounge was still closed. Jess leaned against the wall for a second, listening to the fast hammer of his pulse battling against the booming hiss in his ears, and then looked quickly through the cracked door to see the inside of the lounge.

It was full of rough-looking men, all armed.

"They're coming," Jess said. Dario rolled one of the heavy, tilted tables up to block the door and fired through the glass at the men on the other side.

"Other way," Khalila said. "To the back. We need to find Wolfe and Santi."

"What do they want?" Dario asked. "They can't be here for us. We don't matter!"

"It's the Archivist's train," Khalila said. "At a guess, they want *him*. They will be very upset to find he isn't here."

Once they were through, Jess didn't know how to lock the carriage door to the dining car, but he did the next best thing; he destroyed the controls with a shot after closing it, and then ducked into Dario's room and wrenched a piece of metal from the top of the wall, which he jammed tight in the gap of the door's track. That would slow them down.

They went quickly through the silent bedroom carriages. Jess's door was still shut. He moved on past more cabins marked with the names of their assigned inhabitants. Santi's remaining soldiers had been bunked two to a room, which Jess supposed came as no real surprise; they were used to sleeping rougher than mere students, especially those who'd been wounded.

He passed Wolfe's door, still closed. And Santi's, open.

Wolfe and Santi. Still surprising.

Ahead was the compartment that still had the bloody imprints of Jess's knuckles on it. The compartment where Wolfe had locked him out. As he came closer, it opened.

Scholar Wolfe stood there. "Inside," he said. "Move."

Once the three of them were in, Wolfe touched his gold band to the symbol on the inside of the door. The lock clicked shut with a thick hiss and hum.

"Keep going!" Wolfe said. "Get to the baggage room at the rear.

Thomas, find yourself a weapon when you arrive. The rest of you, extra points for preparation."

"Is there an exit?" Jess asked.

Wolfe's gaze didn't turn from the locked door as he motioned them on toward the back of the train. "Yes," he said. "But whether or not we can use it will depend on the situation. *Go,* I said!"

Santi and his soldiers were gathered in the back with Glain. She was sitting up, her head wrapped in a bloodstained white bandage, and she looked sick enough to drop. Concussion, Jess assumed. Probably not a broken skull or she'd have been on the floor instead of sitting with a pistol in her hands.

"All here?" Santi asked, and answered his own question as he quickly scanned faces and checked them off his mental list. "Burners destroyed the track ahead, and judging from the last lurch the train took, they fired the tracks after we passed. We're trapped here. Library troops have been sent from the nearest available base with a commander I can trust. Toulouse."

"We're still in France?"

"Yes. We're stopped in a park not far from Cahors. When I sent the message, they said it wouldn't be long."

"Too long," Wolfe said. "We're sealed into this compartment, but we're still vulnerable. They can set off Greek fire beneath this car, and we'll roast. We stand a better chance outside."

Santi nodded. "We've enough small and heavy arms to go around. Best to do it now before the search gets this far. My troops go first and secure the ground; the rest of you follow. Maps show that we have about a hundred-meter run to the forest for cover."

"It works better with a diversion," Glain said. She'd leaned forward, and despite the blood and sweat on her face, she didn't seem at all vague.

"We have alchemical smoke, but we'll have to make it count," Santi said. "Since you brought it up, that will be your job, Wathen. Glass tube at your right, on the wall. On my signal, jump out, break the tube in half, and drop it. Don't breathe it in. Can you do that? I will be covering you."

"Yes, sir, Captain."

Glain stood up, but as she did, a sudden strange shudder ran through the train. Not the engines, Jess thought. It felt like something had exploded, but toward the front of the train.

The train attendant, Gretel, checked her Codex, which must have held information about the train. "The engine is burning," she said. "And the lounge. Greek fire, I think." She looked pale now, and shaky, and she grabbed for Thomas's hand. "It's spreading to the dining car."

"We need to go," Wolfe said.

After the dining car would be the first bedroom car. Jess's room.

He didn't think. He just stood and headed for the door.

It took a moment for Wolfe to notice, and then Jess heard him bark out, "Postulant! Where are you going?"

He got as far as the door and reached for the handle. It burned him. He gritted his teeth and grabbed it again. He couldn't hold on. The tube running around the door was hissing like a poisonous snake, bubbling with some liquid.

"Brightwell!" Wolfe pushed him back and held him against the wall. "*Jess.* What are you doing?"

Jess could smell the acrid stench again, the same as in St. Pancras when the Burner had died. The same as in the ancient Serapeum chamber in Alexandria. *The dining car is burning.*

"I left her," he said. "She's still there, waiting for a chance to run. I have to get her out."

Wolfe's eyes widened, and he took a step closer. His fists clenched hard in Jess's shirt. "Are you telling me Morgan is alive? She didn't jump?"

"I have to get her. Open the door!"

Wolfe hesitated for only an instant before he turned and shouted back,

"Nic, go! Get them out!" He slammed his wrist on the seal of the door and said, "Stay behind me. And don't breathe the smoke."

Wolfe locked the door again from the outside and moved quickly down the hall, checking each room as he went. The train seemed eerily peaceful now. Jess touched the sides of the car, and it felt hot, as if it had been in the sun for hours. As they neared the next compartment's door, he could hear what sounded like hissing.

"The fire's spreading," Wolfe said. "Our attackers might already have withdrawn. When I open this, the smoke will spread." *Toxic,* Jess remembered the ghost of a London Garda saying to him, holding him down on the tracks at St. Pancras. "Hold your breath as long as you can."

The door slid aside, and a thick greenish fog reached for them, wisping and whirling. The hissing was louder now, almost a roar, and when Jess tried to brace himself on the compartment wall inside, it singed his fingers. The smoke stung his eyes and blinded him with tears, and it was hard to remember how many doors there were. Which one he needed.

Wolfe was a dim shadow on his left. He found his door and slammed it open, and broke into uncontrollable coughing. "Morgan!" he shouted. "Morgan—" He couldn't see her. There was smoke here, too, a thick, reeking darkness. He scrambled over fallen bedclothes and felt on the bed, all the way to the corner. Then the floor. He yanked open the small bathroom door.

Morgan was on the floor. He picked her up, and she lay limp in his arms. His lungs were screaming for air, shuddering for it, and he had to breathe, but when he did it was like breathing in flames. Jess coughed and gagged and struggled to find some clear air in the miasma. *I can't leave her,* he thought. She was heavy in his arms, and he needed air, but he couldn't leave her.

Somehow, he was kneeling on the floor, with Morgan cradled against him. He didn't know if she was even breathing. The fire was a roar now, and it seemed to him as though the metal of the far wall was soft and sagging in. A silvery tear ran down and caught bright green fire.

Someone grabbed his head from behind, and before he could resist, he felt a suffocating pressure over his face, and then a sudden cold rush of air. He breathed, coughed, breathed again sweet, clean air. Someone had put a mask on his face. It clicked and hissed and glowed with a soft amber light, but all he saw was a thick, blinding cloud of grayish green smoke beyond the glass.

He could breathe. *God*, he could breathe.

"Go!" That was Wolfe's voice. "Go!"

Jess struggled up to his feet. He felt sick and dizzy, and the floor beneath him seemed soft and muddy. He got Morgan into the corridor. One direction was blocked by an eerie, dripping curtain of green flame, melting and burning everything it touched. He went the other way, step after step, breath after breath, and his head began to clear.

Wolfe, he thought, and turned. Wolfe was behind him, but he was failing, and as Jess watched, he slid weakly down the wall and stopped moving. He had no mask. How he'd made it so far, Jess couldn't imagine, but his strength was gone.

Jess put Morgan down and ran back. He gasped in as deep a breath as he could from the mask, then ripped it loose and pressed it to Wolfe's face. He grabbed him under the arms and dragged.

The rest of it came in flashes, like a dream . . . a weirdly beautiful eddy of green smoke, drifting past his face. The shock from the handle of the baggage car door. Holding Wolfe's wrist to the seal.

Dragging Morgan, then Wolfe, across the threshold and sealing the door against the roar and smoke and flame.

I can rest now, he thought. *Just a little. It's all right if I rest.* His lungs felt thick and heavy, and he couldn't seem to clear them.

He tried to close his eyes, but there was shouting, and Captain Santi's face. Glain, bloody and firing a gun. Someone was pulling him along by an arm. Then he was on his feet, running after Captain Santi, who had Morgan in his arms.

He was running, and the world suddenly turned white.

There was an indescribably huge noise, a wave of heat, and as he spun, Jess saw the Alexandrian Express bloom into a poisonous flower of metal and fire. He was flung backward hard enough to stun him, but as he opened his eyes again he saw the huge bloom of flame and smoke rising toward the black sky. Twisted metal sped overhead; some pieces embedded themselves in tree trunks. Smaller trees had been torn to shreds, and some toppled in eerie silence. The whole world went almost silent, with a high, thin ringing on top.

Jess managed to push himself up on an elbow, and by the confusing flicker of the fire, he saw Morgan beside him. He reached over to stroke a hand through her hair, then turned away to cough and retch. Everything came out green.

Someone stumbled over him, a blond giant half carrying a girl with a cut on her head . . . It was Thomas, and the girl was Glain; he was starting to put it back together now. Thomas set Glain down against an undamaged tree trunk and went to roll Wolfe and Santi over on their backs. Santi was moving weakly and tried to push himself up. Dario was there. Khalila.

Wolfe lay where he'd fallen, very still.

Jess crawled up to his knees. His hearing cracked and popped, and he thought that might have been the fire, but he couldn't be sure. Nothing seemed to match up to what he was seeing, and even that didn't make much sense at the moment. His lungs were still burning, and his eyes blurred every time he blinked. His head ached.

With the help of a tree trunk, he got to his feet and found himself staring at a piece of thick metal as big as his arm that had buried itself edge-on in the wood. It was still smoking and black on the edges. Jess took a step and almost went down. Someone caught him; he couldn't see who it was until his helper had moved past him—one of Santi's soldiers.

As the group slowly re-formed around Wolfe's still body, the man opened his eyes suddenly, blinked, and raised his head to look at the inferno of the train. Then his chest rose and fell a few times before he accepted Santi's offered hand to help him to his feet. He bent over to retch up green bile.

Alive. Jess couldn't believe it. He felt a sudden rush of giddiness, and then something else, something acidic boiling in his stomach, and he stumbled into the firelit darkness to bend over and cough more of the poison out of his lungs. Too dark to see if he'd thrown up blood. All too possible, considering the stains on his shirt and the disconnected, weirdly elastic feeling in his body.

He was still on his knees when the Burners found him, put a knife to his throat, and dragged him off into the darkness.

They didn't take him far. He could still see the carnival glow of the burning train through the trees, hear the groans and snaps and hisses as it fell to pieces.

He was too weak to fight and, truthfully, too tired. His lungs burned, and he ached in every muscle. When they finally let him fall, he was strangely grateful.

Dragging him even this far seemed a lot of trouble, if they were going to kill him.

"Which one are you?"

Jess tried to focus. There were three men, two of them standing behind him; one was a burly man in a thick slouch coat who smelled of stale sweat and vinegar, and the other was older, shorter, wearing a knit cap. He tried to remember their faces, on the unlikely chance that he survived.

The third man, the one who'd spoken, he couldn't see very well, until the man crouched down and looked him right in the face. Even then, it was hard to bring him into focus; the smoke had left Jess's eyes blurred and watery, and it took a lot of blinking to make out details.

He had a moment of confusion, because it seemed like he knew this man . . . and then he didn't. The man had thinning, light blond hair, and a familiar line to his nose.

Then Jess made out the light gray of the man's eyes and put it together. "Jess Brightwell," he said. His voice sounded thick and hoarse, and he coughed. "I knew your son. Guillaume Danton."

"Brightwell. He said you were quick," the man said. "My son liked you. You and the Arab girl—what was her name? Khalila. He said you were the best. He wanted to save you."

"Save us," Jess repeated. "Save us from what?"

"From yourselves. From selling your soul to the devil."

Jess sighed. "If you're going to try to convert me to Burner ways, just kill me and get it over with," he said. "We'd both be happier."

"I won't waste my breath. You have to learn how to listen before you will hear."

"They'll be looking for me. Is this all you have left? Three of you?"

Danton reached over and took a handful of Jess's hair. It hurt when he yanked and forced Jess's chin higher. "I want you to tell me who killed my son."

Jess swallowed hard. "He died in an accident. Nobody killed him. It just happened."

"Just happened. Of all of you who went through this Obscurist machine, only my son died. That doesn't just happen."

Jess didn't answer. The hold on his hair was going from painful to brutal. "Tell me what happened. Every detail."

"Guillaume went after Captain Santi, first one of the students. He volunteered to go first. We'd seen how bad it was, and none of the rest of us wanted to do it. *I* didn't want to. Your son was better. He didn't hesitate."

"Did he suffer?" Jess didn't answer, and Danton shook his head like a rag doll. "Answer me! Did my son suffer?"

"Yes," he said. "But it was over fast."

"Did he scream?"

"No," Jess said. He vividly remembered Guillaume's shrieks, those horrible bone-deep cries, but he wasn't going to say it. Not to his father. "He was brave." The hold on his hair suddenly released, and Danton sat back on his haunches. His eyes were wide and glittering. "I liked him, your son. I thought he was clever, and quiet, and smart."

"Did you see his body?"

"He looked peaceful."

"How do you know what happened to him? You said he went first. Someone could have killed him the moment he arrived."

"They were working to save him." Jess's throat seemed worse now, more hoarse, more painful, and he realized that it was the weight of sadness. He hadn't really had time to think about Guillaume's death. About how useless it had been. Strange time to really feel that, when so much else had happened. It seemed like so long ago. "Nobody killed him. He just died. And I'm sorry."

"Sorry," Danton echoed. "He was murdered. Guillaume would have exposed their secrets if he'd lived, and they couldn't let him. Better to kill him quietly, in an *accident*. You all believe the Library's lies so easily. How they are good and kind and lead us all by the hand into the future." He shook his head and stared into the fire. "They turned four million people out of Paris to starve—those they didn't kill outright."

"You've killed."

"You think I've got blood on my hands? The Library's halls run thick with it. Read your history."

"Read yours," Jess said. "Libraries burned. Scholars slaughtered."

"Ah, you know so much. I know things, too, boy. I know about the

Black Archives. About the interdicts. Perhaps you should ask more questions before you choose your side, then."

"I have," Jess said. "It's not yours. Never going to be. This didn't go the way you planned, did it?"

"Greek fire is a powerful thing. Sometimes, it has a mind of its own. We didn't intend to burn the train so quickly. We intended you to have time to leave."

"So you could shoot us."

"Wolfe and his men. Not students. I wouldn't have your blood on my hands."

Jess was angry now, and sick of all of it. All the blood and death and self-justification. "You *blew it up!* You could have killed us all!"

Danton watched him with an odd expression on his face for a moment, and then shook his head. "We didn't set the bomb," he said. "Someone told us where you would be," Danton said. "A message that came from inside the Library. Our own men died when the train exploded. That was meant for you. Scholar Wolfe and his promising young students, all gone." He made a little opening flower motion with one hand, and Jess remembered the train peeling open, the white light of it. It hadn't been Greek fire. He knew what that looked like. A bit surprising, given Wolfe's family connections.

He had a bad feeling that Danton had just told him the truth.

"Monsieur," said one of them at Jess's back. "They're looking. We should go. Quickly."

"Yes," Danton agreed, and stood up.

Jess started to relax, and then he felt the cold pressure of a gun at the back of his head. He flinched, then held himself still, staring straight ahead.

"*Non,*" Danton said. "Too loud."

"Ah," said the man behind him. "I have a knife. Quick and quiet."

Danton looked at Jess intently. "Are you going to beg?"

"Your son wouldn't," Jess said. "I won't, either."

He couldn't tell whether or not they'd just kill him anyway, not at all, until Danton gave a sharp jerk of his head to the man standing behind him, and the three simply . . . melted away. Gone into the woods they probably knew better than anyone.

He could hear the shouts of the searchers now. His name, ringing through the trees.

Time to get up, Jess thought, and managed to stand, somehow. *Someone must have actually missed me.*

He had to go back, anyway. He had to ask Wolfe why the Library had blown up their train.

EPHEMERA

Text of a handwritten note from the head of the Burner faction in London to Danton in Toulouse.

Received your news on the action outside of Toulouse. Destruction of the train serves as a symbolic victory, if nothing else.

It's too bad Wolfe slipped away. Now that we know of the man's family connections, he would be a valuable hostage.

Condolences on the death of your son. He would have been a great asset in the struggle.

CHAPTER THIRTEEN

J ess walked a while before he fell in the ditch on a bed of surprisingly
soft fallen leaves, stayed where he was for a while, until the rain started
to fall. It was a soft, gentle mist, but he knew it would freeze him icy as
the night's chill took hold, so he grimly wrestled himself up to his knees
and then walked until he ran into the line of High Garda searching for
him. Once they spotted him, they reached him at a run. Somehow, he'd
been expecting something else to happen to snatch it all away.

The High Garda men handed him off to Medica staff. He was flat on
his back in a camp bed with his shirt off and a surgeon poking his stomach
when Wolfe threw back the flap on the tent.

"Sterile area," the surgeon barked, and Wolfe stopped a few feet away.
"Talk from there."

He cast her a look but didn't argue. "What happened?"

"Burners," Jess said. "Took me off for a talk. One of them was Guillaume Danton's father. He wanted to know why his son was dead."

Wolfe's expression hardly even flickered. "What did you tell him?"

"I told him what I saw."

"And what did he tell you?"

"Someone told him where to find us."

"Enough talking," his doctor said. "Scholar, the wound in his side was aggravated by the force of the explosion. His stitches tore."

"Will he live?"

"Oh, yes. A few days' rest should put him in good order."

"I'm fine. Tell—" *Morgan,* he almost said. "Tell the others that I'm all right." He didn't want to mention Morgan. Maybe she'd already slipped off in the darkness, found a way to her freedom. He told himself, again, that he wanted that for her.

"Your fellow postulants have been informed. It was all we could do to keep Schreiber from tearing around the woods after you when you disappeared."

"Wolfe," the surgeon said. "Go lie down. I haven't cleared you to get up, and you know it. You've seen the boy. He's breathing and his lungs are almost clear. Now, leave."

Wolfe gave her another piercing look that had absolutely no effect, and left. He tried—and almost succeeded, Jess thought—in making it look like it was his own idea. "He's hurt?" Jess asked, once he was gone.

"Of course he's hurt," his doctor said. "He and Santi both have concussions and internal bruising. Can't keep them down, the fools. The others are all fine. Minor cuts and bruises. Miraculous, considering the shrapnel tossed about."

"There was a girl. Morgan. She's all right?"

"Mmm. Breathed in a lot of fumes from the fire, but she's recovering. No worse off than you."

"What about the Burners?"

"What about them?"

"Did any of them survive?"

"Not the ones we found. They're in pieces."

She called over a waiting assistant, and they inserted needles and fluids, and his constant pain began to recede like a wave pulling out to sea.

The doctor bustled off to see other patients, he supposed, and he floated for a while before Wolfe came back into the tent.

"You're supposed to be lying down," Jess said. "She said so."

"You had something else to tell me."

Jess stirred uncomfortably. He felt sweaty, and the drugs were beginning to be less of a soft cushion. "Danton said they didn't blow up the train," he said.

"Did he?" Wolfe seemed utterly still. "I don't believe we should take the word of Burners for that."

"But if he's telling the truth, someone else did." Jess swallowed the sudden taste of bile. "He said someone told him where we'd be. The explosion was white. Not green. It wasn't Greek fire."

Wolfe considered that, but if he came to a conclusion, he didn't share it. "The doctor says you'll be well enough to travel in a few days. We're fortified and heavily guarded here. There's no risk in waiting. Rest."

He headed for the tent flap, but Jess didn't let him leave without asking the question that had been on his mind since Danton had planted the seed of it out there in the dark forest.

"Scholar? Did someone in the Library just try to kill us?"

"I hope not," Wolfe said. "Because if they did, they'll try again. There's no fighting them. I've tried."

That seemed to beg a lot of questions, Jess thought, but Wolfe was gone before he could even begin to think how to ask them.

The next morning brought him a new visitor, as Jess was plotting how best to stage an escape from being fussed over by the surgeon. He'd just decided to ask Thomas to stage a collapse and draw her off when Morgan stepped into the tent.

He stared at her because he didn't know what to say to her, or how to say it; she had a way of making him feel awkward, as if it was the first time they'd met, every time. Part of it was because she looked different. Instead of wearing her hair up, it was down, soft around her shoulders, and it made him remember how soft and heavy it had felt in his hands. She'd been spending time outside in the sun. He saw a bright splash of sunburn on her nose.

"You really should stop this," she said.

"Stop what?" She gestured around them, at the medical equipment. He nodded. "I should. Funny. Until I met you, I never needed stitching up."

"It's my fault?" She came another step toward him, but only one. He wondered bitterly if Wolfe had fitted her with a restraint again. Maybe the restraint was to keep her away from *him*.

"You make me careless," he said. "I mean that as a compliment. I've always been too careful."

"I never thought that. You always seemed—"

"Impulsive?"

"You never seemed afraid of risking things."

This felt all wrong, all wrong. They were talking like two people who were strangers, and she wasn't coming closer. There were shadows in her eyes and in her smile. Distance.

"Morgan," he said, and heard the longing in his voice when he said her name. He didn't know how to go on from that and wasn't sure he could. "You should have run."

She took a step closer. No more than that.

"Wolfe told me what you did. How you came back. I don't remember any of it. I was hiding and waiting for everyone to leave, and it took too long. The smoke came through the vents. I tried to stand up, and . . ." She let it hang there, then raised her hands, palms up. "Then I was in the forest, and they said you were missing. How could I leave?"

"How could you not? If ever they would be distracted, that would have been the time."

"I know." She came the rest of the way, across the floor, and settled on the foot of his bed. He was intensely aware of her and, at the same time, of the fact that he still smelled of toxic smoke, dirt, and sweat. "I had to know that you were alive. I thought—I thought the Burners had killed you." Her breath caught suddenly, and her eyes widened, and she turned her head to look at him. "That's what it felt like, when you thought I'd jumped. Oh, Jess. I'm sorry."

"Well," he said, "I didn't do it to teach you a lesson."

A laugh burst out of her, and she leaned over and kissed him. *I taste of Greek fire,* he thought, but if he did, she didn't pull away. She relaxed against him, and the sweet taste of her lips drowned all the bitter chemicals. All the bitter memories. He pushed her loose, dark hair back from her face and sighed as she pulled back, just a little. "I missed you," he said. "But I really was hoping to never see you again."

"That is no way to charm a girl." Thomas's voice, from the door of the tent. Morgan stood up in one quick motion, and Jess almost laughed at the expression on her face. Thomas *did* laugh. "Don't you think I know? We all know. We have no secrets, we students."

That was blackly funny in itself, but it didn't incline Jess to laughter this time. *We're nothing* but *secrets,* he wanted to say, but Thomas wouldn't understand.

"What's that?" Morgan asked. Thomas had something in a bag over his shoulder, and it wasn't small.

"Something to keep Jess occupied," Thomas said. "I had time to finish it. None of us but Khalila can beat him at chess. I thought I would make him a proper opponent."

"Make one?"

Thomas set down the bag, looked around, and found a small folding table, which he carried over to sit next to Jess's bed. Then he reached into the bag and took out a large wooden chessboard that sat on a metal box frame almost two inches deep. Jess looked for the drawer where the chessmen would be kept, but the sides were seamless.

"You brought me an empty board?"

"Ach, sorry, no room for the pieces inside." Thomas reached back into the bag and took out a smaller matching box, which he opened. Inside were metal chess pieces in steel and iron. Thomas set them in quick, deft motions. "Black or white?"

"White," Jess said.

"Move."

Jess obligingly pushed a pawn forward and waited for Thomas to do the same. Thomas didn't. He just stood there with that delighted grin on his face.

A piece of black iron moved *itself*, gliding forward two spaces.

"It's an automaton," Thomas said. "One that plays chess. I had Khalila help me with all the calculations."

Jess moved his pawn forward again. The automaton's black pawn slid into his, and his white piece tipped over on its side, rolled off the board, and fastened itself to one side of the metal box.

Taken off the board.

"Magnetic," Thomas said. "If I had more time I would make it smaller underneath so there could be a drawer for taken pieces. Next time."

"It's incredible," Jess said. "It's—"

"It's beautiful," Morgan said. She picked up the piece that had fastened itself to the side and ran it through her fingers. "Did you make all this? How?"

"Yes. Captain Santi was kind enough to have it sent to Toulouse, and the soldiers brought it," Thomas said. "I finished it before we left Alexandria."

"Can it actually play a full game?" Jess moved another piece, this time really putting thought into it, and it was eerie how quickly the machine countered him. *Correctly* countered him.

"That was why it took so long to build," Thomas said. "A chess game has at least ten to the forty-third power of moves."

"How long did it take you, then?" Morgan stood and watched as Jess moved pieces, and the automaton played its side.

"Months, for the clockworks. A few days, for the pieces. *Alles Gute zum Geburtstag*, Jess."

"It's not my birthday."

Thomas shrugged. "I've known you this long. It must be coming sometime. Besides, you need a distraction." A smile spread wide across his face. "Although it seems you have found a very pretty one anyway."

"Flatterer," Morgan said. "Go ahead, Jess. Play."

Jess moved pieces until it became clear that Thomas's automaton was going to trap him in four moves, and, marveling at the eerie intelligence of the thing, he tipped his king.

All the pieces, even the ones that had been fixed to the sides of the board, glided back into place. The board lifted, spun opposite, and the automaton moved white this time.

"You're bloody brilliant, Thomas," Jess said. His throat felt tight with emotion, and he knew it was in his rough voice, too. "I hope you know that."

"I know," Thomas said. "Wait until you see what I have back home at Ptolemy House."

"I thought this was what you were working on."

"This? No. It is a toy. Elaborate, but a toy. What I have there is different." His grin faded, and suddenly, Thomas looked completely serious. "What I have will change the world."

It felt like freedom for the next six days; their wounds healed, and the six of them were much in one another's company. They held a chess tournament and took the Toulouse soldiers' bets on machine versus student; invariably, they made a profit. Khalila played Thomas's automaton to a draw many times and won twice; Jess prized the one time he'd managed to force the machine to tip its king in defeat. Soldiers took a seat. Even Wolfe had a try, which brought the most heated betting of all, but he, too, went down to defeat.

Thomas, curiously, could beat it every time. "I know how it thinks," he said when Jess asked, which was as mysterious as it was maddening.

It began to feel almost benign, these calm days in the sun. When the doctor released him, Jess treasured the hours spent with his friends, individually or in groups. He began to wish it would just . . . go on.

And then, on the sixth day, Wolfe called them to his tent. It was a pretty blue-sky day outside, with a crisp turn of autumn in the air.

Inside that tent the mood felt like winter.

They entered together, the six of them, and found Wolfe seated at a camp desk with his journal open in front of him and a pen marking the center. He closed the book.

"The escort arrives in the morning," he said. "Another trusted commander. Nic has seen to that. We will be traveling in armored comfort back to Alexandria."

The *armored* part Jess didn't doubt. The *comfort* was questionable. Khalila sighed and shifted, as if she could already feel the kinks in her back from the trip.

Wolfe looked tired, Jess thought. There were lines around his eyes and mouth that he didn't remember seeing before. The man hadn't put on Scholar's robes for some time, and Jess had almost grown used to seeing him without them now.

But the robes were out today. They were neatly folded on a chest, ready to don.

It's almost over, Jess realized. *We're going back.* Back to what?

As if he'd read Jess's mind, Wolfe said, "When we arrive, I will be summoned to the Artifex to give him my recommendations for your placements. It's possible that I won't return in time to give them out, but someone will deliver the scrolls if I am unable to attend."

"Unable, Scholar?" Dario asked. "Or do you mean prevented from returning?" When Wolfe looked up, he shrugged. "It's clear that you've got powerful enemies there. You're even worried here."

"Sir," Glain said. "They don't have grounds to punish you. You were sent to retrieve the books from Oxford, and you did exactly that. We will all support it."

Wolfe acknowledged that with a very slight bow of his head to them. "It's been my privilege to be your proctor," he said. "It comes as a surprise, I assure you, to say that; I am the most reluctant Scholar ever to be forced to take on a year's class, and the least inclined to charity. So when I tell you I am proud . . ." He shook his head and smiled. It was a tight, private smile, a little rueful. "When I tell you I am proud, I mean it."

"Sir—" Khalila hesitated, then plunged on. "What happened to Guillaume and Joachim wasn't your fault. We all know that, and if they ask us, we'll tell them you did everything you could. There were risks; we knew that. Life is risk. But you brought us through it. And it is we who are proud. Honored."

She inclined her head to him. Next to her, Dario followed. Then Glain and Thomas.

That left Jess and Morgan.

Jess bowed his head, and out of the corner of his eye, he saw Morgan do the same.

"Honored," Morgan said. "Sir."

Wolfe watched them for a long few seconds and then opened his journal and picked up his pen. "Be ready tomorrow morning by dawn. *Tota est scientia.* Dismissed."

He didn't look up as they filed out, and when Jess glanced back, he saw Wolfe pressing pen to paper.

But the man didn't write a word.

Dinner meant sharing a large, airy tent with the Toulouse Garda crowding the benches, along with the Medica staff they'd brought with them. Wolfe's party was pushed close at one table. Jess had tried to take a seat beside Morgan, but she had been blocked in by Wolfe on one side, Santi on the other, and the best he was able to do was claim a place across from her.

It did give him a chance to study her as they ate. She didn't seem to mind.

The food was better than Jess expected, or maybe his health was coming back; he ate with real hunger and savored the lamb and fresh vegetables and crusty French bread. Wolfe and Santi were, at first, the only ones allowed wine. Santi had only a little, but Wolfe steadily filled glasses, emptied a bottle, then another. He called for a third, and glasses for all of the students. Dario applauded that. Khalila declined, but everyone else accepted.

As the wine was poured, Jess glanced up and saw Morgan watching him. *The last night,* he thought. Tomorrow, at dawn, it would be different. Tonight would be her last chance to run. He wondered if that was why Wolfe and Santi had so firmly blocked her between them.

Wolfe stood up, glass in hand. He didn't seem quite steady. "Postulants," he said, "your attention." He didn't ask, he demanded, and they all gave it. "Guillaume Danton and Joachim Portero. Drink to them."

They all stood then, toasted in silence, and drained glasses. He nodded and they sat again, but he stayed on his feet.

Wolfe clumsily refilled his glass. "And a toast to all of you still here. Congratulations. You're now in the safe embrace of the Library. Good luck." He threw back the entire glass at one long gulp. Santi sat back. He looked concerned.

Wolfe had to brace himself with one hand on the table, as if the room had tilted. None of them spoke. Jess had never seen Wolfe out of control before, and it felt deeply wrong.

"Thank you," Khalila finally ventured. "You've taught us so much."

"Don't thank me for risking your lives. You deserved better than that. Better than me." Wolfe refilled his glass, emptied the bottle, and signaled for another. Santi leaned back to send Wolfe a look behind Morgan's back, but Wolfe didn't seem to notice. "I didn't ask to be your proctor. Saddling me with your class was a kind of punishment. To teach me *obedience*."

"Wolfe," Santi said. "Enough. Sit down."

"No. *Not* enough." Wolfe slammed his glass down on the table with so much force the glass cracked up the side. A dining attendant, who'd come with another bottle of wine, deftly scooped up the damaged vessel and put another one in its place.

"They're no longer my students. No longer my responsibility. All that remains is for the Library to break their hearts, as it broke ours years ago." Wolfe leveled a finger at Santi. "Say I'm wrong."

Santi stood up, put the cork firmly in the bottle, and leaned close to Wolfe. "You're drunk, and this isn't the place or the time. If you don't care about your future, think of theirs. Think of mine."

Their eyes locked for a moment, and then Wolfe blinked and nodded. "I'm sorry," he said. "Forgive me. I'm . . . tired."

"You're grieving," Santi said. "We've all got scars. Don't show them here."

Dario waited a second before saying, "Well, if you're done with the wine and moved on to self-pity, pass the bottle down. That's half-decent French. Not Rioja, but still. Hate to waste it."

Glain, of all people, stood up, retrieved the bottle, and poured herself a very respectable glass. Then she topped up Dario's and passed the bottle down the row. Thomas took a glass. So did Morgan, and then Jess.

Santi guided Wolfe away from the table and said, "I expect you to watch your behavior. Morgan, that tether's still active. If Wolfe's not watching, I will be. We had that double-locked by an Obscurist. Don't even try removing it."

She nodded and picked at the restraint wound around her wrist. She'd been rubbing on it, Jess saw; there was a faint red mark on her skin around the golden coils. He wondered if she'd tried to take it off again. Probably.

Wolfe's soldiers—the five of them who were left—sensibly took the rest of the wine. The mess cleared out, but their table stayed while the kitchen staff cleaned and sent them increasingly irritated looks. Jess only sipped at what remained in his glass, since his Medica surgeon stopped to remind him that his liver was needed for the future.

Morgan was the first to leave. "It's late," she said, and shook her head when the others chorused a desire for her to stay. "No, enjoy yourselves. It's our last night together."

Khalila stood with her. "I'll walk with you," she said.

Dario bowed them off with exaggerated deference. Jess drained a glass of water, watching Morgan go. Another bottle came around again, but this one was filled with fruit juice. He silently shoved it over to Glain. She filled her cup.

"I'm going, too," he said, finally. "I'm still getting my strength back."

"You are missing out," Thomas said, all too cheerfully; his face had gone pink. "Dario is off to find another bottle."

"Not if I get it first," Glain said.

"I will wrestle you for it," Thomas said, and placed his elbow on the table. Glain handily pinned Thomas three times in a row and claimed the bottle, which didn't so far actually exist.

Dario was offering her a game of dice, which was probably far better odds for him, when Jess walked back to his room.

They'd moved him from the medical quarters to something smaller, but it had a comfortable bed, and that was all he cared about. He felt tired, and strangely restless underneath it. Unsettled. Seeing Wolfe come undone, even that much, made him feel that nothing was secure in their strange, new world.

When he stretched out still fully clothed, he heard an unfamiliar crackle of paper, and reached under the thin pillow.

It hid a folded paper note.

I will come at midnight.

She hadn't signed it, but he knew her handwriting, the bold and elegant sweeps of her pen. She hadn't sent it by Codex. She knew those messages would be read by someone—if not Wolfe, then someone hidden back in the Iron Tower.

She hadn't said it explicitly, but he knew she meant to come to say good-bye. That was both sweet and sour at once. He took the note and put it into his personal journal, then took up his pen and let his thoughts run about how he felt. About seeing her. Losing her. About all this coming to an end, and his friends scattering. What had he said to Morgan on the train? Reset the board. Start a new game.

He didn't know if he could, after this.

Jess turned to his journal for comfort. He'd always filled the pages with his feelings . . . fear and guilt, in his earliest childhood. Then guilt, anger, and bitterness. His entries since Alexandria had been about pride and achievement, grief and horror, loss and love.

The last few had been about Morgan. Just Morgan.

Writing about it helped, but it didn't erase the pain completely; he left the journal next to his bed and turned to his blank. He'd loaded it with *Inventio Fortunata*, line after line of careful script, written in a time when every rounded letter was its own work of art. Tales of adventure and discovery from a man long dead.

A blank isn't the same. He remembered holding this book, feeling the history of the leather cover someone had tanned and stretched and cut to fit. The paper that someone had laboriously filled by hand and sewn into the binding. Years, heavy on the pages. Morgan had been reading a copy of it. An original. It felt like the old monk's story was part of his own.

But when he read it in the blank, it was just words, and it had no power to carry him away.

Someone knocked on the board outside his tent door, two quiet raps, and he sat up so fast the blank fell to the floor. "Come in," he said.

It wasn't midnight yet, and it wasn't Morgan at his door.

At the sight of Niccolo Santi, Jess grew cautious. This wasn't the friendly version of the captain; this was the closed, professional soldier.

"What do you want?"

"I know that Morgan's planned to leave. I know she's coming at midnight. I have orders to take her into custody." When Jess started to speak, Santi waved it sharply aside. "Don't bother to lie to me. I know. The question is, how did *they* know? She wouldn't tell anyone else. Just you. Who did you tell?"

Jess glared. "I didn't tell anyone!"

"Then how did the bloody Artifex Magnus already know?"

Jess opened his personal journal and flipped it to the middle, where he'd left the pen as a marker. The folded note slid out. He handed it to Santi. "Maybe someone else saw this. It was under my pillow."

"It's not enough," Santi said. "Anyone who saw it would think it was romance, not intrigue." His stare moved to the book in Jess's hand. "Did you write it in your journal?"

"I—yes. I mentioned it."

"When did you write it?"

"An hour ago, when I found the note. It hasn't left my side. No one read it."

Santi grabbed the journal from him.

"What are you doing?" Jess lunged, but Santi was faster, and kept the journal out of his reach. "You can't!" No one was allowed to read a personal journal without permission, not until the owner's death. Even his brother Brendan hadn't violated that trust.

"I'm not reading it." Santi took out a knife, and that checked Jess's advance, but Santi wasn't threatening him. He slit open the inside of the back cover of Jess's journal and peeled back the paper. Behind the paper was a line of symbols in precise writing, and a splash of something that might have been blood.

Jess knew enough to recognize alchemical symbols when he saw them, but he didn't understand. Not immediately.

"Mirrored," Santi said. "They've been reading everything you write. When did you get this book?"

"I asked for a temporary journal," Jess said numbly. "I got it in the Welsh camp." His mind raced over all the personal and private things he'd written. That was the purpose of a journal, to record a life in all its wounds and bruises, triumphs and sins. It was supposed to be for the *future*. "Who—" His voice cracked, and he tried again. "Who read it?"

"Either the Artifex or someone close to him," Santi said. "Not much time between your entry and the order to stop her."

Jess's neck felt stiff and hot, and the pressure in him was turning slowly from shock to rage. Had he written anything about Frederick? About his brother? He couldn't remember. Jess grabbed the journal back and flipped pages. He hadn't filled many so far, and he scanned each with furious concentration. Every very private thing he'd written cut him. Some went deep. He *had* written about Frederick, and Oxford, but Frederick had left and would be far away by now. Safe, Jess hoped.

Thank God, he'd not written a word about Brendan, or his father. But he'd put in too much about Morgan. Worse. He'd written that Wolfe had known about Morgan. That he'd helped her.

Jess sat down hard on the bed with the book in his hands and fought to keep breathing. "It's my fault."

"It's not," Santi said. "Journals are supposed to be private. You're a Catholic; they're like confession—the law treats them the same. You couldn't have known someone was watching."

"What about Morgan? If mine's mirrored . . ."

"Morgan doesn't have one," Santi said. "I think her father taught her to never trust them. He might be a Burner, but he was right about that." Santi was angry, too. Vibrating with it. "I was willing to let her slip away, as long as there was no proof we were complicit, but that ship's sailed now. They know. It's Wolfe's life if she gets away. And yours."

"What are you going to do?"

"No choice. I have to take her. I know how you feel about Morgan, but it's too dangerous now. I'm not letting Christopher die for her," Santi said, and immediately looked as if he regretted the words. He'd had too much to drink, too. He probably wouldn't have been so direct any other time.

"They won't kill Wolfe. He's a Scholar."

Santi's gaze locked on his, bright and suddenly all too sharp. "They can do anything they like. To anyone."

Jess felt his mouth go dry. "They did try to kill us, didn't they? They blew up the Express. Danton was right. They were blaming it on the Burners."

"Take my advice," Santi said. "Never say that out loud again. Not to me, not to your friends, not to anyone." He took in a deep breath. "I could take Morgan before she comes here, but I won't. I'll take her on the way out. That's a gift, Jess. For both of you."

And then he was gone, and Jess watched the clock hands grind very, very slowly on toward midnight.

M organ didn't come at midnight. Mingled with the disappointment was a sour taste of relief. He didn't know how he could tell her that he'd cost her the only chance she had to be free. If she didn't show, if she ran without telling him good-bye . . . maybe he would have done some good for her by being a distraction for Santi.

If she came, he'd have to tell her that he was the bait in the trap, and watch everything die inside her. He didn't think he could.

She'll understand. She deceived you on the train. And she'd been sorry for it.

He was unprepared when she pulled back the flap of his tent and let it fall behind her.

292 • Rachel Caine

She was fully dressed in thick black trousers and a black Library uniform shirt that was too long in the sleeves. Stolen, he thought. The boots looked like her own. She had a small pack on her shoulder.

"I don't have long," she said. "I figured out how to slip the bracelet. I'll leave it in the privy."

She still thought she had a chance. *You have to tell her,* Jess thought. *It's going to crush her, but it's better coming from someone she trusts.*

Or it would feel like the last, fatal stab in her back, and she'd never trust him again.

"At least it's a nicer privy than the Welsh camp," he said, just because it was the first thing he thought to blurt out. She was too far away, and it seemed to him that she was moving away, even though she was standing still. The space between them was too vast. "So you came to tell me good-bye." She nodded, and he saw a sudden wash of tears in her eyes.

"Yes," she said, and wiped at her face with her sleeve. "I won't tell you where I'm going. I don't want you to have to lie to the others."

He was already lying. He'd said she made him careless. Funny word. *Careless.* It wasn't true. He cared so much more than he'd ever thought he could.

The only thing they had was this moment. This one last moment.

Jess crossed the space—not so big, after all—and kissed her, and she gasped her surprise into his mouth for just a heartbeat, and then he felt her responding with all the heat and desperation he craved from her. *I am careless.*

He pulled back far enough to whisper, "Stay. Just for a while." He kissed her lips, gentle, light touches that turned deeper. "Stay."

"I can't."

"Morgan."

"I *can't.*"

"You won't make it."

"Jess, it's *all right.* I can do this. See this?" She held up her wrist and the golden twist of the restraint. Passed her palm over it, and a whisper of symbols floated up from it. Shimmering orange and red, twisting like sparks from a fire. She stared hard at them, and the swirl of symbols paused and held. "Right there. If I change that one symbol, from gold to iron, I transmute the property of this wire without setting off the alarm. I won't *break* it, and the seal doesn't change. I will just make it something else. I'll slip it off my wrist; they'll be chasing a ghost. And once I'm at the—"

He closed his hand over hers, and the sparks of symbols flew away, collapsing back on themselves. "Don't try it. And don't tell me any more. Please."

"I *have* to try it; you know that. I know you don't want to keep my secret anymore, but I know you wouldn't betray it, either." Her voice was soft. She believed he wouldn't hurt her. Somehow, horribly, he'd made her believe that. "Believe me, I'm sick of secrets. Sick of playing by the rules other people set for us, of being trapped and robbed of choices. I'm sick of it *all*. Aren't you?"

"Yes," he said. And he was, rotten with secrets all the way to his core. But if he let them all go, who was he? He'd never known life without them, the way someone like Thomas lived it. What would that be like, to have that single, unshakeable faith in the world, to not see all the shadows?

"It doesn't have to be this way. You could . . . you could come with me." She said that last in a rush, as if she was afraid to say it, and the high color that flooded her cheeks made him feel even more like a villain. "You don't have to stay here. This is good. We're good. *You're* good."

"I'm not," he said. The clean, crisp smell of her hair made him want to hold it heavy in his hands, but he somehow resisted that. "I'm not good. You know what I am."

She shook her head. Hair moved over her forehead and draped across one eye, and he gently moved it back. She turned her head away. "I know. Jess, I want you to come with me. I didn't want to go to the Iron Tower before, but now . . . I can't let them put a slave collar around my neck and breed me like a prize mare—"

He hadn't heard that right. "What?"

"Obscurists are rare," she said. "Why do you think they want me? I'm a new bloodline to add to their stock. I won't leave the Iron Tower. My *children* will never leave. Once I go inside, I have no freedom left. Not even that."

Jess felt a massive emptiness inside, and then a sick surge of anger. "No," he said. "That can't be true. It goes against everything the Library believes."

"The Library isn't a *person*. It doesn't have a conscience, or a heart or a soul. It does what it has to do to survive!"

"You sound like a Burner."

"Maybe they make sense. You're smart, Jess. You've never hidden from hard truths. You know the Library's not what it once was . . . what we were told it was, from out there." She wiped tears from her face angrily with the back of a hand, and he caught her damp fingers and held them. "Please, come with me. You know I can't stay."

There was nothing left of hope now. *Only this moment,* he thought. He put all his longing into the kisses he placed on her hands and her shoulders and her throat, until they were both breathing raggedly with desire. He'd lied. He'd betrayed her, though he'd never meant to do that. Losing her had made him desperate. It had made him a liar; instead of lying to her with words, he was telling lies now with his body. With kisses and promises. *Just tell her. Tell her that you can't save her, you can't go with her, there's no chance for her at all.*

But he was a coward, and he couldn't.

When Niccolo Santi stepped inside the tent, Jess felt a surge of fury and bitter disgust. At Santi. At himself. At all the dreams breaking into pieces.

Morgan didn't see Santi. She saw Jess's face. He was a good liar, had been one his whole life, but he couldn't hide how he felt in that moment. One look, and she knew. She backed up a step, eyes wide, and whispered, "No."

Behind her, Santi said, "Morgan. Please don't make this more painful than it has to be."

"No," she said again, this time a little stronger. "Jess, you *knew*." The disappointment in her, the look in her eyes, the wounded betrayal . . . It was like knives cutting pieces of him away. "You said *stay*." It was simple, those three words. It was the world cracking open between them.

She lunged at him. He captured her in his arms and held her so tight that she couldn't hit him, couldn't struggle, until Captain Santi pulled her away.

Santi pulled out a pair of iron shackles, and he fitted them over Morgan's wrists. They were a favorite of the London Garda. No Obscurist tricks. Just a key. She went still as she felt the locks click shut, and her face, *God*, Jess would never forget that look as long as he lived. Her stare was as cold as a winter river. She'd have ripped his throat out if she could, and there was no changing it. No going back.

If he'd warned her the second she'd walked into his tent, if he'd told her to run then, maybe it would have been different.

But he'd asked her to stay, and she would remember.

Santi's face was remote and still, as if he was a stranger to both of them. "I know it doesn't help," he said, "but I'm sorry." He walked Morgan toward the tent's exit. Gentle but firm.

Morgan dug in her heels long enough to give Jess one last look. "You told me there were always choices. When did you stop believing it?"

When I didn't have any choice but to love you, he wanted to tell her. But he didn't have the right to say it.

He was the reason she was in chains.

"You're damned quiet," Dario said the next morning. He'd taken the seat beside Jess in the armored carrier—this one had real seats, with padding, which was a vast improvement over their last conveyance. The Library had dispatched what seemed half an army to accompany them home, and yet Jess felt very, very alone.

"Tired," Jess said. He had his eyes shut. There was nothing to see, and he didn't want to join in his friends' chatter.

He felt, rather than saw, Dario bend toward him. "I heard Morgan is in the other carriage. What's wrong? She come to her senses and want nothing to do with you?"

Jess opened his eyes and stared Dario down at very close range. He didn't know how it looked, but he knew he was a hairsbreadth from punching the boy in the throat.

"Not today," he said. "Don't."

Dario lost his grin and faced forward. He seemed suddenly *very* interested in the story that Thomas was telling about a bar in Munich where he'd made a dancing automaton in exchange for his uncle's unpaid bill. It was a good story.

Jess wished he cared.

Khalila was both smiling at Thomas's story and watching Jess in concerned little glances. Her sympathetic, questioning gaze was impossible to bear. Wolfe and Santi hadn't told anyone of Morgan's detainment, and Jess . . . Jess didn't have the stomach.

He rose and shifted farther back from the others to an empty row, where he stretched himself out across two seats and pretended to sleep. He hated the sound of his friends' laughter; it felt like a whetstone scraping his soul open. He wanted to be somewhere else. Gone.

"Shove over," said a voice from over him. He took his arm off his eyes and frowned up at Glain. Her head wound had healed, but there was an angry scar cutting diagonally across her forehead that would probably be with her for life. She was proud of it. Battle scars.

"Plenty of seats up there," he said, and put the arm back in place. She took his legs and pushed them over, and he came upright with something that felt and sounded like a snarl trapped deep inside his chest.

She dropped into the seat beside him. "It's tiring, isn't it? Pretending it's normal. I know about Morgan."

One less person he had to break the news to, then. "Tell them, not me."

"If you want." She let a second or two slip by before she said, "Wolfe's afraid you're going to be accused of Burner sympathies. Makes sense. You went off with them after the train blew."

If she'd been intending to prod him into real anger, she succeeded. He slowly sat up, staring at her. "I didn't *go off with them*. I was taken."

"Then they just let you go free, with hardly a scratch on you that couldn't be explained by the train explosion. Look, I don't say I believe it. I'm telling you that it's easy to paint you that shade. The Artifex sees in-filtrators behind every column in Alexandria. You should take care he doesn't see you that way, too. You've already got enough marks on your record."

"I don't know what you mean."

"I mean your family, *ynfytyn*. I didn't know before Oxford, but now we all do. You don't think the Artifex knows? Even if he doesn't, don't you think Dario would use it if you came up against each other for a placement?"

"Or you would," Jess said. Glain sent him a sideways glance. "We've never been friends. You'd shove me over the cliff for what you want."

"We don't want the same things, so that doesn't matter," she said. "I'm not well suited be a Scholar, but I intend to be Garda Magnus one day. So I'm no threat to you. Nor you to me, I think."

"I'm a threat to everyone right now."

"Mostly to yourself," she said, and paused. Her tone changed, just a little. "Santi says that she's all right. Angry at everyone, but all right. She'll make it. She's strong."

It sickened him that even *Glain*, the least sensitive of all of them, could read him like a blank. "I knew he was coming for her," he said. "She could have escaped. I made sure she didn't."

Glain didn't immediately reply to that, and when she did, her voice was even softer and more guarded than before. "She wouldn't have made it. I spent time drinking with the Toulouse brigade. If Morgan got free, they were to hunt her down by any means necessary and send her back by translation. If we got in the way, they would have killed us."

He turned to look at her. She seemed all too serious. "Bollocks!" Although he didn't think it was, not really.

"It's not bollocks. They'd just say the train fire had no survivors. Letters to our families, so sorry, problem solved. And Wolfe *is* a problem for the Artifex, you know. You heard him at dinner last night."

"He was drunk."

"He was honest." Glain met his eyes squarely, for once, and it wasn't an angry glare. It was almost kind. "It wasn't your fault. She'll know that, eventually."

She patted his knee in a strange, awkward way that he realized was her version of affection, and got up to rejoin the others.

He stretched out across the seat again, and shut his eyes. It was his fault, no matter what Glain said. And even if Morgan forgave him, some kinds of guilt had to be carried, forever.

The convoy traveled far, camped, and Morgan wasn't seen again. Not by anyone. Glain was as good as her word; she told the others, quietly, and by that evening, no one mentioned Morgan to him at all.

No one, not even Thomas, knew what to say, so they pretended it was all fine, that going back to Alexandria was a relief, that everything would be back to normal once they slept in their own beds at Ptolemy House. It was gallows cheer, and Jess was the silent ghost at the table.

He couldn't avoid Thomas the second night, because the big German decided that Jess needed company on his walk through the camp. The elite men and women from Alexandria weren't taking any chances. They had set picket lines, sentries, heavy armaments.

"It's good to stretch my legs," Thomas said. "Not much space for them in those small carriages. Are you all right?"

The question surprised Jess, and it broke through his black shell enough to make him throw a look at his friend. "No."

"I didn't think you were. Everyone wants you to be. That must be worse, that they just think you should be . . . fine."

Thomas wasn't ignoring his pain, and he wasn't poking at it, either. He was just quietly understanding it. Jess let out a slow breath and stopped to look at him. "She's in a cage," he said. "I put her there."

"You didn't. I know you better."

Jess shook his head and started walking again. He wished he could walk all the way to Alexandria. Crawl. Maybe that pain would help clear his head.

"What are you looking for out here?"

"Nothing."

"Jess." Thomas sounded disappointed. "Lie to the others. Please don't, not to me."

"I'm looking for her," he said, and it was the first time he'd even admitted it to himself. "Glain told me she was in one of the carriers, alone. I want to find where it is."

"You can't get her out."

"I know that. I just need to see it."

Thomas shook his head, but he walked along, limiting the length of his strides to match Jess's. "How can you tell? She won't be at a window."

"The guards," Jess said. "Most of these are empty at night. Hers will have guards around it. Not many. They won't want to make it too obvious."

"They'll be warned about you, you know. You won't get close."

Jess nodded. It didn't matter. They walked on, and he studied every carriage they passed. None of them looked right.

"I've been thinking," Thomas said, "that I should go ahead and show you what I was working on before we left Alexandria. Would you mind? Maybe we could work on it together when we are back."

"I'm not much for engineering."

"You need to work. Using your hands helps make things clear."

"You don't need to invent something else. The chess machine is brilliant. You should apply for a Library patent and sell it. I know the Library gets most of the money, but it'd make you a rich man."

"I'm not interested in being rich," Thomas said.

"Rich lets you buy more bits of junk." Jess's mind wasn't on the conversation. *Where are you, Morgan?* Even if he found the truck, even if by some strange miracle he could speak to her, what would he say? It had been said already. *You said stay.*

He couldn't take it back.

"Let me show you what I mean," Thomas said. He pulled out a worn personal journal and handed it to Jess. Pages and pages of intricate drawings, schematics, German writings. Thomas flipped to a diagram, very finely drawn and lettered. Complicated. Jess had no idea what he was looking at.

At least he didn't have to worry about warning Thomas not to ever tell secrets in his personal journal. Thomas was far too focused on his machines to be writing anything about feelings.

Jess handed it back. "Is it another of your dancing automata? Didn't you get enough of that in Munich, paying your uncle's bar bills?" That had too much of an edge, and Jess was immediately aware of it. "Sorry, Thomas. What is it?"

"I had the idea long ago from watching an inkman who copied out some documents for my father. It took so long, even though that was his trade," Thomas said. "I thought, what if it could be done at the simple press of a button?"

"A letter-writing automaton."

"No, no, that is a carnival trick. This is something that could change *everything.* You see, here, this is a matrix on which you place precut letters . . ."

Jess's attention zeroed in on a carrier two down from where they were walking. They passed a large tent that smelled like dinner's leavings; the clatter of pots and pans said that the mess crew was still on duty. Everyone else inside the perimeter was settling down to bunking for the night, but not around that one carrier. At least a dozen heavily armed soldiers were crouched around it. They didn't *look* like they were specifically guarding it, but then again, they seemed vigilant. Too vigilant. "It looks like a children's letter game."

"No, no, nothing like that. You see, you spell out sentences and load the lines from bottom to top. You spell *backward*, because it will reverse. Then this reservoir here—"

Thomas was pointing at the diagram, but the words blurred into nonsense. Jess couldn't focus on it, even though he understood the kindness Thomas was offering. He was a bad friend, but he'd been worse to Morgan, and he felt a fierce desire to . . . to what? Make it right? He couldn't.

Maybe he just needed to know that he couldn't, by seeing it with his own eyes.

Thomas was still trying to explain something about ink and blocks and paper. Jess didn't pay much attention because he knew with a sudden visceral jolt that Morgan was in the carriage just ahead. Locked away, maybe still in iron shackles. She was *right there*, wondering how to escape, and damning him for every moment of her captivity.

He could feel it.

"Well?" Thomas asked, and nudged him. "Would you like to help me? When we get home?"

Home. Alexandria. Where Thomas would almost certainly be made a Scholar . . . and Jess was still the son of a smuggler, with a nasty rumor of Burner sympathy trailing him now. "Sure," he said. "When we get home." There was nothing left in Alexandria for him. How was he supposed to stare at the Iron Tower every day and not think about what he'd done?

Thomas grinned and clapped him on the back.

As they approached the carrier, two of the High Garda troops, both women, rose and wandered in their direction without seeming to react directly. One of them—a small Indian woman, with her black hair knotted into a complex design at the crown of her head—gave Jess a casual nod and smile. "Good evening, sir. Having a nice walk? It's good weather for it."

"It helps to stretch all the kinks out," Jess said, and smiled back as charmingly as he knew how. "Hard travel for you? You came up from Alexandria to get us. That must have been tiring."

She exchanged a rueful grin with her companion, who was taller and broader and had more of an East Asian cast to her features. "Tiring's one word for it," she said. "But we go where the Library needs us. Say, I heard there was a card game coming up on the other side of the camp. You're headed back, aren't you?"

"Of course," Jess said. "Just heading back to the tent. How about you, Thomas? Legs sufficiently stretched?"

"Yes, I feel better." Thomas gave him a look that, Jess suddenly realized, was all too perceptive. "And you? Feeling better?"

"I believe I am," Jess said.

"Good," the little Indian woman said, and strode along beside them at a pace that even Thomas's long legs found hard to match. She seemed to give off wild bursts of energy. "I am Rijuta Khanna. And you are with Scholar Wolfe's party."

"The big one's Thomas. I'm Jess. And your friend?"

Rijuta nodded at the other woman, who had a friendly sort of manner, but watchful pale eyes in a sharp-featured face. "That's Yeva Dudik. Don't mind her; she's not as chatty as I am."

"Ha," Yeva said. It wasn't a laugh. "I've met drunken parrots who weren't as chatty as you."

"It passes the time."

"Someday, someone will shoot you over lost sleep. It could be me."

Jess wasn't fooled. They were excellent at their job, and their job was to misdirect, misinform, and, at all costs, move any of Wolfe's party who got close away from that carriage. Jess didn't care. He'd found out what he needed, because all he had to do was note the number marked on the side. He'd be able to find her now, even among all of these identical vehicles.

He couldn't free her from a locked carrier. He couldn't help her get away. But he knew where she was, and that almost seemed like alchemy an Obscurist would understand: knowing where she was seemed to put them closer.

The Doctrine of Mirroring. As above, so below.

Near their sleeping quarters they parted company with Rijuta and Yeva, who continued on to their likely imaginary card game. Thomas was talking some nonsense about the saturation properties of ink on paper, but he fell silent when Jess stopped replying.

Jess stretched out on his camp bed, closed his eyes, and fell asleep to the dancing visions of ink blots that left bruised echoes nothing could erase.

EPHEMERA

An urgent communication from the Obscurist Magnus to the Artifex Magister.

Our monitors have reported that new information has been added to Thomas Schreiber's personal journal. His drawings are very close to a working model, and a more efficient working model than we have ever seen before, even the one developed by Scholar Wolfe that led to his confinement. Action must be taken to secure his notes and any working models that he might have developed.

Reply from the Artifex Magnus to the Obscurist Magnus.

And so, again, we are at a crossroads.

This is a consequence of allowing Wolfe to live, instead of simply killing him outright as well as destroying his work. If dangerous ideas are a disease, he is the very definition of an infectious carrier.

You must stop protecting him, Keria.

CHAPTER FOURTEEN

rriving in Alexandria was a messy affair. The High Garda force crossed the border in a long convoy, speeding along empty roads, but as they reached the city's precincts the progress slowed, and the last hundred kilometers took hours more than Jess had expected. By the time the carrier finally hissed to a stop on a huge field of evenly paved stones beyond the High Garda barracks, night was already falling on the city, and the day's warmth was chilling fast.

Jess hopped down, groaning from stiffened muscles, and turned to offer Khalila a hand. She didn't need it, but she accepted with a dimpled smile. It didn't move him. The girl Jess was interested in wasn't in this carriage.

He looked up and down the rows, and Glain caught his shoulder as he started to move off. "Careful," she said.

"I know."

"I mean it."

He shook free and walked to the front of the vehicle. The other carriers were parked neatly side by side, with well-practiced precision. The troops were disembarking and forming into lines, but he and his fellow students weren't expected to be so orderly . . . At least, he hadn't yet seen Wolfe appear to order it. So he dodged between forming ranks of soldiers and tried to keep himself hidden from sight as he moved from carrier to carrier, checking identification codes . . . and there, ahead, was the one that he knew held Morgan.

The door was unlocked as he came to a halt, and three armed guards emerged. A beat later, Morgan appeared in the door.

It didn't look like her, except for the silky fall of chestnut-brown hair. She was a pale shadow, drawn and very, very weary. One of the guards—Yeva, Jess realized—offered her a hand, and Morgan accepted it. As her foot touched the stone flagging, she looked up.

She saw him.

He didn't know what he expected from her, or himself; he hadn't thought beyond the simple, visceral need to be there to see her. He hadn't quite imagined what it would feel like to be seen by her in turn.

The girl he'd kissed in the dim sanctity of his tent was gone, and the one who stood there watching him was a stranger.

The small guard—Rijuta—saw him and crossed to him with all the crackling energy he'd seen in her before. No smiles now. Nothing but business. "Go back," she said. "She doesn't want to see you. You will only make it harder for her."

That was probably true. Jess nodded. He cast one more look at Morgan—the last look he would ever have, he thought—but she wouldn't meet his eyes at all.

He turned to go.

A gleaming black carriage was steaming toward them, fast. No ordinary carriage. Definitely not High Garda. It had ornate brightwork, and Jess had a strange vision of the carriage he'd climbed into when he was ten years old, and a man ate a book in front of him.

This was the conveyance of someone important.

The carriage rolled to a smooth halt and hissed a white cloud, and a sharply uniformed footman came around to open the passenger door.

The Artifex Magnus stepped down, and after him, a woman with a gleaming gold collar around her throat. It was intricately, expensively engraved with symbols that flowed together in a surprisingly elegant design.

It couldn't be anyone but the Obscurist Magnus.

Jess heard an intake of breath from the High Garda around him, and spines straightened. *But she never leaves the Iron Tower.* Obviously wrong. Here she was, and walking toward them, surrounded within a single stride by a walking armored shell of six guards. She was a tall, bronze-skinned woman with sharp features and backswept dark hair that fell nearly to her waist, liberally streaked with silver. She was old, at least fifty, but still very striking.

She wasn't coming toward him, after all. She was walking toward *Morgan.* Jess was merely in the way, and at a commanding glower from the Artifex, he moved. Not far, though. And not willingly.

"Stay still," said a voice at his shoulder. Jess looked back to see Wolfe had joined him. He'd donned a flawlessly clean Scholar's robe. His dark hair was down around his shoulders, and his expression was flat and empty as he tracked the progress of the Obscurist. "Stay absolutely still. They'll kill you if you move without permission. Don't meet the Obscurist's eyes directly."

He had the feeling Wolfe wasn't glad to find him here, but he couldn't help that. He'd done what he had to do.

The Obscurist Magnus stopped a few steps from Morgan and bowed just the slightest degree. "I am pleased to find you well, Miss Hault," she said. "I trust your journey here has been smooth."

It was absurd, how socially correct it was, after all the blood and death and anguish. Jess wondered how Morgan managed not to fling it in the Obscurist's face, but then again, Morgan had better survival instincts. "Very pleasant," she said. Her chin rose just a little. "Please don't expect me to thank you."

"Thank us for saving you from a lifetime of running and hiding and unending fear? No, I don't expect that yet. But someday, when you see more clearly." The uniformed footman who had ushered them from the carriage now stepped forward with an ornate golden box, ornamented with the old, traditional inlay of the goddess Nut, wings spread, ankhs of eternal life in both hands. He opened the box and presented it with a formal bow to the Obscurist Magnus.

On a cushion of black velvet inside lay a silvery engraved collar, like the one that the Obscurist Magnus wore. She took it in both hands, and a soft orange glow formed where she touched it. Formulae, made visible and real. The talent of the Obscurists. Morgan's talent.

The collar separated at an invisible seam.

No. Jess could read that clearly in Morgan's eyes, in the shudder that ran through her body. But she didn't try to run from it now.

There was nowhere to go. No one who could help.

The Obscurist Magnus stepped forward and spread the metal around the girl's throat. It gleamed, rare and beautiful, and as she made a graceful gesture with one hand, the symbols hovering around it whirled, spun, and snapped inward.

The collar shut with a tiny singing sound, and Jess saw Morgan lurch as if physically stung by it. She bit her lip on a cry, and tears welled in her eyes. She raised her hands to touch the thing, and Jess realized no one had removed her shackles.

The Obscurist Magnus realized it at the same moment and glared at the guards. "Take those off," she ordered. "There's no need to be cruel."

Yeva came forward and unlocked the irons. Beneath them, Morgan's wrists were red and abraded. She slowly lowered her hands to her sides and with a visible effort blinked away the tears gathered in her eyes and took a slow, calm breath.

"Good," the Obscurist Magnus said. "The worst is over now. You'll be well cared for. Your work will be for the betterment of the Library, and all of humankind. It's a great honor."

"I'm a slave," Morgan said.

In answer, the Obscurist Magnus touched a fingertip to her own collar. It had the feel of a ritual motion, somehow. "We are all slaves to our duty. Is that not so, Scholar Wolfe?" The Obscurist Magnus suddenly turned to face him, and Jess, and her dark eyes seemed as dead as a corpse's. "You, of all people, should know how deep our duty goes."

"To the bone," Wolfe said softly. He didn't move for a moment, but the tension hissed between the two of them. Something dark there, Jess thought. Dangerous. "With your permission, my students would like to say farewell."

Jess realized then that there were others assembled around the two of them now. Dario. Khalila. Thomas. Glain. He'd never seen them look so still or so unexpectedly grim. They'd changed. So had he, he realized. Wolfe *seemed* to have changed, but Jess was starting to realize that he'd just seen him wrong all along.

"Perhaps we owe them that." She crossed her arms and stepped back. The gigantic open ground where the troops had formed into precisely uniform lines by their carriages had gone quiet now . . . so quiet that Jess could hear the hum from the glows that surrounded the stone field.

Glain was the first to step forward, and she offered Morgan an outstretched hand. Morgan took it, and they shook. "*Pob lwc*, Morgan Hault. It was good to know you."

"And you," Morgan said. "Thank you, Glain."

Khalila simply hugged her, clung silently for a moment, and then stepped away with her head lowered. Dario kissed Morgan's hand with all his usual charm.

Thomas stepped forward and, after an awkward, uncomfortable pause, reached into his pocket and drew out a small mechanical bird. The Obscurist Magnus's guards tensed, but she raised a hand to calm them as Thomas wound the clockwork and placed it on Morgan's palm. The tiny thing hopped, whirred, chirped, and sang, and Morgan cradled it with tears glittering in her eyes until the spring uncoiled and it went silent.

Thomas dropped his voice to a near whisper. "I made it without a cage."

She pulled him close and kissed his cheek.

And then it was just Jess.

He came within two steps of her, then closed the distance to one.

He put his arms around her. She felt stiff against him for a moment, then relaxed, and to his relief, he felt her embrace him in return—gently at first, and then as if she never wanted to let him go.

Her lips were very close to his ear, and he felt a shiver when her breath brushed over his skin. Then she said, "I'll never forgive you."

His throat dried up, and he swallowed. Tasted dust. So all he managed to say, in the end, was, "Please find a way." He meant that in all its possible interpretations. *Find a way to forgive. Find a way to live. Find a way to be free.*

Find a way back to me.

The collar around her neck gave off warmth like a living thing. He avoided touching it as he moved his hands up, brushed her silky hair back from her face, and tilted her head back.

Their lips met. Just the once. It was sweet and brief and gentle, and then someone had taken his arm and was pulling him back. He knew by the black shadow's shape at the corner of his eye that it was Wolfe.

"Stop," Wolfe said in his ear, and shook him, hard. "You make it worse."

Wolfe was right, because he'd shaken Morgan's hard-won composure, and tears broke free to run down her cheeks before she quickly blotted them away with the sleeve of her tunic.

The Obscurist Magnus studied him, Morgan, Wolfe, and the rest for a few seconds, and then said, "Artifex. I expect you'll attend to . . . this." She nodded to her guards. "We're finished here. Help our new Obscurist to the carriage."

The sound of High Garda captains dismissing their soldiers echoed over the stones, a rising chorus of commands. The Obscurist Magnus entered the carriage. Then Morgan, followed by the guards.

The carriage steamed away with her in near silence, and Jess let out a breath he didn't know he'd held as it receded in the distance. The Iron Tower was just a dark shadow out there, but the Alexandrian Serapeum stood out brilliantly, washed by colorful lights on all sides.

He blinked when Khalila took his arm, and realized that the High Garda troops were dispersing around them for the comfort of barracks, or homes. Santi had joined Wolfe.

And the Artifex stood watching them all. "Quite a spectacle," he said. "Touching. I'm moved by your collective loyalty to a girl you hardly even know."

"Funny how quickly you get to know someone when everyone else is trying to kill you," Dario said. It was edged, and insolent, and not like Dario to be so careless in his politics. But he was angry. They all were.

The Artifex knew it, and he smiled widely and coldly at them all. "Wolfe. You lost the Archivist's train. He's very . . . peeved."

"He has another," Wolfe said. "And he got what he wanted, didn't he? I mean the books, of course. All those rare, valuable volumes, saved for the Codex."

"Battlefield operations really are your truest calling. Dangerous, though. So easy to be lost on a mission like that." The smile wasn't reflected in the Artifex's eyes in the slightest. "I'll expect your reports on the students tonight."

The old man walked away without awaiting an answer from Wolfe, who didn't seem inclined to give one, either.

"Bastard," Santi said, conversationally; he was standing behind Wolfe now. He'd waited until the Archivist was well out of range to say it. "Come on, all of you. Drinks, and then back to Ptolemy House for a good night's rest."

"You think we can *rest*?" Thomas sighed. "How can we rest if we don't know what's coming?"

"I'll relieve you of that burden," Wolfe said. He almost sounded normal, but it was just off enough that Jess heard the discord. "I'll expect you all at dawn in the Reading Room at the Serapeum. Your scrolls will be ready."

"That's damn well tomorrow," Santi said. "And tonight, I'm alive and off duty, and I intend to drink myself into some very bad judgment. Chris?"

Wolfe's gaze met his and held. "I wouldn't want you to do that alone."

"No," Santi said, and matched his slow, wicked smile. "I don't expect you would."

They found a spot inside the very large, very complicated High Garda compound, which was a short walk from the stone court where they'd parked the convoy carriers. It was an eye-opening experience.

Jess had never quite imagined so many vices being served under one roof. Drink, of course; that was expected. But a significant portion was devoted to the smoking of hookahs and other sorts of tobaccos and weeds, and the smell of it was thick and oddly enticing. Still another section held raised beds and chairs, and artists who tattooed intricate symbols on the bare arms, chests, and other body parts of men and women who seemed to enjoy the pain, or at least endured it in stoic silence.

"We should do that," Dario said, and nodded toward the tattooists. "One for each of us."

"It's forbidden," Khalila said. "Unless it's henna."

"And I wouldn't want to see a single thing mar your perfect skin, flower," Dario said. "But maybe the rest of us—"

"There is not enough wine in the world to make me get matching tattoos with you, Dario," Glain said, and followed Wolfe toward a table in the area of the bar.

It went on from there.

Thomas was the first to disappear; Jess hadn't even noticed his departure, just looked up to find Thomas's seat empty and others still pouring fresh glasses. That led him to finally break free of the celebration and head home.

Stumbling back into his room at the Ptolemy House was like falling through time, to a different life. A different Jess Brightwell, even though in real terms, he hadn't been gone that long. He turned up the glows and blinked at things that seemed familiar and strange together, as if they'd gone ever so slightly out of alignment with one another. Or he had.

The room smelled dusty. Not a surprise. He checked the window and saw that despite the seals, the fine reddish dust of Alexandria had piled up in a creamy pillow along the ledge. Must have been a sandstorm during their absence. He silently shook the bedding clear, kicked off his boots, and fell flat on his back on the yielding mattress. When he closed his eyes, he could have been anywhere. Back on the train, in another bed. With—

Don't, idiot. He opened his eyes again. The room was spinning a little. He'd had at least one glass too much before he'd allowed Dario to win that game.

He'd just started to relax when he heard faint, mysterious hammering sounds from somewhere below. *Thomas. Thomas and his bloody automata.* Not that he didn't admire them, but not now. Not when all he wanted was some sleep.

The rhythmic, distant tapping was going to drive him mad.

Jess launched himself out of bed and jammed his boots back on; they felt damp and unwelcome, but he couldn't venture downstairs with bare feet. Alexandria wasn't the desert, but enough desert creatures crawled their way into it to make bare feet unwise. Scorpions, spiders, snakes . . . even slightly drunk, he didn't feel like tempting fate.

Besides, there'd likely be metal scattered all over the floor, if Thomas was working.

Sure enough, as he stepped off the stairs and into the low-beamed room that had once been a storehouse, he stepped on something hard that bit into his boot. A jagged piece of cut metal. There were a variety of sizes of the things, scattered across the smooth floor. He kicked it free and spotted Thomas's shadow moving behind a drawn curtain. "Stop hammering," he said. "You're giving me a headache."

"Jess?" Thomas pulled the faded green curtain aside and beckoned to him. "I'm almost finished."

"With *what*?"

"What I told you about. The device."

"Oh, the *secret* one," Jess said. He had the beginnings of a headache and was more tired than he'd expected to be. "Not now, Thomas."

"You can sleep anytime. Come. I want to show it to the Scholar to-morrow."

"Thomas—"

His friend didn't give him much of a chance to refuse, and with that big hand around his arm, dragging him forward, there wasn't much option besides a real fight that Jess didn't have the energy to pursue. "Fine," he said. "I'll look."

The thing standing in front of him was no automaton. No windup toy, not even as fine as the little bird that Thomas had given Morgan.

No, this was large, complex, and disturbingly industrial. Not pretty at all.

"You saw the diagram," Thomas said. He sounded absolutely on fire with excitement, and as Jess tried to take it in, Thomas pushed him aside and started pointing things out. "This is the bed, where you place the individual metal letters that form lines, you see? You see how they lock together, with blank spaces between for words? And you slide each line down, from bottom to top, to form a page in reverse. This—" He tapped a large bottle full of dark liquid that he'd engineered from something that had started life as Medica equipment. "This is the ink. It took me weeks to find the right formula, something that holds on the page, dries without smearing . . . Here, let me show you."

Jess stood back and watched as Thomas fixed a large white paper to the top of the machine and flicked a control. Ink sprayed in a long, even line along the letters on the bottom, and then the whole top of the machine, with the paper, came crashing down. For an instant, Jess thought the whole thing had collapsed, but then the top snapped back up, with the white page still affixed.

Thomas turned the machine off, reached in, and pulled the sheet of paper out. He silently handed it to Jess.

It was a neatly lettered page full of the text of the *Argonautica*. A book written by Apollonius Rhodius more than two thousand years past.

"But—" Jess blinked and struggled to order his mind. Too much to drink. Not enough sleep. "Why would you do this? It's a Codex volume. Anyone can read it."

"That's not the point," Thomas said. "You can press any page you like. You can build a book of pressed pages, and you can *keep it*. Privately! No need for hand copying or smuggled books!"

Jess handed the sheet back. The sharp, metallic smell of the ink was unpleasant, but it was more than that. He saw the outlines of something huge in his mind, and he didn't like the shape of it, not at all. He tried to cover it with a light tone. "So you want to take the food out of my family's mouths? I'd hoped you thought more of me than that."

"Think of what the Library could *do* with this," Thomas said. He'd hardly even noticed Jess's comment, so caught up was he with his own visions. "Supplement the Codex so that citizens could order their own editions to keep in their homes. Duplicates of all the unique and rare volumes, limitless duplicates! And no risking fines or prison for owning them. Profits would go to the Library, for selling the pressed volumes.

The Library started out preserving originals, and they kept the tradition, but there's no *need* for it now. We can press duplicates. These are just . . . reproductions; that's all. Cheap. Easy to make!"

"Dangerous," Jess said. His brain was still struggling to take all the implications in, but he could feel the fear soaking in. "Thomas, it takes the place of blanks. It undercuts the entire system."

Thomas brushed that right aside. "The system needs to change; we all said so. This makes it *better*. More able to adapt, and aren't they concerned about the lack of trained Obscurists? And it will satisfy the Burners—what do *they* want? Books they can own. The Library not watching what they read. Freedom. This is *freedom*, in this ink. This page." He paused and said, "It would set Morgan free."

He was right. Thomas was absolutely right about that, and that was what was so damned frightening. Jess didn't even have the words for what it meant, and he just looked at Thomas, shaking his head. He knew he looked as if he didn't understand, but he *did*. That was the whole problem.

"You just said, out loud, that this thing is a gift to the *Burners*, Thomas. To heretics! Think about that!"

"No, no, that's not what I meant. I only meant that it will silence them; it will keep them from—"

"That isn't what the Curators will see," Jess said. "They'll only see the threat."

"But—" Thomas looked lost now, and so disappointed that Jess felt guilty. But not enough to change his mind, not by half. "But surely if it belongs strictly to the Library, it can be a great asset to them. Don't you think so?"

"I think it's bloody brilliant. I think you're a genius. But something like this, something so *simple* and so huge—that can't be controlled. All it will take is a spark, and everything's on fire." Jess looked at the page in his hand. The ink was dry now, and what he saw in it was beautiful. Thomas was right: it would change everything, forever, in the same way the idea and promise of the Library had altered the entire world, gathering together and protecting the knowledge of humankind against wars and persecution and every kind of shallow, mindless violence.

It made him weak at the knees, the blinding simplicity of it. The possibilities.

And it made him afraid.

"Who have you shown this to?" he asked. Thomas blinked. "Anyone else in the class?"

"No. I like to have things finished before I show them. You're the first."

"And the diagrams?"

"I drew them in my personal journal."

Oh God.

His horror must have shown, because Thomas went very still now, very sober indeed. "You think this is dangerous."

"I can't be sure," Jess admitted. "But yes. Very dangerous." There was only one person he felt they could trust. "I'm going to go ask Wolfe." Jess handed the page back to Thomas, and his friend sat down on a chair near his press, holding the paper in both hands. His whole body seemed loose now. Beaten.

"I thought—" Thomas took in a slow breath and let it out. His shoulders sagged even more. "I really thought that it might bring Morgan back to you."

How very like Thomas it was, for that to be his goal. Jess wanted to shake him, and embrace him, and it made his heart ache because it was the kindest thing anyone—even his family—had ever done for him.

"Thomas, you shouldn't have done this, especially not for me. Let me talk to Wolfe," he said. "Don't say *anything*. Can you lock this up? Hide it?"

"I— Yes. You'll have to help."

It was brutally heavy, but Thomas had built it on wheels, and there was a heavy old door at the end of the room that opened into a narrow, abandoned pantry where food had once been stored. A cold room. With the two of them pushing, they managed to fit it through the narrow door and roll it in. It just barely fit. There was a hasp on the outside, but no lock. Thomas hunted around in the shelves and found an old, rusted one that still worked. It helped add to the illusion that the room was long abandoned, at least.

When it was done, the two of them were covered with splashes and smears of ink, and dripping with sweat. Jess had been tired before, but now he was dizzy on top of it, as fear and work burned away the alcohol. He felt sick and filled with a nervous energy that he knew wouldn't go away soon.

Thomas still had the pressed page of the *Argonautica* in his pocket. Jess pointed to it.

"Burn that, then go to bed," he said. "I'll be back before morning."

"Do you want me to go with you?"

"No," Jess said. "We're going to be given placements tomorrow. One of us ought to get some sleep."

"You're a good man," Thomas said, and slapped him on the shoulder hard enough to leave a mark. "A good friend. Thank you."

"Don't thank me yet. Wolfe will tell you to destroy that thing, right down to the bolts."

"Or he might take it to the Artifex, and the world will change for the better. You're too cynical sometimes."

Maybe that was true. Maybe growing up in the Brightwell business had left him with scarred eyes that couldn't see brightness, and afraid of the constantly looming shadows.

Better cynical and alive than optimistic and dead, Jess thought. It was something his father would have said, if his father had thought of it. *And now I'm turning into my father. What a fantastic day this has been.*

EPHEMERA

A handwritten message from Obscurist Magnus Keria Morning delivered to her son, Scholar Christopher Wolfe.

Seeing you tonight has left me restless. You are so angry, Christopher. So hurt. And I have tried my best to protect you, but you knew when you went against the Archivist that you would lose. You are still alive. Please cherish that gift, and stop trying to force change upon the Library. It is ancient and set in its ways, and it stopped changing long ago. None of us can help that.

No matter what happens next, you must think of yourself, and Niccolo, and even those children I saw you with today. You are proud of them — I could see that. The Artifex could see it, and now he knows he can use them against you, too.

We are not the same, but alchemy teaches us that blood is the strongest tie of all. I will not abandon you.

But neither can I save you again.

Give in. Give up.

Survive.

CHAPTER FIFTEEN

—◊◊◊—

Hiring a middle-of-the-night carriage proved impossible, and Jess ended up taking a near-empty public train back to the High Garda facilities, where he hoped he'd still find Captain Santi. He didn't know how to locate Wolfe, and he didn't want to send a Codex message. Someone would be watching.

He reported at the secured gates of the compound and had his Library bracelet flashed, which proved his temporary status was still activated. The presence of guardian statues once again raised his hackles. These were sphinxes, again, the same as lounged on the sides of the Alexandrian Serapeum. They seemed passive, and the guards who checked Jess's credentials waved him through.

One of the sphinxes tracked him, turning its stone head as he passed. He tried not to imagine what it could do to him. It rose from a crouch to pace after him for a few steps, which made him cold to the bones, but it seemed to only be curious. Maybe it smelled the urgency on him, and the fear.

It studied him, and finally settled. The gate slid shut without incident behind him.

That wasn't the end of it, of course. More automata were placed inside, on the large walkway that led to the front of the multistory barracks, the offices, the unit headquarters, and the place they took their ease, the Hive. He took that last pathway, past an automaton that was modeled on a Spartan soldier. Having it look human didn't make it less alarming, especially when the eyes flared red and the whole body twisted into a crouch, spear at the ready. The spear it held was real, and so was the sword. *Could they make an army of them?* Jess wondered. Maybe. Maybe Thomas would be the one to make them.

The thought of Thomas's gifts being twisted that way made him angry.

Jess entered the front doors this time, instead of the back way. It was just as busy, and he paused to get his bearings. It was, if anything, even noisier and more crowded than before, but he pushed his way through to the place he'd been drinking with the others . . . and where he'd last seen Wolfe, with Santi.

They were both gone now, but asking after them among some of Santi's very drunken soldiers got him directions to the captain's lodgings, which were only a short walk from the base gates. That meant braving all the statues again, but having already cleared him, they ignored him this time.

He was feeling bone tired by the time he found Santi's small doorway and knocked. It was well into hours when no sane person made visits, but the captain opened the door and stepped back without any comment. Not even a question. Surely *What are you doing here at this hour?* was warranted.

"I need to talk to Wolfe," Jess said.

Santi paused in the act of tying the sash of his silken robe, but didn't look up. "Presumptuous, but correct, because he lives here. Sit down, Brightwell."

Santi's command tone was out, and Jess found himself obeying the order without question. Santi sat down across from him. He folded his hands on the table and looked at Jess with an unreadable expression.

"Are you going to let me talk to him, or do I have to start shouting?"

"Just listen," Santi said. "I've known Wolfe since we were both postulants. Everyone knew he was to become the next Artifex Magnus, or even the next Archivist. He was brave, brilliant, intuitive, dedicated . . . He had everything the Library wanted. But he had one thing they didn't want: imagination."

Jess was getting more impatient with every tick of the clock, and he found himself picking at a rough spot in the wood, worrying it with his fingernail. "Is there a point to this?"

"Wolfe recognized that the Library had stopped moving forward about two hundred years ago. It wasn't changing. It *couldn't*, because it needed Obscurists to do its work, and as fewer were found, it had to hold tighter to each one. And then squeeze. And then strangle." Santi shook his head slowly. "Wolfe had an idea of how to sweep all that away and rebuild the Library anew. It was brilliant."

Jess was no longer impatient; Santi had succeeded in keeping his attention. "They didn't listen."

"Oh, they listened. He was a well-respected, important Scholar by then. They listened. They took his research. And then he was gone."

"What?"

"Gone. I was told that Wolfe was on assignment. Then on a mission for the Artifex. Finally I was told not to ask again. I kept asking anyway. They persuaded me to stop."

There were scars on Santi's chest. Jess would have thought they were battle scars, but these looked too regular. Too even.

Too calculated.

"It was more than a year before he turned up again. Middle of the night. He looked like he'd crawled out of hell."

A year . . . "Where had he been?"

"He doesn't say, and I don't ask." Santi was quiet for a beat. "They destroyed his research, his personal journals, everything. You'll find no citations for him on the Codex, though Chris wrote hundreds of works before the day he presented to the Archivist. They wiped everything he'd done from the Library's memory. He's a walking ghost. He's been a ghost since the day they finally let him go."

Jess's throat had gone dry, and he heard a click when he tried to swallow. "But they put him in charge of a class. They sent him on an important mission. Why would they trust him with—" He stopped himself. Santi didn't say a word. "They didn't."

"He was never a teacher. They wanted him to find your secrets and turn them over. But he found your secrets, and he never betrayed them. What the Artifex knows, he had to get other ways." Santi smiled a little. "Little rebellions. Wolfe was meant to die on the trip to Oxford. He's an embarrassment and a risk. Living on borrowed time."

"But you're still with him."

"Of course," Santi said, and met Jess's eyes. "Some people you don't walk away from. I know you understand that. But if you're here about Morgan, I can't let you drag him into it. It's too hard for him. He was born in the Iron Tower. He understands what it means to be locked up in that place."

"But—" Jess hadn't thought he could be surprised by *anything* about Wolfe, but he hadn't expected that. "He's an *Obscurist*?"

"Born there, but he doesn't have the gift. He was taken from the tower to the orphanage when he was ten years old, after he was tested. Both his parents are still in the tower. He was set free."

Rejected and rescued, at the same time. Jess couldn't comprehend it. So much of what Santi was telling him was so different than he'd ever expected. He thought he'd known Wolfe. They'd all thought that.

But he was none of the things that they'd assumed. Not a single one.

"It—it doesn't have anything to do with Morgan," Jess said. "I understand—why you wouldn't want him to get involved. But this is about Thomas."

"God." Santi rested his head on his hand for a moment, as if Jess had given him a headache. "Enough. *Enough.* He tried not to care about you and your friends, but he had to, and once he did . . . I don't want him dragged back into this. His position is dangerous." Santi broke off, and his eyes focused on something behind Jess.

The frustration and sadness that spread over Santi's face told Jess what had happened, even before Wolfe's low voice said, "It's my decision, Nic. Not yours."

Wolfe was fully dressed. He'd either not been asleep at all, or he'd slept in his clothes, though these looked too fresh and sharp for that. He slid into an empty chair at the table, and he and Santi held a silent staring contest for a moment.

Santi lost. He shook his head, stood up, and went to the small kitchen.

"You heard?" Jess asked.

"I can guess most of what he told you." Wolfe's gaze was fixed on Santi's back as he went about the domestic business. "I gambled for the soul of the Library. And I lost. Past is past. Now, tell me why you've come."

"Chris, for the love of Amon, don't do this," Santi said. "Class is over. Walk away."

"If you're making coffee, I'd like milk," Wolfe said.

"I know that. Jess?"

"Uh—black, sir." He'd grown up on his father's brew, so bitter and dark that it was like drinking midnight. "Thank you." It was absurd to be thanking him, but it just came out, somehow. Jess felt entirely off-balance between Santi's sudden hospitality and knowledge of Wolfe that he was totally unprepared to handle.

"Go on," Wolfe said to Jess. "Schreiber."

"When we were on the road, he showed me diagrams. I didn't pay much attention at the time; I was thinking of . . . other things." Danger. Death. Morgan, who had somehow come to supersede those other considerations. "Thing is, he built what he showed me. He must have had it ready before we left. He was planning to present it to you. He hoped you'd show it to the Artifex."

"Another automaton?" Wolfe seemed more bored than alarmed. The warm, seductive scent of brewing coffee seeped through the small rooms, and Santi began pouring cups. Wolfe sat back as Santi set one in front of him, then Jess. Jess took the time to gulp down a burning sip.

Jess focused back on Wolfe. "No, sir. Thomas calls it a press."

Wolfe had his cup halfway to his mouth, but he stopped and set it back down, precisely. Carefully. Santi had gone completely still as well. Jess didn't know why, but he knew it was bad.

"A press," Wolfe repeated. "Explain."

"It makes copies of words," Jess said. "In ink. On paper. He calls it a press because it . . . presses ink on the page."

There was a moment of ringing silence. Wolfe's dark eyes bored in on him in unreadable stillness, and then he said, in a very soft voice, "Where is this device now?"

"Ptolemy House," he said. "In the basement."

"And the plans?"

"In Thomas's personal journal—"

Wolfe exploded up out of the chair so fast that he was only a blur. His cup overturned, sending coffee sheeting across the dark wood. Jess didn't have time to do more than scramble to his feet before Wolfe was halfway to the door.

Santi was suddenly barring the way out, and there was real despair in his face. "No," Santi said. "Christopher, *don't.*"

Wolfe lowered his shoulder and slammed into him, but Santi was taller, stronger, and expected the move. He expertly flipped Wolfe aside and onto his stomach on the floor with a hollow *boom* of boards, and held him pinned while Wolfe struggled. "Don't. I won't watch you destroy yourself. I saw the note. I saw what your mother told you."

"Let him go!" Jess said, and took a step forward. That earned Santi's straight focus, and that was . . . chilling. He kept walking, against all the sane impulses to stop.

"Schreiber put his plans in his journal, Nic," Wolfe said.

"His personal journal never went with him to Oxford," Santi said. "They couldn't have compromised it the way they got to Brightwell's."

"Wrong." Wolfe was laughing, but it sounded like tears. "So very wrong. There are ranks of automata in the Iron Tower reading every word. The Library sees *everything*. And the thing they search for the hardest is *this*. This *press*. Because it's the greatest risk in the world to their power. *Damn you, Nic, let me go!*"

Santi finally moved, and Wolfe rolled up to his feet. Santi was still between him and the door, but Wolfe didn't try another rush. Not yet.

"You never told me that," Santi said. "About the journals."

"Would it have mattered?"

"Might have."

"They started after I was arrested," Wolfe said. "Part of the new interdictions. I was afraid you'd change what you were writing. If you had, they'd have taken you. I couldn't let that happen."

"Thomas says it'll change everything," Jess said. "That's true, isn't it? Like your research, something that will change the Library."

"Thomas isn't the first to come up with this idea. Call it printing, or a press, or an ink plate, or movable type. It's an idea that they've been systematically destroying since 1455, when Johannes Gutenberg was a Scholar, and died in a cell beneath the Serapeum," Wolfe said. "Nic, if you ever believed me, believe me now: I have to do this. If I was left alive for a reason, it was this one. To save that boy."

"I know," Santi said. "I just wish you weren't so bloody brave about it."

Wolfe hugged him. It was a sudden, fierce move, and Santi embraced him back. Jess knew what he was looking at, because he'd felt it.

Love, and the pain of knowing that love wouldn't be enough.

"I'm coming," Santi said. "And don't argue with me about how you can't protect me—I know you can't. It doesn't matter. I'm coming."

Wolfe smiled. It was too private a thing, and Jess looked away from it. "Then get dressed," he said. "We won't have much time."

Ptolemy House was silent when they arrived. The whole street was quiet, though in other houses glows burned here and there. Not in Ptolemy. Even the light that always burned over the door was gone, and the household gods shrouded in darkness.

"Who's still inside?" Santi asked. Jess told him. All the occupied rooms were on the ground floor now, and he named off the room numbers and occupants. "Check Schreiber's room first. If you find him, bring him out. We'll get him to safety."

"Safety where?" Jess asked. "This is Alexandria. The Library owns every inch of it!"

"We'll deal with that once we find him. Go. I'll cover the street. Chris . . ." He handed Wolfe a pistol, and Wolfe nodded his thanks. "Watch yourself."

Santi stepped back into shadows and nearly vanished as Jess and Wolfe slipped inside Ptolemy House.

All the glows had been extinguished, and when Jess tapped the first one, which should have raised the rest, they stayed dark. Glows didn't fail often, and this seemed convenient timing. Jess knew Ptolemy House well enough to navigate it in the dark, and he led Wolfe down the hallway, counting doors. Thomas was at the end, on the left.

"Wait," Wolfe whispered. He got a small portable glow from his pocket and shook it to the lowest setting. Then, as Jess eased open the unlocked door, he bent and rolled it into the room, where it cast golden-green shadows on an unmade bed, a pile of unwashed clothes, a blank that had fallen to the floor beside the bed.

And something that looked black and wet on the bedding.

Jess stepped forward, and stopped, because he knew what it was. He could smell the sharp metallic tang of it, like a new-sharpened blade.

Blood.

"Easy," Wolfe said. "Check the wardrobe."

Jess slid back the door and found nothing but folded clothes and tools on the shelves. Boxes of gears and parts. He checked beneath the bed. There was nowhere else in the room for Thomas to be.

Not dead. He can't be dead; that's not much blood. They'd all bled more than that in Oxford, hadn't they?

"Downstairs," he said. "He could be with the press."

"Check the other rooms first," Wolfe said, and handed him a second small glow. "Careful. Try not to wake them if they're asleep."

Jess nodded and stepped out. Across the hall was Khalila's chamber. Empty. Her bedclothes were disarranged, but there were no signs of violence.

Dario's room was likewise empty. So was Glain's. The four of them were all gone.

His heart was hammering fast in his chest, and he checked his own room, simply because he half thought he'd find himself lying peacefully in his bed, asleep and dreaming all of this . . . but it was just as he'd left it. Nothing out of place.

The empty rooms were all still empty.

The basement, then. Jess's nerves were stretched to the breaking point, and when the front hallway door opened as they headed for the steps to the cellar, he flinched. If he'd had a gun, he'd have shot Santi dead as the man eased inside.

That might have been why Santi hadn't given him a weapon.

"Hurry up," Santi said. "Something's not right out there."

"There's blood in Schreiber's room," Wolfe said. "We're going downstairs."

Santi nodded and locked the front door. "They'll know we're here."

Santi seemed relaxed now that things were in motion as he led them down the stone steps into Thomas's workroom. The glows were out here, too. Jess brightened the one Wolfe had given him and tossed it over the railing into the center of the space.

The basement seemed empty. Undisturbed. No signs of blood, or his friends. Thomas had cleaned up the scrap metal that had been littering the floor.

And then Jess's eyes fell on the ancient old door in the far wall. The one he and Thomas had locked.

There was no longer a lock on it.

Santi and Wolfe let him move down the stairs, to the door. He took hold of the cold iron ring and pulled.

There was nothing inside. No bodies. No device. Nothing but fresh scrapes along the walls where the machine had been dragged away. He showed Santi and Wolfe.

"Tagged, most likely," Santi said. "Sent to Archive. They didn't carry it out of here up those steps without breaking it apart. The room's too clean for that."

"Where did they take everyone?"

"Let's go find out," Wolfe said. He turned and led the way up the steps, snuffing the glow with a press of his fingers as he reached the main hall door. He'd forgotten that it was locked, Jess thought.

Except it *wasn't* locked, though Jess had seen Santi do it. The knob turned easily in Wolfe's hands, and the door swung open.

"Halt!" said a voice behind them in the dark of the hallway, and overlaying it was another from outside on the doorstep. Santi whispered a low, vicious curse that only Jess heard, and then raised his hands. "Drop your weapons! You are arrested by authority of the Library!"

There wasn't any choice. Santi and Wolfe both disarmed, and then Jess found himself pushed face-first into the wall. A framed portrait, unseen in the dark, broke loose and fell with a crash. He hoped it was the Artifex Magnus's likeness.

His hands were quickly bound behind him, and he was pushed outside onto the street. Wolfe and Santi were restrained, too, and an unmarked black carriage had been pulled up to the curb. One by one, they were loaded inside by what now in the moonlight Jess could see were High Garda troops. Not Santi's men. He'd never seen these faces before.

The rear of the carriage had been fitted out with metal benches. They were all boosted up into them. Jess took the right side, Wolfe and Santi the left, and in a matter of seconds the doors were shut and locked, and the carriage lurched into motion. The box smelled of sweat and fear and a lingering odor of sick. There was only a small barred window above their heads to admit fresh air, and on this still night it didn't do much good.

"Where are they taking us?" Jess asked. The other men didn't answer.

"I'm sorry, Nic," Wolfe said.

"I'm not," Santi said, and crossed his booted feet. "It was worth every moment of what comes next."

Wolfe turned his face away, and in a flash of passing light from outside, Jess saw that there were tears streaking his face.

That, finally, was what made Jess really afraid.

As much as he hated being trapped in the moving cell, he dreaded what might come next, and when the carriage rolled to a stop, Jess tensed himself for a fight. He wasn't sure how much he could do, given his bound hands; escape was impossible, given the trackers. But he wasn't going quietly.

"Stay calm," Wolfe said. He *sounded* calm, at least. "Jess. Are you listening to me?"

"What if they're dead?" Jess asked. His voice was shaking, and he couldn't seem to control that.

"They're not." Santi sounded sure of it. "Maybe they'd have killed them outside the city. They won't do it here. Don't lose faith."

Faith. Faith in what? He'd believed in the Library, the ideal of it, anyway. He'd believed that it was doing good, and more, that it *wanted* to do good. But now he'd seen the dirty underside, and he couldn't hold on to his faith much longer.

The doors opened, and Jess blinked in the sudden light of glows turned to their maximum brilliance. "Out," a voice in shadow said. "Santi, then Brightwell, then Wolfe. Go."

That was a High Garda trooper, no doubt about it; the tone was one Jess had become familiar with on the road. Jess followed the orders, though he found it harder than he'd expected to step out of the high bed of the carriage with bound hands. He ended up jumping. He heard Wolfe's boots hit the ground behind him.

The glows turned lower, and his eyes adjusted to pick out the soldiers arrayed around them. Six of them to three bound men. At least they had a healthy respect for their captives.

"Brightwell. Come this way."

He hesitated, but Wolfe nodded sharply to him. A guard took him by the elbow and led him away, while the other two were taken a different way. He tried to get his bearings, and finally it struck him just where they were: the Alexandria Serapeum, but on a side of it he'd never seen before. A heavily fortified, highly secured side.

This was the face of the pyramid that held the offices of the Artifex Magnus, and—somewhere in that warren—the other Curators, and the Archivist himself.

"Where did you take Scholar Wolfe?" he asked his guard, who was only a little older than his own age, by appearance. No answer, and the pace picked up as they strode through an ornate outer chamber lined with rare original volumes set behind glass. From there, hallways spread out like spokes, and each had a traditional Egyptian hieroglyph inset with gold atop the lintel. He should have been fascinated, any other time—awed, by walking halls that the greatest minds of the world had inhabited through the ages.

Instead, he could feel only sick anger and fear—and then a wave of relief almost as strong, as he caught sight of the party coming toward him from the hallway marked with the Medica symbol.

Khalila was the first to reach him, and she threw her arms around him with shaking strength. "Thank Allah you're all right! We looked for you—we thought you'd been taken, too . . . Where have you *been*?" Her happiness faded as she realized that his hands were pinned behind him. "Jess?"

Dario and Glain were right behind her. Khalila had pulled on a thick striped robe, and her hijab, but he could tell that she had been pulled from her bed. Dario was wearing a loose shirt and linen trousers that had probably served him for nightwear. Glain had on only a plain nightgown, her feet stuck in the same mud-stained boots she'd worn to Oxford.

"Where's Thomas?" Jess asked. His throat ached with tension.

They exchanged looks. Dario put his hands on Khalila's shoulders. "They told us he was injured in a Burner attack on Ptolemy House. First we knew about it, we were being dragged out of bed and brought here."

"But you're all right?"

Glain nodded firmly. "We're all right." But even Glain's eyes were bright with what looked like fear now. She didn't like this. None of them did. "We asked why Thomas wasn't with us. They didn't say."

"I'll find out," Jess promised, and his guard pulled his elbow to tow him onward. "Find Wolfe and Santi!"

His escort took him down the hallway that was marked with the name of the Artifex Magnus, and he had to turn his attention forward, because all too soon his friends were out of view.

This area of the Serapeum smelled like sandalwood and oils, and at this hour of the night it seemed deserted. There were rooms off to the sides of the halls that held desks at which people must have worked, but Jess had time only for glances as he was marched relentlessly to the end, where a large, ornate door was decorated with the goddess Nut spreading her golden feathers. It stood partially open.

And in the room behind it stood the Artifex Magnus. He paced in front of a large golden desk, in a pale yellow room decorated with old Egyptian gods in the classic Alexandrian styles. Except for the desk and a few chairs, the only other thing the room held was books. Not blanks— original ancient volumes, scores of them, all uneven in size and shape. The room smelled of old paper and leather, overwhelming the rare wood of the hallway.

The guard stood Jess in the middle of the room and, to Jess's surprise, cut his bindings loose. The Artifex nodded to him. "You may go," he said to the guard. "Close the door."

It shut with a heavy *boom*, and Jess heard a lock engage. No escape that way. No wonder they didn't need the bindings here.

"Where's Thomas?"

"Let's set the ground rules now, Brightwell. I ask the questions, you answer, because if you do not, this will go spectacularly wrong for you. Then, if I choose, I will answer one of yours. Understood?" The Artifex's voice sounded calm and cold, and Jess unwillingly nodded. "Now. Why did you go off in the middle of the night in search of Scholar Wolfe?"

Jess wanted to ask about Thomas again, but he knew that wouldn't help. "I needed to ask whether or not he was going to recommend me for a posting."

"You don't strike me as particularly anxious about your future at the Library. Ah, correction. *Didn't*. You have good reason to be anxious now."

"I can't go back home if I fail here. I needed to know for sure that I wouldn't be sent away." The best lie, Jess's father had taught him, was always mostly truth. In fact, this one was completely true, and Jess heard the tremor in his voice as he said it. "Wolfe found out something about my family I didn't want known. I thought he was going to reject me for placement."

The Artifex picked up a marble ball from the top of his desk and rolled it restlessly in his gnarled fingers. "I see. Even if that is true, why did Wolfe and Santi come back with you to Ptolemy House?"

"I was drunk and angry. Wolfe didn't want me on my own, so he and Captain Santi took me back. That's all."

The Artifex Magnus clasped his hands behind his back and stared at him. An old man. An old face. Eyes as sharp as chips of ice. *He doesn't believe me,* Jess thought.

"We have reason to believe that in addition to young Guillaume Danton, may his soul rest in eternal peace, there was another Burner acolyte in your class. One conducting dangerous experiments under the cover of night. Were you aware of this?"

"No," Jess said, and only then realized with a sickening drop in his stomach that the Artifex was talking about Thomas. "What sort of experiments?"

"The sort that result in chaos, blood, and death." The Artifex's pale lips twitched in the cover of his white beard, but he didn't answer directly. "It seems very odd that you were absent from the house when our men arrived. I would have thought you, like your fellows, would have been longing for bed after your . . . adventures."

Adventures. That was one word for it, Jess supposed; the kind of word used by someone who kept his murder at a distance. "I've answered your questions enough. Where's Thomas?"

That earned him a long, long stare, as if the old man was weighing him. Like the Egyptian goddess Ma'at, weighing a man's soul against a feather. "I regret to inform you that the young man succumbed to injuries he sustained at Ptolemy House. Evidence suggests that someone struck him in the head as he lay asleep in his bed. Perhaps his attacker removed the body before it could be discovered. Perhaps we are still searching for it." Those cold, cold eyes froze him from the inside out. "And then, of course, the attacker came back, with accomplices, to clean up after himself. Shall I spell it out for you? I should think you are clever enough to work out the narrative."

"Thomas is dead?" Jess no longer felt clever. He couldn't understand even that one simple fact, though he'd feared it since he saw the blood in his friend's room. "He can't be dead."

"You killed him," the Artifex said. "Or so the story might go. A drunken fight that got out of hand, perhaps . . . common, in all the wrong and sad meanings of that word. Then you panicked. You ran to Scholar Wolfe, thinking he would help you hide your crime. But unhappily for you, young Schreiber survived just long enough to send a message for help to the Garda. They removed the others from the house, for their own safety, of course. Sadly, your friend Thomas expired before he could receive help."

"I didn't—" Jess couldn't stop the protest, but he managed to stop after those two blurted words. It wouldn't matter. The Artifex knew damned well he hadn't killed his best friend. The truth was what the Library wanted it to be. That was the lesson being taught here.

"Of course you didn't kill him. However, I can build a convincing case against you—and the price of that would be your death. And Wolfe's. And Captain Santi's, which is a genuine regret, because he is *very* capable." The Artifex was still rolling the marble ball in his fingers, but now he set it carefully back on its small golden stand on his desk. "Your fellow students might also be suspect."

"What the hell do you *want*?" Jess dimly recognized the tense, gravelly tone of his voice; it reminded him of his father's voice, the day that Liam had been hanged for book running. The day that his father's heart had shattered and been bolted back together as hard as iron.

"From this moment on, you will become my eyes and ears," the Arti-

336 • Rachel Caine

fex said. "*Scholar Wolfe* is a dangerous man, with dangerous leanings, and although he has powerful protection, he can and must be brought down. Your friend Thomas fell under his influence, and his death may be laid directly at Wolfe's feet."

Jess's fists were clenched at his sides, which he realized only when he became aware of the pain. He deliberately loosened them. "You want me to spy on Wolfe. For you, who killed my best friend."

"I think you're a smart, capable lad who has a bright future in the Library, and you'll do what's best for yourself. You understand practical considerations; you were raised by a practical family. Thomas was brilliant, but fatally naive. You won't make the same mistake."

"Do you really think I'll work for you?"

"Oh, I think you'd rather spy than swing like your brother Liam," the Artifex said. He pressed a button on his desk, and the door unlocked behind Jess with a thick metallic *click*. He felt the wave of air as it opened. He looked back to see two Garda behind him. One was taking a fresh pair of binders from his belt. "Yes or no. I need your answer."

"How can you even be sure I'll tell you the truth?"

"Do you really think you would be my *only* source of information? If I catch you in even one lie, you'll hang. Yes or no, Jess. The sand's almost run from your hourglass."

Jess shut his eyes for a few seconds, not because he was uncertain, but because he didn't want to look at the man anymore. He had a sickening, nearly impossible-to-resist urge to grab that marble ball and beat the old man's head in, just as they'd done to Thomas.

"Yes," he said softly. "What will I say to Wolfe?"

"You'll tell him that I questioned and released you. From now on, you will write me handwritten reports when anything of interest occurs regarding Scholar Wolfe. Do you understand? And as I said, there *will* be other eyes watching. I'll know if you try to cheat me."

"Why don't you just kill him?" Jess asked. He opened his eyes now, because he wanted to see the old man's face as he answered.

"With some enemies, it's safer to let them destroy themselves." The man went around his desk, sat, and made a dismissing gesture as he opened the leather-bound blank on his desk. "I expect to hear from you soon, Brightwell. Very soon."

EPHEMERA

Transcript of the questioning of Postulant Thomas
Schreiber by the Artifex Magnus, transferred to the Black
Archives under orders of the Curators.

ARTIFEX: *Explain how you developed the idea for this device.*

SCHREIBER: *I like to tinker with things. My little cousins had wooden blocks I carved for them, with letters on each side. We had a game of spelling words and pressing them into the mud—*

ARTIFEX: *Who encouraged you to build it?*

SCHREIBER: *No one, sir. I wanted to see if it worked. I thought once it did I would show it to Scholar Wolfe.*

ARTIFEX: *And did you? Show it to Wolfe?*

SCHREIBER: *No, sir. I never had the chance. We only just returned and I couldn't sleep, so I worked on it. It only began to work tonight. I was planning to show it to him tomorrow. Sir, I don't understand—have I made a mistake? Doesn't the Library benefit from such a thing?*

ARTIFEX: *Wolfe never saw this machine. And you never showed him plans, drawings, discussed your ideas for it. He never encouraged you in this mission to undermine the Library.*

SCHREIBER: *Sir! No, no, that is not at all what I am doing! I only mean to help the Library, never hurt it. Scholar Wolfe had no knowledge of it. I wanted to wait to show him once it was ready.*

ARTIFEX: *Don't be afraid, Postulant. No one doubts your skill, or your genius. It takes a very bright young man to do what you did, and invent something that is so . . . world-shaking.*

SCHREIBER: *Thank you, sir. I am glad you think so. I can work on it to make it better, if you will give me a workshop and tools to—*

ARTIFEX: *Do you know what happens when the world shakes,*

*Thomas? Cities fall. People are crushed. Empires break. The very founda-
tions of the Library shatter. When I say it is a world-shaking invention,
it is not a compliment. It is a condemnation.*

(SCHREIBER is recorded as silent.)

ARTIFEX: Who else saw the plans? The machine?

SCHREIBER: No one, sir.

ARTIFEX: Is there a hand-drawn copy of these diagrams?

SCHREIBER: I only put it in my personal journal. No one else saw it.

ARTIFEX: We will, of course, make sure you are telling the truth.

SCHREIBER: You're going to destroy the press?

*ARTIFEX: Oh no, boy. We're simply adding it to the warehouse of
many similar inventions. You're not the first to think of such a thing.
Merely the latest.*

SCHREIBER: You're going to kill me.

*ARTIFEX: Some ideas are like a virulent, persistent virus. They must
be ruthlessly eradicated before an infection spreads. It is an unpleasant
rule of medicine that diseased limbs must be severed for the health of the
body. One last time, tell us who else knows, and you may live out your days
in a cell, instead of dying in an unmarked grave.*

(SCHREIBER is recorded as silent.)

ARTIFEX: May whatever god you follow have mercy upon you.

(The Artifex then directed that Schreiber be taken to a place of questioning.)

End of record.

CHAPTER SIXTEEN

When Jess was escorted out of the Serapeum, the world was warming to a clear dawn; the eastern horizon was layered with soft yellow and warm orange, while the western sky still showed indigo. The Serapeum pyramid's top three tiers of stone were bathed in a blazing glow, and the golden capstone shone like the as-yet-unseen sun.

It was beautiful and eternal, and Jess averted his eyes at the sight of it. His head pounded from a mix of tension and weariness, and he felt desperately sick. The guards didn't bind him this time. They escorted him through the courtyard, past rows of guardian statues as thick as an army's column, and out into an area shaded beneath spreading olive trees heavy with fruit.

His friends were there. All but Thomas.

Glain saw him first, and spoke to the others; Dario was embracing Khalila, but he let go when he saw Jess, and they all came at a run to meet him. It should have made things better to be with friends, but he was only starting to realize that he had no friends now. Only people he could ruin and betray.

Thomas is dead.

"What happened?" Dario asked him. "Brightwell? *Jess?* Come on, English, talk."

"Let go, Dario." Khalila was, as always, more perceptive. And she saw the shocked distance in Jess, even if she didn't know what it was. "He's not well. Can't you see that?"

"Too much to drink, like the rest of us." Dario dismissed it, but he did let go of Jess's shirt, and stepped back. "Did you find Thomas?"

Jess shook his head. He couldn't find his voice, not yet.

"Well, then, come on. Wolfe's waiting."

With some enemies, it's safer to let them kill themselves. The Artifex, for all his massive power, was afraid of Wolfe. Why would that be possible?

It hit him as all the small, seemingly random pieces fit together in a blinding flash. Wolfe, born to Obscurist parents in the Iron Tower. Family connections that Monsieur Danton had mentioned. And it had been right in front of him, when Wolfe and the Obscurist Magnus had stood together on the High Garda parade ground.

Christopher Wolfe even *looked* like his mother.

And his mother was the Obscurist Magnus.

"Jess?" Glain put her hand on his shoulder. It wasn't a gentle gesture, as it would have been from Khalila—more of a fellow-soldier tap that simply lingered. "Thomas. Do you know where he is?"

"He's dead," Jess said. He watched her eyes dilate in shock and her expression go flat and lifeless. "Come on. Wolfe's waiting."

He shook off Glain's hand and walked after the others, through dawn's soft light, toward the pyramid steps.

The sphinxes were restless today, red eyes glowing, heads turning as the four of them climbed the endless stairs. Thomas would have joked about it. He'd have offered to carry at least two of them on his back, and he'd have been strong enough to do it, at least part of the way.

His absence felt like . . . a severed limb. An emptiness so large that Jess couldn't yet understand the shape of it.

He counted steps silently, just to keep his mind from chasing the image of Thomas's last moments . . . of the Artifex, watching the cold, clinical execution of his friend. If the climb was tiring, he didn't feel it. His body operated like a machine, like one of Thomas's wonderful automata, and when he finally reached the landing at the top of the Serapeum, he realized that he had left the other three far behind, still toiling through the last third of the climb. His clothing—still what he'd thrown on when going down into the cellar to see Thomas's marvelous press—was soaked through with sweat and clinging to him unpleasantly; his throat ached from gasping. He needed water before the sharp, stabbing aches in his calf muscles turned to crippling spasms.

Instead of resting, he went through the doors and down the hall to where he knew Wolfe would be waiting.

Pain was good. Pain helped.

There was no one else in the Reading Room but Wolfe, who was pacing the end of it in his Scholar's black robe, head down, hands behind his back. Wolfe raised his chin and looked at Jess as he came forward, all the way to the long reading table at the front.

Jess sat down on the bench and said, "Where's Santi?"

"Home. They know where to find him anytime they want, and of course the Artifex made sure that I know the litany of terrible things that could happen to a High Garda captain, regardless of his rank or commendations." Wolfe studied Jess for a beat before he said, "The Artifex told you about Thomas's death."

Jess said nothing, but he looked away.

"He was a brilliant young man. I'd have saved him if I could." Nothing to say to that. He could feel Wolfe's attention fixed on him but held his silence. "Are you all right?"

"I'm fine." He looked up at Wolfe and said, "You can't give me an appointment to the Library. Keep me as far away from you as you can. Send me away."

Wolfe might have asked him why, but by then, Dario was at the door, with Khalila and Glain close behind. They were all still breathing hard from the climb. No time to explain without extra ears listening, and Jess could no longer trust anyone.

The Artifex could have been lying to him, but he couldn't take that risk.

Wolfe's expression had changed again. The mask was back in place as the other three took seats at the table with Jess.

"I had planned to present five scrolls today," he said. "But one will be left ungiven. I am sorry to hear of Thomas Schreiber's passing."

"How?" Khalila's face was tearstained, and her eyes had welled up again. "How could this *happen*?" Dario took her hand in his and silently held it. He was sprawled in his usual posture, but his head was down, hiding his expression.

"I am told he did not suffer," Wolfe said. "It casts a wide shadow over what we must do today, but it can't be helped. I believe he would want us to continue." His dark gaze raked over them, one at a time. Lingering. "Today, you become servants of the Library."

He walked away to a side table, on which sat a sleek black box with the symbol of the Library gleaming in gold on top. It unlocked with a faint click at a pass of his hand, and he took out a tight-wrapped scroll, sealed with wax, and a black box that was a miniature of the larger one. "Postulant Wathen."

Glain came to her feet and to military attention, chin high. She accepted the box and scroll and bowed. "I didn't want it this way," she said.

"Perhaps given that the scroll identifies you as appointed to the rank of Training Sergeant in the High Garda, you should become used to the hard business of losing those you value." He paused for a moment, then added, "Your future was never in doubt. Nor your worth to the Library. Your contract offers you five initial years of service. All you need do is sign the scroll and put on your bracelet. Your Codex will update with instructions on where to report for duty."

"Sir," she said. "Thank you." It wasn't a formality. She really meant it. Her voice was just barely holding steady. "It is my honor to serve."

She sat down.

"Postulant Santiago." Dario wasn't as militarily correct about it, but he stood. Wolfe retrieved another scroll and box and handed them over. No bow from Dario, but then, Jess hadn't expected one. "You are an ambitious young man. If I have any advice for your future, it is to curb that ambition before it poisons you. I debated this. You have flaws. But your performance in Oxford, and beyond, convinced me that you can learn to be a better man. Therefore, the scroll contains an offer for a three-year contract as a Scholar, with a territory and specialty to be assigned by the Artifex Magnus. Sign and put on the bracelet if you accept."

Dario's mouth opened and closed, and Jess could see that he was biting back an acidic comment on the fact that Glain's contract was longer than his own. He nodded stiffly, murmured his thanks, and sank down.

It was Khalila's turn. "Postulant Seif, I am certain that no one would dispute that you have earned this many times over. The offer in this scroll is one that I have only seen a handful of times, and it comes directly from the Archivist. You are offered a lifetime appointment as a Research Scholar, which makes you a gold band, with all the attendant rank and privileges. And I can say that there is no one I would think better qualified to bring credit to the name of the Library." He held out her scroll and bracelet box, and she took them in trembling hands. Her tears hadn't ceased.

Dario touched her gently on the back, steadying her, and she took in a deep, trembling breath to say, "I thank Allah for this chance to bring honor to my family. And I thank you, Scholar. May I ask . . . what was Thomas's offer?"

"The same," Wolfe said. "And for much the same reasons."

Khalila turned to Dario and hugged him hard.

"Postulant Brightwell," Wolfe said. He retrieved another scroll and box as Jess got to his feet. *No,* Jess tried to tell him with a silent, urgent stare. *No, don't give me an appointment—didn't you understand?* "You are many things the Library needs—brave, intelligent, ruthless—and quite a few things that it does *not* need. Your family history is against you. Your recent behavior has called into question your loyalty—"

"What? No!"

"You can't!"

"Jess isn't—"

It was a chorus of three overlapping voices, all protesting: Glain, Khalila, Dario. All on their feet, arguing with Wolfe. *For him.* That surprised Jess. It touched him, too.

Wolfe cut them off with a sharp, intimidating look. "Let me finish! I have since determined that perhaps this appointment will teach you some lessons that dismissing you from the Library would not. You still have promise. I believe you will find your way." He held the scroll and box out to Jess. They felt heavy on his palms. Almost warm. "This contains a contract for an appointment to the High Garda at the entry rank of private, for the period of one year. Should you accept, sign the document and don the copper bracelet."

This wasn't something that Wolfe had done on the spur of the moment. It wasn't done because of the events of the night before; Wolfe wouldn't have had time to draft and seal a new commission, nor to have it approved.

The lowest possible rank, in the one place he didn't want to be. He had no talent for the High Garda, and no desire for it, either. But it would keep him away from Wolfe, and keep him from begging his brother—oh, the irony—for scraps.

Jess put the scroll and box down on the table and said, "I'll think about it."

"Think hard," Wolfe said. "Your family won't welcome you back. We both know that you're of no use to them."

Bastard, Jess thought. Even though he'd told Wolfe to keep him at a distance, this was a deliberate kick in the arse, and they all knew it. Glain had gone red in the face, and only her famous military discipline kept her still. Dario looked tense and angry. Khalila just seemed . . . shocked, as if she couldn't imagine Wolfe saying such a thing.

"Sir," she said. "Sir, Jess doesn't deserve—"

"Dismissed," Wolfe said, and spun toward the black box. He slammed it shut, tucked it under his arm, and strode past them, out through the Reading Room, with his black robe billowing like smoke behind him.

There were pens on the table. Four of them, engraved with the Library's symbol. Jess could feel the others looking at him, clearly unsure what to say to him.

He sat down and broke the seal on his contract. It flared with a little crackle of light.

He picked up the pen and signed his name in steady, flowing script at the bottom. There were Obscurist symbols and a blood drop at the bottom; the contract was mirrored. It would be inscribed somewhere on the Codex, making him a member of the Library, with all the attendant pay, duties, and privileges.

What a bitter irony that was.

"Jess," Khalila said. "Jess—"

"It's done," he said. "I'm glad for you, Khalila. Glad for all of you."

He took off his temporary Library bracelet that had been issued on the trip to Oxford. His skin felt oddly naked without it.

He took the copper bracelet from the box, slipped it on, and clipped it shut. The symbol flared, and he heard a tiny shiver of sound from it as it activated.

One year of service, as a soldier.

Now all he had to do was find a way to survive.

Ptolemy House was no longer their home, and as Jess checked his Codex, he found instructions to pack his things and report to the High

Garda base. He assumed the others had likewise gotten instructions, be-cause when he began assembling his small amount of baggage, he could hear the noise of packing from other rooms.

It was the last moment they'd all be together, he thought. Bittersweet.

His personal journal was still sitting where he'd left it, on the table be-side his bed. He stared at the worn cover, the well-thumbed pages, and for the first time in his life, he wished he had a flask of Greek fire. He wanted to burn the thing into ashes and a dark stain on the floor.

Nothing he'd poured into it was private. Nothing ever had been, from his earliest clumsy scribbles to the last words he'd written. *I have to keep writing in it,* he thought. Wolfe would tell him it was important to keep up appearances. Funny. His father would have said the same thing.

As he picked it up, a folded, loose sheet of paper slipped out of the cover. He grabbed it as it fell and unfolded it.

The note was from *Thomas Schreiber.*

Jess felt a heavy, sickening lurch in the pit of his stomach. He recog-nized Thomas's neat, square writing—not a spare loop or line.

> *Jess, if you're reading this, then the worst has happened. I know it will not happen, because you are always a pessimist and I am not, but some of your pessimism must have rubbed off because here I am leaving this for you. (Also, forgive me for opening your journal. I promise that I did not read it.) Do not blame yourself. I could see that in your face when you left, that somehow you thought this was all your fault, but this time it was mine, only mine.*
>
> *In any case, I have left you something behind the Old Witch. Three seven three. Keep it safe. And destroy this, of course, but you would have already thought of that, because you are clever.*

He could hear Thomas's voice, somehow, in the tone of the message, and for the first time, he felt tears sting at his eyes. Tears of anger at

Thomas for being so *stupid* as to put his diagrams down in his journal for the Library to see. Tears of pain for what was gone.

He read it twice more, then ripped it methodically up into thin strips, put the strips into a copper bowl on the desk, and set them on fire with a match. Once the message was ashes, he crushed the ashes and threw them down the toilet.

Then he stepped out into the hallway. No one there, though he heard low voices from farther down—Khalila and Dario, it seemed. He took the stairs quickly and quietly up to the dusty second floor, with all its closed and locked doors.

And its rows of dusty paintings.

He tapped the glow up just enough to make out the age-dimmed features of the portraits, and the third one on the right was the one he remembered Thomas pointing out. She *did* look like an old witch, this long-dead Scholar; wild white hair, forbidding bone structure, a thin and unpleasant sort of mouth. One of the Magnuses, possibly Medica. He lifted her portrait from the wall and set it aside and counted bricks. *Three across, seven down, three across.* He presumed that was the code, moving left to right, and when his fingers touched the last brick he felt it shift slightly under his fingers. Getting it out required the help of the knife at his belt, but it finally slid free with a soft grating sound.

Behind it, rolled tight, was a scroll. Parchment, by the feel of it. Jess pulled it free and unrolled it.

Diagrams. Plans of the press. Thomas hadn't been as innocent as all that.

Jess let the document snap shut, jammed the paper inside his jacket, and replaced the brick. Then the portrait.

He was halfway down the stairs when Dario passed by on the first floor and gave him an odd look. "What are you doing?"

"Checking my old room," he said. "Just in case I left anything there."

"Did you?"

"Dust." Jess slapped some from his clothes, raising a small cloud, and Dario stepped back to avoid it. "Are you packed?"

"Ready to go," Dario said. "My quarters will be at the Lighthouse."

"And Khalila?"

"The same, thankfully."

Jess met his gaze squarely. "She's too good for you, you know."

"I'm well aware of it." Dario's smile was rueful and a little sad. "Maybe Wolfe's right. Maybe I'll learn to be better and deserve her someday. I'm sorry about—"

Jess cut him off with a shrug. "It's still an appointment. And he's right. I can't go home."

Dario held out his hand, and Jess took it. The handshake was a little too firm. "I will see you again," Dario said. "You can't get rid of me that easily, English. You owe me another game or two of Go."

"You really must be addicted to losing. Scholar."

They parted. Jess went into his room and closed the door. He needed a good place to hide the plans, and after some debate he took one of the original volumes he'd kept—illegal, of course, but most definitely safe from the Library's eyes, which couldn't be said for his Codex or journal. He used his knife to carefully cut a slit in the side of the thick leather cover, and pressed the paper into a thin square. That, he slipped into the make-shift pouch. A little glue, and it was hidden. Invisible. He put it into his bag at the bottom. *I need a hiding place.* But not here, at Ptolemy House, where another crop of postulants would be making an appearance soon enough.

He was closing up his bag when there was a knock on his door. He opened it to see that the others were outside. Khalila silently hugged him, and he let out a breath and held on for a moment. No good-byes.

"We're going to the same place," Glain said to him. "Walk, or share a carriage?"

"Carriage," he said. "I have the feeling we'll have plenty of exercise in the days to come."

She grinned and said, "I'm to be your Training Sergeant after I finish my apprentice orientation. So you can count on it."

"My luck keeps rolling true." But in truth, Jess was a little relieved. Glain would be close. He'd find a way to meet Dario and Khalila. They could all still hold on to their friendship, somehow.

"Do you think there will be a memorial?" Khalila asked. "For Thomas, I mean?"

"Not that we'll get to attend," Glain said. "We have duties now." She extended her hand to Dario and Khalila, and shook. "*Hyd nes y byddwn yn cyfarfod eto.* Until we meet again."

"*O menos que te vea primero,*" Dario said. "Unless I see you first."

As farewells went, it was a good one.

Dario and Khalila took a carriage together to the Lighthouse, that ancient, still-functioning structure that spoke of the grace, beauty, and determination of this ancient place. The beacon still shone from the top of it, guiding sailors safely home.

Jess and Glain took the next conveyance. As they sat together, Jess's Codex buzzed. He opened it.

On an empty page, an invisible hand wrote, **I miss you.**

The message was gone a second later, as if he'd imagined it. Then it was replaced by more letters being drawn, in a hand he knew. Morgan was writing this as he was seeing it. How? How was it possible? Worse, who else could see it? **The connection is open now. You can reply.**

He took his stylus and scribbled as quickly as he could. Glain had given him a glance, but now she was staring out the window, absorbed in her own thoughts. Even so, he wrote too quickly to be neat about it. **Is this secure?**

Yes, she wrote back. **No one else can see it. I've worked out how to do it. There won't be a record. Are you all right?**

He didn't think he was, but he didn't want to say it. **I miss you. Thomas is dead.**

I know, she wrote. Seeing her writing appear was eerily like being with her, face-to-face. I'm sorry. There was a short pause, and he was worried she was gone, but then more letters appeared.

Help me make it change, Jess.

He stared at those letters hard, hard enough that his head began to ache.

She had written, in those deceptively brief words, exactly what he believed. What Thomas had believed. What Wolfe had believed, and been destroyed for daring to try.

The message slowly disappeared, and nothing else followed. She was gone.

He closed the book.

She was right. Everything had to change. But he knew, as the carriage steamed toward the gates of the High Garda compound, that Thomas would be only the first of the cost they were going to pay for that progress.

Continued in Volume 2 of

THE GREAT LIBRARY...

SOUND TRACK

As always, I like to include a list of what I listened to while writing this book. You might like these songs, too, and I think they represent certain aspects of Jess's world very well. A little punk-folk, a little raw Celtic, a little steampunk . . . an unusual mix, even for me. I hope you enjoy the songs, and remember, support the artists by buying (and not just downloading) the music. Artists need support. And rent money.

Santiago	Loreena McKennitt
Come with Me Now	Kongos
The Resistance	2Cellos
Beautiful Decline	Abney Park
No More Stones	Enter the Haggis
Bad Blood	Bastille
Letters Between a Little Boy and Himself As an Adult	Abney Park
The End of Days	Abney Park

Lanigan's Ball	Fiddler's Green
Scheherazade	Abney Park
Farewell to Decorum/Spanner in the Words (Live)	The Killdares
Melancholy Man (Full Version)	The Moody Blues
The Engine Room	Runrig
Rise Up	Abney Park
I'm Shipping Up to Boston	Dropkick Murphys
Not Silent	Abney Park
Rose Tattoo	Dropkick Murphys
Boondoggle	An Dochas
The Anthropophagist's Club	Abney Park
Rose de Lay	The Killdares
Dolan's 6AM	Beoga
And Dream of Sheep	Kate Bush
Waking the Witch	Kate Bush
Jig of Life	Kate Bush
Benedictus	2Cellos
Fierce	Rising Gael
Jealousy	Abney Park
Keep It in the Family	Hybrid
Scalliwag	Gaelic Storm

Things Could Be Worse	Abney Park
The Rocky Road to Dublin	The Tossers
Waiting for You	Abney Park
Balto	Enter the Haggis
Paella Grande	Wolfstone
Ancient World	Abney Park
Supermassive Black Hole (feat. Naya Rivera)	2Cellos
Tam Lin	Fiddler's Green
The Story That Never Starts	Abney Park
The Boys and the Babies/Is Craig Here?	The Drovers
The Broken Pledge	The Drovers
The Oak & Holly Kings	The Dolmen
Elegy	Leaves' Eyes
Mombasa	2Cellos
Oh, Well (feat. Elton John)	2Cellos
Davie's Last Reel	Wolfstone
Cleveland Park	Wolfstone
Ne'er Do Wells	Audra Mae and the Almighty Sound
Wit's End	Skerryvore
Take Me to Church	Hozier
To Be Alone	Hozier